THE FRAGMENT OF
FIRE

By Ben Hale

To my family and friends,

Who believed

And to my wife,

Who is perfect

The Chronicles of Lumineia

By Ben Hale

—The Shattered Soul—

The Fragment of Water
The Fragment of Shadow
The Fragment of Light
The Fragment of Fire
The Fragment of Mind
The Fragment of Power

—The Master Thief—

Jack of Thieves
Thief in the Myst
The God Thief

—The Second Draeken War—

Elseerian
The Gathering
Seven Days
The List Unseen

—The Warsworn—

The Flesh of War
The Age of War
The Heart of War

—The Age of Oracles—

The Rogue Mage
The Lost Mage
The Battle Mage

—The White Mage Saga—

Assassin's Blade (Short story prequel)
The Last Oracle
The Sword of Elseerian
Descent Unto Dark
Impact of the Fallen
The Forge of Light

Table of Contents

Prologue: Elenyr's Friend

Past

The fragment of Fire picked his way up the slope, casting baleful glares at Elenyr's back. They'd been traveling for weeks, and Elenyr had refused to let him use his magic to hasten their journey. His feet hurt, and he mentioned it at every opportunity.

They'd left the other young fragments in Cloudy Vale with Mind in charge, the first time Elenyr had left them alone for such a duration. Fire knew it was his fault for almost killing Shadow. But Shadow had been annoying. Despite Fire's simmering anger, his curiosity got the best of him.

"Where are we going?"

"You'll see soon enough," she replied, and glanced his way. "If you can keep up."

He scowled and picked up the pace, hurrying to reach her side. Ignoring her faint smile, he gestured to the ground at their feet, where plumes of steam curled upward, rising from cavities in the stone.

"Did you know we're standing on a volcano?"

"Of course," she said.

"Why are we coming here?" he asked. "We both know Shadow provoked me."

"I know that," she said.

Surprised, he tripped and struck his knee on a shard of rock. Rubbing the bruise, he rounded on her. "If you knew he provoked me, why are we a hundred miles outside of the claimed lands?"

"Because the cause of your anger does not matter," she said.

"I don't understand."

She circled a plume of steam that reeked of sulfur. "Shadow can be aggravating, but you will encounter many others who are worse. You cannot lose your temper. Not even once. Humans and elves are not as hardy as a fragment of Draeken, and you could kill them on a whim."

"But Shadow—"

"Is teaching you to control your temper." She came to a halt. "But we are here so you can control your magic."

"I *can* control my magic." She raised an eyebrow, at which he scowled and looked away. "Usually."

She resumed her pace, ascending a faint trail up the side of the volcano. "Fire has always been a volatile magic, and many mages have fallen victim to their own power."

"I'm immune to fire," he said.

"Do you wish to kill the barmaid that drops your plate in your lap? Or perhaps the soldier who mocks your armor? Does he also merit a swift death at your hands?"

Her words cut deep, deflating the anger he sought to hold. He'd burned his fragment brothers many times, and even Elenyr had a handful of scars because of him, a legacy of the few times she failed to turn ethereal quickly enough to avoid his temper.

Shadow was the worst of the lot, always poking and prodding, laughing when Fire rose to anger. Shadow lacked remorse or empathy, but Fire had a healthy dose of those attributes, the emotions returning in force whenever his anger faded. He hid behind righteous indignation, but deep down, he still felt terrible that he'd hurt Shadow so badly.

"Is that all you can muster?" Shadow had laughed his annoying laugh. "I thought you were the strong one."

Fire had wanted to scorch him until he could no longer laugh, burn the lips right off his face. Shadow had ducked, the burst of fire scalding his head and neck. Shadow had the gall to mock his own burns, but Fire still felt bad for what he'd done. Fire scowled and looked back at the valley below, wondering if Shadow was behind them even now, lurking, ready to surprise them both, and laugh at their shock.

"He did not follow," Elenyr said.

"How do you know?" Fire demanded.

"His presence would hinder this portion of your training," she said.

He grunted and reached for a protrusion of rock to climb higher. Elenyr had brought him halfway across the world, to train with his magic. But why could they not have trained in Cloudy Vale? Why come to a volcano in the far west?

They reached the rim of the volcano and Elenyr turned ethereal to negotiate a difficult overhang. Her body became transparent and she passed through the stone, rising above like a wraith. Fire had promised not to use his magic, but he cast a rope of fire and used it to scale past the boulder. If Elenyr noticed, she gave no sign, and waited for him on the rim of the dormant volcano.

Fire came to a halt at her side and scanned the empty volcano. The hollow resembled a small valley, with stone across the flat base. Piles of boulders dotted the sides, the stone scorched and blackened. He frowned, confused at its shape, wondering why it resembled a nest . . .

A torrent of fire erupted above their heads. Again, Elenyr turned ethereal, allowing the fire to wash through her body and blast the stone at her feet. Fire stood his ground, the heat washing over him, eliciting a smile. Then he looked to the source of the attack.

A phoenix.

The firebird extinguished the assault and landed on the rim of the volcano. As smoke and cinders billowed about Fire, he gazed upward in awe, marveling at the sheer power to the enormous animal.

In shape the phoenix resembled a hawk, with long, feathered wings and a pointed beak. Powerful legs and claws grasped the stone, cracking it easily, as if it were made of wood. Fire trickled across its neck and wings, wreathing the mythical beast in flames. Then it dropped its head and issued a piercing war cry.

11

Fool intruders!

Archiantial, a voice spoke into Fire's head. *There is no need to antagonize our guests.*

The mental voice was not unlike the fragment of Mind, who possessed the magic to communicate directly with another's thoughts. Mind's voice was distant, like a voice calling from across the street. The firebird's voice carried a timbre of power that caused Fire to wince.

The firebird at their side flapped its wings, shaking them so drops of heat splashed onto the stone. *They are enemies,* the phoenix replied, the voice distinctly female.

One of them is a friend, the first voice said.

Fire turned to the sound of flapping wings, and another firebird landed on the opposite side of the volcano. Whereas Archiantial had feathers of yellow, orange, and gold, the second had wings of bright blue, the fire so hot the stones at the bird's feet turned red. It was twice the size of Archiantial.

"Ancient," Elenyr said, offering a bow to the huge blue firebird. "You have our gratitude."

Fire stared, his jaw open, his eyes wide, until Elenyr pulled on his sleeve. Realizing her intent, he offered a bow as well. He'd never seen Elenyr bow to anyone, not king or queen across the kingdoms.

Hauntress, the Ancient replied. *Your timing is not ideal. After a millennium of waiting, my mate has laid an egg.*

Another firebird burst into view, soaring above the rim before dropping into the volcano. It flared its wings and landed in the largest of the nests, settling over a tiny, red and blue egg. The bird was Archiantial's size, but its coloring was more red, the fires on its wings resembling a dark sunset.

"I am pleased to hear of your egg, Erandisia," Elenyr said, bowing to the new firebird.

The bird released a rumble and did not respond, drawing a mental chuckle from the Ancient. *It is our first in several eras. She is protective.*

"As she should be," Elenyr said.

The Ancient flapped his wings and rose into the air, soaring closer before alighting on the rim near Fire. He brought his beak closer to Fire and sniffed. Fire swallowed in fear and awe. The Ancient was a legend among fire mages, and according to myth, he was the first phoenix, the father of his race. With magic from his own flesh, he'd shaped Erandisia, his mate.

The firebird's beak was taller than Elenyr, large enough to swallow her like a morsel of meat. But it was the grand eyes that commanded attention, the swirling orange irises that conveyed a sense of unmatchable power and intelligence.

This one reeks of magic, the Ancient said, dipping its head to examine Fire.

"Did you hear that?" Fire asked, struggling to contain his excitement. "The Ancient said I was powerful!"

"For this purpose have I come," Elenyr said. "I request your aid."

You have but one favor, the Ancient said. *Are you certain you wish to use it now?*

"I am," Elenyr said.

Then so be it, the Ancient said.

Elenyr swept a hand to Fire. "I wish for my son to learn from you."

Fire swiveled to stare at Elenyr, suddenly realizing why they'd come so far. He grappled with the news, excited, nervous, and oddly sad he could not share it with his fragment brothers. Elenyr did not explain, and continued to look up at the Ancient.

Erandisia flared her wings. *You cannot permit an intruder to enter our flock when we have an egg!*

I would not be alive without the Hauntress, the Ancient declared as he swung his head towards his mate, his voice gaining an edge. *She has one favor to ask, and this I will grant.*

"You saved the Ancient's life?" Fire whispered.

"In my youth," Elenyr replied in the same tone. "I was sent to speak to the firebirds and found a collection of elves had crafted a cage to destroy the bird. Their water magic was impressive, and they had prepared well. If I had not intervened—"

A spear of water would have turned me to ash, the Ancient finished.

"You saved my life as well, you know," Elenyr said.

The Ancient's laugh resembled thunder. *Ask your favor.*

"Train my son," Elenyr said. "Teach him to control his magic."

The human? Archiantial demanded. *He is not worthy of such knowledge.*

I will allow it, the Ancient said.

If he comes near my nest, I will kill him. Erandisia released a burst of fire that engulfed her and the stones of the nest, so hot that some of the stones glowed.

Elenyr turned to face Fire. "I would stay away from her. A brooding mother can be dangerous, especially when the mother is more powerful than a dragon."

Fire was still in shock. "You want me to train my magic . . . with the phoenixes?"

"Their magic is innate," Elenyr said. "As is yours. Treat them with respect and they will impart the true secrets of your power."

Fire looked to the three birds, and spotted a fourth and fifth in the sky above. He sensed the danger of the prospect, that the training could be lethal, yet excitement stirred his blood, eliciting curls of flame up his arms.

14

See, he lacks discipline, a male voice said, sniffing as if in disdain. One of the birds above turned and banked away. *This endeavor will kill him.*

Let us see his power, another male voice said. *We have never encountered a mage with magic like ours.*

Wise words, the Ancient replied. *Rolindious, you will give the first lesson. Teach him to focus. I will not teach a fleshling unless he has the will of a bird.*

As you will, father.

The Ancient turned back to Elenyr. *One year I will give. If he cannot master his magic by then, he never will.*

The new firebird, who seemed to be the smallest of the flock, descended and took Archiantial's place as she dropped off the rim, departing in a burst of heated air. Elenyr stepped into an embrace, hugging Fire fiercely.

"Listen well," she admonished, emotion clogging her throat. "And I will see you in a year."

"Thank you," Fire replied.

Elenyr smiled before wiping the moisture from her eyes. She nodded as if she were attempting to convince herself of the wisdom of leaving Fire with the firebirds. Then she turned and departed, leaving the fragment of Fire to his first lesson. Alone on the rim, he watched Elenyr depart. He wished for Shadow and his sense of humor. He may have been annoying, but he also had a way with amusement. Releasing a long breath, he turned to the firebird.

"I am ready."

The bird dipped its head. *Show me your power, guardian . . .*

Chapter 1: Talon's Well

Present

Fire and Mind crept through the dark forest, advancing on the village of Talon's Well. Positioned just a day's ride outside of Herosian, the large settlement covered two hills, with homes on the slopes. Common structures had been built in the saddle between the hills, all situated around a large well at the center.

Strategically located at a crossroads of major highways, the village was known as a place of respite with an abundance of inns and taverns. Shipping warehouses dotted the two hills, allowing tradesmen to gather and store their wares. Several village walls had been started and abandoned, the growth of the village preventing the completion of a full defensive structure. The remains of the walls had become locally known as Fins, because they resembled the fins of a type of fish that prowled the surface of the nearby lake.

Fire and Mind reached the edge of the village and Fire scanned the northern hilltop, where several large estates occupied the high ground. Situated above a short cliff, one structure belonged to shipping company based in Terros. Operated by a man named Hyren, the estate contained subterranean store rooms and shipped the company's goods into and out of the region. Beneath all the fabrics and goods on the wagons, Fire and Mind had discovered anti-magic weapons. Due to their ability to kill mages, and their high cost, the gnome weapons were strictly controlled by the kingdoms, meaning such smuggling would be subject to prosecution by the guard.

"You still think Hyren is a member of the Order of Ancients?" Fire asked.

"I am certain," Mind said.

They'd traced the anti-magic weapons to the estate days ago, but been unable to find their true target. Normally Mind would have picked the location they sought from a foe, but Mind had been unable to breach the mental shields of the Order's leaders, a fact that drew a great deal of irritation from the fragment.

Fire lifted the pendent from his pocket and held it up to the moonlight. The small crystal could have been dismissed as a trinket, but it carried a powerful charm, preventing a memory mage from reading the thoughts of the wearer. Unfortunately it carried a second charm, a curse that erased the memory of the wielder if removed, a fact only made apparent when Fire had yanked it from the neck of its owner.

"How can you be sure?"

Mind glanced to the crystal. "It's a powerful charm, but I caught glimpses of Talon's Well. And the weapons are being moved through the estate tonight. It's our best chance at finding Serak and Wylyn."

"Why are we tracking these halls?" Fire asked, not bothering to keep the irritation from his voice. "Surely Elenyr or the other fragments would know something by now."

"It's been a week since Shadow destroyed Mistkeep," Mind said. "And Light has disappeared into the north."

"You can feel him from that far away?"

Mind smiled faintly. "His fury was rather potent. I caught a glimpse of Light battling Bartoth in the northern tundra. I think Water is with him."

"And Elenyr?"

Mind shook his head. "I haven't heard anything since we parted ways east of Mistkeep."

Fire grunted and swept a hand to the Lord's estate. "So we're on our own."

"I thought you liked a good fight."

"You know I do," Fire said. "I hate all this sneaking about."

"We must be cautious," Mind replied. "The higher acolytes all carry that pendent, and none of the initiates in the Order know anything. If we don't tread carefully, we could end up with a second pendent and no answers."

Fire pointed to the estate. "Shadow would love sneaking into the estate. It's almost a fortress."

"We don't need Shadow," Mind said flatly.

Fire grinned at his tone. "Is this because of what he did to Mistkeep? I thought it was rather clever to use two contrasting magics to create an explosion."

"He's reckless," Mind said.

"He's always been reckless," Fire said. "So why are you annoyed now?"

"At one time he annoyed you as well."

Fire grinned. "I understand younger brothers are known for that."

Mind stabbed a finger at the estate. "I'll take the servants entrance. You go in through the balcony." He slipped into the night.

"That's it?" Fire called. "You won't tell me why you're angry with Shadow?"

And don't get discovered. Mind thought to Fire.

Mind's words entered Fire's thoughts like a whisper in his ear. Fire never bothered to guard his thoughts, and Mind preferred to use silent communication. Still wondering why Mind was bothered by Shadow, Fire decided the question would have to wait. He stepped out of the trees and turned in the opposite direction.

He descended a short slope and then entered the city, weaving between farms and Fins. The closer he came to the heart of the village, the denser the structures became, forcing him to slow. Winding paths and roads passed through the Fins, navigating around the hundreds of tiny expansions to the village.

18

Distant music and laughter came from around the well, where much of the village populace had gathered for the fall festival. Mind had said Hyren intended to use the festival as a distraction to bring the latest shipment of weapons into the village. It was a good idea. Even the guards had drifted toward the light and music.

Fire came to the base of the hill and looked upward. The other three sides of the hill were smooth in their descent, but on this side, stone had been quarried for the Fins, leaving a rocky cliff. Reaching to a crack, Fire began to climb.

He would have preferred using fire to ascend, but such magic tended to attract attention, so he worked his way up the cliff in the darkness, to a balcony fifty feet off the ground. The wide platform overlooked the south side of the village and was a favorite place to dine for Hyren and his various lady friends.

Fire scaled the cliff to the balcony and levered himself over. Then he crept to the door to examine the entrance. A thick steel door barred entry, likely built so the guards did not have to worry about thieves using it as an entrance. Fools.

Fire snapped his fingers, igniting a flame on his forefinger. Narrowing the blade, he compressed the flame, increasing the heat. The yellow turned from yellow to an intense white. Smiling to himself, he reached out and pressed the blade between the door and the frame. He slid his finger down the crack, the blade gradually slicing through the steel latch.

Drops of liquid metal truckled down the wall as he caught the handle and swung the door open. Slipping into the darkened corridor, he shut the door behind himself and walked into the home of Hyren.

He expected guards and was not disappointed. At the end of the hall he came upon a pair of soldiers talking in low tones. Obviously lamenting their inability to attend the festival, they muttered curses at their low wages. Both turned at Fire's approach.

"I'd rather be at the festival as well," Fire said. "The women of Talon's Well are renowned for their beauty."

The two guards exchanged a look and then reached for their swords. Fire was faster. He dropped his hand and conjured a curving sword of fire from the heat in his flesh. The two guards exchanged a shocked look, and Fire grinned.

"Who needs steel when one has fire?"

Flicking it to the side, he darted in. They raised their swords but Fire deftly knocked them aside, spinning behind them to slap one guard on the back with his free hand. The blow landed lightly, but allowed Fire to attach a charm on his cloak.

Flames burst from the charm, the explosion propelling the guard down the hallway. He slammed into the door and rolled onto the balcony before colliding with the railing, where the force of the fire kept him pinned. He howled in dismay, but the charm only burned one way, preventing any real injury. The other guard looked to Fire in shock.

"No," he pleaded.

"Yes," Fire said with a smile.

He slapped him on the back, attaching another propulsion charm that sent him tumbling down the corridor after his companion. The second man caught the frame of the door and briefly held on, but the force of the magic proved too great, and pushed him outside. Fire listened for sounds of booted feet but none came.

Fire followed the two men back to the balcony and cast a rope of fire, which he used to lash them to the railing. The first charm Elenyr had taught him was how to cast fire that would not burn flesh, and he used that magic to bind and gag the two guards. The propulsion charms on their backs sputtered and faded as he finished.

Not very subtle, Mind said.

"Watching through my eyes?" Fire asked aloud.

The two guards exchanged a terrified look and both shook their heads. Fire ignored them and turned away, re-entering the estate. Passing the guard position, he ascended the stairs into the third sub-basement.

You really should learn how to guard your thoughts.

"Admit it, you like seeing the fun I have." Fire surveyed the dark warehouse, which contained crates in neat stacks.

I'm in the first basement, Mind said. *Hyren is meeting with a group of his men.*

"How did you get in?"

Mind sent an image of the servants walking around him, talking as if he were not present, but Fire knew their memories were being erased as quickly as they were formed. Mind had strolled in like a ghost and descended the stairs to the lower level.

Fire might have asked why Mind had wanted him to enter below, but he already knew the answer. Mind liked to see a target location though two sets of eyes. It provided him the chance to use his gift of strategy. It usually didn't bother Fire, because it meant he could enter the way he wanted, but on occasions Mind's lack of communication was annoying.

I can hear what you're thinking about me.

"That's why you're annoying," Fire said.

There was a mental snort, and then Mind withdrew. Fire passed the warehouse and ascended to the second sub-basement, which teemed with workers unloading wagons. From the empty stairwell, he watched a wagon being driven out through a tunnel in the opposite side.

Anti-magic weapons were taken from secret compartments under the wagons and loaded into wagons marked with the symbol for the Talinorian army. Talinorian soldiers then boarded the wagons and departed. Fire frowned, disliking the suggestion that the Order had gained a foothold in the king's own army.

"Are you seeing this?"

They're not actual soldiers, Mind said. *But their orders and uniforms are real. They must have a high captain in their pocket.*

"Any news of Wylyn's location?"

The question cut to the heart of what they had been searching for. In the last few months they had tracked the smaller Order halls, marking their locations. They had managed to identify many of the Order's homes but had yet to locate a primary hall. They'd failed to find Serak, head of the Order, or Wylyn, the krey woman that Serak had brought to Lumineia.

Hyren has the crystal necklace of a high-ranking acolyte, Mind said. *He must know what we're looking for.*

"How do we get him to talk?"

A few of the guards walked towards Fire, so he retreated up the stairs. Mind dropped him a view of his location. He entered the second sub-basement and worked his way along the back wall, threading the gap between stacks of crates. There he grasped the crate marked with the symbol for a scythe and climbed to the top of the stack. Crawling between the ceiling and the topmost crate, he lay on his stomach next to Mind and surveyed the room.

The sub-basement was large, much larger than he'd expected. Crates were stacked to the ceiling, all bearing the mark of their contents. Most were foodstuffs like grain or potatoes, but cloth, fine wood, and light orbs were also present.

"Thanks for not setting off an alarm," Mind whispered.

"You know I don't like infiltration work."

"You're five thousand years old," Mind said. "You could have learned how to be subtle."

"I don't *want* to be subtle."

Mind released an irritated grunt and then fell silent. Below, Hyren talked to two dwarves who were obviously caravan leaders. Their conversation alluded to Serak and the Order, as well as Wylyn, but avoided naming any locations or other senior acolytes. Standard rules by the Order.

"How do we get what we need?" Fire murmured.

"He has a pendent," Mind said, "so I think we need to get creative."

"You have a plan?" Fire asked.

"I always do."

Fire frowned, disliking the look on his brother's face. "Am I going to like this plan?"

"Nope," Mind smiled in anticipation.

Fire sighed. "Just tell me what you need me to do . . ."

Chapter 2: Hyren

Mind and Fire retreated from the room to gather a few supplies. When they had what they needed they stepped into the open and advanced toward Hyren and his two companions. Hyren turned toward them, his expression one of disapproval. Dressed in a guard uniform, courtesy of one of the guards on the balcony below, Mind walked behind Fire. When they reached Hyren he shoved Fire to his knees and pointed to the anti-magic shackles on his wrists.

"Caught this one lurkin' about," he said with a thick accent.

Hyren barely spared Mind a glance, his attention on Fire. The other two blinked in confusion, their eyes sliding over Mind as if he did not matter. Fire hid a smile, recognizing the impact of Mind inserting an image into their minds, blurring what they saw. It wouldn't work on Hyren due to his pendent, but Fire drew his attention.

"Who are you?" Hyren demanded.

"Just passing through," Fire said airily. "I must say, I'm disappointed with your hospitality."

Hyren stepped forward and struck Fire with the back of his hand. The iron gauntlet caught Fire on the nose and face, spilling blood down his tunic. Fire looked down at the blood and back to Hyren, anger spilling fire on his arms. The flames were quickly siphoned away by the shackles, but not before they were noticed.

"A fire mage," one of the caravan leaders said. "What are you doing here?"

"Perhaps a spy for another trading company?" the second asked. "It wouldn't be the first time they dispatched one to sabotage our stock."

"Dispose of him," Hyren said to Mind, waving his hand in dismissal. "Quietly."

Mind frowned and his eyes flicked to Fire, and spoke into his thoughts. *He doesn't recognize you.*

Stung, Fire came to his feet. Both the caravan leaders reached for their swords, but Fire leaned in and struck one with his forehead. Reeling from the blow and clenching his broken nose, the man tumbled onto his back, his sword clattering to the floor. The second drew his blade, but Fire sidestepped the swing and drew in a breath.

He gathered fire in his throat, the power rising and spilling into a torrent of superheated flames that blasted from his mouth. The dragon's fire was subdued by the shackles, but they sent the man crashing through a crate of cloth and into the aisle beyond. The crate above teetered, and then fell to the floor, shattering and spilling light orbs across the floor.

Shouts came from the room below, but quickly fell silent as Mind made them forget they'd heard the crash. Fire turned on Hyren, who stared at Fire shock. He yanked his sword from his scabbard and shouted to Mind, who caught Fire and again forced him to the floor.

"Get more shackles," Hyren barked. "Before he shatters those."

"As you command," Mind said, leaping away.

Hyren leapt to Fire's back, putting a knee on his spine. As Mind exited the room, he struck Fire in the back of his head, knocking him to the floor. Fire growled as the man leaned down and spoke in his ear, his voice trembling with triumph.

"The fragment of Fire," he hissed. "You are a fool to be caught so easily. Now I get the privilege of handing Serak what he most desires."

"Mistkeep is destroyed," Fire retorted. "He has no cage to hold me."

"You think that was the only cage he built?" Hyren placed his sword on Fire's back above his heart. "He is always prepared."

"I'll escape," Fire said with a sneer.

"He has told us much about you," he said. "Told us how to hurt you but leave you alive. You will not enjoy the journey to Beldik."

Fire laughed, mustering all the scorn he could manage, which was significant. He'd learned from Shadow. "I've never heard of Beldik."

"Of course you haven't." the man said. "None are permitted to go there, not even senior acolytes—not even Wylyn. But we have our orders. If you are captured, that is where you are to be sent. After all the damage you've done to the Order of Ancients, I hope it's not a cage he has prepared. I hope it's a grave."

Hyren plunged his sword into Fire's back, driving the blade through his body. Fire cried out in pain, but mostly in anger, and released a burst of his magic. But the sword was also made by gnome hands, and the black blade siphoned off his magic. With such a deep wound, Fire could not bring the whole of his might to bear on Hyren. He was bound to the floor as Hyren watched him writhe.

"I wish I could see him torture you," Hyren said. "But sadly, I have other places to be."

"Not anymore," Mind said from behind him.

Hyren spun, and Mind drove his blade into his chest. Yanking it free, he casually pushed the dying man to the side and stepped to Fire. Kneeling, he reached for Hyren's sword, and wrapped his gloved hand around the hilt.

"Ready?"

"Can you at least make me forget the pain?" Fire hissed.

"I already am."

Fire grimaced and sensed the suppression of his pain. Even with Mind's magic, the blade *hurt*. Then Mind yanked the blade out of his body and Fire snarled, his vision clouding with darkness. The anti-magic shackles came free and he gingerly rose to his feet. Anger surged forth, and he turned on the sputtering Hyren, unleashing a burst of fire that consumed him, cutting off his scream.

"He was already seconds from death," Mind said. "That was unnecessary."

"I hated this plan," Fire said.

26

"It worked, didn't it?"

With blood darkening his tunic, Fire stepped to the hearth at the side of the room and reached into the flames. Gathering a log, he put the flames on the open wound, searing the opening. He breathed a sigh of relief and then reached over his shoulder to seal the second injury. The burns closed the wound, and he pulled the heat into his flesh, helping his wounds knit.

"Why did your plan include me getting stabbed?"

Mind watched the stairwell. "The caravan leaders were both worried about how Hyren liked to punish his underlings. Their fear implied Hyren liked to gloat. We needed to put him in a situation where he would speak a secret without fear of being overheard."

Fire collected the second log and sucked the heat from it. Tossing the steaming chuck of blackened wood aside, he did the same with the remainder, until the room darkened. Then he shifted his shoulder, pleased to find that he could move it, even if it still ached.

"Time to go," Mind said tightly. "Those below are starting to remember the crash." He motioned to the fallen crate.

"Too bad you can't just erase their memory again," Fire said.

Mind cast him an annoyed glance and his wound began to hurt, reminding Fire that his brother was still suppressing the pain. Mind could not permanently alter memories unless he was touching his target. At a distance, he could only alter memories for a short time, and it became progressively harder each time he altered a person's thoughts.

A shout rang out and then another. Mind and Fire hurried to one of the exits, but Mind caught him and pulled him into the rows of crates. Fire knew to trust his brother and did not resist, ducking from sight just as six guards rushed through the opening.

More below, Mind said. *We're going to have to fight.*

"I wouldn't have it any other way," Fire murmured.

He cast his curved sword and placed a propulsion charm on the bottom crate. Mind drew his sword and darted towards the exit as the

27

charm exploded, sending the crate from its moorings. It crashed into two guards and burst apart. Other crates tumbled to the ground as soldiers dove for safety. By the time they recovered, Mind and Fire were already rushing down the stairs.

"The estate above has most of the guards," Mind said, taking the lead. "Four are on the balcony, six ahead of us. Four seconds 'til they round the corner."

Fire twisted his body and swung his sword through the air. An arc of fire ignited on the blade and came free, spinning down the length of the corridor to strike two guards that stepped into view. Both cried out as the arc of fire caught them in the midsection, plunging deep into flesh and leaving them crumpled on the wall.

The remainder raised shields and charged. Mind struck one shield and ducked a sword swing. Then he reached out and slapped the man on the cheek. He came to a halt, his features growing confused before he rounded on his companion, his eyes wide with fear.

"Kill the demon!"

The confused man swung his weapon and the other guard hastily raised his shield, but the attacker ignored his shouts and struck the shield repeatedly, driving him back. The other two guards came for Fire. He hissed in pain as he swung his sword, parrying his opponents until Mind darted in, his blade striking twice. When they fell, Fire stepped over their bodies and followed his brother.

"If your plan hadn't left me like this, I wouldn't have needed assistance."

"I know," Mind said. "But we wouldn't have a destination without that wound."

Fire didn't care for the casual dismissal of his pain, and fleetingly wondered if Mind would sacrifice him for a victory. Mind glanced back, his disapproving look making Fire feel stupid for thinking such thoughts.

"I'd never let you die," Mind said.

"I know you wouldn't," Fire said.

Fire grimaced, sorry for thinking so ill of his brother, and Mind nodded as if he accepted the unspoken apology. Then they exited the stairs into the lowest sub-basement and sprinted for the balcony. The door was open, with four guards struggling to untie the two bound guards, one of whom was in his undergarments, his uniform on Mind. His eyes widened and he shouted a warning.

"There! Don't let him touch you!"

The fear in his voice made Fire grin. Then he sidestepped a swinging sword and slapped the guard on the chest, placing a propulsion charm. The fire ignited, sending him tumbling backwards. His feet caught on the railing and he flipped into the air, the charm sending him hurtling up and then down and then into the cliff. The man grunted as his body struck the stone below the balcony.

"I *told* you not to let him touch you!" the bound man in his undergarments shouted.

Fire deflected another sword attack and twisted, avoiding a hasty blow from the side. Each motion sent pain lancing through his chest and arm, and he grimaced, avoiding the incoming blows by drifting to the side. Mind filled the gap.

He knocked a sword upward and rotated in, avoiding a swing by his companion. Reversing his sword, he struck once backwards and then whipped his sword forward, killing two before darting to the final man.

Outside the balcony, the man soared upward, the fire on his chest sending him screaming toward the moon. Distracted by the sight of his flying companion, the fourth guard on the balcony didn't see Fire's fist until it slammed into his jaw. He went down hard, his sword falling from his grip.

"You are the fragments of Draeken," the man in his undergarments quavered.

"Indeed," Fire said.

The man swallowed. "Are you here to kill us because of what Serak did to Elenyr?"

Fire and Mind came to a halt. "What about Elenyr?" Mind asked.

29

The man's eyes widened and he shook his head. "Nothing, I just—"

His scream echoed off the cliff wall, the pain sending his body into convulsions. Fire watched Mind interrogate the man until the guard slumped in his bonds, gasping and crying. Then Mind knelt before him.

"I can make you feel a pain you cannot imagine." His voice was as dark as Fire had ever heard. "What happened to Elenyr?"

The man shook his head. "Serak will kill me."

Mind watched him for a moment and then rose to his feet. "Serak thinks he killed Elenyr in Cloudy Vale."

"But I didn't tell you anything," the man protested.

"Yes you did." Fire struck him in the face, and the man lapsed into unconsciousness. Fire rose and turned to Mind. "Did Serak succeed?"

Mind shook his head. "I don't know."

Unnoticed, the guard in the air plummeted to the earth, the propulsion charm on his chest sputtering. He landed in a corn field, flattening several plants, his shout falling silent. As Mind and Fire departed, Mind shared what he'd picked from the guard's thoughts, and Fire's worry mounted.

Chapter 3: A Home Destroyed

Mind and Fire hastened to the secret refuge. Astride two tigers conjured from fire, they rushed across the countryside, igniting leaves on the ground and small branches in their wake. Mind shouted to Fire and he extinguished the fires before they could spread. Otherwise they did not speak.

Mind had shared the memories he'd acquired from the guard, a handful of images where higher acolytes talked of Elenyr's assassination. In the last memory, the guard had stood watch while Serak met with Hyren and a third, masked figure. Named Carn, the man was rumored to have the magic of lightning, the lone power capable of killing Elenyr.

"Stop thinking like that," Mind called over to him. "You're making me worry."

"You're not worried?" Fire demanded. "You saw the memory. If Serak and Carn can surprise Elenyr . . ."

He didn't finish the statement, and Mind merely urged his tiger to greater speed. Avoiding the roads, they rushed through the trees, their fiery feline steeds leaping crags and fallen trees as they worked their way south, to the border of Talinor. Fighting fatigue, both pushed their steeds and themselves until the high cliffs of home appeared in the distance.

Fire imagined finding a body, the thought hurting worse than Hyren's sword. They'd fought countless foes over the ages, and never had he seen Elenyr be in such danger. But Serak was cunning, and the fact he had a lightning mage at his side only made him more dangerous.

"I told you to stop thinking like that."

They reached the cliff and leapt from their steeds. Mind pressed the rune and a hidden door swung open. They hurried into the darkness, the tigers dissipating into smoke and cinders that drifted into the wind.

"I'm not thinking anything," Fire said.

"You keep wondering if we'll find her body."

"Will we?"

There was a hesitation before, "I don't know."

Fire's chest tightened further. Mind had a gift for strategy, and he was the most intelligent of the fragments. If he doubted her survival, then Elenyr could indeed be dead. Swallowing against the burgeoning worry, he sprinted up the dim corridors to the entrance of Cloudy Vale.

"Smoke," he said, slowing and gathering his magic. "I can smell it."

Mind drew his sword and advanced to the threshold, where sunlight streamed into what remained of Cloudy Vale. Fire sucked in a breath as they stepped into the open, and the full breadth of the destruction came into view.

At just a few hundred feet across, the refuge contained a handful of burned trees, the wood blackened and cracked, the leaves gone. The doorways and windows that had lined the surrounding cliffs had exploded, stones and the remains of furniture scattered across the grass, muddying the pond.

Fire turned a slow circle, but his home, and the homes of his brothers, had suffered the brunt of the damage. Beams and stones littered the caves, with gaping cavities where the rooms had once been. Elenyr's home was gone, the porch and balcony shattered, sodden and burned books scattered across the wet ground. An icy wind blew into the empty refuge, as if the wilds were eager to reclaim what had once been their home.

"I don't believe it," Fire exclaimed.

"I cannot sense any other minds," Mind said.

"You cannot sense the dead."

Fire hurried to Elenyr's home and picked his way over the beams and debris, pushing his way inside. Ducking a fallen beam, he worked his way past the ruined entrance hall, pausing at the painting of Alydian, Elenyr's only daughter. The canvas was ripped and burned, the vestiges of the wood poking through the rubble.

"Elenyr!"

His shout was muffled by the ash, and he pushed further, into the library at the back of Elenyr's home. The room was obviously the source of the blast. Bookcases were broken and ripped apart, tomes burned to just their leather bindings, and even the stone walls cracked from the concussive blast.

"She would have survived if she was ethereal," Fire said.

"Lightning magic stops her from turning ethereal."

"Do you have to be so negative?" Fire stabbed a finger at the gaping hole in the fireplace, obviously from a different sort of impact. "She could still be alive in here."

They split up to search the home, sifting through rubble and stone. At any moment Fire expected to see a hand or a foot, partially buried in rocks. He braced himself for the worst, and told himself he would be fine.

But he wasn't.

The thought of losing Elenyr, the woman that had trained them, raised them, loved them, sparked such anger that he trembled. He searched for spots of heat that would indicate a body, but found nothing. All cold.

"Here!" Mind's shout reached him as he sifted through a section of rubble.

"You found her?"

"No," Mind said. "But I found something else."

Fire climbed a pile of rocks to where Mind stood on a section of the balcony at the rear of the room. A hole in the wall revealed a secret chamber beyond, where memory orbs littered the floor, most of them cracked from their fall.

Fire ducked into the space. "Did you know this was here?"

"No," Mind said. "But we always knew she had secrets." He picked up a few orbs. "These were activated recently. I'd say a week past."

"That's when the fire burned." Fire swept a hand at the library.

Mind raised an eyebrow. "You certain?"

"You know mind magic," he said. "I know when a fire burned."

"There wasn't a door." Mind pointed to the entrance. "It was just solid rock. I suspect Elenyr found this cave and used it to store her personal memories."

"What was she looking at?"

Mind frowned as he examined an orb, his eyes flickering purple. "If I'm not mistaken, she was searching for Serak in her memory. That is from a couple thousand years ago."

"She was trying to find him," Fire said.

"It looks that way."

Mind sifted through the orbs, tossing away those that were too damaged to function. Most were intact, probably because the chamber was far enough behind the library that the blast hadn't reached it, but the explosion had knocked the orbs from their stands. Many were broken on the floor.

"She must have come here after we departed for Mistkeep," Fire said.

"Agreed." Mind frowned and examined an orb that still sat on a shelf. "She wanted to study our foe."

"So she was alive when she was here." Fire's attention was on the orb in his hands, and he didn't see Mind slip an orb into his pocket.

34

"Do you think she knows about Beldik? Is that why she came here?"

"I don't know." He pointed outward. "But if they were setting a trap, they would have waited in the grounds outside her home. When she stepped out, she would have been vulnerable."

"She could have departed through the stone." Fire pointed to the back of the chamber, which led north.

"True, but Elenyr likes to see the grounds before she leaves. I suspect it's a remnant of her time before being the Hauntress, when she would walk out the door. Old habits are hard to break, even when you can pass through walls."

They departed the secret room and made their way to the front of the house. It didn't take them long to find where the ground had been scorched by a power other than fire. Fire stooped and examined the large paw prints.

"Lightning," he said. "Probably a wolf entity."

Mind turned and surveyed the house, his forehead knit in thought. "Water crafted a staff for her, and it hung in the guest quarters on the second floor."

"You think she went for it?" Fire asked.

Mind's expression turned pensive. He had an annoying habit of knowing everyone's actions before they took them. Of course, in this instance Fire hoped it led to Elenyr.

"She would have run inside," Mind murmured to himself. "Sought to go to the second floor and retrieve the staff." He took a step forward, his eyes on the ground, where a partial boot print was visible. "She must have been injured, or she would have just turned ethereal."

"Probably a lightning snare," Fire said. "It would keep her from turning ethereal without killing her."

Mind nodded in agreement. "Serak wanted to prolong her death. He's watched us for five thousand years. He wouldn't want to kill her too quickly."

35

Fire's hand balled into a fist. "I won't make that mistake."

"Not if I kill Serak first," Mind muttered, and then pointed into the house. "The fireplace in the library," he said, his voice now tinged with recognition. "The hole at the base was broken *inward*, like a wolf of lightning pursuing a quarry. She must have used the chimney to reach the second floor."

"She managed to get the staff and jump out here," Fire said.

"How do you know?" Mind raised an eyebrow in surprise.

Fire stooped and picked up a broken piece of Water's staff. Then he spotted the scorched section of ground next to where he'd found the shard, the mark a powerful bolt of lightning made when it struck the earth. They both stared at the evidence of Elenyr's final battle.

"It cannot be," Mind breathed.

Anger pooled in Fire's belly like bile, threatening to burst from his pores. He wanted to rend and destroy, shatter the bones of every Order member until he had Serak himself in his grip, and he could squeeze the life from his eyes. Flames gathered across his hands and fingers, spitting sparks.

Mind stood rigid. He stared at the scorched spot, not speaking or moving, just frozen. At the same time he seemed fragile, as if the mountain wind would knock him over. Suddenly his eyes snapped up.

"Someone is coming."

"The Order?"

Mind sprinted to the opening, his blade appearing his hand, Fire leapt after. They flanked the opening but Fire did not cast a weapon. If they were the Order, he didn't want to kill them. He wanted to *punish* them.

Footsteps echoed in the corridor, and Fire's hands balled into fists. He imagined crushing them with his bare hands, extinguishing their life as they had done to Elenyr. The anger built, rising up his throat, the fire threatening to burst into dragon's flame.

They guard their minds. Mind thought. *Could be senior acolytes.*

The two turned the corner, but in the gloom Fire could not discern their identities. They walked with caution, a man and a woman, both human. The woman had a sword while the man carried a bow, the weapons out and ready. Mind was faster.

The moment they stepped into the open he struck, slapping the bow from the man's grip. The woman rotated to Fire, narrowly missing his fist as it swung past her hair. She slashed for his back—and then recoiled.

"Fire?"

Locked in combat, the man suddenly retreated. "Mind? Where have the two of you been?"

Fire finally looked at them and recognized the uniforms of the Bladed, the legendary mercenary force that had exactly one hundred members. Both were highly ranked, obviously well trained.

"Why are you here?" Mind demanded, his voice so forceful that the woman flinched.

"We came on Jeric's order," one spoke hastily.

"To get Elenyr's body?"

The man exchanged a look with his companion, and the woman shook her head. "Elenyr lives. Jeric took her to Ilumidora. We are here to retrieve her sword."

The words washed over Fire, and all the fire in his blood extinguished in an instant, the relief so sharp that he raised a hand to his forehead, and realized he was trembling. He swallowed, and then again, desperate to prevent the tears from leaking into sight.

She's alive.

Mind's mental voice punctured Fire's resolve and he turned away, unwilling to let the Bladed witness the tears on his cheeks. Coughing, he gestured to the devastated refuge, and spoke over his shoulder.

"Tell us everything."

Chapter 4: Xshaltheria

Rynda's consciousness returned slowly, bringing with it a throbbing headache. She'd endured dozens of sleeping charms in her childhood training and knew its effects. But she hadn't endured one since becoming queen, and the anger was sharp. Keeping her eyes shut, she set aside the lingering pain of the magic and focused on her other senses.

She lay in a wagon, that much was obvious. The casual swaying shifted her on her back, her shoulder bouncing against another body. Short. Harry. Probably dwarven. An edge of armor rubbed on her elbow. Definitely dwarven. And since she was here, and other monarchs were being kidnapped, the dwarf was probably the king.

A scowl threatened to push its way onto her lips but she held it in check. She couldn't afford to lose focus. Not now. She was a rock troll queen, taken against her will. Her actions in this moment might make the difference between life and death. Plus she really wanted to crush a few skulls.

She caught a whiff of pine, the air tinged with a cold only felt at higher altitude. The pine indicated they were in Griffin, probably in the far east where villages were scattered. Kidnapping two monarchs drew attention, and while transporting them to a distant refuge was necessary, it also gave her time. If they weren't close to their destination, it would give her a chance to escape.

A muffled clop touched her ears, the sound of horseshoes on rocky ground. Uneven, like the road was ill maintained. They were already outside the stretch of Griffin's maintained highways, indicating they were close to their location. Not much time.

The urge to act rose in her belly, but she chained the desire and continued to listen. More horses, and muffled voices. Ten. Twenty.

More. The wagon had the scent of steel, meaning she was in a box built to contain a troll. Serak had prepared.

A change in the dwarf's breathing indicated he was rousing, and she hoped he would not betray them. She tensed, planning how to act if he began blustering like his kind. If he did, she could use the distraction, but she prepared to knock him out with a single blow.

The wagon suddenly dropped, the wheels clattering onto a bridge. Wooden, like a drawbridge. She risked opening her eyes a crack and saw the interior of the wagon, steel as she'd thought. A tiny, barred window in the door allowed her a view of the sloping ground and towering pine trees. Mounted horses rode behind them, at least a score.

"How many?"

The dwarf spoke in an undertone. Rynda mentally praised him for his reserve. Perhaps he was not an entire loss. She hadn't met the new king, and because of the war with Bartoth, hadn't been to his crowning. But the conclave to decide on the new king had only deliberated for nine days instead of the usual month. That spoke volumes for his caliber. The dwarves never made a decision in haste unless it involved beer or blood.

"Two score," she murmured. "East Griffin. Outside the claimed lands."

"We've come far," he said. "Troll?"

"Rynda."

"Dothlore."

So it was the king. His kidnapping supported what the fragments had been saying, even if she'd never thought she would be one of those taken. The last thing she remembered was the ground opening up beneath her and the sleeping charm robbing her of voice. Serak had planned his attack with care, perhaps even choosing Bartoth's battlefield because it led the rock trolls to select their chosen camp. It had been the only defensible location for miles.

She risked peeking again and spotted walls and battlements through the window, but not of a fortress. Rather the walls lined the road, and the slant of the wagon suggested they were still climbing, probably to a fortress higher up a mountain. The fortifications were old, ancient even, the stone worn by time, the edges rounded and coated in grime.

"I smell sulfur," Dothlore murmured.

"Volcano?"

There were a handful of mostly dormant volcanoes on the far eastern edge of Griffin. According to legend they had once contained settlements, but the people had long since moved to the more arable lands closer to the great Blue Lake.

"I am bound. You?"

The dwarf sounded annoyed, and Rynda realized that he wasn't used to being caged. Her own shackles bound her ankle to the floor of the wagon. Her hands were not bound. Their captors must not fear their escape, or perhaps they didn't expect them to be awake already.

"My feet," Rynda said.

The dwarf shifted, moving with a bounce in the wagon so anyone watching would not notice. The motion allowed him a peek at her bonds, and he released a faint rumble. The dismay was evident.

"Mithral band. Mithral stud."

She resisted the urge to look. Steel she could bend. Mithral would defy even her considerable strength. But it was still bound in the wood at the base of the wagon, and wood might yield if she pulled hard enough. She could even use the spike as a weapon.

A distant clanking of steel indicated a rising portcullis, and she realized they were out of time. If they were to make an escape, it would have to happen now, before they were inside the fortress walls.

She opened her eyes further and saw the mounted soldiers through the window. They were drifting apart, obviously focused on their destination. She shifted her body weight, bending her knees to bring herself close to the stud. If she could brace her weight against the floor, she might be able to wrench the stud free.

She grasped the mithral shackle and leaned back, gradually adding pressure against the stud. Like most fastenings, it would be spiraled, digging into the wood to prevent exactly what she was attempting. But the stud was only as strong as the wood it was fastened to, and it began to pull free, the wood ripping and splitting, groaning under the strain.

A call came from outside the wagon and she gave up subtlety. Rearing back, she yanked on the bond, ripping it from the wood in a savage burst of power. She jumped to the rear door, reaching it as it swung open. The man's face registered surprise, and then crumpled under Rynda's fist. She leapt out and picked up his sword, tossing it back into the wagon, where Dothlore caught it and placed it beneath his own band, using it as a lever to rip the stud free.

Rynda stood on a high road, the slope descending for miles to a long valley. The road passed through aged fortifications until it disappeared into the trees, each section of battlements manned by a small force. She took in the view at a glance and then whirled to the surprised guards.

Rynda picked up a nearby soldier by the throat and launched him at the horse behind, knocking the legs from beneath the steed. Rider and mount crashed in a heap, and Rynda leap to the next horseman. She dodged a hasty swing by his axe and shoulder-bashed the mounted soldier off the road. The horse whinnied in fear and tumbled down a slope, its bulk crushing its rider.

"Rynda!" Dothlore shouted. "Behind you!"

She heard the horseman charging and whirled, raising her hand to the streaking sword. Bartoth had severed her arm below her elbow, but her people had paid a steep price for a group of dwarves to craft a replacement. The steel hand emanated perpetual heat, but it felt like her own flesh. She caught the blade in her steel grip, the blade coming to a halt on the steel. The man cried out in shock as she yanked him from the saddle. Flipping the human sword in her hand, she caught the handle and tossed it to the dwarven king.

"Too small for me," she called.

Dothlore caught it and hurled it at another soldier, the blade spinning end over end before plunging into the man's chest. The man

42

screamed and fell backward, yanking on the reins and bringing his steed to its knees. The horse behind sought to jump but clipped its front legs, sending both horse and rider tumbling.

"Too light for me," the dwarf said. "I need an axe."

"I think that is not necessary," a voice said.

They both spun to find a robed man striding towards them. Silver hair grew on his temples, giving his black hair a distinguished look. He bore no weapon but did not seem concerned that his two captives had killed several men in seconds. Then Rynda's gaze lifted beyond him, to the fortress set above.

The battlements ringed the top of the volcano, the wall interspersed with towers. The wagon had come to a halt just a hundred feet from the main entrance, where the winding road reached a drawbridge and portcullis. Both were open, and soldiers streamed from within. Rynda retreated, but more soldiers charged from farther down the road.

"It cannot be," Dothlore breathed, his gaze on the fortress.

"You know this place?" Rynda asked.

"Xshaltheria," the dwarf said, "ancient forge of my people."

"Indeed," the man said, his grey eyes sparkling with delight. "Abandoned since the first sentenium, when the core of the volcano grew cold. The winters are brutal, but the privacy is unparalleled."

Rynda eyed the two ranks forming on either end. She yearned for her soulblade, the sword she'd forged with her own hand. Armed with the weapon, she could cut a swath through Serak's forces and escape— so she could return with her army and punish them for their arrogance. But she had only empty hands and a dwarf.

"Who are you?" Rynda demanded.

"I am Zenif," he replied. "Second in the Order of Ancients behind Serak."

"What do you want from us?" Dothlore demanded.

43

"You'll find out soon enough," the man said. "For now, I think you must be tired from your journey."

He began to advance, raising his hand to point at them. Rynda recoiled as a wave of fatigue washed over her, the sleeping charm hitting heavy. She growled and jumped to the wagon. She caught the wheel and ripped it from the axle, and the wagon slumped. Spinning, she sent it hurtling at the man, who ducked, the wheel crushing two soldiers standing behind.

Rynda fell to one knee, snarling as the magic worked on her thoughts, robbing her of consciousness. The guards flooded to her, grabbing her arms and shoulders, attempting to drag her down. She caught one by the ankle and used his body like a club, bashing his neighbors. Armor cracked and bent until she hurled the man at Zenif.

She heard a *thud* as Dothlore hit the ground. He managed to free an arm and pulled a knife from a man's belt, using it to stab at an attacker. Then he was overpowered, his growls growing silent. Rynda set her gaze on the mage and drove to her feet. With seven men clinging to her body, she stumbled towards him, her iron hand outstretched, reaching for his throat.

"I'll rip you apart!"

"Don't fight it," Zenif said. "It will hurt less when you wake up."

"I will not be caged!" Rynda bellowed.

In a surge of adrenaline, she closed the gap. The mage hastily retreated, but she grabbed his tunic and slammed him to the road. She had the pleasure of his voice filling with panic, but the magic pressing on her thoughts eroded her awareness, and her body slumped.

"Get her off me!" Zenif shrieked.

Her steel hand twitched, the heat of her steel fingers scorching his tunic as his men pulled him free. Rynda fought to stay awake, willing herself to fight. But her eyes defied her will, and she lapsed into slumber.

Chapter 5: Queen in a Cage

Rynda woke in a cell, her hand going to her forehead, which hurt worse than before. Her blood pounded against her skull, but she shoved the pain aside and scanned the small room to find Dothlore sitting on the second bed. He looked up when she shifted.

"About time you woke up."

She sat up and groaned. "How long?"

"Best as I can tell, it's been two days since we arrived."

"*Two days?*"

She immediately regretted the shout. She grimaced and rubbed her neck, attempting to sooth the ache. The dwarf king grunted and pointed to his own head. "Sleeping charms hurt worse when used on a resistant victim."

"It's not my first time," she spat. "I was trained as a child to resist, but this magic was much stronger than normal. I wouldn't expect a dwarf to know that."

Dothlore scowled. "No need for hostility. We're in this together."

She shook her head to clear it, and then spotted a pitcher of water on a ledge nearby. She reached for it and drained the pitcher, spilling water down her armor, which she saw was the same she'd been wearing when she'd been taken. It now reeked of the road, but at least they hadn't tried to change her clothes while she was unconscious.

"I assume we're in the fortress?"

"Xshaltheria," he said with a nod. "Hasn't seen an occupant in ages."

"Until Serak claimed it."

He watched her slake her thirst and then pointed upward. "It appears Zenif was truthful. He's Serak's top lieutenant, at least according to the others."

"What do you mean, *others*?"

The dwarf strode to the door and swung it open. Rynda followed him through the opening into a large common area surrounded by other cells. Circular and vaulted, the space was high enough for her, its stone walls bare except for bracketed light orbs. Sitting about the space were the other captive monarchs.

Her entrance quieted them, and they stared at her towering figure. The monarchs huddled in small groups, sitting on crates around a makeshift table. She recognized King Porlin of Talinor, King Justin of Griffin, and King Werin, the orc king. King Meroosi of the gnome kingdom walked out of another cell and eyed Rynda with veiled hatred. To Rynda's surprise, there was also a pair of goblins, which she recognized as chieftains of the largest tribes. They recoiled from Rynda and retreated to the threshold of one of the other cells.

"Where's King Numen?" she asked. "And Queen Alosia?"

"Numen was dragged away weeks ago," Justin said. "Haven't seen him since."

"I don't think Serak has taken the elven queen yet," Porlin said, the hope in his voice bordering on desperate.

"Or she's dead," Rynda said, examining the room.

"We never thought he would succeed in bringing you in," Justin said, motioning to the dwarf. "Either of you."

It was a tacit admission that she and Dothlore were considered the strongest of the monarchs, and she did not argue the obvious truth. To be caged with the humans, goblins, and other lesser races was bad enough, but the fact that Serak had bested her—twice—is what rankled the most.

"I don't plan on staying long," Rynda said flatly.

Porlin came to his feet, revealing that he'd lost weight in captivity. His waist was still rotund, but his clothes were loose and ill-fitted. Rynda doubted the food in prison was his usual fare of roast duck and rich bread.

On opposite sides of the room, barred openings represented the only entrances. One led to the hall, where a pair of golems stood well back from the barrier. The two golems were made of fire and water, both hulking creatures as large as Rynda, sentries that would not grow fatigued, or succumb to persuasion.

Rynda strode to the opposite end of the room, where bars covered the opening leading to a balcony. She leaned against the bars, surprised to see the wall of rock blocking her view, the barrier a hundred feet away. It stretched in all directions, but curved inward. Dothlore joined her and motioned to the wall.

"Xshaltheria hangs inside the volcano," he said. "See the chains?"

She shifted and looked upward, spotting a chain as thick as a castle turret fastened to the inside of the volcano. "That supports the entire fortress?"

"Three great chains hold us aloft," Dothlore said.

"You think we can escape?" Porlin's desperate hope returned.

Rynda curled her lip in disdain. "I wasn't built for a cage."

"Neither were we," Justin said, his voice gaining an edge.

"She'll get us killed," one of the goblin chieftains muttered.

"Or she'll kill us herself." The second spat on the floor. "It's what trolls do."

Rynda ignored them. She hated goblins, but only because they preyed on the weak and served the strong. Most of the tribes had allied with Bartoth, and it seemed the two chieftains in their room had refused. Apparently that led to their captivity.

"Have any of you done anything?" she asked Dothlore.

"No need to be so caustic," he said.

She grabbed the bars and tested them, pulling and twisting, but they had no give. When it proved futile she moved on. She prowled the cage like a beast, and the other monarchs wisely gave her space. Being imprisoned with a bunch of useless kings might very well end in bloodshed. She wouldn't be the one bleeding, of course, but she was glad the goblins retreated to their quarters. If they got in her way, she'd snap them like twigs.

One of the doors led to a privy with a small bathing room. She checked the plumbing, hoping for weaker walls, but the walls had been specifically strengthened. The more she searched, the more obvious it became that she was well and truly trapped.

"Can you escape?" Porlin repeated.

"Do you even *have* a spine?"

Porlin reddened and retreated to the table, muttering under his breath. Rynda stepped to the bars and reached towards the golems, hoping she could engage them in a duel. But they remained rooted in place, the fire golem occasionally spilling flames onto the floor, where they died in sparks and smoke.

"Serak prepared for us," Dothlore said, his voice low as he joined her at the bars. "We need to work together."

Rynda rounded on him. "We are not allies, dwarf. We are not friends, or even peers. You are all weak monarchs, used to the comfort of your thrones. Do not think I will free you. If you wish to escape, do so. Otherwise, do not speak to me."

"We stand a better chance together," Justin said, his voice making clear she'd pricked his pride.

"*You* stand a better chance with *me*," Rynda said. "I don't need you."

"Queen Rynda," Dothlore said. "You would escape and leave us all here?"

"Without a second thought."

Dothlore regarded her with a strange expression. "I thought better of you."

He turned and strode away, and she almost struck him in the back. The comment, said so quietly that only she heard, landed heavy. She didn't owe the monarchs anything. Indeed King Justin and trollkind were just a few years from outright war. His expansion into the unclaimed lands had heightened strife among the goblin tribes, and Bartoth's army had further strained relations. If Serak had not intervened, Rynda might very well have been facing the king across the battlefield, instead of trapped in a cell close to his too vulnerable neck.

The kings fell to muttering, cursing under their breath. Rynda hated the touch of guilt and shoved it aside. Most of the men in the room, with the exception of the dwarf, had lied to her on numerous occasions, sought to cheat her, disparaged her kind to their captains and children. Why should she help them?

"They look to you with hope."

Rynda rotated to the source of the voice, and found a dark elf standing just out of sight. Her cell was the closest to the bars at the corridor, her room darker than the others. Rynda had never met her, but knew her to be queen of the dark elves, Queen Erisay.

"I'm not going to save them."

"You should."

"You think to judge me?" Rynda said, heat creeping into her voice. "They hate you as much as they do me."

"Exactly."

The queen faded into her cell, and Rynda remained in place, clenching and unclenching her fists, wondering why she felt so aggravated. She had no love for the monarchs, and would have killed them without a thought on the battlefield. But here, trapped in a cell without any explanation, she found herself with a desire to protect her foes.

Releasing an explosive breath that sent the two goblins scrambling away, she circled the room again, scanning for weaknesses, checking every bar, every crack, every hollow in the stone.

The other kings kept their distance, and the minutes turned into hours. Arguments were frequent in the common room, and simmering tempers flared often. Old grievances were hurled at each other as the others looked on, but it rarely came to blows. Many looks were cast to Rynda, but she largely ignored them, and continued to search the prison. She entered each cell, testing stone and bars, shoving the goblins aside when they protested the intrusion. Without a weapon they could not cause harm, at least to her, and she idly wondered what Serak would do if she snapped their necks.

She expected Serak or Zenif, or maybe Wylyn to come, but none appeared. Only the two golems stood watch. Occasionally a shouted order could be heard, the muffled sound robbed of its clarity by the twisting corridors of the ancient dwarven forge.

By nightfall she'd only found one potential escape, a bar at the back balcony that felt a touch loose. It wasn't much, but it was more than the rest of the prison offered. As the others retreated to their cells, she grasped the bar and began to work, pushing, twisting, and turning. At all times she listened for sounds from the corridor, the silence broken by the faint grinding of steel on stone.

Occasionally the dark elf came and sat at her side, but she did not speak, and Rynda did not break the silence. Erisay had been the first one taken, and had likely been in this prison for weeks, forced to watch as other monarchs joined her in captivity. She probably wished to be around another queen, even if it was just Rynda.

Eventually Rynda turned to speak, but the dark elf had gone, leaving Rynda alone in the common room. Annoyed, she continued to work the bar until her hands ached. Even her steel hand seemed to hurt. Taking a break, she drank her fill from a small fountain set at the side of the room and washed her hands. Her steel hand caused the water to steam, and she put the warm liquid on her neck. After the brief respite, she returned to the loose bar and wrapped her hands around the smooth surface.

The faint grinding continued. A quarter turn left, a quarter turn right. As she pushed against the unyielding stone, her thoughts drifted to Erisay and her comment. Why had she expected Rynda to lead the monarchs to freedom?

Alone in the common room, Rynda shoved the bar, releasing her irritation on the barrier of the prison. She didn't care why Serak had taken them, but if he hoped they would unite while trapped in the same room, he was a fool.

A touch of light brightened outside the balcony, marking the approach of dawn. After ten hours of laboring on the bar, fatigue had risen, and Rynda scowled, annoyed that she would have to sleep in the cell. She'd hoped to escape before the other kings had awoken. For several furious seconds she heightened her efforts, all but slamming the bar against its moorings. Under the constant assault the stone finally yielded, and a tiny crack appeared at the base. Smiling to herself, she left the bar and returned to her cell. She would sleep for a couple of hours and then return, but now she knew escape was imminent. To her irritation, the question remained. Would she escape alone?

Chapter 6: Disturbing Memories

Fire picked up a piece of wreckage and tried to identify where it had come from before tossing it onto the pile. One of his fire golems lifted a long beam and carried it away, allowing him to enter a back section of his personal home. It had survived most of the damage but reeked of smoke.

Fire sighed and scanned the piles they had created. Fire had spent two days rebuilding what had once been his house, sorting burned beams and chunks of stone. He'd managed to salvage a handful of weapons, and his collection of dwarven fire-daggers was intact, but little else had survived the explosion. He sighed in irritation and abandoned the house to return to Elenyr's quarters, where Mind still labored.

"Are you done yet?"

"Almost."

"Why did we not deliver the sword to Elenyr?" Fire asked.

"I saw Elenyr through their eyes," Mind said evasively. "She will not wake for days. There was no need to hasten."

It was the answer he'd given before, which left Fire even more annoyed. "Just how deep were her wounds?"

"Worse than you can imagine."

Fire looked away, uncomfortable with that image. They'd helped the two Bladed retrieve Elenyr's sword and then sent them on their way. Mind had removed the memories of the encounter so they would not know Fire and Mind had been present. The fragments remained in the Vale, sifting through wreckage.

Fire had wanted to depart with the two mercenaries, arrive with them and support Elenyr. But Mind had been insistent they stay behind.

Fire was used to Mind withholding the truth, but this was different. Mind did not want to see Elenyr, not in such a state.

"I hate it when you try to guess my thoughts," Mind said.

"Says the one reading mine."

Mind sifted through a pile of ash, revealing a memory orb. He picked it up and examined the surface. He smiled to himself and tucked the glass sphere into the pouch at his side. Then he stood and motioned to the exit.

"Time to leave."

"It's about time. Did you find what you were looking for?" He swept a hand to the golems and they disintegrated, dropping their burdens onto the ground.

"What makes you think I was searching for something?"

Fire fell into step beside him as they walked towards the exit. "I can't read your mind, but I'm not a fool."

After a moment's hesitation, Mind cast him a look of appraisal. "Have you ever wondered about Elenyr's secrets?"

"Everyone has secrets," Fire said. "That's what makes us human."

"But she is more guarded than most," Mind pressed. "And her secrets led to this."

He swept a hand at Cloudy Vale and both paused on the threshold. Fire's eyes swept across the destroyed homes and gardens, the remnant of his home. He'd assumed they would rebuild, but now wondered if they would abandon the refuge. He didn't care for the prospect.

"You cannot think her secrets led to this attack?"

"Perhaps."

He withdrew a memory orb and tossed it to him. Confused, Fire caught the sphere and activated it by pressing the rune. The light expanded to surround them, and depicted Elenyr sitting at a desk, her features brooding and heavy. She absently tapped her finger on her arm, a habit from when she'd been oracle, when she'd liked to cast magic under her finger where none could see.

"I do not know if I can ever tell the fragments the truth," she said. "Just knowing such a secret will change them, and I fear the consequence of such a change."

She rose and began to pace, staying in range of the orb that was recording the memory. She looked different, younger, more vibrant. Her hair was cut long, a style she had not favored for ages.

"Our first century?" Fire asked.

"See the figurine on the desk?" Mind pointed to the misshapen blob. "Light made that for Elenyr in our eightieth year."

"Do you remember *everything?*" Fire asked, his tone exasperated.

"I try."

"Light was never good with gifts," Fire said. "Remember the figurine he made for my date to the Talinorian festival?"

Mind actually smiled. "It looked like a foot—a broken foot."

"Light said it was her face." Fire grimaced at the memory. "She never spoke to me again."

"She wasn't your best pursuit," Mind said. "And why did you get the piece of Draeken that all women are drawn to?"

"Jealous?" Fire asked, but Mind motioned him to silence as Elenyr spoke again.

"Their training is coming along well, and they are just beginning to master the magic of their fragments, but this secret could destroy them all. Worse yet, I can think of no way to heal them without having the same effect. My only option is to remain silent, and hope they overcome it on their own."

She sighed in regret and reached for the orb, the memory ending in a flicker of light. Fire had always known Elenyr had secrets, but the memory carried a darker tone and implied a secret of much greater magnitude than he'd ever suspected. Doubt sparked in his chest, and he found himself feeling reluctant to see her. He was not usually the one to hesitate, but in this, he wasn't certain he wanted an answer.

"This is why you wanted to wait," he said slowly. "You wanted to find more in her secret room."

"This wasn't the only memory I found."

He stepped into the tunnel and strode away. Fire cast a lingering look at the ruins of his home and then followed, disturbed by Mind's words. Elenyr had always been a constant, always guiding with her soft voice. She fought for them, trained them from the moment of their creation, yet it seemed she had never spoken the full truth.

As they exited the mountain and entered the forest, he scowled and stabbed a finger toward Ilumidora. "Would she tell us the truth, if we asked her directly?"

"You were just questioning whether you wanted to know her secrets," Mind said. "Now you do?"

Fire jerked his head. "What could she know that would make her fear?"

"That's what disturbs me the most," Mind said.

Fire had never seen Elenyr so worried, not even when Shadow was caught by the gnome tribesman for stealing a relic, and they'd nearly killed him. Elenyr had fought with fury born of fear, but even then, she'd only been afraid for Shadow's life. In the memory, Elenyr had been afraid for more than their lives. She feared for their souls.

As they worked their way north, they spoke little, both brooding on the import of what they'd learned. Mind withdrew from Fire's thoughts, and Fire vacillated between angry and distrustful. He continued to have the nagging thought he would never trust Elenyr again. After four days, they neared the bright city of Ilumidora.

The capitol of the elven nation surrounded a lake, with a five-hundred-foot tree on the center island. The sentient tree supported the queen's castle, and the limbs connected to the trees lining the shore of the lake. Rivers floated in the treetops, pouring in waterfalls to the lake, and then rising in plumes of magic. Small watercraft rode the rivers up and down, providing transportation through the multiple levels of the city.

They entered Ilumidora through the southern gates, the guards staring in confusion to each other as Mind erased their memory of his and Fire's passage. Ascending a staircase, they worked their way through the high streets.

"Are we going to tell her we know?" Fire finally asked.

"Not yet," Mind said.

"This is tearing me up inside," Fire said. "How can you wait?"

"I could make you forget."

"My mental shields are not that weak."

Mind didn't respond.

Fire frowned at his silence. "What did you make me forget? Mind? *Mind?*"

Cursing under his breath, he followed his brother up through the teeming streets to the castle. Arrayed in rich robes and fine tunics, the elves of the upper city walked with a haughty bearing. Fire disliked the city of light, not as much as Shadow, but enough that he didn't care to visit. The dwarven cities, full of fire and heat, that was more his style. It didn't help that the male elves disliked his unruly hair and rough clothes, and sniffed in disdain when he passed. The women, though, couldn't take their eyes off him . . .

"Fire," Mind drawled. "Let's try to stay focused."

"Sorry."

They reached the castle and found the guards waiting for them, so they crossed the bridge to the public wing of the fortress. From there they were led into the great hall. With enormous windows of aquaglass and multiple balconies supported by curving branches, the great hall was unique across Lumineia. The guard guided them through the hall and to a set of stairs at the back.

Servants and guards passed them, many more than normal. Fire frowned, eyeing a heavily armed group of battlemages. They carried a host of weapons, anti-magic blades, mithral axes, fire swords, and mirror shields. The patrol eyed Fire and Mind like they were adversaries until they passed.

"Why the increased security?" Fire asked.

The guard motioned to the departing patrol. "The Order of Ancients has been kidnapping monarchs. The captain of the guard has pulled in much of the army to patrol the castle."

Another patrol appeared, this one with a dwarf in their midst. The dwarf strode along, casting heat detection spells along the wall, ensuring nobody could pass without the guards being aware.

"Isn't it excessive?"

"Only King Porlin and our queen remain," the guard said.

Mind frowned and caught Fire's eye, before passing a mental though. *He's worried about King Porlin. Orders are still coming from the throne of Talinor, but he hasn't been seen in weeks. He has also replaced his personal guard with a mercenary group.*

"You think he's been taken?"

Mind groaned and spoke through his mental link. *Can you ever be subtle?*

"Not my style," Fire said.

"What?" the guard said.

"Nothing," Mind muttered, and then thought to Fire, *I suspect only the elven queen remains, and it's only a matter of time until Serak comes for her.*

Fire cocked his head to the side, wondering if they should stay and protect the queen. If Serak was coming, they might not get another chance to strike the Father of Guardians. But doing so might give up their chance to find Beldik.

You think Elenyr is in danger? Mind continued to speak through his magic.

"Maybe," Fire said. "But if he comes for her, she will put up a fight." Then he cocked his head to the side. "Unless he doesn't know she is alive."

We should assume he knows everything we do.

"Probably wise to do so," Fire agreed.

"Are you well?" the guard asked uncertainly when Fire answered the comment he'd not heard.

Fire ignored him. "Jeric is here. He can protect the queen and Elenyr."

He realized he hadn't been thinking about Elenyr's secret, and wondered if Mind had forgotten. Fire didn't like the idea of holding back, and resolved that he would confront Elenyr. He wanted an answer.

Then Mind jerked his head and sent Fire a new thought, a single memory from several days ago, a memory from a guard in the castle, the moment Elenyr had arrived in Ilumidora. Fire faltered in his steps, stumbling on the smooth marble, and sucked in his breath.

He saw Elenyr lying in the bed of a wagon, her leg and arm mangled and burned, scorched black, the flesh torn open. Elves rushed to bandage the wounds but her flesh turned ethereal and the fabric passed through, falling to the wagon bed.

"She's dying!" a healer called. "We have to stabilize her or she won't survive."

Elenyr screamed, the sound ripped from her throat, a haunting howl that caused the healers to recoil. She reached out and struck a healer in the jaw, sending him to the floor. Her eyes were clenched shut, blood smeared across her face, staining her hair and tunic.

"Bind her!" a voice called.

"The bonds do not hold," a healer said, and then glanced over his shoulder to an approaching figure. "Do not let the queen get too close."

"You can't stop me," she said.

Queen Alosia all but shoved the elves out of the way and began to wrap a strange shimmering cloth around Elenyr's good arm. Still unconscious, Elenyr grimaced in pain but her body finally turned corporeal.

"Your grandmother's lightning shroud?" a healer exclaimed, aghast. "It's priceless—"

"It's Elenyr," the queen snapped.

The lightning shroud pulsed, and Elenyr's body remained solid. Healers rushed to bind her wounds, pouring liquid healing magic into her rent flesh. Elenyr finally sighed in relief, and although her arm twitched, the magic of the shroud forced her to remain solid.

"Take care of her," the queen barked. "She's guarded our people for ages. The least we could do is save her life."

The memory faded and Fire realized he'd come to a halt. He was sweating, fire burning on his hands, coursing up his shoulders and spilling down his throat. The guard stood back, his hand on his sword hilt. While Fire had been seeing the memory, a captain of the guard had appeared and stood at the guard's side, his hand on the hilt of his blade. Fire ignored them and turned to Mind.

"That's when she came in?"

"That's what Serak did to her," Mind said. "I found the memory in one of the guards at the castle."

Fire struggled to contain his anger and his magic, for the moment forgetting his worries about Elenyr's secret. He'd never seen Elenyr near death, never broken. Serak would pay for what he'd done.

"She is just ahead," the guard said uneasily.

"You may see her when you are in control," the captain said evenly.

Fire spared him a glance, and recognized him as the eldest son of the House of Runya. He was tall for an elf, and had the bearing of his father. Although still young for his kind, he'd received a captaincy for his skill.

"Horn," Fire said, using the elf's nickname. "I'm not going to burn the castle down."

"That's all I ask," Horn said with a faint smile. He motioned the guard away. "I'll deliver them from here."

"As you order," the elf said. He bowed to Fire and Mind before departing.

"Lead the way," Fire said, drawing in a breath, calming his emotions. But the anger did not dissipate, it only boiled beneath the surface. He would find Serak.

And he would kill him.

Chapter 7: Reunion

Horn guided them down a corridor lined with doors on the right and large aquaglass windows on the left, providing a view of the center of the fortress. With a plume of water rising from a fountain, the center of the fortress contained exterior balconies and winding paths, all overlooking the fountain.

The great tree supported three sections of the fortress. The first housed the great hall, kitchens, and servant quarters. The second branch supported the guest quarters, with its own balconies, fountains, and gardens. The final limb supported the queen's wing, with her own private quarters, library, study rooms, and other chambers reserved for family members.

Stairs of translucent aquaglass and sweeping bridges connected the three wings, granting access to the host of gardens, overlooks, and smaller turrets that interspersed the segmented fortress. At the heart of the citadel, a great fountain cast water into the sky. The plume of water fed the floating streams that curved around the fortress, making the citadel resemble a castle in an orb of glass

As they descended the steps towards the gardens, Fire braced himself for what they would find. Elenyr had been broken, shattered, on the verge of death, but it had all been viewed through the eyes of another. To see it in person . . .

They came down the stairs into a small garden suspended between the guest wing and the queen's wing. On the opposite side, stairs climbed to a small guardhouse, where six armed soldiers flanked a closed gate.

A small tree rose in the center of the garden, the leaves well into autumn, some of the branches displaying bare wood. Flowers and other flora dotted the oval shaped garden, interspersed by comfortable benches, all looking into the heart of the fortress and the grand fountain.

Fire's breath caught as he spotted Elenyr. She was sitting on a bench under the tree, and the bandages on her leg and arm were prominent, as were the handful of other patches of white on her body. Gone was the blood from the memory, replaced by scars.

"Captain," Elenyr said, rising to her feet.

"I believe these belong to you," Horn said.

Elenyr smiled at the captain. "They do indeed."

She embraced Fire, and he fought the well of emotion. She'd always been strong, but now she seemed so frail, like the embrace would crack her in two. He forced a smile, which she returned. She then resumed her seat on the bench, wincing in pain.

"You can walk," Mind said. "That's an improvement."

"I walked thirty steps and I'm exhausted," Elenyr said, her expression annoyed. "Hardly an accomplishment."

Fire motioned to her wounds. "You survived a lot of damage."

"I should remember not to play with wolves of lightning."

Jeric chuckled at her comment, but Fire could only stare. He recalled the damage at Cloudy Vale and what he'd seen in the guard's memory of her arrival. Mind shifted his feet and turned to Jeric.

"Has she been resting?" Mind asked.

Jeric nodded. "I haven't left her side," he added. "She's doing much better."

Jeric spoke easily, and leaned against the railing with a casual air. Fire immediately disliked his tone, even more so given the softness to Elenyr's expression. He folded his arms and fixed Elenyr with a steely glare.

"So you like Jeric now?" Fire asked.

"You are as blunt as ever," Jeric said.

"He saved my life," Elenyr said.

"Are you certain you are well?" Mind asked.

"I am healing," Elenyr said. "And that is enough . . . for now."

Fire saw the simmering anger in her eyes—the same emotion that roiled in his chest. It brought a smile to his lips as he realized he was not alone in his desire for vengeance. He did not envy Serak.

"That's the Elenyr I know," he said, nodding his approval. "So when do we get to go after Serak?"

"First I want to know what is happening." She glared at Jeric. "I have been kept in the dark by my healers."

"They said she needed rest," Jeric said, raising a hand as if to ward off her accusation.

"I've rested enough," Elenyr said.

Fire grinned and launched into their most recent tale. "After leaving Mistkeep we managed to follow several of the members of the Bloodsworn."

He explained how they'd followed higher order acolytes, working up the chain to explore the various halls owned by the Order. Mind took over the story, detailing the challenges they'd faced. After all his reluctance to come, he seemed pleased to be talking to Elenyr now.

"Each hall is isolated," Mind said, "with no knowledge of other halls. Only the senior acolytes understand, but they have been given pendants that block memory magic."

"Serak is prepared for you," Elenyr said, nodding to Mind.

Mind's jaw tightened, betraying his irritation. "Despite his precautions, we've managed to identify a number of their locations. Would you like to see the map?"

There was a nudge at the corner of Fire's consciousness, and Mind's map appeared in his thoughts. Elenyr stared into the distance as she reviewed the mental image. Jeric requested the same and Mind reluctantly passed him the map.

"We haven't explored north yet," Fire said. "But we did learn a location."

"Have you ever heard of a place called Beldik?" Mind asked.

Elenyr frowned. "I do not know the name."

Fire noticed the trace of distrust in Mind's gaze. Elenyr seemed to notice his lapse and he smoothed his expression. He turned to Jeric and gestured an invitation, but the elf slowly shook his head, his features disappointed.

"I have never heard of it," he said.

"Wherever it is, Serak religiously guards the name." Fire absently sparked a flame in his hand and extinguished it, a habit from his early years of training. He wanted to get back into the fight, even more than before. He wanted to hunt the Order members until he found Serak in his hide. Mind snorted as he picked up the thought and spoke through the mental link.

He would kill you.

What makes you so certain? Fire responded in kind, for once.

His caution.

"Beldik is important," Mind said aloud. "That much is clear."

"You've learned a great deal," Elenyr said. "But what is most significant is what you have not discovered."

Fire realized Elenyr had noticed him playing with flames and extinguished the heat. "What do you mean?"

"The Order does not have a presence anywhere close to the Oracle's Refuge."

"He is cautious," Mind said. "He does not want Senia seeing his future, so he keeps his distance."

"Then that is exactly where we should go." Elenyr made to rise but Jeric placed a settling hand on her shoulder.

64

"You aren't going anywhere."

"Are you going to stop me?" Elenyr scoffed.

"A child could stop you," Jeric said with a smile.

She held his gaze, and then settled back onto the bench. "As much as I am loath to admit it, Jeric is right. You and Fire should visit her and learn what you can."

"And if she gives us someone to hunt?" Mind asked.

"Go where she indicates," Elenyr said. "But do what you can to send a message back to me."

"We will," Mind promised.

They spoke of other things, and Fire found his previous anger had eased. He still wanted Serak, but seeing Elenyr alive had shifted that anger to a future date. When he stood in front of Serak.

They spoke of Serak and Wylyn, of the threats they posed and the Order of Ancients, the conversation gradually shifting to the missing monarchs. Jeric seemed to think it was Wylyn's doing, while Elenyr thought it part of Serak's plan.

Eventually the sun began to set and Mind glanced to the sky. "We should go."

"Give my regards to Senia," Elenyr said.

They said their farewells and Fire embraced her. Again he was overwhelmed with how fragile she seemed, and wondered if they would ever fight together again. Deep wounds hurt more than the body, and he worried she would not be as strong as before. Elenyr smiled when they parted, her expression lighter, and he took heart. She was a warrior, and no good warrior remained out of the fight for long.

Fire followed Mind back to the entrance of the fortress, his emotions shifting between fury at Serak and relief for Elenyr. She had survived. Even if there was a shadow to her gaze, she had defied Serak's assault and lived through a devastating attempt on her life.

"Will you permit a request?"

Fire looked up in surprise, and realized Horn had again replaced the guard. Fire hadn't noticed his appearance, and out of the corner of his eye, he saw Mind frown at his lack of attention.

"What do you require?" Mind asked.

Horn looked away and then back. "The people talk like the world is crumbling, and every day there are more rumors of war."

"You want us to protect your family in Talinor," Mind said. Not a guess.

"I know my parents and brothers. When the war begins, they will be in the thick of the fighting. Keep them alive."

"And you think we can do that?" Fire asked.

"I was exiled from Talinor because of Shadow," Horn said, anger tightening his features. "You owe me a debt. I would see it paid."

"We will do what we can," Mind said.

Horn measured his response, and again Fire wondered at his height. The elf seemed to tower over them, and Fire fleetingly imagined a duel with such a soldier. Then Horn accepted his words.

"May Ero watch over your journey."

Fire and Mind departed, and Horn watched them cross the drawbridge. Fire glanced back before the crowd took him from view, and the captain still stood under the gate. He realized they were both trying to protect their families.

"Ero will not protect them," Fire said.

Mind snorted in disgust. "Most of the people still believe him a god."

Fire shrugged in agreement and fell into step beside his brother, wondering about Ero. Few knew his real identity, a member of the ancient race and head of the Eternals, the organization that protected

Lumineia from the Krey Empire. Fire had met him a couple of times, but knew little about his purpose or life.

"Why aren't the Eternals taking a greater interest in Wylyn's presence here?" Fire asked. "They failed, and Wylyn managed to reach us. Surely that would merit Ero coming to deal with threat."

"They sent Lira," Mind said absently.

Fire considered the presence of Lira, the barbarian body mage that had joined the Eternals at the end of the Dawn of Magic. She had traveled with Water to the west, and Fire wondered why the Eternals had only sent one to their aid.

Mind answered the unspoken question. "Why would they send anyone else? Elenyr and the fragments of Draeken are strong enough for nearly anyone. In just a few months we've killed Wylyn's son and most of her dakorians. It's only a matter of time until we finish the threat."

"And you still think Wylyn will be with Serak?"

"Wylyn is a stranger in these lands," Mind said. "Serak gave her a home in the Order of Ancients, but she would view herself a royalty. She would not be satisfied with less than his primary hall. We find Serak, we find Wylyn."

"And if we don't?"

Mind shrugged. "If we find Serak and destroy the Order, Wylyn will be homeless and friendless. She will be easy prey."

Fire pondered the exchange all the way until they were outside the city, and only then realized he had never asked Elenyr about her secret. He frowned, recalling the moment Mind had revealed the memory of Elenyr's arrival in Ilumidora—right before they'd spoken to Elenyr.

In that moment, Fire realized Mind had purposefully given him the memory of Elenyr. It had not been to prepare him for seeing her, but to keep Fire from mentioning what they'd learned in Cloudy Vale.

He spun and grabbed Mind's wrist, yanking him to a halt. "You *manipulated* me."

"I always manipulate you," Mind said, pulling his hand out of Fire's grip. "And I couldn't have you talking to Elenyr about her secret. Not yet."

"When?"

"When I'm ready," Mind said, so coldly that Fire came to a halt. Mind continued walking.

Fire watched his brother continue down the road. Mind was not inclined to anger, but what he'd seen in Mind's gaze left Fire disturbed. Fire had no doubt that Mind knew more than he revealed. He always did. But in this, Mind felt something deeper.

Mind felt betrayed.

Chapter 8: The Anger of Mind

Fire and Mind traveled north in silence. Seething, Fire imagined all the ways he could burn Mind without leaving a scar, taking note to visualize each and every action. Mind would see them in his thoughts, and there was no need to say a word. Unfortunately, Mind ignored him.

They stopped in an inn a day's ride from the Oracle's home, and Fire used the flames from the hearth to cast a bed. Relaxing on the flames, he tried to sleep. His rest was fitful, and he dreamed of punching Mind in the face. When dawn finally lit the room, Mind groaned.

"Will you stop with the mental blows? Even in your sleep you want to punish me."

"You deserve it."

Mind reached for his boots. "Let's just go."

"Senia would be mad at you too."

"You're going to tell her?"

The surprise in Mind's voice was small consolation, and Fire jerked his head. "I won't break our oath."

Five thousand years, but the oath still stood. Fire and Mind had promised to keep each other's secrets. It was a promise between brothers, except they were more than brothers. They were fragments of the same soul. As angry as he was, he wouldn't betray Mind.

They left the inn behind, the innkeeper appearing confused as they turned in the keys to their room. Once they were on the road Fire conjured two tigers out of flames and they mounted. Then they sped their way north.

Taking the road to the oracle's refuge, they hurried their way toward the elven forests that marked the border between Talinor and Griffin. The great forest of Orláknia was renowned for its beauty and tranquility, and travelers frequently slowed their journey simply to enjoy its light. Fire, too, felt as they did, but when they reached the towering trees cultivated by magic, his irritation remained.

They reached the path that veered towards the oracle's home and left the mounts behind. Grand trees grew on either side, their branches shaped and curved in artistic patterns, their leaves filled with glowing light.

Mind abruptly caught Fire's arm, bringing him to a halt. "I'm sorry."

"For what?"

Mind rolled his eyes. "Don't make me explain."

"You're going to have to," Fire said, folding his arms. "Because you treated me like an errant child."

"Do you ever look at Elenyr and think she's been lying to us?"

His blunt question drew a surprised look from Fire, and he snorted in amusement. "And they say I'm the angry one. What's got you so rankled? So she has secrets about us. Does it matter? You've listened to the thoughts of countless mothers. Surely you know by now that they keep secrets about their children."

"She knows what we are!" Mind shouted. "Don't you understand? She knows what we *really* are—and she's *afraid*." He yanked a memory from a pouch at his side and raised it as if in proof. "Elenyr uses us for her own purposes."

"She taught us to help others."

"What if that isn't what I want?" Mind demanded.

Fire stared at his brother. "What else would you want?"

"I want the choice to be *mine*."

Fire had never seen Mind so angry. He was always controlled, always thinking ahead. But the ground had begun to tremble, and leaves fluttered even though there was no wind. The magic Mind could not yet control bubbled out of him, unrestrained.

Nearby trees bent at their waists, the trunks groaning, the bark cracking. Limbs snapped off and flew away. Mind clenched his fists, and the trees stilled. But the birds had gone silent, as if afraid to voice their song in the presence of such power.

"Perhaps she has reason to fear what we will become." Fire spoke quietly.

"We treat her like family, but she is not."

"Elenyr is practically—

"—our mother?" Mind snapped. "She would have killed us."

Fire stared in shock and then laughed. "Why?"

"If we'd fallen to our magic," Mind said, "she would have killed us. She said it in her own words." He dropped the orb on the ground and it shattered, the memory rising for a final time.

The light magic rose and revealed Elenyr standing in her hidden room. She wore the same armor she'd used when Draeken had first awoken, even the same braid in her hair. Fire realized it was the same day she'd agreed to train Draeken.

"I understand my duty," Elenyr said quietly, speaking to another out of sight. "If Draeken falls to his magic, and loses his wits, it will be my duty to kill him. He is too powerful to let live . . ."

The image sputtered as if it had been damaged by the fire, and then faded away. In the silence Fire turned to Mind, who stared where Elenyr had stood, his features fixed in anger. Fire reached out to him and placed a hand on his shoulder.

"Would she have done it?"

Mind nodded. "That was why she became our trainer, to kill us if we fell to the guardian charm. It was only later that she became our mother."

Fire tried to shrug the revelation aside. "We were more dangerous then. And every other guardian had fallen to madness."

"You don't know that."

"Water would say we should trust her," Fire said, grappling with the swelling emotions.

"Water isn't here," Mind said.

"He is still part of us," Fire said. "Perhaps we should listen to him."

"That wasn't the only secret I found," Mind said evenly.

"What could be worse than that?" Fire asked, his stomach filling with dread.

"The orb was damaged," Mind said. "But she spoke of a realization about the fragments, and a desire to keep us separated."

"She doesn't want us to become Draeken?"

The revelation was a surprise. It went against everything Elenyr had ever said. From the beginning she'd sought to train them separately, so they could survive as Draeken. So they could remain in control. Or that was what she'd claimed.

Unable to accept the gravity of Mind's thoughts, Fire looked south, towards Ilumidora. "Let us wait and see. We must not act in haste."

Mind gave a sour chuckle. "That is usually what I say."

"You are the fragment of intelligence," Fire said. "You don't have *all* of it."

Mind regarded Fire for a moment and then inclined his head. Turning, Mind continued down the road, and Fire fell into step beside him, wondering why Elenyr would fear Draeken, but not the fragments. Each of the fragments had weaknesses, and it had taken them a thousand years to understand and control them—Mind even longer. He possessed memory magic, and the magic he had yet to master when he was angry.

But Draeken? The few times Mind had merged with all the fragments, his magic overpowered his will, causing damage and devastation. They were guardians, their power beyond that of normal mages, but Draeken's power surpassed them all. Is that what she feared? Draeken's power? Mind answered as if he'd spoken aloud.

"Guardians like us descend into madness, unable to control the raw power in their flesh. We've lived a thousand times longer than other guardians—and still do not know what will happen when we merge as Draeken."

They reached the side trail leading to the oracle's home. The trees continued to lighten, the soft rays of the afternoon sun filling the breadth of the forest. Tree trunks contained streaks of color, the purple, pink, and blue threaded into the wood and leaves. All the trees of the forest were cultured by elven plant mages, but the trees surrounding the oracle's home were cultivated by the oracle herself, and each generation was expected to add to the rich tapestry of magic.

The sun set but the light only brightened. Mind strode through trees lit from within, the blues and white blending to shine on the path. Birds sang even at night, adding their approval of their new homes.

"I wager Light could stay awake in here," Fire said with a snort.

"It's beautiful," Mind agreed, but his voice was distant, still occupied by thoughts of Elenyr.

They passed through an invisible line and the forest retreated, leaving manicured paths of crushed white stones, interspersed with beds of flowers. Senia favored lilies and exotic flowers, and their scents filled the air. The fruit trees were a vibrant green, the fruit imbued with light. A handful of families had come to speak to the oracle, and their children ate the fruit, giggling at the glow in their mouths.

Ahead, a trio of enormous trees grew intertwined, the thick trunks hollowed out to form the multi-leveled structure. More chambers lay beneath the ground, and all were guarded by elven Honor Guard. Dressed in the ceremonial blue of their rank, the elite soldiers recognized Fire and Mind on sight, nodding to them as they entered the structure.

The main hall was not overly large, the chamber just a hundred feet across. A sweeping staircase curved up the side, leading to the receiving hall where Senia accepted patrons. It was the end of the day and a family was descending the stairs, their features bright with awe and wonder. In their midst, Senia walked.

Wearing a flowing white dress with blue highlights, the woman seemed regal and imposing. Her blond hair contained red streaks, a mark of rebellion that drew a measure of ire from the elven elders. Senia motioned the guests to depart and strode to greet the fragments.

"I foresaw the arrival of a friend," she said with a smile. "I didn't know it was you."

Chapter 9: Oracle Senia

"Oracle," Fire said, stepping forward to embrace Senia.

The woman smiled and returned the gesture. "Always a pleasure to see you, Fire. How is Elenyr?"

Fire and Mind exchanged a look, and Mind smiled faintly. "She still wants you to find a love."

Senia rolled her eyes, looking much younger than her two hundred years. "Once a mother, always a mother," she said. "But I have yet to find someone as handsome as Fire." She winked at Fire, eliciting a grin.

"Can we speak in private?" Mind asked.

Her smile faded as she looked between them. "Why the serious expression? Surely it can wait until after I've been given my hug."

Mind permitted a smile and stepped into the warm embrace. Senia had a gift for putting one at ease, the talent hiding an indomitable spirit. Only twice had someone infiltrated the home, the second time by a member of the Assassin's Guild. Senia had left him writhing on the floor before marching him personally to the Assassin's Guild to demand answers. The duke that had dispatched the assassin was heavily punished, and the assassins had sworn never to come for an oracle again. She'd been fourteen years old.

"Senia," Mind said, "you're as beautiful as ever."

She smiled and gestured to the flowing dress. "It's the outfit," she said airily. "And how I envy yours." She pointed to their warrior garb. "Please tell me you've come with tales of adventure and intrigue."

The dismissive attitude was a show for the benefit of those present, a persona to ease concerns in case anyone was listening. Elenyr had the same habit, but Senia didn't seem aware of what had happened to Elenyr.

Her eyes sparkled with mischief, as if she thought their visit merely a prelude to a challenge. Fire abruptly noticed she had a handful of freckles dotting her nose and cheeks. Unusual for an elf, the marks gave her a younger look, making her seem softer.

"This way," she said.

She guided them up the stairs and onto a balcony, where a large, gilded cage hung from a wispy branch. They climbed inside and the cage lifted them gracefully into the lofty branches, away from the prying eyes of the patrons or Honor Guard.

The spacious loft was high in the tree. Like a private cottage hidden in the boughs, the room sat nestled between a trio of branches, the walls made of thin aquaglass to permit a view of the night sky. Stars were just coming out, twinkling between cottony clouds.

Couches and a desk sat around the space, and a small bookshelf extended from one corner. Without stairs to reach the space, it was obviously meant as a private retreat, likely built by the oracle's own hands.

An opening at the rear led to a set of stairs going up, leading to a second platform. This one was circular. and contained an assortment of weapons and magical sources, a space for the oracle to train for combat.

"This is new," Mind exclaimed, admiring the refuge.

"It is," she said, and stabbed a finger at Fire. "So don't burn it."

"That happened one time," Fire protested.

"Don't let it happen again," she said.

"And that?" Mind asked, pointing to the training platform.

"Decoration only, I assure you."

Fire chuckled at her evasion. "I wager the elven elders do not know about your taste for sharp decorations."

"I may have neglected to mention it upon their latest visit," she said, her smile widening. Then she gestured to the couches and claimed a chair near her desk. "Now, what brings you to my door?"

"Ero paid us a visit," Mind said.

"*Personally?*" Senia asked, her eyes wide. "He never leaves the Hall of the Eternals."

"I'm sure you are aware of the krey invasion?" Mind asked.

"Two krey is hardly an invasion."

"It is when they have the support of the Order of Ancients," Mind said. "And the wars are spreading."

"I'm aware of the empty thrones," she said. "And I watch the future for Queen Alosia closely."

"So you know of Serak?" Fire asked.

"Less than I would like," she said, a frown creasing her beautiful features. "The elven council has been given many duties, and there is little time to follow the future for everyone. The waves of the sea remain clouded because of him."

Fire recalled that every oracle saw the future differently. Elenyr had seen a vast tapestry, while her daughter had seen an endless forest. Senia described her farsight as waves rising and falling, the surface of the water containing images of people and events, moments yet to be. But like all oracles, her ability to see the future was limited by indecision. With the climate of fear and the rumors of war, many would be uncertain about their futures.

"Serak is the Father of Guardians," Mind said, "the first to endure the guardian charm, and it seems, one of the most powerful."

"A dangerous foe indeed," Senia said. "But a fool to think he can best Elenyr and the fragments of Draeken."

Mind shook his head. "He came for Elenyr. She is in Ilumidora, recovering."

77

For the first time, Senia's eyebrows pulled together. "You make it sound like she almost . . ."

She went rigid, her eyes going wide. Fire glanced to Mind and guessed he was giving her the same memory of when Elenyr had arrived in Ilumidora. Her jaw clenched and for an instant rage rippled across her features. Then she reined it in and passed a hand over her face.

"My apologies," she said, her voice clipped. "I was aware of the conflict but my duties have occupied my attention. The elven elders requested I focus my extra time watching the future for Queen Alosia."

Mind's brow knit in sudden anger. "What if Serak did not take Queen Alosia because leaving her in Ilumidora *kept* you occupied?"

Senia regarded him with doubt. "A bold plan. If I had looked at the future of any other monarchs—"

"But you didn't," Mind stated. "Did you."

Senia looked away, her jaw working in anger. "I have not."

"It's what I would have done," Mind said, his voice tinged with his own anger.

"The conflict has escalated quickly," Fire said, his tone conciliatory. "You cannot blame yourselves."

"My birthright is to protect and watch over the people," she said, rising and beginning to pace. "I have not watched the waves enough, and now the monarchs have been taken and Elenyr is . . ."

She came to a halt, her back to the fragments. Fire recognized the rigidity to her frame and knew the anger and fear in her heart. Senia's mother had died when she was a child, and Elenyr had frequently visited, helping train Senia for her life as an oracle. Elenyr was as much a mother to Senia as she was to the fragments of Draeken.

Senia turned and sank into a seat, her eyes piercing. "Tell me everything."

Mind, his expression troubled, leaned back in his seat and motioned to Fire, who detailed the events of the last few months. As the current

78

oracle, Senia carried the weight of knowledge, just as Elenyr had when she'd been high oracle. The woman knew all about the Eternals and the krey, and the true secrets of Lumineia. Several times Mind interjected, but when they reached the part about the battle with the dragons she leaned forward, her expression going hard.

"They sought to break the treaty?"

"Not anymore," Mind said, gesturing south, towards Ilumidora. "The Hauntress exacted an oath from the new king."

Senia chuckled sourly. "The dragons call themselves fearless, but I wager they experienced a touch of terror at Elenyr's hand."

"What is disturbing is not how easily the dragons would turn on us," Mind said. "They've always been ones for greed. What is disturbing is the rise of the Order of Ancients. Serak has remained hidden for thousands of years, yet built an organization large enough to kidnap kings. They also have the dakorians to bolster their ranks."

"The dakorians do not know how to fight magic," Fire said, thinking of when they'd fought.

"They are learning quickly," Mind said.

"They would," Senia said. "From what I know, they are bred and trained for war, and if Wylyn has a Bloodwall, then she is truly powerful."

"You know of the Bloodwall?" Mind asked, a trace of surprise in his tone.

She settled back in her seat. "How much do you know of the Krey Empire?"

Fire shrugged. "They live in the stars and mankind are their slaves."

"A fair summation," she said with a faint smile. "What you may not know is that they occupy thousands of worlds, all owned by one of the krey houses. The houses are ranked according to wealth and power, with the largest receiving favors from the empirical house. Only the strongest houses have a Bloodwall, a dakorian gifted with a perfect body, so they can protect the head of the house."

Fire scratched at his chin, considering Tardoq, Wylyn's Bloodwall. Shadow had spoken of him after the battle at Mistkeep, and how it seemed he'd allowed Relgor to die in the swamp. Was he really as strong as Senia described?

"The other fragments are dealing with the Order," Mind said. "For now, we are hunting Wylyn and Serak."

Senia was nodding. "And you wish to know what they seek."

"It's possible they hide in a place called Beldik," Fire said. "Do you know of it?"

Her smile was grim. "After what you have shared, my time to join this war is past due."

"You cannot intend to join the conflict," Mind said. "Since the other oracle bloodlines were destroyed, it is forbidden for you to—"

"Don't tell me what I can't do," she said, all trace of civility gone. "Councils may seek to control me, but I carry the mantle of my office, and my fate is my own."

Fire laughed, the sound filled with admiration. They both shot him a glare, which he ignored. If Senia joined the battle against Serak, how long before he was destroyed? How long before the Order lay in ashes and Wylyn dead?

Or she could be killed, Mind thought to him, the mental voice bordering on a growl. *She has no children and her mother is dead. If she dies, the world loses its last oracle bloodline.*

Fire ignored him, and Senia nodded to Fire. "I am not as gifted in farsight as my predecessors. I may see what comes in the next few months but anything beyond a year . . .?" She jerked her head. "Nevertheless, I will see what I can do. And after you depart, I will prepare myself for war."

Her gaze settled on Mind and he wisely held his tongue. Fire tried not to grin. Senia settled into her chair and closed her eyes. The magic of farsight, unique to oracles, allowed her to see glimpses of the future. Elenyr had said it was due to their ability to see every type of magic.

80

Fire could only imagine what such power would feel like. From his perspective, it felt a lot like waiting.

After a few minutes of silence he grew bored. Rising, he turned and strode up the steps to the training circle to browse the blades. Most were elven but he found a few fashioned by dwarves, and tested their steel. Just as he picked up the axe, an image exploded into his thoughts.

He flinched, the axe falling from his fingers, clattering on the floor of the training platform. The sound never reached his ears, his eyes on the images flooding his skull. The memories came from Mind, a torrent of thoughts pressing against his consciousness.

Fire instinctively knew Mind did not intend the assault, the mental link bordering on instinctual. Fire opened his mouth to call out to his brother, and then he began to register what he was seeing.

Unable to resist, Mind had extended his thoughts into Senia's consciousness, dipping his magic into her thoughts. Memory magic was tricky, and if the recipient was aware of the intrusion they could fight back. Mind usually didn't infiltrate the thoughts of a friend, but oracles had a habit of avoiding the full truth, and Mind's curiosity drove him to attempt watching her vision. Perhaps motivated by what they'd learned about Elenyr, Mind had slipped into Senia's farsight. And what he'd seen had broken his mental reserve, the images flooding to Fire.

Senia stood on the surface of an endless ocean, the image like seeing the interior of a house through a dirty window. Still, the scene was clear enough to show Wylyn speaking to Tardoq, both standing on the surface nearby, the waves rising up to shape their bodies. They argued about the Stormdial. The image faded to fog so Senia turned to another wave.

This time the image was of a black tower rising from the sea, piercing the heavens. Its sheer size drew a gasp from Mind, and Senia turned, nearly spotting Mind in the clouds. Senia frowned and walked around the image in search of another.

Fire sucked in a breath, struggling to control the torrent of memories. It was as if a dam had cracked in Mind's thoughts, spilling the last few seconds into Fire's own mind. Faster and faster the images came.

81

Mind saw himself receive the keys to becoming an Eternal while Elenyr stood at his side. She looked on, her expression inscrutable. The room was dim, but a large Gate stood behind them, the silvery surface reflecting Mind's features, which seemed darker, more like Draeken.

The next image came in a rush, depicting all the fragments merging as Draeken, becoming a single whole—and remaining stable. Fire realized the potential future showed they had triumphed over Wylyn. The prospect of standing united with all the fragments, as a single whole, elicited a surge of pride from Mind—and abruptly the image flickered.

The potential future darkened, with a storm rising overhead. The patches of fog grew thick with lightning, crackling and arcing into the ocean. Standing behind the shocked Senia, Mind watched a Dark Gate appear, and a hooded figure rise above a great mountain.

Dark figures poured from the opening and flooded into Lumineia, slaughtering with abandon, the innumerable horde becoming an unstoppable force that rolled across the earth, laying waste to armies and villages. Four great generals led the way, each with powerful artifacts.

The specter of Death hunted leaders, claiming lives before the people could unite.

Famine stripped men of their flesh, their bodies wasting away to an unquenchable hunger.

Plague sent disease into the ranks of the gathered armies, watching them fall to ruin.

And a mighty general of War, whose sword cut through steel and stone.

Mind stared at the scene of carnage that swept the earth, horrorstruck as he realized he was witnessing Lumineia's fate. If they failed to stop Wylyn, Lumineia would fall, and no race could stand against the horde lurking behind the Dark Gate. Then he spotted the figure standing at the head of the army.

Shock bound his tongue, and he stared as the person removed his cowl, turning to face Senia. Fire sucked in his breath, dread spilling into his veins as he waited to see the face—but abruptly the images evaporated, leaving him standing over the axe at his feet. Mind was stumbling up the stairs to him, while Senia remained in her chair, her features fixed in a forced calmness, apparently unaware of what Mind had witnessed.

Fire darted to Mind's side and pulled him out of view of Senia. "Mind?" he hissed. "Who was he? Who led the army?"

Mind rotated to face him, his eyes flicking to Senia, but she was still deep in her farsight. Fire's expression darkened as Mind struggled to speak, and Mind pulled him to the far edge of the platform, behind a rack of weapons.

"You don't understand," Mind said, grimacing. "The future she saw, that we saw . . ."

"Are you afraid?" Fire fought to keep his tone quiet. He'd never seen Mind act in terror. "What did you see? Was it Wylyn? Or Serak—?"

"Neither," Mind hissed, his eyes finally turning on Fire.

"Then who?" Fire asked. "Who led the slaughter?"

Mind shook his head, and passed the image to Fire. Again Fire saw the cloaked figure standing at the head of the horde, watched him turn and reveal his features. Fire's eyes widened, and he finally understood why Mind had lost control of his magic.

"Us?" His voice was barely above a whisper.

"Draeken." Mind shuddered as he spoke the name. "Serak and Wylyn aren't the villains. We are."

Chapter 10: A Chilling Future

"Us?" Fire hissed. "How could that be?"

"I don't know," Mind growled. "But it was real enough."

"Is that all you saw?" Fire asked.

Mind passed a hand over his face. "Did you *want* to see more?"

"How could we become an Eternal and then destroy Lumineia?" Fire said. "It doesn't make sense."

"An oracle's farsight is hardly fact," Mind said. "What she foresaw *might* come to pass, or none of it could occur."

Fire heard the trace of desperation in his voice, and wondered if it matched his own. They'd spent lifetimes battling people like Serak. To bring an army in and simply slaughter the people they'd fought to protect? And who were the dark creatures coming through the Gate? Then another question came to mind.

"You said the image first showed Draeken becoming an Eternal?"

Mind jerked his head, and Fire caught another trickle of thoughts. Mind fleetingly wondered if the future had altered *because* he'd been watching, because he'd seen it. Knowing Senia, she would have revealed only half truths to them, and Mind would not have reacted the same way. Had he destroyed the future, simply because he'd seen it?

"It's not your fault," Fire said. "But whatever brings about that future, we need to stop it. Quickly."

"But we could become destroyers," Mind whispered.

"That doesn't make sense," Fire said stubbornly. "We protect Lumineia. Why would we harm it?"

Mind and Fire argued until Senia exited her farsight. She looked pale and worried, and both Fire and Mind tried to feign ignorance. The oracle ascended the steps to join them, and Fire felt Mind forcefully withdraw, the leak snapping shut like the steel door of a prison.

"All is well. I believe you will find what you seek in the southeast. Beldik isn't a city, but a mine once owned by the dwarves. It has been abandoned for ages, but it lies to the southeast, beyond the Wilds." She hesitated, and then added, "But remember, as fragments you can fight this war on multiple fronts. Perhaps it's best you not join together as Draeken in this battle."

"Wise advice," Mind said. "And thank you. We'll take our leave."

"Be careful," Senia said. "Your futures are . . . uncertain."

She clearly didn't want to reveal the whole of what she'd seen, and Fire and Mind didn't want to reveal that they'd seen everything. Both gave the oracle a quick embrace, and in moments they had departed. When they stepped outside the refuge Fire lowered his voice.

"Does she know?"

Mind jerked his head. "She was never good at mind magic. And she mistook our reserve for a desire to head to the battle. She's also distracted by her own plans to join the conflict."

"What have we done," Fire breathed. "The oracle is joining the fight, and we may very well be the ones she will face across the battlefield."

"It won't come to that."

"She *saw* us," Fire growled. "She *saw* what we could become. She's going to take measures to stop us unless . . ." He stared at Mind. "Please tell me you didn't erase her memory."

"I did when I hugged her."

"You erased her knowledge of her vision?" Fire released an explosive breath. "You can't do that."

"You want that idea floating around?" Mind growled. "It's a *possible* future. Now let's get to work and make sure it doesn't become reality."

Mind lapsed into a brooding silence, grappling with what he'd witnessed. Several times Fire made to speak but ultimately held his tongue, and Mind did not expound on his fears. Turning east, they journeyed through the night to reach the highway that would take them southeast.

Knots of people dotted the road, with caravans rushing to complete their journeys before the winter snows made passage difficult. Fire wanted to yell at his brother—but seethed in silence. He'd expected Senia to smile and point out the locations of Wylyn and Serak, not find a future where he and the other fragments become the greatest butchers of life that Lumineia had ever seen.

"What were the creatures that came out of the Dark Gate?" he asked.

"You *want* to talk about a future where we destroyed hundreds of thousands of lives?"

Fire stepped over a root in the road. "You always say we have to know our foes to defeat them."

Mind cocked his head to the side, his silence suggesting Fire had struck a chord. Fire disliked talking about the potential future, but ignoring it could very well bring it to pass. He shuddered and looked away, wondering what would happen to him if Draeken became whole forever. Would he be erased?

It was a strange fear. He'd been a fragment for most of his life, and remembered snippets when he'd been joined to the others as Draeken. But when he was part of the whole, he was not conscious, and only afterward did he remember.

"Do we matter?" Fire blurted.

"What do you mean?" Mind asked.

"As fragments," he said. "Do we matter? Or are we just part of Draeken?"

86

Mind released a long sigh. "I don't know," he murmured. "Two thousand years ago I would have said that we were merely part of the same being, that eventually we would be forced to become one. Now?" he shrugged, clearly having no answer.

"If you could choose," Fire said, glancing to his brother. "Would you be Draeken? Or you?"

"A difficult question," Mind said. "For we cannot deny Draeken's power."

"You would choose him?"

"Do you ever miss the pieces you lack?" Mind asked. "Do you ever wish you had honor, or a sense of humor, or luck?"

"I did," Fire admitted. "Still do, sometimes."

They passed a small family. The couple drove the wagon, while three boys wrestled and argued in the back. Fire wondered if they would ever have such a conversation. Would they grow up to be friends? Or rivals?

"I envy your strength," Mind said.

"But you're the intelligent one," Fire said.

Mind sighed in regret. "When Elenyr needs a wall shattered, it's you she turns to, and I've always wondered what it would feel like to possess such might."

"I feel stupid all the time," Fire admitted. "You talk with such intelligence, and even kings respect you. Me? I'm the brute they wish would *stop* talking."

"Only to their daughters," Mind said, a slight smile appearing on his features.

Fire laughed. "Probably true." His smile faded, and for a moment he hesitated to voice the question. "Is Draeken evil?"

"I don't think so," Mind said, his voice pensive. "When we are joined, we fight for Elenyr's cause. But there's something about our joining that makes us more inclined to ambition and cruelty."

Fire considered his answer as they left the highway behind. They had entered southern Griffin, a region known for its mountains and mines. Caravans loaded with ore ambled down the narrow roads, their riders and guards hurrying to complete their shipments before the snows came, muddying roads and freezing rivers.

Fire would have liked to cast tigers and rush through the forest, but he found himself reluctant to reach the next fight. Were they on a path that led to the Dark Gate? Or had they already changed the future?

They trudged down the winding roads, working their way south and west. Scattered inns and villages were common, as were bandits seeking easy marks. A trio sought to relieve Mind and Fire of their coin. Annoyed by the intrusion, Fire ignited their cloaks, and they fled, shouting as their cloaks turned to ash, leaving their skin lightly burned, but otherwise unharmed. Mind didn't even speak as they trudged down the road.

"Have you ever heard of the Dark Gate?" Fire finally asked.

Mind hesitated, and then nodded. "Actually, I have."

"Really?"

"One of the senior acolytes we interrogated," Mind said. "He caught a glimpse of Serak's archive, and remembered seeing the phrase. Apparently more than once."

"So Serak has something to do with the Dark Gate?"

"I think he wants to open it," Mind said, "and he needs us to do it."

Fire considered the prospect, his scowl deepening. "No."

"No what?"

"No," Fire said. "I refuse to join him. I don't care how, I don't care when. I'm not going to help Serak kill innocent people. And I'm not going to be Wylyn's pet."

"You just want to protect the women."

Fire stabbed a finger at him. "It used to bother me that everyone liked Water, but I've adapted. You once told me we could overcome what we lack, and so I'm going to do that. Serak can do anything he wants, but I'm not becoming his servant—as a fragment or as Draeken."

Mind measured his words and then grunted in agreement. "Perhaps you are right. A decision is a powerful thing, and just deciding we will fight might be sufficient to defy Serak's designs."

"Then let's go find him," Fire said. "I'm tired of trudging through mud. Let's find Beldik and put an end to the Father of Guardians."

"And Wylyn?"

"We'll kill her as well," Fire said. "Bloodwall or not, she deserves her fate."

Mind chuckled and pointed to the sky. "I wish you could craft wings for both of us."

"Do you have any idea how hard wings of fire are to cast?" he retorted. "It's riding a tiger or walking on foot."

"I'll take the tiger," Mind said.

A caravan rounded the corner ahead and Fire pulled the lingering heat from the ground, the ground becoming icy as he cast a pair of tigers. As the guards of the caravan cried out and scrambled to defend themselves, Fire and Mind mounted the steeds and darted into the trees.

Fire, now eager for the fight, turned his face forward, and failed to notice his brother's expression. Pensive and troubled, Mind stared into the distance. Fire didn't see the dark glimmering in Mind's eyes, or feel the intense anticipation in his own chest.

Draeken had seen the vision as well.

Chapter 11: An Unexpected Visitor

Elenyr flicked the reins, guiding her horse through the gates of Herosian. News had come shortly after Fire's and Mind's departure that Shadow was preparing a strike on Wylyn. Too late to recall Fire and Mind, she'd sent Jeric instead. She'd never imagined it would lead to Jeric taking King Porlin's place.

She'd recovered enough to travel, and so she'd thanked Queen Alosia for her hospitality, and the woman had given Elenyr a horse. For several days Elenyr rode across the plains of Talinor toward Herosian, listening to the rumors of the people regarding the events in the capitol. An unnamed group had attacked Wylyn in the fortress, but the woman had escaped after claiming control of the Order of Ancients. In the ensuing confusion, Jeric had revealed the medallion of the Steward, allowing him to take the throne. As Elenyr guided her mount into Herosian, the streets were buzzing with the news.

"An elf sitting on the throne." One man shook his head as Elenyr passed.

"He's probably loyal to the elves," came the reply.

"But he was named Steward by King Porlin," a third protested. "Surely the king had his reasons for trusting the elf."

The three men went back to shifting crates out of a wagon, and Elenyr continued on, brooding on the sudden shift in the conflict. Until now their focus had been more on Serak, but Jeric's latest message had found Elenyr on the road, and the import had been clear. Wylyn now controlled the Order of Ancients.

Although the assassination attempt on Wylyn had failed, it seemed Serak had withdrawn from the conflict. She scowled, her brow furrowed in confusion. Just when they were starting to understand the Order, the entire organization of their foe had changed.

Wylyn wanted to raise the Shard of Midnight, the Stormdial of the ancient race. Elenyr knew Serak could rejoin the conflict, but suspected that he would not. He would wait until Wylyn was either victorious in opening a Gate, or defeated by Elenyr and her fragments.

As she approached the fortress, the guards were on high alert, obviously on Jeric's order. She considered the thought of Jeric—an elf—sitting on the throne of Talinor. But these were strange times, and much had changed.

Jeric had informed the guard of her arrival and they'd permitted her passage, so she directed her steed towards the stables. The stablemaster himself stepped out of his office and reached for the reins, a smile on his bearded face.

"Hauntress," he said. "Never seen you arrive on a steed."

She smiled and swept a hand to the sky. "Overcast skies make for a pleasant ride."

He guffawed heartily and held the mount so she could step out of the saddle. She dismounted on the opposite side, preventing him from seeing her ginger movements. She'd healed well, but not entirely, and her leg still hurt. She had no wish for others to know the severity of her injuries.

She straightened as the man guided the horse into a stall and patted his flank. Then he motioned to one of the stable boys to care for the animal and joined Elenyr, walking her back to the courtyard.

"The Steward is expecting you," he said.

"First I'd like to meet with Light, Shadow, and Water," she replied. "I understand they are staying in the fortress?"

"They are," he said.

"Have them meet me on the southeast tower." She pointed in the direction of the turret.

"As you will," the man replied.

He motioned to another stable boy, and Elenyr stepped outside. Leaving the scents of horse and hay behind, she strode to the stairs and began an arduous climb. She could have turned ethereal, but passing through solid objects was still painful. Besides, it would take some time to reach the summit of the turret. And it gave her a chance to brace herself for the truth.

She would have preferred to speak to Fire and Mind first. They were considered the eldest fragments. But unfortunately they had departed and Elenyr felt compelled to tell the others. Better to give the truth of the fragments to them, and let them decide. It had haunted her for long enough.

She'd made her decision after Jeric had departed, when she'd been thinking of Mind and Fire's visit. Mind had been reserved, and it had taken her a few days to suspect that he knew the truth. Of course, he might not know the whole truth, but Mind's reserve could mean only one thing. He'd been to Cloudy Vale. If that were true, Mind could very easily have found her secret vault amidst the ruins.

The burden of Draeken's secret weighed heavily upon her, and she feared speaking to the fragments. But if Mind began to distrust her now, they would all fall to ruin. And Serak would use everything to divide her from the fragments.

The stairs curved up the turret, growing silent as she passed patrolling guards. The men and women spoke in low tones, muttering about the fact an elf had mysteriously become the Steward of the kingdom. Elenyr wanted answers as well, but such truths would have to wait.

She reached the final curve, where the stairs rotated around a storeroom reserved for arrows and signal flags. The door ahead led to the summit of the turret, where she would wait for the fragments. It seemed to loom large ahead of her, and she didn't see the storage door open.

A hand caught her shoulder and yanked her into the room. Then the door slammed shut. On instinct, Elenyr rotated and drew her sword, catching the tunic of her attacker and slamming them against the wall. Her blade settled upon the throat of the attacker.

"Senia?" Elenyr asked in surprise. "What are you doing here?"

"Trying not to die," Senia said, eyeing the blade.

Elenyr withdrew the sword and sheathed it, before closing the gap and embracing her descendent. She hadn't seen the woman in years, and the oracle had grown into her mantle. Senia returned the gesture.

"You've recovered well, I see," Senia gestured to her injures.

Elenyr retreated and lifted her sleeve to how the bandage. "Almost whole. Do the elders know you left your home?"

"They are rather upset," Senia admitted, a small smile on her lips.

"Of course they are," Elenyr said with a laugh. "It is forbidden for you to depart your refuge without permission. They fear losing the oracle bloodline."

"And you?" Senia asked, straightening her warrior's garb.

"You know how I feel about caging an oracle," Elenyr said, her lips thinning. "But you've picked a dangerous war to join."

Senia's smile faded. "More dangerous than you know."

"What have you foreseen?"

Senia reached out and touched Elenyr's cheek. Although she lacked Mind's gift with memory magic, she still possessed all types of magic, and a handful of images appeared in Elenyr's mind.

Elenyr sucked in her breath as she saw a great horde of creatures pouring from a Dark Gate, and four mighty generals leading a slaughter of Griffin. The final image showed the source of the invasion, and it wasn't Serak or Wylyn.

"Draeken?"

She reached back and caught a crate to brake her fall, sinking heavily onto a barrel. After everything she'd done, Draeken would become what she most feared. She fought to breathe as she was assailed by guilt.

A patter of footsteps came from the hallway, and Elenyr recognized them as the fragment of Water. He was eager, hurrying up the steps and past the door. Elenyr rose and leapt to the door but Senia caught her hand and spoke in her ear.

"That's why I've come. They are not ready for the truth you wish to share."

Elenyr brushed her off and spun. "You think to admonish me?" she hissed. "We both know your gift in farsight is lacking."

Senia winced, and Elenyr immediately regretted the words. Senia was a strong oracle, even stronger than her mother had been. She had many talents, and she was gifted with farsight—when the events were not far distant.

"I'm sorry."

"A hard truth," Senia said quietly. "But true nonetheless."

Elenyr passed a hand over her face. "I still shouldn't have said it."

"If I had the gift you once possessed, perhaps I could have stopped this conflict before it grew so dire."

Elenyr reached out to the oracle in apology. "Serak and Wylyn have planned with caution, even for you."

"That is what Mind said," Senia replied. "He suspected Serak left Queen Alosia alone in order to draw my gaze, allowing the others to be taken."

Elenyr frowned at the truth to her words. "Serak is more cunning than we gave him credit."

Senia sighed. "I came to you because I saw what you would tell the three fragments. They would not react well, and Shadow particularly would fall to distrust."

"He has reason to distrust." Elenyr sucked in a breath and reclaimed her seat on the barrel. "I have lied to all of them."

"We both know how damaging the truth can be," Senia said.

"Lies cause more harm," Elenyr said, and then met her eyes. "Did you see what I would tell them?"

Senia gave a slow nod. "I did."

"Then you and I know the truth of Draeken," she said, and then amended. "Us and Serak." Senia grimaced, prompting Elenyr to frown. "What?"

"I suspect Mind and Fire saw my vision."

"They what?" Senia flinched at the heat in her voice, and Elenyr lowered her tone. "They saw what Draeken could become?"

"They reacted strangely," Senia said, "and Mind tried to erase my memory of the moment. At least I think he did. I started wearing my mother's pendant, and as you know, my grandmother added a charm, preventing the one wearing the Book of Oracles from having their memory manipulated."

Elenyr clenched and unclenched her hand. The prospect of Mind and Fire knowing a potential future made her cringe, yet she wondered if it could very well be of benefit. They would certainly try to prevent such a fate. She hoped.

They shared a moment of silence until a flicker of shadow appeared under the crack in the door, suggesting Shadow had arrived. When Light joined the others they would expect Elenyr, and she was just below them, shackled by indecision.

"What should I do?" Elenyr murmured.

"You ask me?" Senia gave a humorless smile. "You know far more than I, and I'm just now starting to understand the threat we face. You are the Hauntress, an ethereal warrior, mother to five powerful fragments, protector of our world, guardian of secrets."

"And Serak almost killed me," she said.

"Almost dead is not dead," Senia said.

Elenyr stifled a laugh and then shook her head. "What do you suggest?"

"I've spent every night searching the waves," Senia said. "And it seems evident that we have two wars. The one with Wylyn, and the one with Serak."

"They are not the same?"

"They never were," Senia said. "Wylyn wants to enslave us all, while Serak's purpose remains a mystery. I do know that he seeks to open the Dark Gate."

Elenyr shook her head. "The one from your vision?"

"I only know it from my visions of the future," Senia said. "But it is of ancient make, so we need to ask a krey."

"Ero," Elenyr said with a nod.

"I suspect he has the answers we need," she agreed.

"With my home destroyed, I have no means of contacting him," Elenyr said.

"In time," Senia said. "For now, I believe you should focus on Wylyn's war. She desires to open her own Gate, and lead her army to our lands. It's only a matter of time until she raises the Stormdial from the sea and uses its power to accomplish her desires."

"And while I deal with Wylyn?"

Senia swept her hand east. "I prepare for Serak."

"Alone?"

She grinned and shook her head. "There is a certain white dragon that needs to join this battle. I go to speak to him."

Elenyr thought of the images of Draeken leading the vast horde and shuddered. "I cannot let that future come to pass."

"We won't," Senia said, and embraced her.

Elenyr clung to her descendent, grateful for such a woman to be the oracle. Senia was wise and strong willed. If anyone could help stop the calamity of the mysterious Dark Gate, it would be her. But would it mean fighting her fragment sons?

Another set of footfalls rushed by, the fragment of Light. He skipped up the stairs and Senia reached for the door. Raising the cowl over her features, she closed her eyes, obviously checking the immediate future to see if she could slip out of the fortress unseen. Then she looked back.

"I won't see you for a while. When the first snows fall, go to the King's Library in Terros and see what you can learn of the Stormdial. Fire and Mind will meet you there." She sighed. "I don't know how long you'll have to wait."

"And the other fragments?"

"Get them ready," Senia said. "Battles have been fought, but the war is just beginning."

With that Senia slipped out the door, and Elenyr stood in silence. She felt alone, worried, and angry, but all three settled into a cold resolve. She would not let Serak take her sons, even if it cost her life.

Chapter 12: Tale of a Titan

"Where are we going?" Water asked.

It was the morning after Elenyr had spoken to the fragments, and she'd asked Water to join her. Without knowing the destination, the fragment had agreed, and followed her into the city. Then she'd turned her path to the secret entrance of the Assassin's Guild, where Elenyr, Fire, and Mind had battled the Bloodsworn.

"Did your brothers tell you of the fall of the guild?"

Water grinned and pointed upward, in the direction of Shadow's quarters in the king's castle. "Shadow has been very vocal about his victories."

Elenyr's smile turned soft. She hadn't known at the time that Shadow had been present during the conflict, and only later heard his tale. But Shadow's presence had saved them from Gendor's strike.

The tunnel wound its way deep beneath the city, the darkness broken by dim light orbs. As the sole survivor of the Assassin's Guild, Lorica had begun rebuilding the order, and although she kept her efforts hidden from the others, Jeric—being Jeric—had learned she had already recruited a new member to her fledgling guild.

Elenyr again wondered about Jeric. In her recovery she'd examined him in a new light, surprised to discover she knew very little about the man. He was an adventurer, had been since the day they'd met in the bandit camp. But the more time they spent together, the more Elenyr realized just how much Jeric hid.

The elf had been two hundred years old when Elenyr had encountered him, but she'd never heard tales of him before that day, an oddity for someone so connected. In addition, he seemed to understand more of the events in Lumineia than she did. She knew it had something to do with the Bladed, because the mercenary guild frequently sent messengers to him. They were disguised, of course, but warriors of such renown could not hide their ability. In every stride, every look, even their carriage, they displayed a legacy of training.

"Elenyr?"

She realized she'd lapsed into silence and shook herself. "My apologies. Just thinking about Jeric."

After a moment's pause, he asked, "Do you love him?"

She sighed. "I do not know. I care for him deeply, and believe I always shall. But there are questions about his identity that are too pressing to ignore."

"Like how he saved King Porlin's father, and the king gave him—an elf—the mark of a Steward?"

"Questions like that one," Elenyr said.

"You think he is not who he claims to be?"

As much as Elenyr had considered Jeric, she had never thought of that solution. She'd assumed he merely liked his secrets, just as she did. She frowned, wondering how it could be possible. She'd known Jeric for nearly seven hundred years. Even when they had not been together, tales of his exploits were renowned across the kingdoms. But was it possible?

"I'm sorry," Water said. "I don't mean to pry."

"Your question has wisdom." She smiled wryly. "And I will consider your words."

He swept a hand down the tunnel. "We're headed to the old Assassin's Guildhall. Does this have to do with Wylyn? We still haven't found the location of the Stormdial."

"We will soon enough," she said.

"Jeric has the royal historians combing through the king's archives," he said. "I've been searching as well, but Shadow and Light are not much help. I don't think they realize what is at stake."

"They never do," Elenyr sighed. "But there is something I must show you. When we are finished, you can return to your search, and I will be departing."

"So soon?" he asked. "You just arrived."

"I will travel to the King's Library in Terros," she said, and raised a hand to him. "I want you to stay here. If either of us finds the Stormdial, we will meet there, and face Wylyn together."

He obviously didn't like the plan, but he nodded in agreement. They reached the end of the tunnel, which opened into a giant cavern situated directly beneath the castle of Talinor. Thick supports were partially buried in the walls of the cavern, providing the foundation for the fortress above. The light orbs of the cavern had started to go dim, but they carried enough illumination to reveal the remains of the Assassin's Guild.

A lake filled the base of the cavern, the current entering from an underground stream and exiting on the opposite side. The island at the center contained seven piles of rubble around the exterior, each the destroyed tower of one of the assassins. Shadow had mentioned that Lorica had burned everything after her sister had perished in the battle, but this was the first time Elenyr saw it with her own eyes.

Lorica had lost her sister in the battle and razed the Guild to ash. Elenyr wondered what she would do if she lost one of the fragments to Wylyn or Serak. One look at the towers told her exactly how she would respond.

"It still smells like scorched stone," Water said.

Elenyr led them onto the stairs into the cavern. "It has only been a few weeks since Gendor destroyed his own guild."

Elenyr noticed his gaze drawn to the giant statue, half fallen into the lake. The enormous soldier retained his sword, its bare upper torso curving with stone muscles. It had stood above the council chamber until Gendor's strike had destroyed the chamber, dropping the statue on its side.

"And that's . . ." he motioned to the statue.

"A Titan."

Water released a whistle of appreciation. "I never thought I'd see one with my own eyes."

Elenyr lifted her eyes to the enormous statue. "At the close of the Mage Wars, the Verinai built five Titans. This was the first, a test of whether such magic could be done. Tens of thousands of charms made its flesh and body, and were woven together to create its mind."

"How can such an entity exist?" he asked. "The first rule of entities is that the larger they are, the more unstable they become. That's why the dragon entity is considered the pinnacle of entity crafting—yet the Titan is twice the size of a dragon."

"It's not an entity," Elenyr said. "It's a sentient."

Water balked. "A mind that size? That would have taken thousands of mages working in concert, and a sentient would never function with so many different minds being the creator."

"Magic creates what we have the courage to imagine," she said. "Control is gained through discipline and practice."

"What does that have to do with the Titan?" Water's voice echoed in the cavern as they crossed the bridge to the small island.

"Creating the Titan required a sacrifice," Elenyr said, advancing around the crumbled council chamber to the feet of the great statue. "A single individual, placed inside the machine, gave up her consciousness to become the weapon."

Water's expression hardened. "The Verinai killed her."

"Yes."

"Was she willing?"

101

Elenyr experienced a surge of pride for Water. He did not ask about the person's power or their magic, he wanted to know if the woman who had sacrificed her life to become the Titan had been willing, or had she been killed by the Verinai. He wanted to know if the woman had honor.

"This Titan was joined to a woman named Heleen. She was a powerful mind mage, and the Verinai thought the charm would require a mind mage to succeed. They put her inside and forced her consciousness onto the Titan. She fought, and both perished."

"That's why it sits down here," Water said. "They thought they'd failed, and left it here to rot."

"What the Verinai did not know is that Heleen succeeded," Elenyr said. "The magic did bond, and her consciousness was transferred. But Heleen fought the magic, so the Titan never moved. The Verinai assumed it a failure and built four others, this time with willing participants. Those four attacked my home in the final battle of the Mage Wars. All were destroyed."

"What happened to Heleen?"

"I killed her."

Water swiveled to face her. "What do you mean?"

"When I encountered the Titan her consciousness was deteriorating." Elenyr imagined that moment, of speaking to the Titan, of Heleen's broken and failing mind, and her plea. "The Titan charm was never meant to endure, and she knew her mind was failing. She worried that in time, she would lose herself to the magic, much as the guardians before Draeken. She feared rising through Talinor and destroying the city, so she asked me to sever the link between her and the enchanted flesh."

Elenyr spoke distantly, like the moment had happened to another. Elenyr had refused, of course, and sought a way to heal the woman. But she was already dying, and her body was gone. Ultimately Elenyr had fulfilled the woman's plea. But not before she'd brought the woman's great grandchildren to the chamber, a last chance to say farewell. A final moment of joy before the end. The family had been grateful, and the surviving patriarch had vowed to forever help Elenyr. Their descended now owned a shop in Herosian.

"Why did you never tell the fragments?" Water asked.

"Because some burdens should not be shared."

For several moments there was quiet. Then Water shook his head. "I don't understand. Why tell me this now?"

"The Titan is essentially a giant body, one that now lacks a mind. He is much like you, and is essentially a guardian charm. The flesh awaits a consciousness of another, but none born of flesh could wield the magic."

She swept a hand to the Titan. "It was built to destroy, just as all the guardians before you. Serak knows what you were born to do, and although I do not know his intention, he has made his desires clear. He wants Draeken."

"Draeken is not for sale."

She chuckled at his quick answer and turned to face Water. "Serak reminds me of the Verinai. He has the same arrogance, the same power, the same willingness to disregard the lives of the people. But what I fear is what sets him apart. We may have to fight Wylyn at the moment, but Serak is patient and calculating. What's more, his actions speak to a larger plan, one with a goal that may not be what we first thought."

Water cocked his head to the side. "What are you saying? He can't be an ally, he tried to kill you."

Elenyr spared a smile for Water's simple perspective. He always looked at things with such clarity. "When he brought the krey here, I assumed Serak to be our foe, but he has allowed the krey to fight us, ultimately leading to Relgor's death. Most of the dakorians have been slain, and Wylyn controls the Order. If Serak is fighting a war, he's given up a lot of ground to Wylyn, and watched her stumble as she tried to control it."

"You think he *wants* Wylyn to fail?"

"Fail by fighting us," Elenyr said.

103

Water furrowed his head in thought. "But why? Why bring Wylyn here just to see her battle the fragments of Draeken?"

"That is what I do not understand," Elenyr said. "He has gathered for a war but has not fought one. It is almost as if the conflict he has prepared for has yet to arrive."

"And that is the war where he wants Draeken's allegiance." Water was nodding.

"I believe there will come a day when Serak tries to force Draeken into his service. To do so he will have all five fragments together. If that moment comes, you must fight, just as Heleen did. Draeken is more powerful than even a Titan, and if he turns to follow Serak—"

"That's not going to happen. I won't let that happen."

"Nevertheless," she said, "if the moment comes when Serak has the five of you together, your honor must be stronger than Draeken's will."

"Why are you telling me instead of Mind?" Water asked.

"Whatever happens with Wylyn," she sighed and looked away, unable to meet his gaze, "I need you to be prepared. Serak spoke to Draeken through you. I am doing the same."

His features hardened. "Serak sought to manipulate me."

"Draeken has heard Serak's voice," Elenyr said. "And I want him to hear mine. From you, I seek your aid. To him, I issue a warning. Water's honor is the strongest element in the fragments."

Water regarded her with a closed expression. Elenyr knew she was pushing him, but she needed Water to understand what was at stake. Serak was winning. She didn't know how, she didn't know why, but Serak's plan was working exactly as he desired. All except her survival. If Serak came to kill her again, Elenyr needed her voice to be heard by Draeken, even if she had to endure Water's anger.

"Why does it feel like I am just a pawn in this conflict?"

"Because to Serak, you are." She patted him on the arm. "But a pawn can still choose their own fate."

She cast the Titan a final look. Heleen had been a pawn as well, but she'd refused to yield. She'd been a simple woman who cared about family and love. As a Titan, she could have fought in the war with Alydian, and the presence of one more Titan could have made the Verinai victorious. One choice had changed the war. One day soon, Water and the fragments would face a similar choice. More than anything else, Serak was preparing for that moment. Subconsciously she reached up and touched the pendent on her neck, the one containing her treasured memories of the fragments. What Serak did not know, what the fragments did not know, is that she too was preparing for such a moment. She just hoped that when the time came, Water's honor would prove the victor.

Chapter 13: The Wilds

Fire trudged through the rain, wishing for a nice fire in an inn. But there was nothing, because they'd left civilization days ago. After departing from the oracle's refuge, they'd journeyed southeast, skirting the towering barbarian mountains. That's where a lightcast bird from Light reached them, revealing the events of the attempt on Wylyn's life, and Jeric claiming the Talinorian throne.

The news of Serak's withdrawal and Wylyn's takeover filled their conversation as they passed through the mountains and beyond the borders of occupied lands. Then they left Griffin behind and entered the Wilds.

Rugged and hilly, the region was known for its ravines and small valleys. Sparse vegetation grew across the uneven landscape, the broken ground discouraging exploration or farmland. The Wilds extended for miles and lacked any natural resources worth pursuing. Expeditions had been sent and returned empty-handed, and many had dismissed the region as barren.

Rain sluiced off Fire's cloak and he shook it in vain. Mind trudged ahead of him, slowing as he approached a shallow ravine. Less than twenty feet deep, the ravine was choked with icy water, and they were forced to ford the freezing creek at the base. Winter could arrive at any moment, and the rain flirted with becoming snow.

"Stop thinking about how miserable you are," Mind said irritably. "There's nothing we can do about the situation."

"I hate being cold," he said.

"*You* don't get cold." Mind shivered. "*I'm* cold."

"I can almost feel the chill." Fire showed his hand, which lacked the usual red tint to his skin. "See?"

Mind whirled and showed his own hand. "I *do* feel the chill."

His hands were trembling with the cold, and almost white. Fire grimaced and cast a thread of heat into Mind's gauntlets, warming his fingers. Mind didn't comment, and merely turned away to climb the bank on the opposite side of the creek. Fire reached for the shelf of wet stone to pull himself up, imagining the last inn they'd stayed in and the woman in the tavern who'd eyed him from across the room.

"And stop thinking about the woman in the last tavern," Mind said.

"She was pretty."

"She wanted to steal from you."

Fire began to laugh. "I know. Doesn't mean she didn't find me attractive."

Mind grunted, the sound a confirmation that she'd desired Fire. He climbed up the ledge and surveyed the next section of crags and gulleys, his annoyance returning. Aside from an encounter with a pack of ravenous moordraugs, they'd encountered nothing. They'd been hiking the Wilds for long enough that his feet actually hurt, and he'd begun to wonder if they would ever find Beldik.

"Do you ever think positive thoughts?" Mind asked.

"Not when I'm this wet."

Mind actually laughed, and Fire realized his brother was equally as miserable. It actually made Fire feel better that he was not the only one that hated this particular journey. But then, only Water or Shadow would enjoy such weather. He frowned, recalling Mind's previous anger at Shadow.

"Why were you so upset with Shadow before," he asked.

Mind pulled his cowl tighter. "Isn't it obvious?"

"It's never obvious," Fire said.

Mind sighed and swept a hand to the landscape. "We've done dangerous work before, but Shadow allowed himself to be caught. It was a risk that could have led to all of us being captured by Serak."

"So?"

"So he could have gotten hurt."

Fire chuckled as he realized the truth. Mind had been upset with Shadow for nearly being killed. Under other circumstances Fire would have been teased his brother about loving Shadow, but the weather just didn't make it sound appealing.

"I was worried about him too," Fire said.

"It's strange," Mind spoke softly, as if to himself. "I worry about the other fragments like you're brothers, but we are parts of the same being."

Fire wondered what it would be like if a fragment was killed. How would that affect the others? Would it make them weaker? Or stronger? And would they all be able to feel the death? Distracted, Fire collided with Mind when he came to a halt.

"Look at this," Mind said, stooping and pointing to the ground.

"It's just more mud," Fire said.

Mind threw him an annoyed glance and then wiped his hand across the mud, revealing a smooth stone, perfectly square. Curious, Fire stopped and examined the object. Obviously built by hand, the stone was set next to three others, the pattern suggesting they belonged to the same object. Cracked and worn, the stone had smoothed with time.

"It's a road," Mind said, rising and looking in both directions. "Or it was, at one time."

"A road to Beldik?" Fire asked.

"Maybe," Mind said. "I've spotted the stones a few times, and I wager there was once a road connecting Griffin."

"All the way out here?" Fire was dubious.

"Senia said that Beldik was a mine. I would guess that it had a large deposit." Mind pointed southwest. "One valuable enough that building a road through the Wilds made sense."

"The Order certainly isn't using a road."

"They probably have a tunnel underground," Mind said. "We know they have connections in the Deep, and those tunnels connect to every region."

"You mean we could be traveling through a warm tunnel?" Fire pointed to freezing rain. "Instead of walking through this?"

"It would have been guarded," Mind said dismissively. "This is the only way they would never expect us coming."

"Because it's *terrible*," Fire shouted, his voice lost in the storm.

"Exactly."

Mind turned and picked his way across the stones. Fire considered throwing a ball of flames at his back, but Mind would see it coming and dodge. Releasing an explosive breath, Fire trudged after his brother, deeper into the storm.

The remnant of the road lead to more stones, and they did their best to follow the vestiges of the highway. Bridges were all gone, and other sections had washed away, the stones taken into the depths of rivers, but at several points it was clear the highway had been grand and broad. Well traveled.

"Wagon ruts," Mind said, pointing to a particularly grooved stone. "The road was used for several decades, and wagons were heavy laden."

"I'm not as interested in the road as you are."

But he was, and Fire found himself intensely curious about the mine itself. Senia had known nothing about the settlement except its name, yet the evidence spoke to a heavily trafficked mine, large enough to sustain decades of labor.

They camped under an overhang where water had washed away the rock. Cold and wet, Fire cast a roaring fire where the rain could not touch them, and for once Mind did not complain that it could be spotted. The next night they were forced to camp in the open, and the next day in a tiny cave, barely large enough for the two of them. A week went by, and still they slogged down the ancient road.

"I'm guessing gold," Mind said.

"I thought the same thing," Fire agreed.

It was a lie, but Mind didn't call him on it. Fire appreciated that his brother didn't usually call him on his lies. It would have been enormously irritating to have a brother do that. Mind flashed a faint smile, as if agreeing with the thought. Then he slowed and pointed to the side.

"The road is coming to an end."

"How can you tell?"

They stood next to a small escarpment of rock. The stone rose up to their right, jagged and pitted with crags. But it was high enough to partially block the storm, and in the shadow cast by the formation, square foundations were just visible rising through the mud.

"A place of respite," Mind said. "Likely an inn or tavern. Its size suggests we're within a day's ride from Beldik."

"So we're only a day away?" Fire sighed. "Lovely."

"Maybe closer."

They continued to follow the road, and Mind began speculating on what sort of mine would be located so far away from the claimed lands. Fire tried not to get annoyed. Mind liked to talk about Lumineia and often wondered about the lands outside the known kingdoms.

"Imagine how much is out there," Mind would say. "There must be room for hundreds of kingdoms and thousands of cities."

Mind had gotten the ambition of Draeken and always wanted more. Fire cared nothing for such ambitions and was content with a warm fire and a beautiful woman, followed shortly by a battle. Or preceding. Fire wasn't discriminating about when the conflict occurred.

He wondered if there would be another pack of moordraugs. The last one had been small, probably split off from another pack. Their giant throats, all lined with teeth down to the stomach, made them terrifying to humans, but Fire loved fighting the creatures. They fought as a unit, presenting a challenge.

Fire. Mind's words intruded on his thoughts. *I can tell when you're not listening.*

"Good," Fire said.

Mind frowned. "The nature of the mine could be important."

"And we'll find out when we get there," Fire said with a shrug.

"Indulge me," Mind said.

Fire rolled his eyes but allowed himself to be drawn into a conversation about Beldik and its possibilities. It seemed less likely that it was for a type of ore, such as silver or gold, as they discovered enough rusted metal rings to indicate barrels of some kind. Mind seemed to think it would be stonesap, the liquid dwarves used to power their machines.

"Wouldn't the mine be empty?" Fire asked.

"Of course." Mind swept a hand to the road. "It would have been depleted ages ago, and mines are usually not remembered as well as cities. People remember where they lived, where they spent time with family and friends. Where they worked? Most try to forget."

"Does everyone hate their occupation?" Fire asked.

Mind eyed the approaching hill, which the scattered stones of the road ascended before descending out of sight. "Most."

"What about the nobles?" Fire cast a look at the storm, which had finally abated, and then returned with snow. "Do the royals hate their jobs?"

"More than you'd think."

They passed through a gap where a squat plateau had been cut to allow room for the road. Runoff over the years had worn the right side into a river, forcing them to walk along the left. The flurries drifted into the crashing water and settled on the grey stone. Fire yawned, growing tired and wondering how long until they arrived, almost missing the shape detaching from the wall at their side.

"Mind!"

Mind turned, and then flinched, the action saving his life. The shape swung a length of steel, carving a line that would have taken Mind's head. Fire opened his hand and flames poured from his flesh, forming a long, curving sword. Leaping in, he evaded the makeshift sword and sliced upward once.

His blade cut deep, slicing the figure from foot to neck. Cut in two, it fell out of the shadows and landed in the dim light, revealing a broken golem. Fire spun, searching for other targets, but there was none.

"Your neck intact?" he asked.

Mind touched his throat. "I expected there to be human sentries."

The surprise in his voice made it clear Mind had not anticipated the attack, an event rare enough to make Fire grin. It was not often his brother failed. He motioned to where the golem had hidden in the cavity of shadow, where it resembled a boulder.

"I did say we should look out for sentries."

Mind threw him a withering glare. "You don't have to be so smug."

"Yes. I do."

Mind pointed to the odd shaped left hand, which looked like a squirrel attached to his wrist. "It's not a sentry," he said. "It's a warning. If you hadn't dispatched it so quickly, it would have gone ahead to warn of our arrival."

"Is it that hard to say I was right?"

Mind groaned. "You were right. Now put that sword away before it's spotted."

Fire dismissed the blade. "I *love* being right."

Ignoring him, Mind pointed to the golem. "It's hollow, not solid, and old."

"I'm still right."

Mind rolled his eyes and stepped over the golem. "Keep your eyes open. We have to assume there are others."

As they worked their way up the slope, they spotted several humanoid shapes in the surrounding rocks, and took great care to avoid the sentries. Mind insisted they needed to be silent, but Fire guessed he didn't want Fire reminding him of how he'd been wrong.

As they approached the top of the hill, a faint glow was visible through the falling snow, and Fire tried not to accelerate. His sodden boots would slosh with every step, and golems would probably descend upon them like rats on a fallen wedge of cheese.

By unspoken accord they slowed as they reached the top of the hill. They crouched behind a boulder too small to contain a golem and surveyed Beldik. Fire's eyes widened as he examined the sprawling ruins, and then glanced to Mind.

"At least we found it," Fire said.

Mind lowered his voice. "Now what do we do with it?"

Chapter 14: Beldik

Fire and Mind took their time surveying Beldik. Placed in a small valley between hills, the mine covered the breadth of the hollow. Ancient structures were packed against each other, the walls becoming the walls of neighboring structures. Towers dotted the mine, pipes and pumps attached to the exterior and twisting out of sight. While the rest of the mine lay in ruins, the pump towers were relatively new, the pipes replaced to working order.

"Wylyn or Serak?" Fire asked.

It was the question both had wondered. Would they find Wylyn or Serak at Beldik, now that the Order had been usurped by Wylyn? Mind's expression was pensive as he examined the mine, the light from the fires illuminating his expression.

"This wasn't built overnight," Mind said. "I suspect this is a location Serak has kept hidden from the Order."

"Hyren said as much." Fire rubbed the spot the man had stabbed.

Fire grunted in irritation. He'd hoped to kill Wylyn and move on to Serak. But perhaps all was not lost. After what Serak had done to Elenyr, he deserved every bit of punishment Fire could deliver. But the mine did not look like a refuge, and Fire realized that their goal was destined to be a disappointment.

"He isn't using the mine as a refuge," Fire said.

"Obviously."

"I hate it when you say that."

"Sorry."

Fire listened to the clank of gears and watched the pumps turn. He'd visited stonesap mines in the dwarven kingdom until he'd been banned for nearly exploding the entire underground. He sparked fire into his palm, wondering what a spark would do to Beldik.

"Don't," Mind said. "We need to see what's down there first."

"I can't just destroy it?"

"Even if you could," he said. "We shouldn't."

"Is that a challenge?"

Mind shifted and pointed to the nearest pump tower. "Each layer of that pumping turret contains safeguards to prevent explosion. You ignite one thing and the entire mine will shut down."

"Are you an engineer now?"

"I learned from Dothlore before he became king," he said.

Fire knew better than to disagree. Mind wasn't arrogant, not like him and Shadow, but he was confident. If he said the pump towers could not be destroyed easily, then Fire trusted him. He reluctantly extinguished the fire in hand. Then he spotted a pair of golems laboring on a pump tower, repairing a leaking pipe. The dark liquid covered half their bodies and one slipped, falling forty feet to shatter on a building. Another appeared and scaled the exterior, taking its place.

"There aren't any workers," Mind said, picking up on his thoughts. "Golems must run the entire mine."

"They can't run everything," Fire said. "They would have to have someone leading them."

"Not necessarily," Mind mused aloud. "Serak is a guardian of water and earth, and given enough time, he could have crafted golems for specific purposes, each built to repair, work the pumps, or fill barrels."

"Golems only have a single purpose."

"And those probably have a single task, repair that pipe. Others work over other sections. Or act as guards. There must be thousands in the mine."

"That would explain why no one knew this location," Fire said. "But some tasks would still have to be done by human hands. There is a limit to what golems can do."

Mind met his gaze, and Fire provided a memory of trying to get a golem to play a musical instrument. His fire golem had burned the instrument to ashes, and the house to the ground. Fire could still recall Elenyr's glare as they watched the home burn. Fire's female companion screamed hysterically as she watched the flames devour her bedchamber. It hadn't been Fire's finest moment.

Mind nodded slowly. "Perhaps you are right."

Fire peered into convoluted pumps and pipes of the ancient mine. Many roofs were broken or outright missing, and through the holes Fire made out the interior. Golems appeared and disappeared, going about their tasks with exactness. After several moments he noticed a shuffling movement through a window of a pump tower.

"There," he said.

Mind squinted through the falling snow. A plume of fire came from the top of a pump tower, the brief illumination revealing a dwarven face. Dirty and disheveled, he worked next to a human, both laboring over a series of levers at the base of the tower.

"Not servants," Mind said, his tone darkening. "Slaves."

"We need to get a closer look," Fire said.

They exchanged a look and then stepped away from their vantage point. Working their way down the slope, they avoided several spots of shadow. Used to seeking such places to avoid discerning eyes, Fire's skin crawled as he walked out in the open, his entire framc illuminated by the bursts of fire as the pipes burned off the higher pressures of stonesap.

"Easy," Mind murmured. "Golems cannot see, and will sense the vibrations in the earth. If we walk too close to the boulders, we will find ourselves quickly surrounded."

"I can handle golems."

"Not this many," Mind said.

They finally reached the base of the slope and entered the city. They kept their pace slow, but it quickly became apparent that the mine lacked defenses on the interior. Golems passed them by, so close that Fire could reach out and touch them. Oblivious, the golems inside Beldik worked to carry out their assigned tasks.

"The fortifications must be outside," Fire murmured.

"More golems would be beneath," Mind replied, pointing to a set of stairs, which led to rumbling and clanking beneath the ground. "They will come if summoned, but otherwise we should be well."

The interior of Beldik was an odd mixture of ancient and modern. Most of the structures were ruined, the stones rounded by age, gaping holes in the roofs. Pipes were new and glistening, golems laboring over them, quick to repair damaged sections.

"Serak spent a great deal of time repairing this place." Mind pointed to a section of pipe that lay on the ground, a new section taking its place. The metal looked old and well used.

"We've heard nothing of Serak or Wylyn gathering stonesap," Fire said. "Why would they need it?"

"He could raze an entire city," Mind said, "or even level a castle."

"But why?"

Mind didn't answer, and Fire scowled. Mind didn't know, and Fire disliked anyone being smarter than his brother. Fire had grown used to feeling like Mind always had a plan, always knew more than their foe. But Serak? He was the Father of Guardians, an enemy unlike any they had faced.

"We need to find a slave," Mind murmured. "They should have some answers."

They crept through the city, working their way through buildings that had once been homes, the vestiges of stone furniture still visible. The structures were so densely packed that new paths had been created, winding through holes in walls and over piles of rubble. The labyrinthine ruins were dotted with golems, most of which were obviously worker golems.

The worker golems had hands like a human, their bodies squat and built for strength. Powerful enough to undo pipes without tools, they crawled up and down the pumping towers, keeping them operating smoothly. Gouts of flame occasionally cast light upon the mine, revealing broken golems and dilapidated structures.

While the worker golems ignored them, Fire and Mind steered clear of the soldier golems. At six feet tall, the golems carried shards of steel like rough-hewn blades. Terrible to wield but effective, they prowled the ruins hunting for prey.

As they approached the center of the city they were forced to move more slowly, frequently halting to permit patrolling soldier golems to pass. Then they encountered their first brute. Towering over the others, the brute golem was fifteen feet in height and carried two large hammers. Obviously a sentient, it searched the ruins for intruders, sniffing about like a hunting hound.

Workers, soldiers, and captains, Mind thought to Fire. *Serak has built a city.*

Fire didn't like to speak mentally, but this time he responded with a thought. *Those brutes took time to cast. There won't be very many.*

We need to stay out of sight, Mind said. *If we are discovered, the whole of the force will descend upon us.*

Fire eyed the brute as he absently destroyed a wall in his way and passed through a building. In the distance, another brute climbed onto a roof to survey the surrounding region before dropping from view. The snow had turned to rain again, and through the sleet Fire noticed what lay at the heart of the Beldik.

118

A dozen pumping towers were placed at irregular intervals, and a mostly intact structure sat between them. Domed and large, it towered over the city, and had obviously been built in the last few decades. A smaller, knobby building sat adjacent to it, the roof repaired, the walls barred.

"There," Fire murmured. "I suspect they keep the slaves housed in that building."

Look at you being all thoughtful.

"I'm not stupid," Fire said, a touch too loud.

One of the brutes turned as if he'd heard Fire and began to advance in their direction. Fire shrugged in apology, and the pair retreated, ducking around a wall as the large golem plowed through the wall to search where they had stood. It turned about, its expressionless features searching. Fire resisted the urge to conjure his fire sword, and Mind shook his head, confirming the restraint.

The brute abruptly rotated and scaled the wall, using the hook at the end of its blade like a hand to reach the broken walls. With more agility than seemed possible, it picked its way across the broken roofs, searching the ruins beneath.

Fire and Mind followed what had once been a road, advancing beneath a ceiling of pipes. A patrol appeared ahead, led by a brute. Mind and Fire ducked into a fallen structure. Through a back door, Fire and Mind found an alley, and then worked their way through a succession of buildings, using holes in the walls that Fire now guessed had been made by golems.

As they approached the slave quarters, Fire spotted a group of them. Watched over by three soldier golems, they worked to fix a particularly complicated section of piping next to a pumping tower. Thick, dark liquid spilled onto the ground, and a dwarf shouted to the others, his voice tinged with warning.

Fire and Mind passed them by and darted across a larger street. Fire caught a glimpse of two wagons being loaded with barrels at the end. The golems placed the barrels into the back, while other golems pulled the wagon towards a large cave. At least that explained how the volatile liquid was being shipped out.

They reached the two intact structures, the giant one and the smaller prison. Obviously built from a section of ruins, the building had an assortment of old and new walls. Much of the newer construction had used stones from neighboring buildings, making them easy to climb. Catching a hold, Fire began his ascent in the shadow of the structure.

The stones were smooth and slick with icy water, so he cast needles of fire out of his fingers. The tiny spikes pierced the stones, granting him a solid grip as he came off the ground. Mind followed, and they navigated a pipe and approached a large, barred window. Set beneath an overhang, the window looked over the gloomy ruins.

Fire ducked under the overhang and gripped the beam supporting the roof. It trembled, so he shifted back to the wall. Mind joined him, and together they peered into the interior. Well lit by light orbs, the room contained hundreds of humans, with a smattering of elves, dwarves, gnomes, and other races.

Private quarters were positioned around the outside, surprisingly well made. Fire expected the slaves to be listless, but they were not as despondent as he'd expected. There was an air of fatigue and resignation, but not despair.

The window sat at the end of the large room, and some of the slaves were nearby. Realizing he and Mind would have to get inside, Fire cast a finger blade at the tip of his finger and placed the glowing fire against the steel bars. The light reflected into the interior, and a nearby woman looked up. She closed the distance in a single step.

"Don't," she hissed. "If you cut that bar, you'll kill us all."

Chapter 15: A Caged Friend

Fire withdrew his hand and extinguished the knife. "How?"

The woman issued a low whistle and everyone in the room perked up. Men stood and ambled about, taking up positions next to doors and other windows, obviously lookouts. Others continued to talk, speaking a touch louder as they cast furtive looks in Fire's direction.

"The entire building is filled with stonesap," she said. "Others have tried to escape, and their buildings are in ashes around us."

Fire spared a look to the north and spotted a cavity adjacent to the slave quarters. He'd assumed it was just part of the ruins, but now he noticed the epicenter of a single blast, not the weathering of time.

"Who are you?" Mind asked.

"Along the wall and up to the roof," she whispered, stabbing a finger upward. "I'll meet you up there."

She stood and shuffled away. Fire eased out of the overhang and climbed above the arch, where he and Mind scaled to the roof. Picking their way up the cracked and broken tiles, he spotted a chimney and worked his way to it. Just as he arrived, the woman poked her head into view.

"This way," she said. "They keep finding our exits and sealing them with stonesap."

She disappeared again, and Fire reached for the edge of the chimney. Mind caught his arm, and Fire looked back, raising a questioning look. Mind was glancing about, as if searching for a trap.

"What?"

Mind shook his head. "There's another mind here. Someone . . . powerful. They're subdued, so I can't get a full read on who they are."

"I trust her." Fire jerked his head towards the woman.

"That's because she's beautiful." Mind folded his arms.

"I didn't get a good look."

That's a lie. Mind thought back.

"Have I told you I hate it when you do that?"

Mind grinned. "Many times."

Fire caught the top of the chimney and levered himself up. Inside, he found a makeshift ladder built out of scraps of pipe. He climbed down with great care, not wanting to fall on his face, not in front of the mysterious woman.

He couldn't define it, but the woman commanded attention in a way he'd never experienced. In the window below she'd spoken with authority and conviction, an inner fire that seemed to call his name. The shadows had not permitted a full look at her features, but she was human. Then she'd poked her head out of the chimney and Fire had been at a loss for words.

He reached the base of the fireplace. The slaves had covered the opening with cunningly placed pieces of wood, stone, and sections of piping. Fastened together, they formed a door that looked like a section of wall.

Fire stepped out—and stared. The woman stood with her arms folded, regarding him with a curious expression. Two men flanked her, both older, both with beards. Grizzled and obviously soldiers, they carried no weapons, but they appeared ready for a fight. Fire dismissed them outright, his gaze on the captivating woman.

She was shorter than expected, her head just reaching Fire's shoulder. Her hair was red—he'd always liked redheads. Dressed in pants and a tight vest, she had piercing green eyes that held him fast.

"I'm . . . er, what's your, . . . I mean . . ."

122

"Is he always so articulate?" she asked, glancing to Mind.

Mind smirked as he stepped out of the fireplace. "Usually not." Then he mentally added to Fire, *Are you actually flustered?*

Fire shot him a glare and managed to find his voice. "I'm Fire. This is Mind."

We usually use our personas, Mind thought dryly.

Fire winced and responded in kind. *Sorry.*

"Those are your real names?" she asked.

"Actually they are," Mind said aloud. "Who are you?"

"Soreena," she said.

"That's your real name?" Fire grinned.

She stared at him. "Yes."

What was wrong with him? Where was his legendary smooth smile that made the women melt? He was the fragment of passion, and the woman was just another in the long line of women he'd wooed—

Don't lie to yourself, Mind thought to Fire. *You think she's stunning.*

Fire shook himself. "Did Serak bring you here?"

"We rarely see him," one of the men said.

"Boaz and Billet," Soreena said, motioning to them. "They help me keep the others safe."

"You're in charge," Mind said, a trace of surprise in his voice.

She lifted her chin. "Have been since my father was killed."

Mind's features hardened, and Fire recognized the expression. He'd picked a memory from Soreena, and his eyes flicked to Fire, transferring the memory to him. Fire watched a giant golem with four arms crush a man beneath his foot, while swatting others aside like they were insects.

123

Liquid in form, the golem's body bore an odd sheen to its skin. Someone screamed and Fire realized it was Soreena before she sprinted to the golem. It caught her easily, lifting her into the air and bellowing in her face. In the reflection of the liquid, Fire saw the tears streaming down her cheeks.

"Lead your people, woman," the golem snarled. "Or you can die like your father."

Then he dropped her next to her father, and Soreena scrambled to his side. He raised a hand to her cheek, just as the giant golem plunged a flaming dagger into his chest. It did not ignite his body, but the fire burned through his blood, until he turned to ash in Soreena's arms. The young woman held the ashes, crying, the memory tinged with a burning desire for revenge.

The memory faded, retuning Fire's vision to the interior of the prison, and the woman regarding him with thinly veiled distrust. Fire coughed and managed to keep his voice normal to ask the obvious question.

"What is the golem from your—"

"What's the creature that leads the golems?" Mind asked, and shot Fire a warning look.

"Serak calls him the Incinerake," Soreena said, "a sentient crafted out of stonesap."

"Couldn't we just detonate the golem?" Fire asked, igniting a blade of fire in his fingers.

"Would that it would be so easy," Boaz said, eying the fire blade. "We've used fire enough to know he doesn't burn unless he wants to."

"How long have you been here?" Mind asked.

"Twelve years," Soreena said.

"A long time," Mind said.

"We were brought in to replace another tribe of druids," she said. "They died trying to escape."

"Druids?" Fire asked. "Why druids?"

Someone whistled a warning, and Soreena darted to the chimney, motioning Fire and Mind inside. They ducked out of sight while Boaz and Billet replaced the false wall and set up a small table, where they began to play dice. Mind picked the image from one of them, allowing Fire to watch through Billet's eyes as a brute and two soldier golems entered the room. They picked up a pair of men by the door and dragged them from the room. Another entered and walked to Boaz, grabbing him and taking him as well. Billet scowled but did not protest.

"Follow me," Soreena whispered, and began to climb.

Fire jumped to follow, and they scaled up the chimney. Before reaching the top, Soreena shifted a section of the stones, swinging it aside to reveal an access into the rafters. She climbed inside, guiding them through the beams to the hallway outside the room.

"The golems come all the time," she said. "The Incinerake likes to keep us working, to remind us that we are slaves."

"You've tried to escape?" Mind asked.

"Several times," Soreena said. "The furthest we've gotten is outside the city, but there is nowhere for us to go. We'd never survive the Wilds to get back to Griffin, and the tunnel is too well guarded for us to escape in that direction. Did you sneak past them with your magic?"

"We came through the Wilds," Fire said.

She paused and looked back, regarding them with new respect in her eyes. "You're stronger than you look."

"How weak do we look?" Fire protested.

She looked him up and down, wrinkling her nose. He dropped his eyes to his cloak. Spotted with mud and drenched, he looked like a rat caught in the rain. His hair was disheveled, his cheeks smudged from the road.

"We just walked six days," he protested. "And you don't look that much better."

He pointed to her. Her cheeks were also smudged with grime, her clothing stained, her red hair blackened with soot. She regarded him with thinly veiled annoyance until Mind nudged his shoulder.

Very smooth.

Fire growled under his breath and swept a hand forward. "What does Serak want with all the stonesap?"

"We don't know," she said.

They climbed over the hallway to another large room across the hall, where more slaves were present. She leaned over a rafter and whistled a combination. A man looked up and nodded, and then passed on the message.

"Our entire tribe was brought here together," she said. "The mine was already set up with golems. The Incinerake is like their general, and the mine was all set to work. Once we helped get it moving again, they've been loading barrels every day."

"Serak must have harvested tens of thousands of barrels," Mind said.

"And still going strong," she said. "Only two of the forty pump towers have gone dry. As long as the engine keeps going, we could go for another decade." She flashed a grim smile. "Unless we escape, of course."

She reached the opposite end of the structure and scaled through another secret door to the roof. From there she led the way to the pinnacle of the building, where the entirety of Beldik was visible.

The rain had stopped, but the air retained a chill that nipped at Fire's cloak. Mind shivered, but Soreena seemed impervious to the cold. She leaned against a broken section of roof and pointed to the Wilds.

"Your turn. Why are you here?"

"Hunting Wylyn and Serak," Fire said. "It looks like Serak guarded this location with a great deal of care. We assumed he'd be here."

"He never has human guards." She pointed to the crawling golems. "Probably suspects they would eventually need to return to their families."

"He is the only one that comes?" Mind raised an eyebrow.

"None but him," she said. "The dwarves in our group guess he spent more than a thousand years preparing this place. Some of the golems are certainly that old."

"He doesn't want to risk it being discovered," Mind said, frowning and pointing to the building they stood on. "But why go through all the effort to ensure secrecy, and then bring a group of captives that will surely attempt to escape?"

"To fix the mine?" Fire asked.

Mind shook his head. "The golems do that, or most of it. Why are you really here?"

"We help fix the mine," Soreena said. "But he's right. That's not our primary purpose here."

"Then what is your purpose?" Fire asked.

"To keep the engine going." Soreena's expression was grim.

"What engine?" Fire asked.

Mind spoke before she could, his breath releasing in shock. "It cannot be."

Soreena cast him a strange look and then turned back to Fire. "The mine was depleted ages ago, but there was more stonesap deep in the earth. Serak is using an abundance of fire like a lance, keeping a hole open without igniting the sap."

"That would take an inferno," Fire said, "and a conscious mind to control it . . ."

He froze, realizing what Mind had gleaned from Soreena. Anger and worry flooded his frame and he shook his head, refusing to believe the only possible answer. Soreena frowned at their reaction.

"You already know. Don't you."

"A phoenix." Flames spilled onto Fire's fingers and he clenched a fist. "Serak trapped a firebird."

Soreena regarded him and then nodded. "Come with me. I'll show you his cage."

Chapter 16: A Plan to Escape

Soreena took them over the roofs, avoiding pitfalls and worn sections, to reach the giant structure at the heart of the mining city. Numerous pump towers were close to the domed structure, forcing them to keep their path slow or risk being spotted. Eventually they reached a loose section of roof that Soreena shifted, allowing them a view of the interior.

Huge and open, the interior of the domed space resembled a cage, with the walls covered in a special metal that absorbed heat. At the base of the building, giant chains coiled around the legs of an enormous bird.

Half on its side, the phoenix did not rise, as if it lacked the strength to do so. Its wings were no longer bright, now graying and dark red, like rust on an old metal figurine. Abruptly the bird lurched to its feet and issued a war shriek. Flames sparked and fell off its back and wings, only to be siphoned away by the chains. Its power leeched by its bindings, the bird again fell on its side, its eyes fluttering shut.

Fire clenched his hands into a fist, so tightly that sparks tumbled from his fingers. The bird was a creature born of magic, its power surpassing dragons and reavers. To see it caged spilled anger into Fire's blood, compelling him to act.

He recalled his year of training with the birds, where he'd learned lifetimes of lessons. Fire had gained their respect, even calling a few of them friend. He could not stand idle while one sat in a cage, bound to Serak's machinations.

"Fire," Mind spoke softly. "Do you recognize him?"

"You know the phoenixes?" Soreena asked, eying the veins of fire pulsing in Fire's arms and neck.

"They are friends," Fire said, his voice rigid.

"Do you know him?" Mind pressed.

Fire leashed his billowing anger. There would be a time for such conflict later, when he could wrap his hands around Serak's throat and watch him burn, watch the flames curl up from his eyes and his magic disintegrate into sparks.

"Fire," Mind's voice turned sharp.

Fire clenched his jaw and reined his magic by force of will. Then he took his hand off the metal roof, leaving a steaming handprint where the metal had begun to melt. Soreena stared at the spot.

The firebird was male, that much was clear. The females all had a tinge of orange in their feathers. It also was older, its size marking his age. Then the bird shifted, revealing a distinct pattern of scratches across its beak, rising past its eyes to its head, the legacy of a battle with elven mages seeking to trap the bird long ago. A flutter of magic appeared, and abruptly the fiery wings burned from red, to white, to blue.

"It's the Ancient." Fire sucked in his breath and cursed.

"Are you certain?" Mind asked.

Fire threw him a withering glare. "He is the only one with magic strong enough to make his wings blue. I'm certain. He is the oldest phoenix, the father of his race."

"We need to get down before we're spotted," Mind said, and then mentally added, *and before you melt your way through the roof.*

Fire watched the caged firebird before striking the roof with his fist. Then he reluctantly turned and followed Mind and Soreena back to the slave quarters. The distance did not cool his anger, rather it fueled it, so by the time the trio dropped into the slave chambers, he was almost spitting flames.

"We have to free him."

"And us?" Soreena challenged.

"You're a given," he said, motioning in dismissal. "The Ancient has never attacked humankind. And you have no idea the role he played in the Dawn of Magic."

"Fire," Mind said. "We need to think carefully."

"*You* do the thinking," Fire stabbed a finger at him. "*I* burn things to ash."

Soreena whistled to her group, and a man joined them. She murmured an order and he nodded before departing. Then she turned back and folded her arms, regarding Fire and Mind with wary eyes.

"Who are you, really?"

"Just enemies of Serak," Mind said smoothly.

"Don't lie to me." Soreena's voice had turned dangerous. "You're stronger than a normal mage."

"We're going to help you escape," Mind said.

Other slaves had taken up positions around Soreena, subtly picking up lengths of pipe and stones fastened to sections of steel. Makeshift weapons. Abruptly Fire realized that Soreena now viewed them as a threat, a realization Mind seemed to also notice.

"We are not here to harm you," Mind said quietly.

"Do you know what will happen if you attempt to fight and fail?" Soreena stabbed a finger toward the building that had been destroyed. "Two other tribes have sought to escape, and each time—"

Fire groaned. "The Incinerake killed your father, stabbed him in the chest and let heat burn him from the inside out. We know. Can we get on with this?"

Soreena's eyes widened. "How could you possibly know that?"

Mind glared at Fire. "We cannot explain—"

"We're fragments of an ancient guardian," Fire said. "Serak is as old as we are, and we want to kill him. Enough?"

131

"Fire." Mind passed a hand over his face as if suddenly weary. "You really need to learn to shut your mouth."

"That was never my talent," Fire shot back, and held Soreena's gaze. "Enough truth for you?"

Soreena stared at Fire long enough that, despite his anger, he experienced a flutter in his chest. She really was captivating, her fire forged through years in captivity, keeping her people alive, and plotting their escape. A warrior, a leader, a soldier, and so beautiful.

Would you stop telling the woman our secrets?

Mind's thoughts were tinged with heat, but Fire ignored his brother. This was not the time for subtlety. They needed to move, and quickly. It was only a matter of time until the golems discovered Fire and Mind, and they needed to strike before their presence was known.

One of the men hefted a makeshift maul. "Soreena?"

"Bring Boaz and Andel," she said. "Let's go to the pump house."

The man scowled. "It's taken two years to build that refuge, and you want to just give it away? They could be Serak's men."

"They aren't." Soreena pointed to one of the women. "Cover for my absence with the golems."

"You only have thirty minutes until the next patrol," the woman said.

"Then let's make them count," she replied.

The other captives dispersed, while Boaz strode to the door and whistled. Soreena took them to the opposite corner of the room, to a cunningly placed section of flooring that covered a tunnel. Fire dropped in behind Soreena while Mind and Boaz brought up the rear. They crawled through the tunnel for thirty paces, winding deeper and then turning away from the Ancient's cage. Fire tried not to stare at Soreena's form in the gloom, vacillating between bursts of rage for the Ancient, and attraction to the woman.

You need to control yourself, Mind mentally growled.

132

Fire ignored him.

The tunnel was small, obviously dug by hand, and reeked of stonesap. When they reached the end, they climbed into a large, rusted pipe, and from there they descended into an abandoned chamber. They exited the pipe through a broken section and then continued to descend through a series of rubble ladders to reach an underground section of the mine.

Through cracks in the metal, Fire spotted an abundance of pipes. The clanking of metal echoed in the distance, a constant hum of sound that matched the pulse of heat washing across Fire's skin. If the circumstances were different, Fire would have loved to explore the place.

Pipes and machinery protruded from the walls, aged, and rusted. Some sections were absent, the pieces salvaged for other machinery. When they reached an observation room, another woman was already present, this time a dwarf.

"Andel." Soreena nodded to the woman as she stepped into the room and motioned to Fire ascending the steps behind her. "This is Fire and Mind, our visitors."

"So the rumors are true," the dwarf said, eyeing Fire. "I can smell the fire magic on you."

Boaz claimed a position at the window overlooking the subterranean section of the mine. "Looks like we're clear."

Soreena stooped and retrieved a roll of parchment hidden inside a broken section of piping. She proceeded to unroll it on a valve wheel at the center of the room, using stones to brace it from moving.

"We've been planning our escape since the day we were taken," she said. "And with your help, we might be able to pull it off."

"And the firebird?" Fire asked.

"He was not in our plan," she said evenly.

"I'm not leaving without him."

133

Andel cast Soreena a look. "He's a charmer."

"Apparently he knows the bird," she said.

"My sympathies," Andel said. "But there's no way to free the bird."

Fire folded his arms. "I don't need your help."

"You will if you want to survive," Soreena said. "No matter how much magic you have, this city is crawling with golems, by our count, over five thousand workers, and the same in soldiers."

"Another thousand of the larger ones," Andel said.

"The brutes?" Mind asked.

Andel nodded, and pointed to strategic points on the map. "The brutes, as you call them, are sentients, crafted to be captains. They patrol certain sections of the city, and the soldiers follow their orders."

"What about the scout we found outside?" Mind asked.

"A few thousand scout golems are hidden around the mine," she said. "We don't have an exact count."

Mind shook his head, incredulous. "Serak has over fifteen thousand golems here? It would take a thousand years to cast them all."

"Some bear the mark of other mages," Boaz said, glancing back from the window. "I wager he hired a few dwarves to build some."

"Indeed," Andel said.

"And the Incinerake?" Mind asked.

"A powerful sentient of stonesap." Andel pointed to the window. "He is usually down here, but likes to patrol the entire mine. He's as smart as we are."

"Smarter," Andel said. "He has found dozens of our escape routes, and whenever he discovers one, we are punished."

"Tell me about the tunnel," Mind said.

134

Soreena put her finger on the map. "Here. More guards are inside, we believe in the hundreds, maybe thousands. None of us has ever made it inside and returned alive."

"Fifteen thousand golems," Mind mused. "Led by a sentient of stonesap, all designed to cage the phoenix and harvest a king's ransom of stonesap."

Andel stepped to the window and pointed to the firebird cage. "Most of us act in shifts, keeping the bird subdued. He has two chains on his legs, one siphons his magic, the other is ours, keeping him partially unconscious."

"Does he ever speak to you?" Fire asked.

"They speak?" Soreena asked in surprise.

"Through your thoughts," Mind said, his brow furrowed as he examined the map.

The trio fell into a conversation of tactics, and Fire tried not to pace. The Ancient had taught Fire, asked his family to teach him, and now the regal bird had been caged like a beast. He recalled the firebird's once lustrous feathers, now grey and sputtering magic. He looked frail, and that brought Fire's anger surging back.

"We work in shifts," Soreena was saying. "Each group reinforcing the enchantment on the chain. Those not working sneak into the mine, gathering tools for weapons, digging tunnels, or other work. We now have a network throughout the mine."

Fire noticed the two exchanging a look, with Andel obviously wanting to say more, but Soreena shaking her head. Noticing the exchange, Fire frowned, but Mind scowled, obviously picking the truth from their thoughts.

"That will make things more difficult," he said.

"What?" Fire asked.

Mind swept a hand to Soreena. "Your thoughts are easy to read. Care to enlighten my brother?"

"Stop reading my memories, mage." Then she grimaced in irritation and turned to Fire. "There's one more thing you should know about the bird."

"What's that?" Fire asked, disliking the apology on their features.

"Serak has increased our efforts in the last six months," Andel said. "He's pulled more and more magic from the bird. As it stands, there isn't much left."

"He's the Ancient," Fire said. "He's born of fire magic, and possesses enough to burn a city."

"Or power a mine for a decade," Soreena said.

"It's obvious he's weak," Fire said.

Soreena shook her head. "I'm sorry, but the bird is dying."

Chapter 17: A New Arrival

The first week of Rynda's imprisonment yielded little but frustration. No one visited except a water golem that delivered food. Still, Rynda waited at the bars any time she heard footsteps, ready to strike. But hitting the golem proved pointless, and merely spilled their food into the hall. Her actions garnered no small amount of derision from the other monarchs. It was muttered, of course, since none in the room would dare speak aloud against her.

She spent much of her nights at the balcony, working the loose bar against its moorings. It could turn with ease now, and she rocked it up and down, cracking the rock further. The metal was too rigid to bend, but the stone could not withstand the repeated blows, and the cracks gradually expanded.

The dwarf offered to help, but she refused. He was stronger than the other races, but no match for her. Alone, she shoved the bar up and down, side to side, until the cracks continued to expand. She guessed she had two or three days before it gave way.

During the day she listened to the others bicker. She'd rarely spoken to the other monarchs in the past and in the prison she avoided them, mostly because she might kill them by accident. Or on purpose. She listened to them argue, wondering if it was allowed to knock them unconscious. It would be easy, a tap on the head with her steel hand. It would certainly bring her more peace.

"I'm telling you," King Justin was saying. "He wants our kingdoms."

"Then why hasn't he come and spoken to us?" Werin said, his words thickened by his orc accent. "I've been here for weeks."

Dothlore grunted in irritation. "You're just sore they took you first, and none of the other kingdoms noticed."

Werin cursed in orcish and stalked to his room. If he had a blade he probably would have struck the dwarf, but he'd already tried that a few days ago, and Dothlore had put him on the floor. The orc king still nursed bruises from the encounter.

"Then why are we here?" Porlin demanded.

Of all the monarchs, he looked the worst, and Rynda sniffed in disapproval. After a lifetime of excess, a few weeks in a cell had left him looking haggard. He'd lost more weight, and his clothes hung on his frame, rumpled and dirty. They'd been given new clothes shortly after Rynda had arrived, but Porlin still looked unkempt.

"They argue like children forced to sit in their room," the dark elf queen murmured.

"Kings and queens do not make good friends," Rynda said.

"Even those used to a throne need a leader."

Rynda cast the dark elf a long look. Erisay did not often leave her quarters, and spoke little. Oddly, Rynda found that she respected the woman. She may have come from an often-maligned race, but she spoke with grace and conviction.

"I don't care about them." Rynda sniffed in disgust. "Or their kingdoms."

"You should," Erisay said.

"Why?"

Rynda motioned to Werin. The orc had returned and was glaring at Justin, arguing over a grievance from years ago, when Justin's father had broken a trade agreement. Justin was just as quick to accuse Werin of allowing Bartoth to steal a shipment of anti-magic spears.

"You are a race of combat and war," Erisay said. "But you are surrounded by brothers and sisters that do not fight. Kill them, and you would be alone."

"Would that be so bad?"

138

"No one wants to be alone," Erisay said softly.

A faint echo of footfalls came, and Rynda shifted through the bars. She assumed it was just a golem, but then she heard two pairs of boots, one shuffling, the other strong. Another captive? She pressed herself against the wall, the other prisoners growing quiet as they saw her stance.

Down the corridor, a human guard approached with a second human at his side, shackled, his head down. But they did not approach the gates of the common room, and instead turned up a side corridor. A moment later, a set of bars clanked shut over the goblin chieftain's rooms. Both chieftains rushed to the bars, as did Rynda, who shoved them away. On the opposite side of the room, the wall retracted into the ceiling, and a man was pushed through the opening. Then the door closed and the bars lifted at the entrance.

Rynda leapt past the new captive and felt along the back of the room, searching. The hidden door had a seam, but it was cunningly built so she could not even get a fingertip into the gap. Scowling, she turned to find the man sitting on the bed, the rest of the prisoners crowded in the door.

"Numen?" Porlin cried. "Is that you?"

"Porlin?" Numen stood and wearily embraced his neighbor king. "How long have you been here?"

"Long enough to lose weight," Porlin laughed, but no one else did.

"It's been months since you were dragged from the cell," Justin said. "Where did they take you?"

"Wylyn wanted to speak to me," Numen said, and shuddered. "She asked about our military strength, our resources. She spoke to me like I was a slave."

"These are *our* quarters," one of the goblin chiefs growled.

"You want to die in them?" Rynda snapped.

The goblin retreated, and Dothlore motioned Numen out. Rynda followed as well, curious to learn more of their captors. The moment she was out of the way, the two goblins claimed their room and shut the door.

"How long were you with her?" Porlin asked.

"I arrived in Xshaltheria shortly after Werin." He pointed to the orc. "Erisay came next, and then one of the goblins."

Rynda studied the man, disliking him already. His hair had grown in captivity, and now looked unkempt and matted. It gave him a dangerous look. The way he moved implied he was comfortable with a blade. His kingdom of Erathan was in the west, and lacked the size and strength of Talinor or Griffin. Werin returned from his room to lean against the door.

"And your daughter?" Porlin asked.

"Serak is taking family?" Rynda asked.

They all turned to her. It was the first time she'd directly addressed the entire group, and it seemed to take them off guard. Numen too, seemed surprised, and he glanced to Porlin as if in support.

"My daughter was taken with me," Numen said.

"You're the only one that had family kidnapped?" Rynda asked, glancing around.

The others shook their heads, and since the goblins did not come out, Werin said, "The goblins were kidnapped alone. Why do you ask?"

"Serak is a tactician." Rynda stared beyond them, considering the battlefield. "He plans for war, considering every tactic, every gambit that will bring victory."

"I thought you didn't know him," Werin sneered.

"I know his work," Rynda retorted. "He has enlisted my sworn enemy to his cause, taken kings, sets himself against the legendary Hauntress, and battles the fragments of Draeken. For what purpose? One does not act in such a manner without cause."

"Who are the fragments of Draeken?" Werin asked, but his question went ignored.

"Serak has a cause," Numen said, his voice rough. "He wants to defend Lumineia against the krey."

"He is the very one that brought the outlanders to our shores," Dothlore scoffed. "He has *allied* with the krey."

"Perhaps not," Rynda wondered aloud. Again, all eyes turned to her, and she grunted in irritation. "Do *any* of you study battle tactics?"

"We study war," Erisay said from the door of her cell. "We do not live for it. Perhaps you can enlighten us."

A twist of a smile tugged Erisay's lips, the expression a challenge, an invitation, yet also a plea. Rynda realized this was what the woman had meant, and for the first time understood a simple fact. As queen of the rock trolls, she knew combat better than anyone in the room, but Erisay—and probably the others—knew far more about people. Erisay had said the captives needed a leader, and she'd seen the opportunity to provide it. Her words, her expression, all the conversations in quiet and attempts at gaining her respect, had been to bring Rynda to this moment. So that she could lead the captive kings.

She grimaced at the distasteful task, yet could not help but admire Erisay's skillful maneuvering of the conversation. If it was a battle, Erisay would have drawn first blood, and that deserved respect.

"Serak invited Wylyn, but does not always behave like her ally. Wylyn is alone on Lumineia, and I suspect Serak could have helped her accomplish her goal months ago. Instead Wylyn has seen her forces blocked at every turn, and the Order of Ancients is being defeated."

"You think he's smart enough for such a tactic?" Justin's voice was dubious.

Rynda folded her arms. "How often have *you* sent an envoy of friendship, while sending an army of blades to a flank?" They shifted uncomfortably and Rynda bared her teeth in a look of disgust. "If you're smart enough to employ such a tactic, Serak certainly is."

"Rynda speaks with wisdom," Dothlore said.

"Of course you side with her," Meroosi sniffed. "You and the rock trolls are always allies, always killing my kind when—"

Rynda picked him up by the throat, but resisted the urge to knock him into the wall. "Your petty grievances are only useful to your foes, gnome. In here, you are all allies."

"Even you?" Erisay asked.

Unwilling to answer, Rynda sidestepped the question. "Serak allied with the krey, but alliances are always temporary. He has brought a foe to our doors, forced us to pay attention, to fight. We battle the left flank, while the right destroys our camp."

Numen was nodding, his long hair falling across his face as he did. "I was brought here now because Wylyn has claimed the Order of Ancients."

"She what?" Justin came to his feet. "I thought Serak led the Order."

"He did," Numen said. "But it appears while Serak focused on the fragments of Draeken, Wylyn garnered support among the senior acolytes of the Order. She has seized enough support to eject him from his position."

"Did Serak fight?" Rynda asked.

Numen jerked his head in confusion. "He let her take it. Shadow gathered allies and attacked Wylyn in Porlin's castle."

"Is my keep intact?" Porlin burst out.

"It's just a fortress." Numen frowned in disapproval. "They nearly killed Wylyn before Serak arrived. They argued, and Serak let her be. That's when I was taken here."

"Xshaltheria must still be in Serak's control," Rynda mused.

Rynda considered the revelation. The Order had fractured, with a portion following Serak and a portion following Wylyn. But how could she use the division to her advantage? And what would both parties do on their own?

142

Erisay drifted closer to Rynda. "In recent weeks the forces here have seen an increase."

"How did you know that?"

"I hear them training and marching," Erisay said.

"Never doubt elven hearing?" Numen asked with a faint smile.

"Indeed."

Rynda noticed a trace of evasiveness in her answer, and wondered what the dark elf queen held concealed. She was smart, that much was evident, and also patient. All monarchs were adept at concealing the cards they possessed, and the dark elf would be no exception. But what did she hide? Still, the greater question was Serak. If the man had been increasing his forces in Xshaltheria, that implied he knew of Wylyn's impending betrayal, yet chose to allow half his Order to be taken by his supposed ally. What did he gain from such a tactic?

Draeken and the Hauntress would be forced to deal with Wylyn, that much was clear.
Serak's action was a sacrifice gambit, and granted Serak time until Wylyn was killed. But why did he need time?

"You spoke well," Erisay murmured.

The other captives had fallen to arguing about Serak and Wylyn, but Erisay had remained at Rynda's side. Rynda grunted in irritation and strode to the front bars to peer down the hall, listening for the sounds of footsteps. Erisay followed.

"You should trust them," the dark elf said.

"I trust the dwarf to be pragmatic and good with an ax," Rynda said. "I trust the gnome to be paranoid and irritable. And I trust the human kings to speak an earnest lie while they hide the truth."

"They are not always so deceiving."

"Are you so different?" Rynda challenged, and lowered her tone. "Or are you going to tell me how you *really* heard the arrival of Serak's troops. Even elven hearing could not do that."

143

Erisay studied Rynda for several moments, and then raised a finger as if in warning. Instead, a sliver of orange light streaked from her finger and pierced Rynda's ear. She recoiled and instinctively raised a hand to strike the queen. Instead, an ocean of sound washed over Rynda. She heard the guards down the hall, human, judging by their heartbeats. One was scratching an itch in his armor, the other muttering about the guard change.

She heard a plate falling into a sink from upstairs, and the distinct clang of blades in a training room. Even further, she heard the sounds of rain outside, falling in sheets onto the stone parapets of the fortress. Then the sounds faded and Rynda stared at Erisay.

"Trust must be given, before it is earned," Erisay said softly, and then walked away.

Chapter 18: Tardoq's Offer

For the next several days, Rynda watched Erisay from a distance. The dark elf made no effort to close the gap, seemingly content to stay on the threshold of her cell. At night Rynda continued to work on the loose bar, which was getting closer to coming free. The gap would not be enough to get her out, but she could use the bar to pry against the others. As she worked, she considered what she'd learned of the dark elf queen.

Erisay possessed sound magic. That much was obvious. What came as a surprise was the fact that Rynda had never heard of her ability. As a rule, monarchs showed their strengths against other races, as much for appearances as for self-gratification. Rynda herself had no qualms about reminding her neighbors of the might of her army. The gnomes and orcs in the west, and the goblins and giants to the east, were all afraid, as well they should be. Even Griffin and the dwarves were wary of attacking the troll nation. A queen with the ability to hear conversations, even strike with debilitating curses, made queen Erisay formidable. So why had she hidden her magic?

She was clearly strong. The single charm had amplified Rynda's hearing a hundredfold, enough that she could hear much of the goings on in the fortress. Did Erisay's children know her ability? Did her people?

Rynda jerked her head, continuing to twist the bar. Rynda hired spies in all the kingdoms. Such an act was necessary in order to stay abreast of current threats. Men were also quick to betray their kind for coin. But her spies in the dark elf nation had not known of the queen's magic. So Rynda could only conclude that Erisay had kept the talent to herself, possibly even from her own children.

The secret was a powerful one, especially for a monarch. She would be able to hear the whispered conversations at the edge of the room, listen to enemies in the street, even hear the approach of an assassin. Yet she'd given the secret to Rynda.

Rynda yanked on the bar, abruptly frustrated. Erisay had given Rynda the highest of trust just days after they'd been imprisoned. Why? Rynda was as likely to betray her as use her, and the truth gave Rynda an advantage.

She sighed and leaned against the bar, resting as sweat beaded her forehead. Rynda disliked the trust Erisay had given, but she hated even more the trust she felt for the dark elf. It rankled to feel like Erisay was kindred.

A faint patter of feet warned her that another prisoner was awake, so Rynda slipped back to her quarters before one of the goblins exited the room. From the shadows of her bed, Rynda watched the goblin prowl the room before drinking from the reservoir and returning to their quarters. Shortly after, another king rose and Rynda consigned herself to waiting until the following night. Despite her haste to escape, she found herself curious about the dark elf.

She slept lightly, as she always did. Like the rest of her kind, she'd learned as a child how to wake at the slightest hint of danger. At the age of six, she and her peers had been taught a game, to creep upon each other during slumber. Drawing blood represented victory, yet if the victim awoke before blood was drawn, they were the victor. She still recalled the frustration of being fatigued through daily training, yearning for sleep. She'd been bloodied by her peers. Then she'd grown hardened, and become accustomed to sleeping among foes.

"Someone comes."

The words were no more than a whisper. She snapped awake and was on her feet, striding to the bars in the hall. The words had come from Erisay, who leaned against the wall of her cell, her expression tense. She'd clearly left a remnant of the charm in Rynda's ear, making it possible to activate if she had need. Under the current circumstances, such an overture was only prudent, so Rynda resisted the urge to rip at her ear.

The other monarchs were awake and sitting by the makeshift table, most grumbling about the upcoming meal. After so many days of captivity they'd grown lethargic and resigned. Fools. Still, they noticed Rynda's sudden tension, and Dothlore came to his feet.

"Queen Rynda?"

She didn't respond, and continued to peer through the bars down the corridor. The two golems, water and earth, stood across from her, as still as twin statues. Rynda glanced to Erisay, an unspoken request, to which the dark elf gave a slight nod.

Rynda's hearing heightened, and she heard the footfalls of one approaching the corridor. The two human guards around the corridor recoiled, shying away from the visitor. Rynda frowned, recognizing the weight of the steps could only come from someone heavy. A large shape rounded the corner and strode down the hall, coming to a halt in front of the bars, and several of the kings cursed, with Numen all but fleeing to the opposite side of the room.

"It's Tardoq," he spat, trembling. "Wylyn's Bloodwall."

Rynda regarded the dakorian, unflinching under the gaze of the outlander. She was tall, even among her own people, but Tardoq was even taller. He stood at ten feet, bones growing from his flesh, forming armor and spikes. Horns grew from his head, and his musculature revealed a powerful frame.

He carried a hammer on his back, the head and shaft glowing with runes. From what the fragment of Water and Lira had described before the battle with Bartoth, the weapon gained power with every impact, and the power could be released up close or from a distance. Beyond the weapon, Rynda had expected a legacy of battle on the dakorian's flesh, but was disappointed. Only a handful of chips and scars were visible, although some wounds were recent.

"I expected more scars," she said evenly.

The dakorian motioned to his chest. "My body has been perfected, and scars do not last. What you see are only my wounds of the last year."

"Or you're not as good as I've heard."

147

Tardoq actually laughed, the sound tinged with anticipation. "You are everything I have heard."

He motioned to someone out of sight and Rynda heard the clank of a lever. The bars dropped into the floor. Both golems moved for the first time, rising and flanking Rynda. She resisted the urge to strike and remained in place, a single step from freedom.

"Where is Wylyn?"

"She and Serak are not currently allies," Tardoq said. "I am seeking to remedy the breach."

"She let her dog off its leash?"

Tardoq's sneer came quick. "I do not belong to her."

"Then why are you here?"

"To see for myself the strength of your race. You can, of course, stay in your cell . . ."

It was an invitation to duel, a surprise, yet not an unwelcome one. She'd been itching for a fight and here it came, from a supposed perfected warrior, no less. Dothlore called out to her, his tone an edge of warning.

"I wouldn't."

"I would," Rynda said.

She stepped into the hall and the bars slid upward, sealing the monarchs in their cage. Without sparing them a look, Rynda fell into step with the golems on either side. Tardoq took up the rear, putting him at her back. She would have been concerned, but it was obvious what he wanted. And killing her in the hall would not suit his purposes.

"They say you've lived a long time."

"Forty thousand years," he replied. "Perhaps more. You lose track after a while."

"And when did you gain a perfect body?"

Her voice was casual, curious, like a friend asking a friend in a tavern. Tardoq chuckled, making clear he understood the duel had already begun. Information about a foe granted power during combat.

"Dakorians lives for a thousand years," he said. "Much like those you call elves and dwarves. Dakorians that prove their loyalty to a house are given a perfected form, and some rise to the coveted rank of Bloodwall."

"I don't know what that means."

"You and your people get sick, you scar, you age," he said. "All this comes from imperfections in your flesh that eventually wear your body into death. The krey have perfect forms, and they grant that power to dakorians, a chosen few."

Rynda followed the water golem, absently memorizing the turns, the stairs, and the number of soldiers they passed, most of which were men or women, although golems and other races were also present. The revelation of Tardoq's ability was significant. He'd likely been training for longer than Rynda's people had existed. A dangerous foe.

"Any other abilities come with this perfection?"

They came to a portcullis barring a hall and waited for it to be opened. "I heal quicker, and can feel less pain. My mind is sharper, my senses even more so."

"Did arrogance come with the changing?"

He chuckled again. "You are wise to learn of me."

"You are unwise to reveal so much."

They stepped into a large chamber, empty except for racks of weapons on the wall. One was prominent, her soulblade, hanging on the wall opposite her. She hadn't seen it since she'd been kidnapped, and her blood sang at seeing the glittering weapon.

"It will not matter," Tardoq said. "You are superior to a normal slave, but your body still carries the same flaws."

"And that is what you came to see?"

149

She strode to her blade and removed it from the rack as the golems flanked the door. Like all her people, she'd fashioned it herself to become Warsworn, and forged it with metals of her own choosing. She could wield any weapon, but her soulblade was an extension of her life. Five feet long, light, with a handle that could accommodate two hands or one. Its single edge had been honed to the pinnacle of sharpness, while several spikes extended from the spine of the blade. The spikes added a menace to the otherwise elegant weapon, and a large sapphire socketed into the hilt added a touch of beauty.

Tardoq remained a distance away, unhurried, obviously wanting to enjoy the conflict. He wanted to study Rynda at her best, and that was probably the reason he'd given Rynda her soulblade. She picked up her sword and swung it in a tight circle, relishing the weight, the spin.

"I hear the humans and fragments have killed many of your dakorians," Rynda said.

"They are no more my people than you are," he said.

The comment spoke volumes, and there was a faint sadness to his tone. Rynda was careful not to reveal what she'd heard in his voice, an emotion that surprised her. Tardoq could have spoken with scorn or arrogance, but instead he spoke with sorrow? Why?

"He is lonely."

Erisay's voice was just a whisper, like one murmuring over her shoulder. Rynda hid her smile by examining her sword, pleased to find the dark elf listening, and responding. But why would such a formidable opponent be lonely?

She took her place across from the dakorian and spun her sword, lazily, as if she didn't care about the duel. The act hid her eagerness, for she craved such a fight. They both knew that she would kill Tardoq, if she could. She doubted Tardoq had come to execute her, so the duel gave her an advantage. As much as one could have against someone like Tardoq.

"My people have a saying." Rynda watched her foe but the dakorian did not draw his hammer. "We are the flesh of war, and train for life . . . to fight to the death."

150

He chuckled, the sound echoing off the walls and weapons of the room. He still did not reach for his weapon, and merely stood in place, haughty, dismissive. Like she was beneath him. Then he motioned in invitation.

"Then kill me, if you can."

Rynda smiled, and surged into a run. Towards the door.

Chapter 19: A Master's Duel

Tardoq didn't move, the surprise evident on his face as Rynda fled. Whatever he'd thought she would do, that was not it. He recovered quickly and darted forward, but Rynda was already at the door.

The two golems rose up before her, and she ducked the rock golem's arm, spinning and sweeping her blade across the water golem, slicing it in two. Leaping through the water, she kicked the stone golem into Tardoq's path and raced down the corridor. Her purpose was not to escape, but explore the cage that held her bound. The bar in her cell would come loose, and when it did she would need to know the layout of Xshaltheria, the twists and turns, where it was safe, where the guards bunked. Knowledge was the most potent of weapons.

"Well done," Tardoq praised, leaping the golem. "You seek the greater victory, rather than a duel with me."

"Don't mistake my flight for fear," Rynda called back.

She turned a corner and accelerated towards a portcullis. Two men flanked the barrier, and both turned white at her appearance. One fumbled his spear and jumped to the lever that would shut the gate. Rynda hurled her sword, the giant weapon turning end over end, plunging into the man and sending him flying backward. The other man leapt to pull the lever, reaching it as Rynda close the gap.

She picked the man up by the throat and hurled him at Tardoq. Then she yanked the lever and sprinted up the steps, pulling her sword free from the corpse as she passed. She cast a glance backwards and saw Tardoq slam into the portcullis. She flinched, half expecting the dakorian to break his arm. But the steel snapped from its moorings and tumbled down the hall, colliding with the stairs.

Rynda scowled and hurried to put distance between them. She knew he would catch her, and the guards of the fortress were already raising the alarm, shouts and answered calls erupting from every direction. But it didn't matter. Her tactic had already yielded fruit.

Shaped like an upside-down cone, the lowest part of the fortress was the smallest. Her cell was near the bottom, as was the armory where Tardoq had thought to have their duel. Each higher level had forges, curiously shaped in a circle at the center of the fortress. The forges had tubes extending toward a center column. But the dwarven forges were now dormant, their hearths cold.

The fortress was expansive, large enough for a city, with streets circling the hearths, and homes placed on the outside of each circle. Between the individual quarters, shops and taverns were built with typical dwarven austerity. Grand staircases ascended to each level, and dwarven ascenders were evenly placed, providing quick ascent and descent.

"The descender is filled with soldiers . . ." Erisay's whisper came over her shoulder.

Rynda veered away from the ascender, leaping up the curving stairs just as the doors swung open and a score of armored soldiers appeared, each bearing bows and nets, weapons intended to capture, not kill. So they didn't want to kill her. At least not yet.

Tardoq plowed through the men, shouts ringing out as he knocked them aside. He'd closed the gap to thirty feet. She raced down a wide tunnel illuminated by stonesap torches. Most of the rooms were empty, and she guessed the fortress had only a fraction of the forces it could actually support.

She took the next steps four at a time, entering a garden level. Growing plants filled the entire floor, all for food. The fortress was obviously built to sustain itself for a siege. Serak had prepared for everything.

She reached the next set of stairs as a score of soldiers closed ranks, their overlapping shields becoming an unbroken wall, spears pointing out. Rynda leapt up and to the side, catching a statue of a dwarf carved into the stone wall. Her steel hand closed on the helm of the statue and she swung over the guards, landing at their back. They howled in dismay—and shouted in pain as Tardoq charged through their shields, spears snapping on his bone armor, weapons clattering to the floor.

Rynda charged around the circle of the fortress, breathing hard from her reckless run, Tardoq just twenty feet behind. The last stairs approached, but hundreds of soldiers clogged the steps. Rain fell on their armor, and she caught a glimpse of the stormy sky. She skidded to a stop, swinging her sword at Tardoq, who dodged with ease.

In the middle of a wide corridor, soldiers raced to close off any avenues of escape, their ranks thickening, until over a thousand soldiers blocked the way to the center forges, the barracks on the outside, and the two ends of the curving corridor. They formed a ring around Rynda and Tardoq.

"You thought to escape?" a guard taunted.

"Of course not," Tardoq said. "She wanted to see the fortress. One cannot escape the unknown."

"One cannot kill the unknown," Rynda said, noting that Tardoq too, was out of breath. He did not tire easily, but he was still made of flesh.

"You are more intelligent than I anticipated," Tardoq said.

Zenif rushed into view behind the ranks of soldiers. Still wearing his robe, the mage pushed his way through, his features furious. When he reached the open ground he stabbed a finger at Rynda.

"Take her back to her cell!" he said. "Serak will not let her escape!"

"Remove her and you take her place," Tardoq barked.

No one moved, and Zenif scowled. Rynda spun her sword, controlling her breathing. Tardoq began to circle, yet still did not draw his hammer. Rynda watched her peripheral vision, and spotted the dwarven ascender. Only five ranks of men barred the way to the open doors. Foolish.

She charged Tardoq, whipping her sword down and up, before spinning and slicing for his throat. He ducked and spun, agile and smooth, avoiding the flashing blade. She feigned being out of breath, just a touch, so he would not suspect, and slowed her swings.

154

"You are smart," Tardoq said, "But weak. I doubt you could even draw blood."

She lunged, feinting high—before reversing her blade along her arm. Spinning towards him, she flicked her blade out—and then struck with her free hand. Her steel hand, perpetually held in liquid form by dwarven magic, changed shape, and spikes extended from her knuckles. Spinning away from her sword, Tardoq did not see her fist until it was too close, and it struck him across the jaw.

An audible gasp came from the onlookers, and Tardoq came to a halt. He lifted his hand and touched his cheek, his fingers coming away bloody. He began to laugh and inclined his head to Rynda, a mark of respect.

"Your use of magic is a source of constant surprise," he said.

"I hope you'll think the same when you're dying."

He began to chuckle, and finally drew his hammer. "You are skilled, but you have much to learn."

He darted in, spinning his hammer at her side. She leapt over the swinging weapon and rolled to her feet, closer to the ascender. He placed his hand higher up the handle and swung with unprecedented speed, the hammer and the shaft coming at her as he pressed the assault.

She ducked a swing of a hammer and rose into a retaliating strike, ignoring the subtle shift of his feet, the swing of the hammer shaft. He wanted to land a blow, to teach her a lesson. And she let him. It struck her in the chest and sent her tumbling into the crowd of soldiers. They were quick to part, but some were not quick enough, and they landed beneath her.

She'd known it was coming, even planned for it, but it cracked a rib. Not since training in her youth had she been struck so hard, and for a moment her thoughts scattered. Gritting her teeth, she shoved herself to her feet, ignoring the two soldiers groaning on the floor.

"I expected better," Tardoq said, stalking forward.

Rynda smirked despite the pain. "So did I."

The blow had knocked her close to the ascender, into the five ranks of guards. She whirled and leapt to the ascender, bursting through the remaining line of soldiers. Unprepared for her charge, they were knocked aside, their helmets clattering off the stone. She caught the grate that formed the entrance and wrenched it from its moorings, hurling it over her shoulder.

Tardoq batted it aside and it fell into the soldiers, the shards of steel cutting flesh and trapping several. But Rynda was already inside the ascender shaft. Dwarven ascenders were a marvel of engineering, but known for a methodical ascent. The roof of the ascender was little more than a thin layer of wood, allowing easy access to the machinery off the shaft.

Rynda leapt to the controls and placed a foot on the housing of the levers, using it to leap to the boards. She crashed through the aged wood and levered herself upward. Thirty feet of empty air separated her from the top of the fortress, and she launched her sword upward, aiming her throw so it would land point down close to the mouth. Then she began to climb.

Tardoq blasted through the remaining wood, his armored bulk leaving bits of wood scattered into the ascender. Soldiers shouted for order, and many rushed for the stairs, hoping to cut her off above. Tardoq had slung his hammer over his shoulder and begun to climb.

"You used my blow to claim a position," he called up the shaft. "Clever."

"A battle is won in the mind before a blade is drawn," Rynda called, reaching for another gear, using it to jump to the lip at the top, grimacing at the throbbing pain of her ribs.

"But what if I had landed a killing blow?"

Tardoq was just inches from her feet, and she resisted the urge to kick him. The dakorian would anticipate that, and could catch her leg, pulling her back into the shaft. She couldn't risk that. She reached the top of the shaft and clambered over. Rolling onto the surface of the fortress, she stood and picked up her sword.

"That's not why you wanted to fight," she called, sprinting towards the exit.

Circular and enormous, the top of Xshaltheria was a large courtyard. Holes dotted the surface, most leading to other dwarven ascenders or stairs. At the center of the fortress, a giant hole bored through the structure, and a plume of heat rose through the opening, suggesting it led all the way to the volcano far below. The shaft was probably the source of power for the dwarven forges.

A wall circled the courtyard. A gate in the wall was open, leading to a bridge that spanned to the mouth of the volcano. A second wall was built on the top of the volcano, obviously the first line of defense. An attacking army would have to breach the outer wall and then fight across the bridge to reach the fortress. Any soldiers unfortunate enough to fall into the gap between citadel and volcano would tumble between the volcano wall and the fortress until they plunged into the magma beneath.

A storm darkened the sky above, with scattered rain falling on Rynda's shoulders. The wind carried the bite of winter, and she noticed the guards on the two walls wore furs over their armor. Well maintained, well organized.

Soldiers rushed to close the gates, and a portcullis clanked into place. She guessed that five thousand soldiers, all loyal members of the Order, were stationed in the ancient fortress. As they repositioned themselves around her, she recognized many with similar features, the symbols on their uniforms also matching. Families. These were generational servants to Serak, likely gathered over time from the corners of Lumineia, gradually taken and placed here. They had probably lived their entire lives apart from the races, trained from birth to worship Serak. The idea made her grimace in disgust. Serak had taken more than just their lives. He had enslaved entire generations.

She turned as Tardoq appeared and stabbed her sword at the gathered army. "Is this what it's like in the Krey Empire? Children born and raised to be slaves?"

"It has always been so," Tardoq said, coming to a halt out of reach of her sword.

"These people deserve lives." Rynda spat into the dirt.

"Are they not lesser races to you?" Tardoq asked.

"They are not beasts," she said, raising her sword in challenge. "And I'd rather die than be a slave to you."

Tardoq regarded her with a curious expression. "I'm sorry to have to kill you."

She braced for his charge but another voice called out to them. "That's gone far enough, Tardoq. You've had your fun."

The sleeping charm came quickly, and Rynda fought the magic, even though the effort was futile. She had no desire to see more of Tardoq, or of the soldiers gathered around. She'd learned what she came to learn, and her time to escape would come soon enough. Then she'd bring an army against the fortress.

"You are the least like a slave I've ever met," Tardoq said, his voice quiet, intended for only her ears.

"And I thought you had honor," she said.

She fell to her knees, and then to her stomach, the impact eliciting a groan before the sleeping charm claimed her consciousness. She'd learned a great deal, surprised her foe, and made plans for her future escape. But witnessing Serak's army left her with a simmering anger. Escape was no longer enough. She wanted to see Serak hang.

Zenif approached and she spotted his boots nearby. "Take her to her cell, and bring King Numen to me. Serak wants to interrogate him again."

"As you order," someone replied.

Many hands reached for her, and her vision clouded. But she saw Zenif's boots, just within reach. What a fool. A surge of anger brought a fleeting moment of clarity, and she reached out with her steel hand, catching his ankle. He bellowed in fear and she snapped the bone, earning a shriek of pain. She smiled as she heard Tardoq laugh, and then she succumbed to the sleeping charm.

Chapter 20: Soreena's Secret

Fire and Mind spent the day with the captives, and then the next. Much to Fire's rising irritation, Soreena insisted on waiting to prepare the captives for the escape. Fire spent much of the time prowling the underground tunnels, learning the layout of the mine for the impending battle.

The captives' quarters were oppressive. Every hour the golems came and took four druids, bringing them to the firebird to reinforce the charms keeping the Ancient subdued. Occasionally repair golems came and took others to perform work they could not. The rest of the time the captives were left alone.

Soreena kept her people busy. Some crafted makeshift weapons, while others slipped into the tunnels and searched. Mothers cared for their young, some of which had never known freedom. The most important were the lookouts and the scouts, both trained with a complicated pattern of whistles.

Golems occasionally searched the captive quarters, and a lookout whistled a warning. The golems stomped through the quarters, kicking the ramshackle walls used to cover homes, and pulled apart anything that was suspicious. On one of Serak's visits he'd crafted a quartet of highly focused golems, each designed to sniff out escape routes. Soreena had sought to hide the routes at first. Then she'd done the obvious, and blinded the golems. They could not feel pain or speak, so they discovered nothing before departing. Some still had the shards of piping in their heads. It would only work until Serak returned, but Soreena hoped to leave before that occurred.

Fire could not avoid Soreena and found himself surreptitiously watching her. On the night after Fire's arrival, while the rest of the captives slept, she quietly rose and slipped to one of the secret exits, disappearing. Curious, Fire rose and followed.

I wouldn't, Mind thought to him.

Fire turned and noticed Mind awake. "I'll be careful."

I don't want her to hurt you.

Fire grunted at the mental barb. Then he turned and slipped into the secret tunnel, using the same loose stone that she did. He dropped into the tunnel. Just large enough for a person to crawl, the space disappeared into darkness. Serak had provided an allotment of light orbs to the captives, and half were used in the network of tunnels. He listened to the faint scratching of a body sliding through the tunnel and then lay down.

He conjured a sled of fire, adding six wheels. Then he ignited a touch of fire from his boots, driving him forward. The wheels of fire made no sound as they rolled across the uneven ground, and he angled his path to follow Soreena.

She took three turns and then disappeared. He came to a stop at an intersection, confused as to where she could have gone. The sounds of crawling had faded, but she could not have gone far. He blinked and shifted into his magesight, the tunnel turning into a pattern of heat. He cast about, but there was nothing until he looked up at the ceiling. Twenty feet above, a blob of heat climbed a ladder.

He chuckled to himself and returned his vision to normal. Then he searched the ceiling of the tunnel until he found the hidden clasp. The roof swung open, and he climbed into the cavity above.

The basement contained dust and debris, and smelled of stonesap and age. He spotted the stairs in the corner, and the crumbling remains of furniture. Broken barrels sat in one corner, the wood rotten away, the rings covered in rust. He cautiously ascended the steps to the first floor, which was empty except for a ladder in the corner. He strode to it and climbed to reach the attic.

The space was large and open, probably owned by a wealthy individual before the mine had been abandoned. Unlike most of the ruins, the roof was intact, albeit a pair of holes allowed moonlight to enter. He drifted into shadow, watching Soreena.

The woman sat on the edge of the attic, at the center of the one of the holes in the roof. The opening faced the Wilds, providing a view that extended to the horizon. He cocked his head to the side, waiting and watching. Then he heard a faint scratching at his side and turned—to find himself facing a giant throat, with teeth all the way into its stomach.

He recoiled and cast a sword of fire, but the moordraug darted to Soreena. He called a warning and jumped, swinging his blade, but Soreena came to her feet, stepping between them. She raised a hand to Fire, her eyes holding him fast.

"It's unkind to kill a druid's animal companion."

"A moordraug?" Fire demanded. "You bonded with a *moordraug?*"

"Keep your voice down," she said, and resumed her seat. The moordraug growled a warning but she soothed it with a touch. Then it retreated back into the shadows. Fire turned to watch the beast.

At six feet tall, it was hardly more than a youth, and would grow to fourteen feet when adult. Its hind legs were bent like those of a wolf, while the arms ended in large pincers, their ends flattened from contact with the ground. The creature's mouth lacked bones, allowing it to open large enough to swallow its prey whole. Rows of tiny teeth lined the throat all the way to its stomach. Two stubby horns grew from the skull.

"Sit down," Soreena said. "You're making her nervous."

"It's an alpha," he realized.

Moordraugs lived in packs, with a female alpha at their head. The beasts could swallow a man whole, chewing him all the way down its throat. And a pack? They were as deadly as reavers. Elenyr had taught the fragments that moordraugs had complicated social structures, with a specific order of leadership between the alpha female and the betas. She'd also taught them that they were born killers.

"I don't like being followed," she said.

"Sorry," he said. "But you are rather captivating."

She snorted and cast him an appraising look. "Don't tell the others about her."

"She doesn't kill you," he said, taking a seat beside her.

"Of course not," she said. "She's my Joré."

"But she's a moordraug."

"How much do you know about druids?" she asked.

He hid a smile. He'd lived for five thousand years, and he'd been trained by a former oracle. He knew more about magic than she would in her entire life. Still, it wouldn't be nice to attempt proving his superiority. That didn't work out well with women. He'd learned that very early.

"You can speak to all animals but typically bond with a single creature, your Joré." He motioned to the moordraug. "But I am surprised you bonded to a moordraug."

"She was growing quickly, and became a threat to her pack," she replied. "When she was cast out, she found me."

"They are killers."

"They are born hungry," she said. "And the hunger only grows with age. It's not their fault that they are predators."

"Would you say that as you're chewed and swallowed?"

"Probably not."

They shared a smiled. "We killed a pack not two days ago. Hers?"

"Maybe," she said. "They are frequent in the Wilds, and hunt mountain goats and deer."

The moordraug approached and put its neck on her shoulder, like a dog placing its head on its master's lap. But this dog was massive, with the strength of a troll, and a hunter's instinct. It made him chuckle.

"She cares for you," Fire said.

"She is my companion."

"The others do not know about her?"

She shook her head. "They would not understand. Druids bond to bears and lions, sometimes the noble elk and deer. Bonding to a moordraug would be seen as a dark mark on a person's soul."

"There was once a rock troll that bonded to a reaver," he said.

"Really?" she rotated to face him. "When?"

"In the Age of Oracles."

"A fascinating time," she said. "One that few understand."

"Some more than most," he said wryly, thinking of Elenyr. She'd lived through it, survived its battles. Even faced a sea dragon.

"I've spent most of my life in this city," she said, motioning to ruins outside the window, and the Wilds beyond. "I don't know what it would be like to be free."

"I can show you, if you'd like."

She laughed lightly. "You? I could see at a glance that you like to pursue women. Half the females in our tribe practically lost their heads the moment you stepped into the room."

"I didn't notice."

"How could you not notice?"

"My attention was drawn to another," he replied.

She laughed again, this time softer. "See? But one like you does not settle down."

"One like me?"

She raised an eyebrow. "How many women have you loved?"

None.

The answer was easy, but he didn't voice it. For all the women that had loved him, he'd never loved one in turn. He was the fragment of passion, not permanence, and the relationships had never lasted. Water had the ability to love, as did Light, and probably Mind, although he

163

never allowed himself to get that close. When Fire did not speak, Soreena frowned.

"I did not mean to offend."

"You are much less forceful here," he motioned to the attic. "Why is that?"

"There I am chief," she said. "Here I am me."

"You are the alpha," he said.

The moordraug released a rumble as if in agreement. Fire knew that druid companions gained attributes of their masters, a sentience they lacked before the joining. Soreena, in turn, would gain the strength and speed of the moordraug, and maybe its hunger. It did explain why she was so captivating.

She patted the beast on the head and she rotated her neck so she could scratch beneath its throat. The motion was soft and intimate, the touch of a master to her beloved companion. The moordraug crooned its gratitude.

"What's her name?"

"Sherarend."

"She's beautiful."

Soreena thanked him with a nod and then stood. He did as well, but Soreena did not depart. Instead she motioned out the window, to the endless expanse of the Wilds. The gates of the city were open, the walls crumbling.

"It's almost time."

"For what?"

"For why I come here," she said.

"Not for her?"

The moordraug cast him a look before retreating back into the shadows. "Not the only reason," Soreena said, her voice hardening.

164

He watched out the window with her, the seconds passing in silence. Then a flicker of movement appeared and a giant shape detached from the city. It was the size of a giant, with smooth, reflective black flesh. Six horns grew from its skull, and four muscled arms swung at its sides.

"The Incinerake," she murmured.

"The one that killed your father?"

"And many others."

The Incinerake advanced into the Wilds, ascending a small hill to stand at its summit. With the moonlight at its back, it was imposing and fearsome, a golem of tremendous power. Across the distance, Fire sensed the magic, and yearned to fight the creature.

"It comes out every night," Soreena said. "I've often imagined going out there and striking at its back."

"It would kill you."

She did not disagree. "I've seen it pick up golems that weigh more than a bull and rip them apart with its bare hands. But it prefers casting a blade from its flesh and stabbing deep, before igniting the fire, burning them from the inside. It *loves* to kill."

"A stonesap sentient," Fire said, absently casting a dagger in his hand and then dismissing it. "Designed to ignite but not be burned. Serak is indeed powerful."

"If he crafted that thing, then yes, he is the one to fear. We have never so much as injured it." Her jaw clenched.

"We'll kill it," he said.

He reached out and caught her hand, but she pulled away. Then she met his gaze. "I hope so," she said softly. "Because if you do not, I will live my life here, caged as much as your firebird friend. And when he dies—because he will—then the Incinerake will kill my entire tribe."

"I'm not going to let that happen."

165

She reached up and touched his cheek. "Passion won't kill him, nor will fire. What else do you have?"

"Trust me," he said.

"I do," she said. "And that is what scares me."

She turned and departed, and Fire cast the Incinerake a long look. He ignited a dagger in his hand, sharpening the magic until it turned blue, the heat so bright the moordraug retreated. The light shimmered off Fire's face as he spoke.

"They say you cannot be burned, but you're still made of stonesap. Let's see if Serak's magic is stronger than mine . . ."

Chapter 21: Unchained

The captives had stashed weapons throughout the ruins, and it took time to gather them. At Mind's suggestion, Fire used his magic to sharpen the pieces of steel, making them considerably more dangerous against the golems. Even with the weapons, an attempt to escape would be risky. There were just three hundred captives from Soreena's tribe, against an army of golems. Their only advantage would be surprise, that and the last member of their group.

"Are you certain the Ancient will fight with us?" Soreena asked. "We've kept him bound for years."

"He will know who to fight," Fire said.

The captives were only permitted entry four at a time, and were watched over by a quartet of soldier golems. The druids reinforced the magic on the chains for an hour before they trudged out of the room to make room for another group. It required constant magic to keep the mighty phoenix contained, and if he was too weak to fight, their plan would be for naught.

Fire and Mind did not mention the other part of their plan. With the firebird's ability to connect with another, he'd likely spoken directly to Serak, and could know more about his plans than anyone, even his own acolytes. The Ancient might know how to locate Wylyn, at least.

Fire spent as much time as he could with Soreena, but the woman spoke little. She led her people with precision, shifting weapon caches every time the golems appeared. Using a complex series of whistles, they sent warnings to each other, and Fire learned to live on his toes. He hated hiding from a threat, but in this instance, he understood the wisdom. If Serak could cage a phoenix, the fragments of Draeken were just as vulnerable.

Two days after Fire's arrival, the fragments gathered with Soreena and Boaz. Mind and Fire were both dressed as druids, the ragged clothing hanging over their finer cloaks. When the soldier golems came for the next shift, the foursome were ready, and Fire fell into step behind Soreena, his head down.

The group trudged down the corridor and out the stairs. Then they turned and followed a winding trail through the rubble to reach the door into the domed cage. Four more guards flanked the opening, as did four more inside. These carried large hammers fashioned of stone and stood like statues, their heads rotating to follow Fire's movement. Fire resisted the urge to cast his blade and cut them apart.

The short tunnel ended inside the dome, and for the first time he raised his eyes to the smooth, reflective walls. The heat was unbearable for the others, and even Mind started sweating immediately. Fire merely smiled, drawing the heat into his flesh, breathing it into his lungs. The chains siphoned the firebird's magic, but plenty lingered in the air, and Fire relished the ambient power.

They were led between two piles of rubble to the bird's claws, where the quartet stooped and placed their hands on the chains. The claws were huge, each talon as large as Fire's body. But the smooth black talon was now pitted, grey, and cracked. Up close the bird looked even worse, his feathers and body appearing like an old dishcloth soaked in rainwater. Fire clenched his fist on the steel chains.

Don't lose control now, Mind shot into his thoughts. *At least not yet.*

Fire gritted his teeth and pretended to push his magic into the chain. The spell to subdue an animal was a common one for a druid, but against a phoenix, it was like dripping water on an inferno. Boaz and Soreena both strained to add magic into the bindings, even as Fire pushed heat into the steel.

The metal began to glow, and one of the guards took notice. He garbled an order to the golem next to him, and both advanced. Fire shoved heat into the steel, willing it to melt, to pour onto the ground in a cascade of molten metal. The golems approached as steam wreathed

168

Fire's face, and just as they reached for his shoulder, Mind drew his sword.

Hidden beneath his tunic, the blade came free in a whisper of steel, and Mind swung twice, removing both of the golem's heads. The golems crumpled without a sound, but the other soldiers whirled and charged. Mind dispatched them with ease, cutting them apart with fluid bladework until a brute appeared.

The brute took a step into the tunnel and raised his hammer, before swinging with enough force to crack a Talinorian shield. Mind ducked and spun inside his guard, his sword cutting into the brute's side. As footfalls pounded outside the tunnel, the two dueled, and the chain continued to melt.

Liquid metal dripped onto the ground, the steel succumbing to Fire's magic, until finally the link came apart, the chains groaning as sparks of druid magic sputtered and dimmed. The metal clattered to the floor.

"That's it," Fire barked. "Wake him up."

Soreena and Boaz leapt to the phoenix and placed their hands on the claws, this time their charm working to counteract the curse. Fire darted to the second chain, the one designed to be impervious to heat, impervious to even a phoenix.

"Running out of time!" Mind called, plunging his blade through the golem as two more brutes appeared.

"He won't wake up!" Boaz shouted.

Fire spared them a look. Both were sending their magic directly into the phoenix's claw, attempting to break the decade of subduing curses. But the Ancient did not move. Then Soreena reached up, wrapped a hand around the shaft of a large feather, and yanked it from the bird's stomach.

The screech rattled the dome, sending bits of rubble tumbling to the ground. The bird's claw scraped the ground, nearly ripping Boaz in half. He flapped his wings, filling the air with charged heat.

169

"He's not fully conscious!" Soreena shouted, diving away from a curl of flame. "We need to wake him up so he can fight!"

"He may not be able to!" Boaz cried.

"He's the Ancient," Fire called.

He gave up trying to sever the chain and raced up the slope of rubble against the wall to the phoenix's head. The great eyes spun, the iridescent gold, yellow, and red spinning as if he could not see Fire's body. Then Fire cast his favorite sword, and sliced across the beak.

Fashioned of pure fire, the flame was as a sharp as any sword, but against the Ancient it merely nicked the bird's beak. All at once the eyes focused on Fire, narrowing as the pain breached the sleeping charms.

"I'LL KILL YOU FOR WHAT YOU'VE DONE!"

The mental assault knocked Fire away, saving his life as the firebird lurched to its legs and snapped its beak where Fire had stood. Flames burst from its head and poured on Fire, but they were siphoned off into the second chain on the bird's leg.

"We need to cut the chain!" Boaz cried.

"He has to do it on his own!" Fire shouted, and then jumped back to the Ancient's head.

He seemed disoriented, his wings flapping, sending flurries of fire spinning in the confines of the dome. Mind continued to fight, slipping through the miniature tornados and knocking a golem into the path of the next. The cyclone ripped the stone apart, leaving pieces of arm, leg, and head, the rest melting on the floor. Heedless of the potential damage, the other golems rushed the bird, attempting to drive past Mind.

Fire swerved to avoid the large wing. "Ancient!" he bellowed. "You have been caged and your captors stand outside this dome. Rise forth and punish them for their impudence, burn them to ash and let them behold your might!"

Your voice is known to me . . .

170

The firebird fell to the side, crashing into the wall before righting himself. Fire dropped to the ground and poured heat into the feathers of the right wing. The bird stood again, breathing in the flames.

The fragment of Fire, the Ancient growled, his mental voice thick, like he'd drunk too much ale. *Why are you here?*

"I'm here to free you," Fire shouted. "But if you do not fight, this cage will be your tomb!"

The phoenix swiveled and seemed to notice the golems flooding into the cage. Mind held them at bay by force of skill, his blade spinning left and right, carving through the stone figures and leaving pieces at his feet. Boaz and Soreena flanked him, desperately attempting to keep the thickening throng from gaining entry.

My captors . . .

The phoenix tossed his head. His wings flared but a hiss came from the mighty bird's beak. Then he seemed to notice Fire, still standing on the rubble nearby. In a moment of lucidity, the firebird snapped its beak.

Where is the demon called Serak?

"Gone," Fire called, sparing the entrance to the cage a look. Mind, Soreena, and Boaz were being driven back. "You've been trapped here for twelve years. Serak's army of golems control this mine, and the only thing keeping you from revenge is that chain." He pointed to the remaining chain coiled around the phoenix's ankle.

The bird dropped his gaze, his mental words gaining a chilling edge. *First the chain. Then I claim the blood of my foes.* He lowered his head towards the chain and pointed his wings downward, just feet from Mind.

"Look out!" Fire shouted.

Mind heard his warning through his thoughts, and grabbed Soreena by the shoulder, shoving her clear. Then he dove to the ground. The phoenix leveled its beak to the opening and unleashed a torrent of flames.

171

White hot, the fire ripped through the ranks of golems, melting them in place and filling the tunnel with piles of molten stone. The chain still attached was quick to leech the magic, but not before the corridor became a graveyard.

The Ancient stumbled back, lowering his scarred head to examine the chain that bound him. More fire spilled from his maw, but the chain was enchanted to absorb magic, and it merely pulled the heat inward. Releasing a bellow of fury, the phoenix tried again, the flames burning yellow, through white, and then into the supreme blue spectrum. Boaz, Soreena, and Mind fled to the farthest side of the dome as the heat in the room mounted.

Fire shouted in victory as the chain began to crumble, the mighty blue fire beginning to melt the enchantments. But the blue fire began to dim, and Fire realized the Ancient did not have enough magic left to destroy the chain. Heedless of the phoenix, he leapt into the spilling flames.

Soreena shouted a warning as Fire charged into the phoenix's fire, but such heat washed over him like an ocean wave. He breathed in the inferno as Soreena stared, frozen in disbelief. Surrounded by the flames spilling off the chain, Fire pulled from the ocean of magic and forged a hammer of pure, blue fire. His body turning elemental, he roared and struck the weapon into the partially melted chain.

Built to absorb heat, crafted by Serak himself to prevent even a phoenix from breaking free, the chain could not withstand both a phoenix *and* a fragment of Draeken. Cracks appeared in the metal, expanding and glowing. Fire unleashed an assault on the chain, sparks and flames billowing about him until abruptly the link snapped.

The Ancient yanked on his clawed leg and the two halves of the link came apart in an explosion of sparks and drops of molten metal. The flames being absorbed by the chain rebounded and covered the phoenix. He spread his wings to the breadth of the cage and released an ear-shattering war cry.

The Ancient was free.

And he wanted revenge.

172

Chapter 22: Fury of the Ancient

The firebird launched itself off the ground and burst through the roof, rising into the air in a triumphant shriek. The sound galvanized the other druids, who barricaded the doors to the two prison rooms and rushed to the secret exits, threading into the tunnels as golems poured toward the city.

In the midst of raging flames, Fire bared a grim smile and watched the Ancient turn on his captors. Then he stepped free of the flames and returned to flesh, striding to Soreena and the others. She stared at him with wide eyes. Fire casually wiped the lingering flames off his shoulder and offered an exaggerated bow.

Mind caught his arm and pointed to the still burning entrance. "The golems will be occupied with the Ancient. We need to get out before they return for us."

Fire pointed to the inferno and the flames parted, opening a path through the center that would be safe for the others. Mind took the lead and sprinted through the tunnel. Fire and the others fell into step behind them and rushed outside—only to recoil when a pump tower exploded.

Flames blossomed from the tower, rising into the sky in a plume of thick black smoke. In a groan of steel and falling sparks, it tipped to the side and crushed a building. Even as repair golems feverishly sought to fix the breaks, the tower tumbled into a set of ruins, the entire turret detonating. The Ancient soared through the smoke as fire poured from its wings, ripping into another tower.

"He's using too much magic," Fire said. "If he keeps this up it will kill him."

"He won't stop until he's destroyed Beldik," Mind said. "We need to get the others out."

"Still think it was smart to bring an enraged phoenix to the battle?" Boaz muttered.

"You wouldn't be escaping without him," Fire snapped.

"On to the next phase," Mind said. "Fire, you ready?"

"I'm going with him," Soreena said.

"That's not the plan," Mind said.

They all flinched as another explosion rocked the mining city. "I'm going with him," she insisted.

"Your people need you," Fire said. "I can handle the Incinerake."

She folded her arms, her features set in a firm line. She didn't even blink when a tower nearby pulsed with rising pressure, and then shattered. Her hair waved in the heated wind, a vision of beauty.

Fire smiled. "Don't get caught in the battle," he warned.

"Don't get yourself killed," she retorted, and then turned to Boaz. "Get the others out as we planned. Make sure you're not spotted."

"As you order," Boaz said, clearly reluctant to obey the order. Then he turned and slipped away. Mind cast Fire a warning look before following.

If you get her killed, he thought to Fire, *they will blame you.*

"I'm not going to get her killed."

Mind grunted in irritation and departed. Fire and Soreena turned in the opposite direction, and slipped into the ruins of Beldik, dodging eruptions of fire and hordes of golems. With smoke pouring across the city and golems dying in droves, he couldn't help but smile. He loved a good battle, especially with a woman at his side.

"I could use a weapon," Soreena said, intruding in his thoughts.

"What type?" he asked.

They ducked into a fallen building as an entire company of brutes rushed by, only to suffer a fireball from above. Fire grinned as golems shattered, others melting. The surviving golems continued on, ignoring their fallen comrades.

"A hammer would be best against the golems," she said. "But won't do any good against the Incinerake."

He pulled from the abundance of heat in the air and forged a hammer of fire. He also added a shield across her tunic and pants, the material shimmering red for a moment before going dim. She accepted the hammer and swung it experimentally.

"It will do."

He grinned and cast his own sword. "Mind said the Incinerake would come for the phoenix, but how will he get the Ancient back on the ground?"

The Ancient will fall on his own, Mind's mental words were distant. *When he comes down, defend him.*

Fire scowled, suddenly realizing that was Mind's intent all along. "You want us to use the Ancient as bait? I would never have agreed to that plan."

That's why I didn't tell you. Mind replied.

I'm getting tired of being manipulated. Fire responded through the mental link.

Only way to victory, Mind replied, and then withdrew.

"What's with the angry face?"

"Brothers can be annoying."

She flashed an amused smile. "Usually. Then they come through for us and we are forced to realize they're family."

"You have a brother?"

"Boaz," she said. "And he can certainly be annoying."

The Ancient screamed again, but the war cry was tinged with fatigue. The fires on his wings had begun to cool, revealing the grey and haggard feathers. The bird was still in the air, but it was only a matter of time before he came down.

"We need to move," Fire said.

"As long as you keep me from catching fire."

"I should probably tell you I have a reputation for burning things."

She chuckled, the sound overshadowed by a burst of flame. "You make it sound like you're a disease."

"Oh, I'm definitely a fever."

Fire, Mind mentally called, his voice irritated. *Can you stop flirting and focus? You're as distractible as Light when there's a woman around.*

Fire grimaced at the insult but did not give Mind the satisfaction of a response. He did turn his attention to the battle. Pump towers were exploding on all sides, the pressure from the stonesap building beyond the fail safes. Pipes exploded, golems melted in the streets, and still the firebird raged.

The Ancient poured flame into every street, every structure, intent on leveling Beldik to the ground. Fire caught Soreena's hand and pulled her through the ruins, extinguishing fires in their path. The armor he'd given her would keep her alive, but would not last.

A pipe exploded in the ground nearby, the gout of flame catching Soreena and knocking her into the wall. Flames licked at her clothing and her jaw clenched, but the fabric didn't burn, and she brushed the fire off with her bare hand. The armor shimmered as it came in contact with the heat. Even encased in a fire shield, being engulfed in a blast usually led to panic.

"I'm fine," she said. "Let's go."

He admired the look of flames across her body and then shook himself. Mind was right. He was as distractible as Light when a woman was around.

176

I told you. Mind called.

You don't have to be smug about it.

Mind's smile was evident through the link. *Yes. I do.*

They worked their way north and east, towards the firebird. Everything was on fire, the pump houses, the ruins, even the giant cage and the slave quarters. There was so much on fire that Fire recast Soreena's shield, strengthening it against the billowing waves of heat. The shield also protected her against the smoke, igniting every time cinders bounced off her frame.

Fire caught a glimpse of Mind and Boaz leading the captives out of the mine. Scattered golems tried to stop them but the druids fought with unmatched ferocity, tearing the golems apart as they sprinted for the nearest exits. In the chaos and focus on the Ancient, the golem army could not stop them, and the captives breached the outer wall and fled into the Wilds.

Fire turned his attention to the firebird. The Ancient sunk low in the sky, his wings struggling to hold him aloft. Flames continued to ignite but they were now a dull orange. After another defiant war cry, the firebird dropped into an empty street. Golems were quick to swarm him, but the flames were too much, and they melted before they got close.

Fire and Soreena hurried to reach him, and came to a halt in a building adjacent to the street. Through a giant hole in the wall, they surveyed the battle, and Fire watched for a place to join the conflict. Before he could, the golems withdrew.

"What's happening?" Fire asked.

"The Incinerake." Her tone was rigid.

The golems lined up on the sides of the street, so Soreena pulled Fire up the crumbling steps to the second floor of the structure. The roof and walls were mostly gone, but there was enough for them to choose a vantage point at what had once been a window.

Through the glow of fire and haze of smoke, a giant figure strode into view. The Incinerake advanced up the street as if it did not fear the Ancient and came to a halt just thirty feet away. Fire expected the

177

Ancient to burn him to ash, but instead he trembled in fury and spread his wings to release a defiant shriek.

"Your magic is failing," the Incinerake spoke in a voice like flowing tar, thick and heavy. "You were a fool to escape."

I DO NOT FEAR DEATH!

The firebird's mental scream was heard by all, but still the great phoenix did not strike the Incinerake. Fire shook his head and glanced to Soreena, but she too appeared confused. Why did the Ancient not punish his captor? What held him in check?

"Kneel," the Incinerake commanded.

The Ancient released flared its wings. Fire growled and clenched a fist, mentally asking why the bird did not kill the Incinerake. The bird's head swiveled to Fire in the window but he did not answer.

The Incinerake advanced another step and raised a hand, the dark liquid turning into a blade—that it pointed to its own stomach. The Ancient went still, and Fire almost stood and shouted. Soreena caught his arm.

"*Kneel,*" the Incinerake commanded again. "Or he dies."

The Ancient knelt. Folding his wings along his back, extinguishing the magic across his frame, the father of phoenixes, the first firebird, knelt before Serak's minion. Fire shook free of Soreena's grip and leapt through the window.

He landed in the ranks of golems, but a blast of his magic sent them tumbling away. He darted into the street, coming to a stop between the Incinerake and the Ancient. Raising a hand to the Incinerake, he faced the firebird.

"Why will you not fight?" he growled.

I cannot.

The golems surged forward but the Incinerake made a motion and they came to a stop.

178

"You are the *Ancient*," Fire roared.

You do not understand, fragment.

"Then I will do what you cannot."

He turned to the Incinerake but the Ancient lowered its beak and flames spilled from its throat, looping in a line around Fire and keeping him from the Incinerake. More confused than ever, Fire stood in a ring of phoenix flames. They could not hurt him, but the bird took a warning step towards him, his claws extending.

Beyond the wall of fire, the Incinerake stood its ground. Its thick chuckle made Fire's skin crawl. Then it reached to its stomach and the dark liquid parted, revealing a large red and blue egg.

My son, the phoenix said, his words tinged with hatred and, shockingly, fear. *The Incinerake has my son.*

Chapter 23: The Incinerake

The Incinerake smiled, the stonesap closing around its stomach, sealing the egg inside its own body. It began to chuckle, the sound dark and menacing as it advanced on Fire. It stepped through the wall of flames the Ancient had cast and came to a halt.

"Your identity is known to me, fragment," it said. "My master warned that you might come. I must say I hoped you would, if only for the chance to kill a piece of Draeken. He said I should not, but my purpose is to kill those who disobey, and I do relish my purpose . . ."

It extended a hand and the stonesap flowed outward, turning into a long, bladed staff. He then cast a second staff, wielding it with his two left hands. The Ancient released a rumble and shifted in place, clearly disliking the idea of Fire battling the golem. The Incinerake gestured in dismissal.

"Don't worry firebird," it rumbled. "It's not like he's going to break your egg, especially as I have no intention of fighting fair . . ."

The golem horde charged. Hundreds became thousands, and the golems poured toward Fire. He didn't wait for them to close the gap and darted toward the Incinerake, spinning his sword. The curving blade passed within in an inch of its throat. The Incinerake sidestepped and struck Fire in the back.

The staff hit hard, sending Fire into a knot of soldier golems and brutes. Fire collided with a brute and both went down. He sliced the brute across the midsection, and rose to stand on its chest. Holding the hilt of his blade with both hands, he ripped the sword in half, giving him two swords.

He spun, using both blades to whirl through the golems, his blades slicing through stone like it was flesh. They crumbled around him but more came from behind, the relentless ranks charging his back.

He could have taken to the air but his anger mounted, and he craved the heat of battle. He added a detonation charm to his blades, and then struck the nearest golem. The blow left a glowing dot on its chest. Fire stepped away as it detonated, shredding nearby golems.

He gathered magic across his arm and morphed his second sword into a hammer, which he hurled into the midst of the golems. It struck a brute in the head and remained in place—before exploding. As the hammer detonated, Fire leapt into the air and conjured another hammer, using a burst of fire on his boots to soar high above the golems. He hurled the hammer, and another, the spinning weapons landing in the golems, blasting arms and legs in all directions. He landed on the rubble and struck the ground, flames billowing outward, shattering those nearest.

But for every dozen he killed there was a hundred behind, inching closer, their thick arms reaching for Fire. He bared his teeth in a snarl and struck left and right, sending flying hammers into their ranks, cutting others with his sword, and detonating those that drew close. Still they inched closer.

Fire stepped through the flames and smoke, bellowing a challenge as the tide of golems cascaded upon him—his roar ending in a grunt as a blow struck his back, knocking him sprawling.

"An ember dies away from the flames." The Incinerake laughed and withdrew into his ranks.

"I *am* the fire," he retorted.

He rose again and fought, catching a glimpse of the Ancient where he prowled in the street. Bound by the Incinerake's captive, he nevertheless sent threads of fire coursing across the ground, giving magic to Fire. He recognized the gift for what it was, a desperate hope. The Ancient could not directly fight the Incinerake, so he helped Fire. Using the power, Fire blasted and struck, unleashing an inferno upon the army. A moment later the Incinerake stepped from the ranks of golems and again struck his back, disappearing from view by the time he rose.

He fought his way to a clearing again and roared a challenge. "Do you fear to face me?"

181

"My purpose is to kill," the Incinerake called. "But I prefer my prey weak and bloodied."

Fire wiped blood from his cheek and conjured another hammer. He'd been knocked about, driven away from the street and into the rubble. This time he hurled the explosive hammer at a pump tower, the weapon blasting through the pipes and igniting the stonesap.

The explosion rippled through the city, shaking the earth and flattening walls. Golems nearest to the blast were torn to shreds, others perished as a building collapsed, and a fireball illuminated the region.

He bared a grim smile and used the flames to conjure a tigron, a fire-breathing tigron. The animal was enormous, twice the size of its smaller cousins. It released a snarl, flames curling from its jaws before it charged, breathing dragon's flames into the ranks of golems, sowing discord and chaos. Fire's moment of triumph was cut short when the staff slashed across his back. He growled in anger and crashed to the ground, the Incinerake towering over him.

Fire managed to roll onto his back. The dark staff came down on him and he raised his sword to block. Fire blasted him with flame but the Incinerake shrugged aside the heat, the fire washing over the liquid meant to explode.

"Your magic means nothing to me," the Incinerake rumbled.

"Mine will."

The fragment of Mind darted in, his blade flicking up, striking the Incinerake's arm. Then he leapt and caught one of the six horns. Already flinching from the sudden strike, the golem was not prepared for the mental assault. It growled and recoiled, and Soreena struck from the side, her fiery hammer coming down on one of the Incinerake's four arms. The weapon smashed an elbow, spilling stonesap onto the ground.

"I could have killed it," Fire growled, rising to his feet.

"Others deserve the kill," Soreena said, slicing a pair of golems in two. Her moordraug charged into view and caught a golem's throat with its pincers, snapping the head clean off. Mind leapt through the gap, alighting at Fire's side.

"Do you ever think before you start a war?"

"Not usually," Fire said, turning and letting the others cover his back.

The Incinerake had withdrawn into the golems, and the group of four fought the golem army, turning together and climbing over the bodies of broken foes, the golem corpses piling like fallen statues.

"It has a powerful consciousness," Mind said. "I can't take it down."

"Don't worry," Fire said. "I have a plan."

"You?" Mind asked, incredulous.

"Yes," Fire said.

Mind raised an eyebrow as he caught the idea. "I like it. Could get you killed."

"That's what makes it fun."

"Don't get killed," Soreena said.

"Are you worried about me now?" Fire asked.

"That's not the word I would use," the woman said.

If you kill my child, I will tear you apart and burn you to ash.

Fire looked to the Ancient. "I'm assuming that's good luck?"

The firebird released a plume of flames, and Fire grinned. Conjuring his tigron again, he sent the creature ahead and summoned the wealth of heat, shaping wings of bright red, the flames falling off his shoulders, dripping onto the ground in liquid drops. Then the fire ignited on his boots, carrying him skyward.

He winked at Soreena, the woman flushing as he soared into the sky and banked after the Incinerake. The giant golem looked up and spotted Fire, and bared his teeth in a snarl. With one arm broken from Soreena's attack, he cast a trio of blades and whirled to face Fire. On a small hill between three pump towers, the Incinerake raised his swords and snarled.

"You are no match for me."

Fire folded his wings, and blasted his boots, diving into the golem. Striking hard, he knocked the Incinerake through a building. Stone and dust billowed upward as the roof crumpled on top of them, and Fire rolled away. He came to his feet and leapt, his sword coming down on the golem, but the creature slashed at Fire, his weapons attacking on all sides.

Fire fought to parry but the blows rained down upon him, cutting his flesh, drawing blood. He reached for the wealth of fires to heal but the Incinerake kept up the assault, driving Fire back—into the pump tower.

Fire flashed a grim smile and spun. Using his sword like a scythe, he sliced across the large pipe. Stonesap burst from the pipe, covering them both. The Incinerake recoiled as it recognized Fire's intent.

"You were made to burn," Fire snarled, and plunged his flaming sword into the stonesap.

The liquid exploded, the fire devouring the stonesap across them both, and reaching into the pump tower. The tower detonated, the flames billowing outward, engulfing Fire and the Incinerake, belching smoke into the sky.

Fire closed his eyes and breathed deep of the flames, relishing the heat, letting it wash across his skin. The flames receded, and through the burning smoke the Incinerake rose to its feet. Stonesap burned across its body, its three arms, and the six horns, turning it into a demon out of nightmares.

"You think to destroy me with fire?" it chuckled. "My skin is impervious to such magic."

Dismayed, Fire darted in, but the Incinerake reached to the side as a brute appeared. The brute held a struggling Soreena and tossed her to the Incinerake. The Incinerake caught Soreena and held her aloft, the flames on its body burning upward, spilling across her back. Only the fire shield kept her from roasting alive.

"I'm sure you know what I did to her father," he said. "Now you get to see it for yourself."

He dropped Soreena against a wall and reared back, a shining dagger flowing into shape in his hand. Gripped by fear, Fire scrambled forward, lunging as Soreena screamed. The gap was too far, the Incinerake on the opposite side of the destroyed building. He reached a hand out, and caught a glimpse of Mind in the crumbling doorway, his hand also outstretched.

As the Incinerake's dagger fell towards Soreena's heart, an unseen force shoved Fire, propelling him across the distance. He stumbled, and passed between the dagger and Soreena, the blade piercing his chest instead of hers.

Fire cried out as the dagger plunged into his body, the stonesap spilling into his blood, attempting to ignite and burn him from the inside. He bellowed, but not in pain, for his body was already made of fire, and instead of igniting his flesh, his body burned into the dagger. His innate fire climbed passed through the blade, burning the stonesap to enter the Incinerake's hand . . .

Chapter 24: Born of Fire

"No!" The Incinerake stumbled backward.

The giant golem clawed at its hand as flames appeared inside the fingers, the cracks brightening and expanding up its wrist. The Incinerake collapsed into a wall, crushing stones as it sought to tear its own limb from its body. But the cracks had already reached its shoulder, expanding into its body.

"You cannot kill me!" the Incinerake bellowed. "I am forged to be impervious to fire."

"Apparently not on the inside," Fire wiped blood from his nose and smiled grimly.

The Incinerake ripped at its arm but the veins climbed higher, the flames devouring the stonesap inside its body. It cried out as if in pain and bellowed its defiance, but the sound was tinged with fear.

"I am the Incinerake! I caged a firebird and became his master!"

You were never my master.

The Ancient's voice was tinged with satisfaction as the Incinerake stumbled into the street. The stonesap golem growled and picked up a shard of pipe, placing it against his stomach. Soreena was faster, and leapt to the arm. Her blade swung, severing the cracked limb and spilling stonesap across the street.

Fire followed the golem as it shrieked and fell to its knees, the other golems following suit. Like their minds had been damaged, they crumpled, their bodies thudding onto the piles of rubble, many with limbs still burning.

"You are just a fragment," the Incinerake protested, the cracks rising up its neck into its face.

186

"A fragment of *Draeken*," Fire spat.

The light spilling from the cracks became blinding, and Fire raised his arms to form a shield. Soreena and Mind jumped behind, as did the moordraug. Then he clenched his eyes shut against the glare . . .

The Incinerake released a final, unholy scream, and then shattered, the blast devouring half the street, the adjacent buildings, and part of the slave quarters. The flames consumed the stonesap from the inside, leaving only broken sections of the skin to clatter onto the ground, like glass on rock.

When the light faded, Fire released his shield and advanced, peering into the cavity where the Incinerake had stood. He spotted what he sought, but the egg lay in pieces, and for an instant, Fire was seized with fear. Then a small pair of wings began to flap, and a new firebird rose from the ashes.

Behold my son, the Ancient said.

The bird passed through the smoke and cinders, the wings a burnished copper, and soared above the fallen golems. Regal and beautiful, the bird conveyed an air of power amazing for its size. It alighted in the street before the Ancient, a tiny son beside his father.

Born of fire, destroyer of the Incinerake, son of a king, the Ancient said. *You deserve a name that speaks to royalty.*

I am at your service, Father.

The Ancient bowed his head and put his beak on the tiny bird. *In fire and in ash, your name will be Reiquen.*

The new firebird spread his wings wide and released a plume of fire from his beak, accepting his new name. Then the Ancient sighed, and sparks fluttered across his wings, unstable, and igniting flames on the street. Fire recognized the damage and grimaced.

"We must go."

"Now?" Soreena asked, her eyes wide.

"The Ancient is dying," Fire said. "And when a phoenix dies, all their magic is released."

Soreena tore her gaze from the scene. "Can we not save him?"

I have lived many lifetimes, little one, the Ancient said. *Do not mourn my passing.* Then he swiveled his head to Fire and Mind. *But I make a request of you, that you will exact vengeance from Serak.*

"I swear it," Mind said.

The bird bowed his head, and Fire reached up to touch his beak. Emotion clogged his throat, bitter and sharp. The Ancient was a power unlike any on Lumineia, a remnant from the Dawn of Magic, one of the last. And now Serak had killed him.

Mind caught his arm and dragged him away, and Fire realized the feathers on the firebird had begun to pulse, the magic inside growing more unstable. Reluctantly, he allowed Mind to drag him away, but picked up a bright blue feather on the way. The feather remained charged with the Ancient's magic, a sliver of power that had fallen from the Ancient during his battle. Tucking it into his pocket, he followed the others from the city.

They wound through the streets and climbed over piles of golems, all of which had fallen when the Incinerake had died. They still possessed magic, but their purposes had been linked to their general, and without the bidding of the great golem, they were just lumps of stone.

They wove through a building and out a hole in the opposite side. The ground began to tremble, the shaking growing more violent by the second. By unspoken accord the trio and the moordraug picked up the pace, and sprinted out of the mine, rushing up the nearest slope.

In the center of Beldik the Ancient flared its wings and released a thundering shriek, the sound defiant, even in the face of death. Mind and Soreena raised their hands against the glare, but Fire bore witness to the final moments of the great phoenix.

The bird did not explode, rather fire poured from its body, faster and faster, rising like a well of heat that spilled into the ruins of Beldik.

Everything it touched melted. Remaining pump towers exploded, their stonesap consumed by the expanding flames. Then the light within the phoenix rose until it resembled the sun at noonday, and finally the phoenix shattered.

The explosion ripped apart the city, leveling every wall, every stone. The concussive blast rocked the earth, almost taking Fire from his feet. The explosion swallowed the city, erasing it from existence, a final act of destruction from the fallen firebird.

When it subsided, the mine of Beldik was nothing but a sea of fire and smoke. Stones melted, metal dripped like honey, and golems disappeared into the magma. A chunk of the Incinerake's face floated on the surface, its skin still impervious to the heat.

A small figure flapped out of the fire and smoke, rising and banking towards them. Reiquen soared close to Fire and slowed, coming to a hover above them. Even the size of an eagle, the firebird exuded power.

Your deeds this day will be remembered, the bird said.

Fire pointed to the destroyed mine. "I'm sorry. We tried to save the Ancient."

A guardian imprisoned my father, killed the father of my race, and there will be retribution.

"Serak is your foe," Mind said. "Not us."

Soreena's expression tightened with regret. "And we were forced to keep the Ancient in his cage."

The Ancient spoke of you, Reiquen said, his words considerably softer. *You resisted Serak's command, and many lives perished because of your defiance. Know that I am a friend to the druids.*

"As we are to you." She bowed to the hovering firebird.

The bird swooped down to Fire, his copper wings washing heated air across him. *Father said the Incinerake spoke with Serak often. If you truly seek him, you must find the Shard of Midnight, the Stormdial of the ancient race. He and the krey woman would see its return.*

189

"Do you know its location?" Fire asked.

In the center of sea, where land fears to be.

Reiquen flapped his wings and soared away, leaving the group where they stood. None spoke until the bird had disappeared from view, and then Mind released a long sigh, turning back to survey what had once been Beldik.

"The anger of a firebird will last for eons."

"We failed to save the Ancient," Fire said.

"Will the Ancient not rise again?" Soreena asked. "I thought firebirds could not die."

The group turned and descended the hill as Fire shook his head. "Everything can be killed. A phoenix is impervious to age. When they grow old, they perish in ash, and are born again, retaining all the memories of their past lives. But like any other creature, they can endure only so much damage." He pointed to the destroyed mine. "Even the Ancient had a limit."

The trio approached the collection of druids. The haggard group had survived the escape. As Beldik continued to melt and burn, Mind set about bandaging their wounds. He did not have healing magic, but like every other trade, he'd picked up the skills from the minds of others.

The realization that they were free settled in, and the children began to play, calling out and running through the boulders, their laughter echoing in the Wilds. Mothers smiled and fathers talked of the future. Through it all, Fire stood with Soreena.

"We will help you return to Griffin," Fire said. "It's six days north and east of here. Then you can return to your homeland."

"Our village is gone," she said. "I think we must find a new home."

"The forests north of Heth are beautiful," Fire said.

He didn't add that they were accessible from Blue Lake, and close to the dwarven mountains, allowing him easy access to visit. She smiled up at him, the expression turning coy, and then abruptly leaned up and kissed him on the cheek.

"What was that for?"

"You have so much power," she said. "Yet you used it to free captives and fight the oppressors. I'm grateful people like you exist."

"I'm glad I exist too," Fire said.

"Will you visit us?"

"More often than you'd like."

She laughed lightly. "And when you are away, will you be visiting other women like me?"

"There are no women like you," he scoffed.

I could use your help down here, Mind thought to him.

You're just annoyed she's falling for me.

I'm annoyed you're *falling for* her, Mind corrected. *We have a job to do, and do not forget what Draeken could become.*

He snorted, the sound dubious. *We've already changed that.*

Do not be so certain.

"What is that expression for?" Soreena asked.

"Brothers can be annoying."

Her laughter rang out over the boulders, and Boaz looked up. He ambled over and swept a hand to the tribe, which had begun packing their things to depart. "We are just about ready, but we lack food for the journey."

"There's plenty on the way," Fire said with a shrug. "Deer and goats and . . ."

191

Boaz's expression was disapproving, and he folded his arms. "Did you forget what we are? We are druids. We bond to animals. We do not eat them."

Soreena grinned at Fire's forlorn expression. "There will be plenty of vegetation for us to eat."

"Rabbit food," Fire muttered.

"One of my best friends was bonded to a rabbit," Soreena said.

"How many rabbits have you eaten?" Boaz glared at Fire.

"He's eaten thousands," Mind said, approaching with a sly smile on his face.

"They're delicious," Fire said defensively.

Boaz's expression darkened but Soreena laughed. "Gather the men and organize them into groups. Place the children, injured, and weak in the middle, those that can fight on the outside. Then we'll move."

"As you order."

As Boaz strode away, Fire questioned why he was falling in love with a woman that only ate vegetables. What would life be like without meat? He shuddered, and tried not to think of how much he hated broccoli. And carrots. And the purple vegetables. Who wanted to eat food that was purple?

Soreena looped her arm through his. "If I didn't like meat, I wouldn't have bonded with a moordraug."

Fire released an explosive sigh. "You have no idea how grateful I am to hear that."

Mind pointed ahead. "Fire and I should scout ahead. We can help you all avoid any predators we come across."

Soreena nodded, and Fire gathered her into his arms. Leaning down, he brushed his lips across hers. She did not pull away, and leaned into a kiss that had more heat than Beldik. When they parted she smiled.

"When this is done, I want to know if you really are the fragment of passion."

"Challenge accepted."

Mind groaned and pulled him away. Laughing, Fire joined his brother and they went ahead of the tribe. While Mind used his magic to scan for animal minds in the vicinity, Fire dared to wonder what a life with Soreena would be like.

"You cannot be with her," Mind finally murmured.

"Why not?" Fire asked.

"You are a fragment of Draeken," Mind said. "And she will die within sixty years."

"I'll take sixty with her over a million alone."

Mind snorted. "Passion has no intelligence."

"It's not supposed to," Fire said.

Mind scowled, his expression annoyed, and the two fell silent. Fire continued to wonder about a future with Soreena, and ignored the touch of anger in his chest. A life with Soreena would be wonderful, but it would be a life without battle. He shoved the doubt aside, too excited for the future.

Chapter 25: The First Snowfall

Elenyr swung her sword and darted in, feeling the rush of the air through her body. In her ethereal form, she leapt through the practice figure and turned corporeal on the opposite side. Then she plunged her blade into its back. Feeling the thrill of battle, she leapt to the next, whirling between the blades in their hands, turning ethereal and then back to flash, slashing them apart, dancing away from imagined blows.

After weeks of recuperating, the rush of battle returned, sweet and vibrant, intoxicating. She'd never realized just how much she enjoyed being a warrior, and relished the test of her skill. It was not a desire she'd ever shared with anyone, not even her husband when she'd been oracle, or her daughter. The fragments might have guessed, especially Mind, but she kept it to herself. She loved being the Hauntress.

"You're beautiful when you fight."

She came to a halt and turned. Through a curtain of straw settling to the floor, she spotted Jeric leaning against the door. He wore the medallion of the Steward around his neck and was dressed in a tunic and pants befitting a king. He'd never looked so handsome.

She sheathed her sword, wondering why her love for him had cooled. He'd saved her life, brought her to Ilumidora, but something about his evasive behavior left her rankled. Then he'd revealed that he possessed the Steward's medallion of Talinor, a gift only the king could give, granting the wielder a place on the throne in his absence.

"How fares the kingdom, your majesty?"

Jeric's smile turned sour. "I never wanted this."

"Neither do the people," she said with a laugh. "They don't like an elf sitting on the throne."

"It was either that, or watch your fragments kill a few hundred castle guards and start a war."

She sighed, abruptly tiring of the secrets between them. "How did you earn it, Jeric?"

"I cannot say."

She used her sword to point at him. "You know, I'm beginning to wonder if I ever knew you."

He remained silent as she strode to the water basin set at the back of the room. She drank her fill and wiped cool water across her neck. Dressed in her armor and cloak, she was ready to depart, but had wanted one last exercise before leaving.

The private training room was small, and contained a group of practice figures made out of straw and wood, most of which were now in shreds. A training circle and a handful of weapons were also present, all illuminated by the light orb in the ceiling, and the bright sun cascading through the window. The room connected to her quarters.

"You don't have to go."

"Yes I do," she said, glancing out the window. The sun was shining, but snow had fallen the previous night, the first of the season, and Senia had been clear. When the first snow fell, she was to go to the King's Library and meet Fire and Mind.

"Elenyr."

His voice was soft, prompting her to rotate and face him. He had entered the room but stopped short of reaching her. His features were conflicted, doubtful. She'd never seen him not confident.

"What?"

"There's something I should tell you."

"There are a lot of things you should tell me."

He looked away, his brow furrowing in regret. "True. But one thing in particular."

"What is it?"

She folded her arms and waited. She wasn't being very patient, but he didn't deserve much. She'd been in the castle since speaking to the fragments, and Jeric had hardly spoken to her. He'd claimed it was because he was busy, but she had lived long enough to recognize when someone was avoiding her. It was only now as she was ready to depart that Jeric appeared, wanting her time.

Jeric sighed and sank onto a bench. "You must understand. This is a secret I never thought I'd share, not with anyone, especially you."

"Especially?"

He winced. "We both know I've been avoiding you. But I think it's time you understand why."

"Spit it out," she said. "I'm all healed and the next fight awaits."

He leaned back against the stone wall. "You're not making this easy."

"Good."

He sighed. "I'm trying to apologize."

"For ignoring me for days? Or lying to me for years?"

He stood and swept his hands wide. "Are there not things you guard about yourself? That you keep from everyone around you? To keep them safe?"

"Plenty," she said. "But I don't lie about who I am."

"It was never supposed to go this far," he said. "I never meant for this to become my life."

"Becoming the Steward? It's just a persona."

"Some personas last longer than intended," he said bitterly.

She frowned, curious despite her irritation. The way he spoke, it seemed his secret haunted him, and for longer than she could have thought. Jeric had lived many different lives, donned many personas. Even when they'd met, he'd been operating under the guise of another.

She thought back to that day, when she'd stormed a bandit refuge, where he'd been completing a deal. The bandits had known him as Jeric, a name Elenyr did not know, despite his reputation.

"I've heard of him," Mind had said with a nod. "Does deals with anyone with coin. He's clever, but harmless."

Jeric had drawn a knife and flicked it past Elenyr, the blade sinking into a man about to strike her back. "Hardly harmless," Jeric said, indignant.

The memory faded and she examined Jeric in new light. "What's going on?" she asked, taking a seat at Jeric's side.

He didn't answer, but she could see the wrestle on his face. She'd experienced that emotion before, the conflict of wanting to speak, but being afraid of the consequence. Grunting in irritation, he rose and began to pace.

"I've wanted to tell you this for a long time," he said. "But I couldn't bring myself to do it. Everything I've ever held back from you, everything I've kept hidden, all links to one truth—but once it is shared, we can never go back."

He came to a stop and motioned to her. "You and I? What we have between us will forever be changed, and it's entirely possible that what you feel for me will break forever."

"What are you talking about?" Elenyr asked, also on her feet.

The door swung open and Water and Shadow entered. Elenyr gave Jeric an apologetic look before turning to them. She'd requested both to come so she could say farewell, before she'd known that Jeric would come.

"I hope we're interrupting," Shadow said, his eyes flicking between Jeric and Elenyr.

"Not at all," Jeric said, his customary smile on his face.

"Blast," Shadow said.

"I was going to ask if you were ready," Water said, eyeing the destroyed practice targets. "But it appears you are back in shape."

"Straw doesn't hit back," Shadow said.

"I'll miss you as well, Shadow."

He grinned. "That's all I wanted to hear."

"Are you certain you must leave without us?" Water asked. "Shadow has grown bored, and we know what he does when he gets bored."

Shadow laughed. "You only bled for a minute, and you should have seen your face."

"It's not fun when you have to regrow an eye," Water said sourly. "Do you have any idea how much that hurts?"

Shadow shrugged and picked up a piece of broken shield. "I am itching for a fight right now. These little halls of the Order are so disorganized without Serak it's almost easy."

Using the map Fire and Mind had provided, the other fragments and the Talinorian army had sought to destroy the Order hall in the region. The prison cells below the castle were full of Order members, some of them culled from the leadership in the city. In a few months the Order would be all but eliminated from the kingdom, assuming they found Wylyn.

"I know it's been easy," Water said. "Doesn't mean I would set a trap that takes your eye out."

"I gave you the water to heal you," Shadow said.

"It stained my face pink," Water growled.

Shadow's features lit up with amusement. "Right. I'd forgotten about that."

Elenyr listened to them argue, pleased by the banter. She could have very easily taken them with her, but she had a deeper reason to go

198

alone. After Serak nearly killed her, Elenyr found herself bound by a measure of trepidation. She was afraid, and the only way to overcome it would be to go out alone, and dare Serak to risk another attempt.

"I don't like you traveling alone," Jeric said. "One of them should go with you."

"I will be fine," Elenyr said. "I will find Fire and Mind and join them. You should stay here in case Serak or Wylyn comes after Jeric."

"Wylyn has been very quiet since taking the Order," Jeric said. "I expected her to attack or retaliate for what we've been doing, but there has been nothing."

"There is always a calm before a hurricane," Water said. "And her losses are just slaves to her. She only wants the Stormdial."

"Agreed," Elenyr said, and then realized there was one absent. "Where's Light?"

"He and Willow were at the House of Runya," Shadow said, his tone annoyed. "Of course they like *him*."

"You did get their son exiled," Water said.

"Only one of them." Shadow grunted in irritation, and then brightened. "Perhaps Jeric could—"

"There are limits to what a Steward can do in the king's absence," Jeric said.

"Blast."

Elenyr swept a hand to the fragments. "Keep taking down the Order halls, but stand ready for an assault on the Stormdial. I'll message you when we have its location."

"My historians are still searching," Jeric said.

"If King Porlin had information on the Stormdial," Water said, "you would have found it by now."

"So we fight and wait," Water said, glaring at Shadow. "And no more traps."

"I figured you were going to leave without talking to me," Jeric said, his voice quiet enough so only Elenyr heard.

"Never."

She offered a tentative smile. Whatever his secret, they still had a war to fight, and what he had to share could wait. She hoped.

"This could work," Jeric said, nodding in approval. "We suspect the Order still has quite a few soldiers in their pocket. If we eliminate their halls in Herosian, it could help us clean out the corruption, maybe even find out where King Porlin is being held."

"Eager to give him his throne?" Shadow asked.

Jeric's expression was distasteful. "As soon as possible."

The door burst open and Light entered. "Am I late?"

"Right on time," Shadow said, clapping him on the back. "But there's something I need to show you in my room."

"The thing that took out Water's eye?" Light laughed. "I wish I could have seen that."

"Are you certain I cannot come?" Water asked, his voice pleading.

"I'm sorry," Elenyr said. "Do what you can to keep them in line. Once I meet up with Fire and Mind, I'll send a message back. Be safe in my absence."

She embraced them all, grateful her sons had survived the conflict with Serak. She couldn't shake the sinister thought that one of them wouldn't survive, or all of them. Or perhaps she would be the one killed by Serak.

"We'll accompany you to the edge of the city," Water said.

"I'd like that," Elenyr said, and turned to Jeric.

They shifted uncomfortably for a moment. "We'll talk later," Jeric finally said. "There are more important things happening right now than us."

"Are you certain?"

He nodded, all trace of his former conflict gone from his features. Had she imagined his tension? But she knew she hadn't. Whatever he intended to reveal, it was serious. But she'd waited so long for the truth from Jeric, and a little longer would not hurt.

"Be safe," Jeric said. "There's no telling if Serak will come for you again."

"I hope he does," Elenyr said evenly.

Jeric held her gaze and then stepped into a quick embrace. They parted, and Elenyr followed the fragments out of the training room. She cast a look back at Jeric as she left, but he remained in place, his expression somber. She gave a nod of assurance and then departed.

She listened to the fragments talk on her way to the city gates, considering the strange conversation with Jeric. At one time she'd been in love with him, and after her rescue even more so, but now she began to wonder if she knew anything about the elf. Ever since seeing him again, he just seemed more and more mysterious. And what did he mean about "some personas endure longer than intended" . . .

She came to a halt, stopping so quickly that Shadow had to jump aside to avoid running into her. She didn't hear his complaint, and instead reviewed Jeric's words. He'd spoken of a persona like it was a burden, one that he'd carried for a long time. Water called Elenyr's name but she didn't hear. Instead a shocking thought held her bound. What if the persona he spoke of . . . was his own? She felt a chill across her flesh as she sensed the truth.

Jeric wasn't his real name.

But if Jeric was the persona, then what was his real identity?

Chapter 26: The King's Library

Fire descended the slope into Outer Terros, his thoughts on Soreena and the events at Beldik. The air carried the tinge of fresh hewn wheat, the nearby farmers rushing to complete the harvest before winter. Great towers dotted the farms and villages, while the walls of Terros rose in the distance. Beyond the city, the waters of Blue Lake stretched to the horizon. Distracted, Fire almost didn't notice the boy run up to Mind and hand him a piece of parchment.

"Who sent this?" Mind asked in confusion.

"Your mother."

Fire and Mind exchanged a look of surprise. "Elenyr is here?"

"She didn't give her name," the boy said. "But she did pay me well."

That sounded like Elenyr. After so many years the woman had plenty of coin, but she had a habit of giving it away to anyone that appeared in need. As the boy scampered away Mind unrolled the parchment and scanned the lettering. Fire peered over his shoulder.

"Do you have to do that?" Mind asked. "You can wait until I'm done."

"What does it say?"

"I swear you and Shadow were born to be annoying."

Fire grinned. "We try."

Mind swept a hand to the parchment. "Senia met up with her and told her we'd be coming to Terros. She's in the King's Library."

Fire noticed a trace of doubt on Mind's features, and realized he was worried Senia had revealed the true contents of her vision to Elenyr.

202

But Mind had erased the memory, right? Fire jerked his head, unwilling to consider what Elenyr would do with such knowledge.

"It appears we are expected," Fire said, excited at the prospect of seeing Elenyr back in fighting shape.

"Indeed."

They wound their way through the trees and then stepped into the open. From their vantage point, the breadth of Terros sprawled out before them, the outer farms reaching to the city, which sat on the bank of the great Blue Lake.

Griffin had been steadily expanding its borders and the population had soared, necessitating growth to the capitol. The city itself was segmented into districts that each served a unique purpose, the Blue District housing the bulk of the merchants, while the Red District contained the seat of the Griffin army.

Instead of building new districts, the city had expanded into a village outside the city walls. Homes, businesses, and other trades were built into curving rows, following the hills of the region. No outer wall protected the area, but enormous towers had been erected, each built with a host of dwarven-made ballistae on a myriad of balconies.

Other trades had built towers as well, with the Mining Guild boasting the largest structure. At the petitioning of the people, a school had been built at the center of Outer Terros, the building becoming known as the King's Library.

Initially intended as a place of learning history, the building had expanded and the huge structure had become the one of the largest edifices throughout the kingdoms. A central tower rose to an impressive three hundred feet, with smaller towers placed around it. A host of arched walkways connected the towers of the King's Library, providing paths and support for the buildings.

Mage guilds had a presence in the towers, as did various guilds of trade, each dedicated to training young minds wishing to follow in their craft. The only school absent from the library was combat, and the elders that controlled the King's Library refused to permit the building of a tower dedicated to swordcraft.

As they approached the Library, Fire and Mind were met by the Griffin guards. Initially the post had been seen as one of honor, but guarding a bunch of youths and children quickly became a chore, making it the most derided posting in the army. All the more seasoned soldiers had been pulled away in the search for King Justin, who was still missing.

They passed through the outer wall, receiving barely a glance from the bored soldiers. The north entrance was flanked by the weaver and stonemason towers, their exteriors decorated with banners and work that reflected their crafts. A quartet of giant dwarven statues stood around the stonemason tower, each carved by students.

Wide cobblestone paths wound between the great towers, leading to courtyards and gardens. The elven plant guild boasted the brightest gardens, while the guild of water magic helped care for the streams that gurgled in the courtyards.

"When did Water help you teach at the Water Tower?" Mind asked.

"Sixty years past," Fire said, glancing up at the tower that boasted a slide of swirling water beneath the stairs, allowing students to float down the outside of the structure.

"I can still see the damage on the stone," Mind said, peering upward.

Fire grunted in irritation. "They should have a tower for fire magic."

"Fire mages are notorious for burning things down," Mind said, glancing back at him, a faint smile on his lips. "I doubt they want a group of untested dwarves handling the archives in the Library."

Fire grinned. Still, it rankled to see so many youths running about, each wearing the robes of their respective towers. Water had taught the youths, their eyes wide with wonder at even the simplest of charms, and Fire had been envious. His attempt to garner praise from the children had caused no small amount of damage.

The pair of fragments passed the Druid Tower, where several brown-robed instructors were teaching a group of children how to properly approach a bear. The beast sat contentedly while a young boy hesitantly reached out to touch its fur. Fire's smile was soft as he thought of Soreena, and wondered how they would react if she and her moordraug walked into the library. When they passed beyond the tower marked by the symbol of elk, the Library Tower came into view.

Built of pure white granite, the structure had the inscription of the royal seal of Griffin, the eagle wings spread, the lion's body raised as if for flight. Above the insignia, banners hung from brass rods, each showing the white and gold colors of the library. The banners bore the same inscription.

All are welcome. All must learn.

"Try not to burn anything," Mind said.

"I would never burn the books here," Fire said, indignant.

"How many times have you burned Elenyr's library?" Mind asked.

Fire glared at him and Mind flashed a smile that made him look like Shadow. Then he led the way into the magnificent edifice. Fire lifted his gaze to the interior of the building, his eyes lifting to the legendary machinery of the King's Library.

Entire rooms ascended the exterior of the tower, the chambers moving around the outer wall as they rotated to the pinnacle three hundred feet above. There they detached from the wall and descended down the center of the tower, the rooms held aloft by thick dwarven chains. With so much movement and the whisper of gears, the King's Library felt like the inner workings of a giant clock.

Each chamber contained bookshelves, couches, comfortable desks and alcoves for study. Students of every age sat in the chambers, while the rooms climbed the outer wall, passing in front of great windows.

Staircases were cleverly built between the chambers, each gradually flattening to a platform at the top of the tower before reversing into a descending curve. Students and teachers, unperturbed by the perpetual motions of the library, walked up and down the steps, or murmured in soft tones as they waited to connect to a higher level. The outer towers had bridges that linked them to the tower, the great archways allowing entrance and exit at various points along the great height.

Built from a combination of magic and dwarven engineers, the interior of the library tower inspired awe, each turn and swivel, gear and step, all working in perfect harmony to continuously elevate the students to new heights, before bringing them back to the base to begin anew.

"I love this place," Mind said.

Fire agreed with a nod. "It's like a machine out of imagination."

He took a step forward but Mind caught his elbow, his tone suddenly serious. "Can we keep our questions about Elenyr to ourselves, for now?"

Fire met his gaze and shrugged. "For now."

Mind nodded. "You have my gratitude."

After the battle at Beldik, Fire realized he was less concerned about Elenyr's secret. Serak had enslaved entire tribes, crafted the Incinerake, and caged and killed a firebird. How bad could Elenyr's secret really be?

"Let's find Elenyr," he said.

A librarian looked up at Fire's voice, his features brightening. He was a human, but dressed in the robes of a water mage, an uncommon talent for one of his race. Still, he had the knots of a master, visible as he raised a hand in greeting.

"Ah, the Heckle brothers," he exclaimed, using the persona Elenyr currently used among the populace for the fragments. "She said you'd visit."

"Do you know where—"

"This way," the librarian said, and hurried to the stairs.

The man hopped to the floor, a spry move for one that looked well into his seventies. His hair had gone grey instead of bald, a thick collection that made him appear handsome and wise. He smiled broadly at Mind.

"Did your brother come to teach my class again?" He looked about for Water before seeing they were alone.

Mind motioned upward. "Unfortunately our time is short. Will you point us too—"

"She is searching for the records on the Shard of Midnight." The man's eyes sparkled with interest. "The fabled tower of the ancient race. I have a few minutes before my next class. Why don't we see what we can find?"

"Thank you, Talis," Mind said.

He didn't flinch at Mind knowing his name. He turned and led them to the nearest stairs and pointed to a chamber several rooms upward. Fire realized then that there were actually several tracks for the chambers, four to be exact, each with separate rooms gradually ascending the outer wall.

"Any information we would have on the ancient structures would be found in the seventh archive," he said. "Elenyr has been there for several days. It is restricted to masters and upper level journeymen that have received special permission. As you'll see, the books are quite fragile."

He doesn't want you to burn the books, Mind thought to Fire.

Fire snorted in irritation. Mind smirked and Fire gave him a tiny shove. Both straightened when Talis glanced back. The steps were moving with the rooms yet felt perfectly stable, the railing fashioned of an odd gold material that bent and turned with the movements of the chambers. Fine carpet softened their steps, and paintings hung from the exterior of the chambers.

As they ascended the steps past one of the archives, Fire looked up at the number 5 above the arched entrance, the sign glowing as if imbued with light. Passing it and the sixth archive, they came to a great, ironbound door that blocked the entrance to the seventh. Producing a key, Talis unlocked the door and swung it open.

A crackling fire burned in a hearth, while dusty tomes sat on the bookshelves that lined the exterior. Small couches and desks were also present, although the air had a musty scent, indicating the room was rarely frequented. Elenyr sat in the chair by the fire, next to a pile of books. She smiled when they entered and rose to her feet.

"It's about time you arrived."

"We had to finish our business in the south," Mind said, his voice vague as he glanced at Talis.

Fire crossed the space and embraced her, pleased to see her healthy and whole. No trace of her lingering wounds was visible, and she looked ready for the fight. When they parted she smiled up at him.

"You shouldn't look so worried."

"He nearly killed you," Fire said.

Elenyr's eyes flicked to Talis, who looked on in interest. "I am well," she murmured. "But there is much to read. You should join me."

Taking the hint, Mind and Fire sat at the table, and after a moment Talis inclined his head. "I'll leave you to your work." He walked to the door and departed, and the moment the key turned in the lock, Elenyr dropped her smile and leaned in.

"Show me."

Mind settled into his seat. "We started with Senia . . ."

Elenyr frowned, her expression distant as Mind shared the highlights of their tale. Fire had been on the receiving end of Mind's memory tales before, and knew it could take time to condense weeks of memories into a few minutes. This time it seemed Mind was in a hurry, because the images came fast and sharp, the memories culminating in the Ancient's death.

Elenyr's features tightened in real pain. "Serak has committed an atrocity. The Ancient was one of the great soldiers of the Dawn of Magic, and now even he becomes a casualty of this war."

"At least his son survived," Fire said.

"Indeed," Elenyr said. Then she shook her head and motioned to them. "As much as I would like to seek Serak for what he has done, we have a more pressing matter. I have learned that Wylyn and the Order of Ancients are close to raising the Shard of Midnight. We must discover it before they do."

"What have you learned?" Fire asked.

She stood and strode to the far back wall. "The Shard of Midnight was the most feared of the ancient structures, with many claiming it controlled the very storms in the sky. Any ships that tried to approach were scorched with lightning, the bolts tearing through ships like they were toy boats.

"We do believe it was located on a body of water," Mind said. "The question remains, which one?"

"No one knows," Elenyr said, glancing at him before brushing off the spine of a book. "The story is now considered a fable, with most agreeing it never existed."

"And you?" Fire asked. "What do you believe?"

"I believe there was such a tower," Elenyr said. "And it was probably somewhere in Blue Lake or out in the Southern Sea. Most of the knowledge we have about the Shard came from sailors, indicating at least that part was true. Ah, here they are."

She stopped and pointed at a row of large tomes. "This is what they have from the Dawn of Magic."

"That shouldn't be too hard to read," Fire said.

Elenyr reached to the side of the bookshelf. Pressing a rune, she activated hidden machinery and the bookshelf rotated, another row appearing from beneath the floor, and then another. The ones at the ceiling disappeared into it.

"*All* of these are from the Dawn of Magic," she said.

Elenyr and Mind quickly fell into a deep conversation about the events at Beldik, and Fire reluctantly reached for one of the books. Before long the others resorted to reading as well. Growing frustrated,

Fire rose and walked to the row of books, staring at the hundreds of archives, annoyed.

The other fragments, even Light and Shadow, enjoyed reading, but Fire found it to be an onerous duty. He preferred reading the tales of bards, the stories too epic to be real. Reading history was nearly as dull as hearing it from a historian.

"Fire," Elenyr said. "We have a lot to read."

Fire sighed and chose a book. Then he found a seat by the fire and dived into the text. To his surprise it was rather enjoyable, and detailed the description of the supposed ships the ancients had used to fly in the sky. He wished he could have seen the ship Light had discovered in Bartoth's refuge. But Light had destroyed it. Because he destroyed everything.

Fire browsed its contents and picked another, quickly becoming absorbed in tales of the first mages. History spoke of a time when magic had not existed, until Ero had activated the Forge of Light, giving all the races a touch of power, that very power leading to the death of the ancient race.

The three of them read throughout the day and deep into the night, when fatigue drove them to retire. Talis provided them quarters, his face turning a shade of pink when Elenyr thanked him. When he departed, Fire grinned at Elenyr.

"Looks like you have an admirer."

"She already has Jeric," Mind said.

"Perhaps not," Elenyr said cryptically, before leaving for her own quarters.

Confused, Fire looked to Mind, who shrugged and removed his boots. Fire claimed a bed in the fireplace, relishing the heat as he thought of Soreena, his thoughts bleeding into his dreams, where he imagined standing at her side, little Firelings running about their feet.

They rose early and returned to their search, diving into forgotten texts and dusty tomes in their search for any reference to either the

Shard of Midnight or the Stormdial. Although many spoke of them, it seemed the historians all knew their locations, so they were not written.

Their studies pushed into a second day, and then a third. By the fifth day Fire would have given anything for another battle with Serak's golems, and decided the chairs in Chamber 7 should be burned. Day after day they were lifted up and down the King's Library, the mechanisms raising their chamber to the ceiling at the top of the tower and then down to the floor.

On the sixth day, Mind leaned back with a sigh. "This doesn't make sense. Some say the Shard of Midnight was fifty feet high, some a thousand. Others say it pierced the heavens like a blade."

"They must have known its location," Elenyr said.

"Blue Lake," Mind said, pointing to his current text. "That much seems clear. But after the krey perished, the tower abruptly vanished. Many sailed in search of the structure but it was never found."

"I found it," Fire said in surprise.

"You?" Mind asked.

"Don't sound so surprised," he said, and hefted the book. "This record contains the account of a sailor who said the tower plummeted into the sea. He watched it fall from an Azure ship, at the heart of Blue Lake."

"It fell?"

"No," Elenyr disagreed, pointing to her own book. "It descended."

Fire frowned. "That still doesn't explain where it is, unless there's a place in Blue Lake where waves to not go."

Elenyr closed the tome with a thud, her eyes wide with excitement. "I know where it is."

The door abruptly opened and Talis entered, his appearance making Fire realize they'd been studying for several hours. The sun had long since descended below the horizon, and the lights in the library were dim. Then another figure followed him inside, a hulking shape that towered over the older man . . .

Chapter 27: Aradig

Fire was on his feet in a second, pulling fire from the hearth to fashion a sword. Then he lunged for the shape. Talis cried out in surprise but the newcomer removed the hood of his robe, bringing Fire to a halt.

"Do you dislike my presence?" the troll asked.

"Sorry," Fire said hastily. "I thought you were someone else."

The troll nodded. "Many do not like my kind. They prefer my rock troll cousins, despite their warlike nature."

"Aradig has been with us for decades," Talis said, eyeing the flaming sword in Fire's hands. "He is a peaceful troll."

Realizing his sword was about to touch a book, Fire extinguished the blade and offered an apology. The troll bowed and smiled, the expression failing to light his black eyes. His immediate forgiveness sounded hollow to Fire but the others seemed to take it in stride.

"Aradig teaches our only history class on the ancient race," Talis said. "He'd been visiting friends the last few months but I spoke to him regarding your search. He was quite eager to assist."

Aradig bowed his head, revealing the sand-colored skin of his race. His head was shaven, making it difficult to determine his age, while his clothes were grey and white, the robes of a master in history.

"Talis said you seek the Shard of Midnight," he said.

"We would like to find its location," Elenyr said.

"A mystery for the ages," Aradig replied, his eyes lighting up with interest. "I believe it once stood in the center of Blue Lake, although my peers dispute my theory."

"We will have to return another time to continue our search," Elenyr said, smoothly scooping the book and placing it back on the shelf.

Fire noticed her glance his way, and he saw the warning in her eyes. After a thousand conflicts together, Fire did not need to read her mind to know Elenyr's thoughts. She did not trust Aradig. Mind too seemed to notice, and he gathered his books, returning them to the shelf.

"You are already departing?" Talis asked, in dismay. "But there are still many books to explore. And I brought sweet rolls!"

Elenyr smiled and shook her head. "Perhaps we will return tomorrow."

She inclined her head to Aradig and strode around him, giving him a warrior's berth. Fire and Mind did the same. When Fire looked back, Aradig had Elenyr's book in his hands, and he browsed the interior. When he spoke over his shoulder, all three of them halted at the door.

"The Shard of Midnight was fabled to be the creator of the great Blue Lake," he said softly. "Did you know that?"

"I did not," Elenyr said.

"A handful claim that the ancients built the lake for the people," he said, "giving fresh water to any in need."

Talis looked between the two groups, his expression uncertain. "Aradig believes they were not the hated tyrants the histories describe."

"Our records are sadly tinged by the voices of hatred and anger," Aradig said. "There is little enough that has survived the ages, and truth has become distorted."

"Who are you?" Elenyr suddenly asked.

The troll smiled but did not look up from the book, and spoke as if he had not heard her. "You know, I have read this passage many times, yet never noticed what you saw this day."

"I saw nothing," Elenyr said.

" . . . the Shard descended into the sea like a sword into its sheath, the water falling still, forever tranquil without the Shard's magic."

"Forever tranquil?" Fire blurted, and Elenyr shot him a warning look.

Aradig chuckled and finally looked up, his gaze falling on Talis, who looked decidedly confused, and uncomfortable. Returning the book, Aradig reached up and began to remove his cloak. When it fell off his shoulders, he revealed tight armor and a wind bow, the curving weapon snapping into place as he pulled it from his back.

"Talis," Aradig said, causing the man to flinch. He'd been staring at Aradig's clothing in surprise. "Have you heard of the spot on the sea where no waves ever seem to form, even in the greatest of storms?"

"The Azure call it the Devil's Maw," Talis said. "Why do you wear the armor of a warrior?"

"Because I am a warrior," he said. "The moment I heard who had arrived, I knew my time here was complete. I did enjoy your lectures, but my allegiance lies with the Order of Ancients."

"The Order?" Talis asked, retreating a step. "I thought that was a myth."

Fire glanced to Elenyr and she had her sword in hand. "It exists," Elenyr said. "And the Order does indeed want to see the return of the ancients to power."

"But the ancients are dead," Talis protested.

Aradig chuckled and notched an arrow to his bow. "Not anymore, Talis, and soon you will kneel at their feet. You have been a friend, so I will ensure you are treated with mercy."

"Who is your master?" Mind asked. "Wylyn or Serak."

"A member of a race of gods? Or an abomination created by mages?" His chuckle was dark. "But it seems he is not the only guardian that survived the Age of Oracles."

"Talis," Elenyr said quietly. "Evacuate the library. Quickly."

215

"What are you going to do?" he asked, scurrying to the door.

"Kill him before he can tell the Order what he learned," Elenyr said, and Fire knew what she meant. Before the Order told Wylyn.

The man departed, shutting and locking the door as if that would stop them from exiting. The jangling of his keys was followed by a curse, and then the faint footfalls of him fleeing. When he was gone Fire stepped away from Elenyr, while Mind took the opposite flank. Aradig did not seem concerned.

"Elenyr," he said. "I always wondered if I would get a chance to face you."

"You know who I am?"

"Of course," he said. "I may not be ageless, but I do have a gift for the dragon's sleep, and I've lived long enough to notice the hand of a former oracle." His features tightened. "And when Wylyn claimed the Order from Serak, she revealed even more."

"Then you know us?" Mind asked.

"You and Serak are the same, two failed experiments." He gave a derisive snort. "Perhaps as Draeken you could defeat me. But as fragments?" His lip curled into a sneer of anticipation, and Fire noticed the staff taking shape in his hand. Like smoke turning solid, the air magic turned sharp, the weapon a wicked curve on the end meant to take limbs.

"Fire?" Elenyr called.

"Yes?" he answered without turning his head, his gaze fixed on the troll.

"Don't burn the books."

He recognized it as permission to fight in the library, and smiled in anticipation. He started forward but Aradig raised his hand. He cocked his head to the side and listened, and Fire did the same. Dozens of booted footfalls echoed within the empty library tower, followed by several shouts, the voices distinct in their accent.

216

"Dakorians," Mind spat.

"My friends have arrived," Aradig said. "Now we may begin."

In a flash of movement the troll raised the bow and fired, sending a bolt straight to Elenyr's heart. She turned ethereal, the arrow streaking through her body to strike the door—blasting it outward in a plume of smoke and fire. Elenyr had partially returned to flesh and the explosion knocked her into a table.

Fire charged, leaping the gap as his favorite sword appeared in his hands. He brought it down on the troll but Aradig spun and tossed the bow into the air. The weapon unfolded, becoming two bows crossed at the center, forming an X. A new arrow appeared in the opening at the junction and pointed at him. He'd seen the weapon before, and he scowled at the memory.

"The Assassin's Guild," he said. "You were there with Gendor."

"I'm glad you remember," the troll said with a smile. "I hope you enjoy my bow. He *loves* to kill his targets with an arrow to the heart."

Fire cast a shield out of fire and raised it, the arrow breaking the barrier and sending him across the room. He blasted through a set of shelves and rose to his feet, dazed. As he raised the shield again he cursed Aradig.

Although an entity acted as an extension of the mage, a sentient took much longer to cast. The wielder gradually added a framework of consciousness, giving the being a mind and a purpose. Usually sentients were fashioned after living creatures because the mind naturally took the form of the shape. To force a consciousness onto a weapon required enormous skill and patience.

The dual bow turned and fired at Mind, but he'd anticipated the weapon and dived out the door, disappearing into the library. The arrow soared outside and then flipped midair, streaking back at Elenyr. Back to ethereal, Elenyr shouted at Fire as the arrow detonated around her.

"We'll stop the incursion," she called, following Mind out the door. "Don't let him escape."

"With pleasure," Fire said.

217

He sucked the flames off the books around him, casting a new shield to replace his broken one. Then he jumped into a flip and fastened his feet to the ceiling, using the heat to lash himself upside down. He sprinted across the ornate surface, jumping as another arrow came at him. Then he dropped and released the bond, landing in front of Aradig.

Fire struck the floor, sending flames blasting outward. Aradig was knocked into a bookcase, snapping wood and sending books scattering. His features contorted in irritation and he stood, twirling his bladed spear.

"I look forward to killing you," he growled.

"I could say the same about you," Fire said.

Aradig darted forward with poise that belied his large frame, and swung his spear at Fire's neck, a swing meant to take his head. Fire ducked and twisted, sweeping his sword at the spear to knock it upward. Then he kicked off a table and drove his blade toward the troll's chest.

The troll swiveled to the side, allowing the fireblade to dig into a bookcase, biting into the wood and scorching it black. Then the troll swung the staffblade at Fire's wrist, forcing him to release his blade and withdraw.

Fire retreated and cast a chain, the links snapping into place in a burst of sparks as they connected to the sword. Yanking on the chain, he pulled the blade free and whirled the chain, gathering momentum into a whirlwind of fire. The sentient bow released another explosive arrow but it was knocked aside by the spinning sword and exploded on the chimney, sending ornaments tumbling away. Aradig charged through the fire and brought his staffblade down on Fire, but he was no longer there. He'd used the cover to leap into the fire. Sucking it dry, he wreathed his body in flames and cast a horde of tiny squirrels.

Aradig laughed. "You want to strike at me with rodents?"

Fire smirked as the little creatures swarmed the troll. He reached up and swatted one away—and it detonated, knocking him through a table and onto the steps leading to the door. He snarled and retreated as the other squirrels ascended his legs, biting into his flesh. Another

218

detonated, sending him tumbling through the door and over the railing. The sentient bow folded together and darted after its master, and Fire sprinted to follow.

He reached the balcony to find their chamber was halfway down the tower. So smooth was the motion that he could hardly feel its downward motion. Aradig had jumped down a level, entering an archive two chambers below. Squirrels detonated and he roared his frustration. Fire smiled.

"They never fear the rodents," he said. Then he spotted the battle.

The base of the tower was pure mayhem. Elenyr and Mind fought with a handful of Griffin soldiers, teachers, and a pair of students who had gotten caught in the tower. Order members in dark armor, their faces masked, fought with a patrol of dakorians, the giant figures standing over a dozen still figures.

He spotted Elenyr locked in a deadly duel with the very same Order that had tried to kill her in Cloudy Vale. The image of her on her deathbed came unbidden to his thoughts, of her deep wounds, of the damage they had done . . .

Anger pooled in Fire's body and flames arched up his arms. Pulling from every source of fire in the structure, he gathered it around his body until the flames turned white hot, the railing glowing red. Then he leapt toward the dakorians and released a bellow as he plummeted into their midst.

Chapter 28: Elenyr's Gambit

Fire landed on the ground and struck the floor with his fist. Flames blasted outward, sending the dakorians tumbling backward. The stones of the floor cracked from the heat and the fires burned into the nearest archives, igniting bookshelves and their contents.

Their bone armor scorched and blackened, the dakorians rose to their feet and regrouped, and then Fire noticed they no longer carried their hammers. Long, black swords glinted in the light, the metallic sheen distinct for the anti-magic charms. The gnome magic was expensive and rare, and Fire guessed the Order had helped procure the blades for the dakorians. The thought was fleeting and crushed beneath Fire's rising fury.

Wreathed in flames so hot they turned white, Fire converted the flames into fireflesh, encasing his body, lifting him off the ground and until he matched them in size. Heedless of Elenyr's shout, he charged the group. A dakorian swung his sword and Fire flowed around it, knocking it upward and slicing the soldier across the midsection. The bone armor was no match for the sword, and he cried out.

Another dakorian came at Fire and he parried, sparks spilling across them both as the anti-magic blade struck the blade of magic. The dakorian leaned in and struck him with his free hand, but grimaced in pain as his hand came away burned. Fire reached up and caught his wrist, twisting it and forcing the dakorian to his knees.

"You think you are mighty?" Fire snarled.

He plunged his fire sword into the Dakorian's back and he fell away. Then he rotated to parry another sword. Other dakorians rushed to surround him, their blades coming at him from all sides. Those behind plunged their blades into Fire's back, only to see their anti-magic blades brighten, the fireflesh overpowering the anti-magic until they shattered, sending the wielders into the wall of an archive, shards of burning steel lodged in their bodies.

"All your flesh and training are naught," Fire said, his voice distorted with anger.

He twisted to gain momentum and hurled his sword, the blade spinning end over end to impale a dakorian in the gut. Then Fire cast his chain and yanked the blade from the dying soldier, sending it into a lethal spin, forcing the dakorians to withdraw. The Order members were not so fast, and the bladed chain sliced through them like a scythe through autumn wheat, cutting them down, their masks tumbling to smoking stones.

"Fire, you must stop!" someone shouted, but he was too far gone to hear it.

"This day you learn your place," Fire growled.

He yanked on the chain and it returned to his hand. The blade spit and sizzled, all the impacts with anti-magic swords robbing it of heat, the white turning yellow and orange. Dimly Fire recognized his fireflesh was equally as damaged but he did not care. Every impulse drove him to punish the intruders that had dared to threaten Elenyr.

"FIRE!"

The word pierced his thoughts and he looked to Elenyr, who pointed at Mind. The fragment stood on the stairs to the center archive, fighting for his life. Four Order members forced him to retreat upwards. His face was twisted in rage but not at his foes, and when their eyes met Fire realized where his anger was directed.

He took a step towards Mind but it was too late, and the railing had begun to warp. Answering to Mind's power, the metal twisted and bent, snapping inward to strike one of the Order members, knocking him screaming from the ledge. Then the entire archive began to rise.

Metal and stone groaned as the chambers strained to escape their bindings, but the Order members didn't notice. Heedless of the damage, they charged at Mind, one stabbing his shoulder with his dagger, another plunging his sword into Mind's arm. Blood and purple light leaked from the wounds and Mind issued a disturbing roar.

The sound grated like a sword on glass, primal in its fury and power. Even the dakorians paused to look up at Mind, to see his eyes had gone dark, the irises turning a bright purple. The very archives leaned away from him as if they too feared his wrath, and then Mind lifted off the ground.

His boots lifted an inch, floating like the earth had lost its power over his flesh. The Order members finally hesitated, stumbling as the stairs where they stood began to shift and separate, the stones floating away.

Mind grimaced as if he struggled to contain the surge of magic, and the Order fled, but it was too late. Their bodies were slammed into the walls as a pair of chambers ripped free of the machinery, the great rooms dropping down the stairs, crushing the Order soldiers and the dakorians.

Fire shouted to the professors and shoved the nearest away, and then leapt to safety as the rooms crashed into the floor, the shock reverberating through his bones. He sprinted and dodged as the giant chambers bounced off each other and struck the floor, dislodging others from the machinery, sending more to the floor.

Fire spotted a student running with a professor. They sprinted for safety but an entire archive fell towards them. Fire picked up a stray stone and sent it spinning to them, striking the man in the back. He cried out and went down, taking the student with him, their fall saving their life. The archive bounced over a broken section of stone and rolled above them, nearly crushing them to dust. A dakorian caught on the other side was not so fortunate, and he disappeared into the rubble, his anti-magic blade clattering from his fingers.

The shaking finally came to a stop and Fire stood, instinctively looking upward. The lower half of the library was in ruins, with one chamber hanging on its side. Others were broken and leaning, while the rest were on the floor. A grinding of gears echoed from somewhere in the walls, the tower attempting in vain to lift what had fallen.

Flames licked at the broken archives, books burning, their cases broken into kindling. One archive was filled with flames, the interior little more than a burning husk, smoke rising from the cracks in the top.

Fire spotted Mind where he lay on a pile of stones, and raced to him. He leapt a pile of rubble and landed at his side, catching his arm to lift him up. Fear spiked in his gut, but the fragment groaned and reached for his skull.

"I couldn't control it," he growled. "I tried and failed."

"Easy," Fire said. "You're wounded."

Mind ignored him and pushed himself to his knees. Catching a piece of stone, he levered himself up and cast about, clearly searching for someone. Confused, Fire did so as well—and then spotted the group by the door.

Aradig stood with the remaining Order members and a quartet of dakorians, who held Elenyr bound in shimmering chains. The bonds sparkled and crackled, lightning arcing off them as they kept her ethereal form caged. Unconscious, she looked small and frail.

"Power without restraint is doomed for self-destruction," Aradig called, motioning the dakorians out the door.

Fire clenched a fist, but the fires on his body had faded, and sparks fluttered from his fingers. Elenyr had always been the rock of wisdom, never flinching, never failing. To see her so helpless—again—filled Fire with fear.

"I'll cut you apart," Fire growled.

Aradig smiled and reached up, catching the crossbow that flew into his hands. "You have already failed."

"They came for her," Mind murmured, his voice weak. "They may have wanted the Stormdial but they came for her."

"Why?" Fire demanded, taking a step towards the troll.

Anger and fear curdled in his gut, and the urge to leap across the chamber and strike at Aradig was overwhelming. Only Mind's hand on his arm held him fast, his fingers firm despite the weakness in his voice.

Aradig smiled. "You are like unruly children, striking about and destroying everything you touch."

"Is that why you're a member of the Order?" Mind asked. "To stop the unruly races?"

Aradig gestured to the destroyed tower. "What have we done with our freedom? Since the Dawn of Magic we have fought and killed each other, our wars wreaking havoc on every race. When the ancients return such conflicts will be abolished."

"You wish to be a slave," Fire spat. Mind tightened his grip.

"We are already slaves," Aradig said. "You to your power, me to the color of my skin. The people do not see me, they see a troll. Even after teaching children for years in this school, the people still look at me with fear in their eyes."

Scorn twisted the troll's features and he looked away, and Mind sent Fire a mental suggestion. Fire nodded, and cast the charm his brother requested, the tiny mouse of flame burrowing into the dust and disappearing before Aradig looked back.

"To them, I was always a brute," Aradig said.

"Aren't you?" Mind asked. "You lurked in their midst as a friend, yet in your heart lay betrayal. They did not know, but they sensed the truth."

Aradig scowled, but the distant sounds of boots caused him to glance outside. In that moment the fire mouse darted from the dust and climbed onto Aradig's boot. It disintegrated, leaving a scorched scar on the boot that faded from sight.

"You will see in the end," Aradig said, turning back. "And before you die, you will kneel before the krey and call them master."

"I'd rather die," Fire said.

The troll smiled, the expression dark and foreboding. "I know," he said.

He turned and left, and Fire leapt to follow. Again, Mind restrained him, preventing him from charging after those that had taken Elenyr. Fire whirled to face him but the fragment was weak, barely able to stand.

"Why do you restrain me?" Fire asked.

"You're a fool," Mind spat. "You didn't stop Aradig, and then you blasted in without thought to the consequences."

"I killed them," Fire growled.

"It's not enough to claim their lives," Mind said. "We must deprive them of what they most desire."

"Then why can I not go after Elenyr?" he growled.

"She *allowed* herself to be captured," he said. "She *wants* us to follow them."

Mind shared Elenyr's thoughts of the last few minutes, and Fire felt like a fool. Mind had caught their intent from their thoughts, and agreed to the plan. During the fight, she'd made her choice, and risked herself so they could find Wylyn. And Fire had all but leveled the King's Library.

A groan from nearby drew Fire's attention and he spotted one of the professors that had been fighting. Half buried, he struggled to pull himself free. Fire stepped to help but the man's features filled with fear.

"Please," he said. "You must go. You've damaged enough."

Fire scowled and made to retort, but the words failed him. The man was right. Despite his best efforts, Fire had damaged the Library because he couldn't listen to Elenyr or Mind. He jerked his head and turned away. Gathering Mind, he retreated, leaving the library just as soldiers swarmed the building.

Mind was nearly unconscious, his wounds leaving droplets of blood on the stones. Fire had fought in numerous wars, conflicts, and battles, yet never been so alone. He'd failed to stop Aradig, failed to notice Elenyr's plan, and failed to keep from burning the books in the library. Oddly that last was the most stinging, and made him question if he could be trusted at all. Leaving the destruction behind, he helped Mind through Outer Terros and to the woods. There he set him against a tree. Then he turned northward, where a faint pulse of heat drew his gaze. Aradig may have escaped, but Fire had left a brand, and Fire was more than ready for a second fight.

Chapter 29: Wylyn's Offer

Elenyr's first thought was of pain, lancing down her side, her arms, and back, and even into her fingers. It was an ache that spoke of past injuries. She grimaced and focused her scattered thoughts before opening her eyes.

She lay sprawled on the floor of a cell, as if she'd been unceremoniously tossed inside. She still wore her clothing from the battle in the King's Library, but it was soiled and torn, bloodied from the conflict. She sat up, touching the wounds through the cuts in her tunic.

Allowing herself to be caught was a gamble, a potentially lethal risk, but Mind had gleaned the purpose of the attackers from their thoughts, and she'd seen the opportunity. They needed Wylyn, and it was likely Aradig would lead them right to her.

Her memories of the battle were hazy, but she recalled rising from the ground and turning solid, striking at the back of a dakorian. The next thing she knew a net of lightning had been cast over her body. On instinct she'd turned ethereal but the bonds had filled her with pain, forcing her to remain in the flesh.

The scene of battle washed over her and she recalled Fire battling in the midst of foes, while Mind retreated up the steps to the center chambers of the tower. Beyond them, the professors, students, and guards unfortunate enough to get caught in the melee were retreating towards a back door, desperately trying to stave off being surrounded.

"The net was created specifically for you," Aradig had said, stooping to face her. "I do hope you resist."

Anger filled her and she lunged against the net, attempting a third time to phase to ethereal. This time the excruciating pain robbed her of consciousness, and the last thing she saw was Mind shouting to Fire.

Their eyes met, and Elenyr sent a mental thought before darkness claimed her.

Make sure you follow.

Rising to her feet in the cell, Elenyr looked about, unsurprised to see a thread of power crackling in the stone barrier, extending into the ceiling and the floor. Even the door contained the threads of lightning, the unmistakable arcing occasionally appearing and disappearing. There was no window.

She growled in anger, but the sound betrayed her fear. Lightning magic had already been used against her, and the scars went to her bones. Carn, the lightning mage that served Serak in the Order of Ancients, could be present. At their last encounter he'd nearly killed her, and would not hesitate to finish the job.

She phased to ethereal and attempted slipping through the floor, easing her body into the stone like it was icy water and she was dipping her toe into it. Instantly the pain appeared, her booted feet sparking. Grimacing, she moved to a different section and tested it as well, working her way around the room.

Thorough and slow, her search proved what she most feared. The lightning barrier had no cracks she could exploit. Just as she was checking the door, a set of footfalls sounded in the distance, and she retreated to the back of the cell.

A key sounded in the door but it crackled rather than clinked, and then the door swung open. With the lightning net in his hands, a dakorian entered first. He smirked when he saw Elenyr's rigid form. Then he stepped aside and two more figures entered. Aradig came first, and Elenyr's eyes flicked to Aradig's feet, where the faint glow of a brand marked his boot. The last person to enter the cell was Wylyn herself.

The krey woman stood tall and removed her cowl, regarding her with eyes that glowed with triumph. Elenyr remained in place, recalling their last engagement at the home of the king of dragons. Aradig took his place behind them, lounging in the doorway, his eyes on Elenyr.

228

"Hauntress," Wylyn said. "It is good to see you alive after what Serak attempted."

"I am glad to disappoint," Elenyr replied. "How is Serak, by the way? I understand he is no longer your ally?"

Wylyn scowled, a touch of red appearing in her eyes. "I was forced to take the Order of the Ancients for myself. He took his loyal and left like a coward."

"And Tardoq?" Elenyr glanced to the nameless dakorian. "Where is your Bloodwall?"

"He went as my envoy to Serak. He should be returning shortly."

Her eyes remained red, as if she were irritated at Tardoq. Elenyr wondered if that meant their relationship was strained, or if Wylyn knew what Shadow had witnessed at Mistkeep. Did she know Tardoq had let Wylyn's son die?

"Serak is still dangerous," Elenyr said.

"More than you know." Wylyn swept a hand at the room. "This is one of several rooms he created to cage you, if the need arose. Carn's magic is truly one to admire. A pity he does not have the temperament of a slave."

Elenyr folded her arms. "We have been destroying your Order in Talinor."

She waved airily. "They are sheep, easily scattered. Now that we have what I desire, it will be a simple matter to conquer all the kingdoms."

Elenyr kept the dismay from her face. Wylyn knew where the Stormdial had descended into the sea, a glance at Aradig confirming it. But why seek to capture her? What did she have to gain from speaking with the enemy?

"What do you want?" Elenyr said.

"Peace," Wylyn said. "I want your races to end their pointless wars and join my house."

"To be your slaves."

She motioned to Aradig. "You helped Aradig discover the location of the Stormdial, and we will depart here to raise the tower. Before his death at the hands of Shadow, my son gathered the resources to assemble the Gate, and it will be easy to use the Stormdial's power to open the Gate to my home. It's over."

"Nothing ends while the free continue to fight."

"Do not be foolish," Wylyn said. "You have a royal bearing, and you must understand the battle has been lost. I will leave through my Gate, and return in your skies. Those who fight will perish—including the fragments of Draeken."

"So you can have us as slaves?" Elenyr folded her arms. "Does your greed have no end?"

"Do you even know what you possess?" Wylyn asked. "Magic is so dangerous, yet so enticing. It is a wonder you have not utterly destroyed yourselves."

"We are not without integrity," Elenyr said.

She snorted but did not disagree. Then she gestured to Aradig. "I have learned much of your ways in my time here. Magic, with all its myriad possibilities, is truly fascinating. And my time as head of the Order has proved very enlightening."

"Is that why you cast Serak out?" Elenyr asked. She glanced to Aradig's boot. The brand was slightly brighter.

"I cast him out because he created an organization that worshiped *me*." Her eyes burned red with sudden anger. "And he was always away. The Order didn't need a leader, they craved a god."

"And what did you ask of them?" Elenyr asked.

"The truth." Wylyn took a step forward, and the dakorian bristled at their proximity. "They showed me their magic, showed me their records. Since the attempt on my life at Herosian, I've learned everything about magic. And everything about you."

Elenyr's laugh was mocking. "Kings are the most arrogant before they are killed."

Elenyr hated the way she described magic, as if it was an experiment, its wielders merely subjects to be studied, like they weren't sentient creatures. Wylyn would look at a human child the same way Elenyr would view a rodent caught in the house.

"Royalty are entitled to their pride," Wylyn said.

"They are entitled to serve the people," Elenyr said. "That is what mages do with their magic. We serve those who are in need."

"Those with power should not serve," Wylyn said. "They should conquer. Such magic, such power, such potential, wasted on helping other slaves. It is power squandered, especially for the oracles." Wylyn shook her head, her voice gaining a touch of awe. "I understand they have the ability to see the future? Such an ability has been sought by my people for eons, to no avail."

"You think to understand magic in just a few months?" Elenyr asked. "I've spent lifetimes studying what magic can do, and still there is much to learn."

"And that is what is most fascinating," Wylyn said, her eyes dark with desire. "The krey believe themselves superior because we have cleansed our flesh of every imperfection, allowing us to live forever."

"Unless you are killed."

Wylyn held her gaze and then nodded. "We can be killed, yes, but perhaps with magic, that can be changed."

Elenyr's eyes narrowed. "Everything can be killed."

Wylyn chuckled and shook her head. "Ero used the imperfections of your race, granting you abilities we can only dream of. Now that I know what you are, I cannot destroy an asset of such value."

Elenyr's expression hardened. "You think to control us? It would be easier to cage the dragons."

"Even they will be tamed," Wylyn said coldly.

Elenyr kept her fear in check. Wylyn spoke as if she'd already won, and now that she knew the location of the Stormdial, she had everything she needed. A simple journey in a ship and then raise the tower. But the tower had not been raised yet.

"What do you want with me?" Elenyr asked.

"These people will need a ruler," she said. "And they all trust the Hauntress. Former oracle, ageless like the krey, you can become their Gorwhip, slave master for an entire world."

"And servant to you."

She scowled at Elenyr's tone. "The position is highly sought after by slaves."

"You think to entice me with a promise of power?" Elenyr laughed, the scornful sound causing Aradig and the dakorian to shift. "Do you know how often I could have claimed power from the kings? As High Oracle I could have laid waste to kingdoms. As Hauntress I could have killed the kings and taken their thrones. And the fragments of Draeken? I could have raised them to be killers, almighty soldiers leashed to my will. You can take your offer and shove it—"

"How dare you speak to an ancient that way," Aradig snarled.

The troll crossed the room and caught Elenyr's throat, slamming her into the wall, but she phased ethereal and passed through his body, surreptitiously drawing the dagger from his side. Wylyn smirked as Elenyr flitted to an empty corner of the room and leveled the weapon at them.

"Your dogs cannot hurt me," Elenyr said.

Aradig bristled but Wylyn motioned him to silence. "You are a formidable woman, Elenyr. If it is not power, perhaps it is wealth you seek? If you will lead the people, many more will live, increasing my profit a thousandfold—"

"I would sooner die than help you do anything."

"This world is doomed to fall," Wylyn said, her voice now dangerous. "And when it does, many will be slaughtered. Those that

232

remain will become my slaves. It is inevitable. If you join me, you can ensure the people are cared for, and minimize the loss of life. Power and wealth I offer, but it is the blood of those you protect that should be your price."

"I heard your offer," Elenyr said. "And I refuse. I will not permit you to build your Gate. You will live out your days here, hunted as an exotic, the last of the ancients."

Elenyr's anger mounted as she spoke, her body turning into the Hauntress. Her skin turned green and translucent, the smoke gathering around her and forming a cloak and cowl. The dagger in her hand turned ethereal as well, the blade igniting with green light. Her voice gained a prophetic timbre that chilled the very air.

"Continue on your crusade and I will see your corpse flung into the depths of the ocean, your name never to be known in Lumineia, and forgotten among the Empire you call home. Learn to fear, *krey*, or I will show you the true might of those you call slave."

Her words echoed into silence, and for several moments none moved. Wylyn and Aradig, even the dakorian, all stood frozen, staring at the enraged Hauntress they had bound. Transfixed, Wylyn's features registered a flicker of doubt. Then her gaze hardened and she motioned to Aradig.

"Bring in the prisoners."

Aradig disappeared, and a moment later returned with a struggling man and a young woman. Both were thrown to their knees and the troll pressed them against the wall. Air flowed around his arms, enchaining them in clear bindings. Then the air solidified into a long spike, aiming at the young woman. The girl's eyes widened in terror as she saw the weapon ready to pierce her eye.

"King Numen," Elenyr exclaimed in surprise, gliding toward the bound man.

"I wouldn't," Aradig said, the blade advancing to touch the girl's throat. Then he reached up and removed the gag on the man's mouth.

"*Please*," he plead, tears streaming down his cheeks. "Please don't hurt my daughter."

"Serak gave me Numen and his daughter as a peace offering," Wylyn said. "He believes they could serve me."

"They don't have anything to do with this," Elenyr said, gauging the distance.

Wylyn swept a hand to the struggling man and crying girl. "You believe in families, an archaic notion, and so you should desire their safe return. This is the blood price."

The man looked to Elenyr with a tinge of hope. He was thinner than the other kings, and built like a warrior. Trained by his father's elite soldiers, he'd proven himself their equal and then their superior. He was strong willed and ambitious, but here he was a captive.

"There must be something I can give you," Elenyr said, unable to deny the fear of the young woman.

Wylyn's eyes glowed with triumph, as if that had been her aim since the beginning. "Since you will not join me, you will instead tell me how to subdue the current oracle, Senia is it?"

Elenyr's gut tightened. "I would never betray Senia."

The blade dropped towards the girl's throat, stopping just short of piercing skin. Wylyn shook her head in disappointment. "They told me you were a defender of the innocent, yet here you are, condemning them to death. Your choice is clear, let this girl die in the presence of her father—and trust the current oracle to defend herself—or tell me what I wish to know."

"Why do you want the oracle?"

"Isn't it obvious?" Wylyn asked. "I want what no one in the Empire possesses. I want the future."

Elenyr saw the truth. With the aid of an oracle—even one forced to support her cause—she could rise through the ranks of the Empire, even take the throne. The Empire would not be able to stop her.

Elenyr shook her head. "I choose neither."

Then she hurled her blade and burst into motion . . .

Chapter 30: The King of Erathan

Elenyr's dagger struck the spike of air in front of the young woman and it disintegrated, the pieces slicing shallow lines across one cheek before the dagger embedded into the wall—right into a shard of lightning.

Now severed, the thread of lightning streaked into the room, striking randomly. The dakorian instinctively raised a hand to shield himself, growling as a bolt struck his leg. Wylyn jumped behind the dakorian while Aradig retreated out the door.

Elenyr leapt to the captives and grabbed their hands, yanking them toward the opening. Wylyn shouted an order and the dakorian flung the net. Elenyr ducked and felt the charged material pass over her head. Then she was out the door. A shout came as the net snagged on the door and a bolt of lightning struck Wylyn, who shrieked in pain. Elenyr skidded into the hall to find Aradig raising his bow.

"I'm not going to let you—"

Elenyr struck the troll in the chest. Backed by her considerable strength and fury, the impact sent Aradig crashing into the wall, where he slumped, wheezing. His weapon rose in the air but Elenyr knocked it away.

"You can't stop me," she said coldly. She turned and ushered the captives down the hall. "This way," she urged.

"Thank you," sobbed the girl, and King Numen clung to his daughter, hurrying them along.

"I can't believe you got us out," he said, his voice tense.

"We're not out yet," she replied, hearing a crash behind them.

The corridor reached a set of spiral stairs and they hurried upward, sprinting up the steps into what was evidently a narrow turret. Elenyr had expected them to be in Terros, but when they reached the top of the turret and stepped outside, she came to halt in surprise.

"We're in the castle," she exclaimed.

The city of Terros lay sprawled below her, the district reserved for the nobles directly beneath the turret. Other districts were steeped in shadow, the lights from elven light orbs illuminating the city. Beyond the city walls, the towers of Outer Terros expanded into the hills, with the King's Library in their midst. Smoke rose from the library, suggesting their conflict was just hours old.

Ominous clouds filled the sky, and a rumble of thunder heralded rain. Droplets landed on her cheeks and she pulled the king and princess along the upper fortifications of the castle wall, looking for a place to escape.

"We need to flee," she said.

"Too late," King Numen said.

Elenyr glanced his way and found his hands reaching to the sky. More thunder rumbled, and then a bolt of lightning appeared, streaking across the sky and descending to her. Elenyr shifted to ethereal and leapt away, but the bolt struck where she'd been standing.

Her vision went white, her body tumbling from the battlements to land in the gardens below. She struggled to move, to speak, to flee, but her body refused to cooperate, every muscle clenching. In the back of her mind she realized the truth. King Numen had not been a captive. He was her captor, and was the very lightning mage that had helped build the cell.

King Numen was Carn.

She managed to roll onto her back as booted feet descended the nearby steps. King Numen stalked forward, lighting crackling up his right arm. His daughter hung back in terror, obviously shocked to see her father behave in such a way.

"Do you have any idea how long it took to prepare your death?" he growled, all trace of the former fear gone. "How long it took to plan your execution in Cloudy Vale?"

"I thought you served Serak," she said, her words distorted through her jaw. "Why are you here with Wylyn?"

"I was *ordered* to stay with Wylyn, to feign allegiance and seek a chance to finish what we failed to do in Cloudy Vale." King Numen's features were dark with anger. "That chance was now, when Wylyn thought to use me as bait. What a fool. She thinks all will follow her because she is krey."

Aradig dropped from the battlements above, a gust of wind slowing his descent and allowing him to land. Trees and brush bent away from him, the wind snapping their branches. The storm continued to mount and rain fell, splattering Elenyr's cheeks. Numen turned and hurled a bolt at Aradig, sending him scrambling backwards. The dakorian from the cell appeared and a lightning bolt shattered the stones at his feet, forcing him back inside the turret.

"My fragments will find you," Elenyr said.

"They are scattered," Aradig said. "And Serak has his own plans for Draeken."

Elenyr had regained some motion and pushed herself up onto her elbows. Her features contorted in anger. The man recognized that she was recovering and gathered his lightning, the sky crackling with power.

"It is a pity you would not join us," he exclaimed. "But Serak is right. You are too old and set in your ways."

Elenyr spotted the glow on Aradig's boot and smiled. "And you have no idea who you've challenged."

He frowned and followed Elenyr's gaze. Then he recognized the brand on Aradig's boot, the same type cast by a mage so they could be tracked. Numen growled in recognition and reached for the sky—just as a massive ball of fire appeared over the battlements. Aradig saw it

238

coming and dove for cover. Elenyr just managed to turn ethereal as the ball struck, the fire passing through her to detonate on the ground.

Fires spilled outward, scorching a boulder and shredding nearby trees and brush. It licked at the castle wall, sending smoke billowing skyward. King Numen rolled on the ground but the flames had ignited his tunic and burned his face, his shrieks filling the garden. Aradig rose and looked to the battlements, expecting Fire to appear. But the fragment had not fired the weapon.

He *was* the weapon.

In the depths of the crater Fire rose to his feet, flames cascading off his body, swirling up his arms and torso. His eyes burning like coals, he turned on Aradig. He swept his hands downward and flames flooded up the hill, rising like a wave that broke on the boulder. Aradig bolted, racing to escape the inferno that ripped through the gardens, leaving smoking trunks in its wake.

"Fire!" Elenyr shouted. "We must retreat!"

The fragment turned on Numen, who was rising to his feet. Half of Numen's face was blackened and burned, the ugly wound too large for a healer to fully repair. The king raised his hand to the sky and pointed to Elenyr.

"I will not fail a second time!" he cried.

"Elenyr!" Fire shouted, and tossed her a sword.

She reached up and caught her sword, and sprinted to the lightning wielder. A bolt of lightning dropped towards her but she fell into the earth to evade the charge, rising into the castle wall before bursting from behind her foe, driving her sword into the man's side.

He cried out and went down, the distraction costing him control of his volatile magic. Elenyr stood over King Numen and pointed her sword at his throat, her chest heaving from rage and pain. She'd thought the man a friend, an ally against those who sought to usurp the kingdoms. And he'd betrayed her. The blade pressed into his throat but his daughter cried out.

"Please!" she shouted.

She appeared from behind the turret and stumbled to her father's side. Her features were filled with fear as she knelt and raised a hand to Elenyr, and plead for the life of her father. As the Hauntress, Elenyr stood over the man that had betrayed Lumineia, and yearned to take his life.

"I spare your life for the sake of your daughter," Elenyr finally said. "But know this, from this day forth you are no king, and if we meet again, my blade will find your heart."

"I will see your corpse rot," the man snarled.

Without taking her eyes off the dangerous king, Elenyr looked to Fire and pointed upward, an order to retreat. Fire leapt to the steps, ascending out of sight and dropping over the castle wall. Elenyr kept her sword pointed at the man.

"How many of your kingdom's threats have I eliminated for you?" she asked. "A dozen? A hundred? All while the true danger lurked at my side. We even saved you from an assassin."

"You and your fragments did save my life," Numen growled. "And I saw their power. I knew then that they were a danger to all life on Lumineia, that *you* were a greater threat than bandits or killers, for you had the power to destroy us all."

She abruptly noticed that the castle guard and a handful of nobles and peasants stood at the edge of the burned gardens, staring in shock and terror. They looked on in fear, as if Elenyr was the attacker, and likely thought she threatened the king of Erathan.

"You *dare* to attack a king of Lumineia?" one of the nobles cried.

From within the cowl of her cloak, Elenyr faced the terrified people and realized she stood on a precipice. Since taking Draeken as her charge she'd sworn to protect the people, but the Order had infiltrated the kingdoms, quietly preparing for the time they would oppose her. Her time of hunting bandits and fighting for the kingdoms was at an end. She pointed her sword at the man, her voice soft and deadly, sending a chill through those gathered.

"I am the Hauntress, punisher of oathbreakers, slayer of the unjust and ungodly. Nobles you may be, but your secret works are known, and I am your judge. Betray your oath to the people, and I will see your crowns taken, even if I must take your head."

The man swallowed and fell silent. Elenyr glided backward, passing into the wall as the people gasped and cried out, calling her a devil, a demon. Elenyr reached the outside of the castle and Fire fell into step beside her, his expression worried.

"I arrived in time," he said.

"You did well," Elenyr said. "Where's Mind?"

"Wounded," he said. "I placed him in a stables nearby."

"Alone?" she asked.

"I had to," he replied. "He's barely conscious and I didn't know how to help him."

"We need to send a message to the other fragments," Elenyr said.

"Mind already said we should." Fire nodded and pointed south. "I sent the message as soon as we left the library. They will meet us at the Shard of Midnight."

She noticed the worry in his voice and bowed her head. Fire had always been protective, and this time, he'd been her protector. She touched his arm in gratitude and Fire offered a tight smile before helping her walk.

"You saved my life," she said. "Now we must retreat before our foes can regroup."

She looked up to the castle, and spotted Wylyn standing in the opening of a turret. She glared as Elenyr fled, the red in her eyes burning like embers. The dakorian stood behind her, and then the pair retreated into darkness.

Elenyr lowered her cowl and turned into flesh. Then she dropped a few coins at a street weaver and picked up a stretch of cloth she used to create a makeshift cowl, one too colorful to belong to a fugitive. First, escape the city. Second, the Stormdial. But the storm was picking up.

Chapter 31: Betrayed

Fire led Elenyr to where he'd stashed Mind, weaving through streets to a small structure behind an inn. His brother sat where Fire had left him, in an empty horse stall. He'd managed to find cloth in the stables and was tying it around his wounds.

"Elenyr?" Mind asked.

"She's watching for patrols," Fire said. "But there's more."

Fire passed his memory of the battle with Carn, and Mind's head snapped up. "King Numen is Carn?"

Elenyr burst through the wall of the stables. "We must go. The city guard has begun searching the city."

"Wylyn attacked us," Fire growled. "We should go back and end this."

"The people saw me about to kill the king of Erathan," Elenyr said. "The army is coming to arms and Wylyn will have the Order's forces gathering."

"We need to get a ship," Mind grimaced in pain. "The only thing that matters is reaching the Stormdial before the Order. We cannot let Wylyn open a Gate." Mind caught a barrel in the stables and used it to stand.

They hurried out of the stables and entered the main street. Clogged with people rushing to complete their business before the storm struck, the streets were filled with shouts and rushed footfalls. Shopkeepers shuttered windows while children retreated to the safety of their mother's cloaks.

"We're going to be remembered," Fire said, spotting a group of women staring at Mind's bloody bandages.

"Not anymore," Mind said.

The women turned away and ushered their children towards the shelter of an inn, and Fire grinned, grateful for his brother's gift. Then he spotted a patrol of guards down a side street, the captain barking orders to spread out.

"Mind?" Elenyr called.

"I can't erase all their memories," Mind said. "There are too many."

"Get Mind to the waterfront," Elenyr said. "I'll lead them away."

"But they think you're a killer," Mind said.

"Doesn't matter now."

Elenyr's tone was grim as she disappeared into a building, a scream indicating a woman had seen the Hauntress before she burst into the alley. The guards scrambled to follow, and raced away from Fire and Mind.

"Numen serves Serak," Fire growled as they worked their way down the street. "The guards should be chasing him."

"I saw what you saw," Mind replied. "But the people are quick to fear. Their king has been taken, and now they see the Hauntress standing over a king from an ally kingdom. The rumors are already spreading."

"But she is their protector," Fire all but snarled.

"As are we," Mind said, his voice the darkest Fire had ever heard. "But they will fear us as well. Those that know of our identity have long thought we were dangerous. This will confirm what we are."

"You never told me that."

"We are the ones with power," Mind said. "And the people always fear those with power."

Fire wrestled with his anger all the way to the docks. The streets were rapidly thinning, the people fleeing to the interior of their homes.

The clouds had darkened to midnight, lightning crackling in the darkness.

"More guards are coming," Mind said. "We need a ship, and stop thinking about the brand on Aradig. You can't hunt him now."

Fire turned away from the pulsing brand. He could feel the brand calling to him, like a flicker of light in the distance, but they needed an escape first. Mind stumbled to stay with Fire, who reached out, helping him stay upright. Together, they made their way to the waterfront district and Fire turned towards a ship.

"Not that one," Mind said.

"I thought you said we need to hurry."

"Not that one," Mind insisted.

"Why not?"

"We're going to need something fast."

Mind's face tightened in pain and Fire did as he requested. Other sailors and dockhands cast them strange looks, and blood dripped down Mind's cloak. Mind pointed to them and their gaze turned upward. Then they rushed to lash crates and move perishable goods out of the street.

"That one," Mind said.

Fire veered towards the ship, an empty vessel bobbing near the north of the waterfront district. The captain stood on the nearby dock, peeling an apple with a knife as he watched the storm. Fire pulled Mind to a halt.

"How much for the ship?"

The man regarded them with an unblinking expression. "Buy or rent?" he finally said.

"Buy," Mind said.

"Four hundred gold."

"That's absurd," Fire said. "I could buy two ships with that."

"It's enough to buy my silence when the guard comes asking about you."

"Done," Mind said, and mentally added for Fire's benefit, *Coin we have. Time we don't.*

Fire would have preferred to intimidate the man, but instead he helped Mind onto the deck and pulled out a writ from the moneychangers. Scribbling a note, he passed it to the man, who examined it like it could be false. Seemingly satisfied, he pointed to the deck.

"You're well stocked, but I wouldn't go sailing in this gale. It's likely to—"

"I thought we bought your silence," Fire snapped.

The man shrugged and walked away, still peeling his apple. Mind groaned as Fire helped him aboard and placed him against the steps leading below. Fire checked his wounds but Mind scowled and pointed to the city.

"Elenyr is coming. Get the ship ready to sail."

Fire leapt away and undid the sail. In moments it filled with wind, straining against the ropes that bound it to the dock. He yanked it free, undoing the knot, and the ship leapt into the sea. They passed other ships sliding into port, their sailors shouting in warning. Fire ignored them and glanced back to shore.

Elenyr burst from a warehouse, passing right through the wall before racing onto the water. Still ethereal, she streaked across the sea like a vengeful wraith, eliciting cries of fear from sailors and shouts from the guards. Then Elenyr reached their ship and entered through the hull, rising to join Fire.

"How many did you kill?" Fire asked.

"They aren't our foe," Elenyr said.

"Perhaps they should be," Fire muttered.

"Take us north," she said. "We'll find an inlet to weather the storm. Then we travel to the Stormdial."

The clouds cracked open and rain poured upon them, sluicing off the deck and pouring off Fire's shoulders. He shook himself, steam rising from the water as it burned away, his innate magic repelling the liquid, but leaving him miserable.

"I'm going to check on Mind," Elenyr said. "You have the ship?"

Fire grunted in agreement and sailed north, hugging the coast as close as he dared. Storm swells lifted their hull and brought them crashing into troughs, and Fire gripped the helm so tightly the wood blackened. Ten minutes felt like a lifetime before he spotted a sheltered inlet and banked them towards it. The swells faded as they passed inside, the nearby hills partially blocking the wind. Then he dropped anchor and ducked inside, grateful for the heat coming from the interior cabin. At least Mind had started a fire. As rain battered the deck and the ship pulled against the anchor, Fire stepped into the galley to find Elenyr and Mind sitting at the tiny table.

"How much did you see of King Numen?" Elenyr asked.

"How do you know I saw anything?" Mind challenged.

She offered a weary smile. "Why do children never think their parents notice?"

He snorted and looked away, his simmering anger burning on his face. "They don't deserve us."

"They never did," Fire said, brushing water onto both of them and eliciting a round of protests.

"I know how you feel," she said. "And it's not the first time I wanted to abandon the people."

Fire looked to Elenyr in surprise, and found her expression hard. It wasn't exactly anger, but the expression made it clear she felt betrayed. Fire leaned back in his seat and folded his arms, surprised to see the normally serene woman so disturbed.

Elenyr sighed and passed a hand over her face like the motion would ward off their foes. "I became ageless because I wanted to be free," she said. "I'd grown tired of the constraints on being an oracle and wished to choose my own fate. Then the mage wars began and the opportunity came. Yet I was unprepared for the life it would bring."

Her eyes and voice were distant as she spoke, and Fire realized she was revealing an aspect to her identity that she'd always kept hidden from the fragments. She'd always been their infallible protector, their parent and friend. But now she spoke as if they were equals.

"For a long while I lived the life I had thought," she said. "We went where we pleased, fought who deserved fighting. But over time . . ." Her features darkened. "Everyone I knew began to die, their children knowing only tales of me. Then they perished and their children spoke of me as if I were a myth. Even Senia looks at me as though I'm a relic from an age forgotten. I did not anticipate the sense of solitude."

"Griffin probably has a bounty on us by now," Mind said. "You won't feel alone when you are hunted."

Fire grunted in annoyance. After all the work they'd done for the kingdoms, they would now find themselves the ones being hunted— because the thrones had become corrupted. He wondered if Soreena would like a man with a bounty on his head.

"The people don't deserve us," Mind said. He hesitated, and then added. "And I'm tired of doing what we do."

Fire rounded on him in shock, but Elenyr surprised Fire by laughing. The sad sound filled the galley before she shook her head and swept a hand south.

"What else would we do?" she asked. "We are fighters, and fighters need a foe."

"I can't exactly cook," Fire agreed.

"This is a time of turmoil," she said. "Not just for the people of Lumineia, but us as well. I suspect that when this conflict ends, each of us will be forced to find a new place to stand."

248

She stood to leave, but Mind called her back. "Do you know what you want?"

Elenyr paused with her hand on the door before turning back. "I may not know the foe, but I want to fight beside my family."

Fire grunted and pointed south, towards the oracle's refuge. "I'm sure Senia is available."

She stabbed a finger at him. "You may think I saved the five of you by taking responsibility for your lives, but you kept me from solitude. You are my family, and I hope that whatever happens at the end of this, we remain so." She turned and left, the door clattering shut.

"I've never seen her like that," Fire said.

Mind leaned in. "She knows about Senia's vision."

"What?" Fire straightened in his seat and banged his head on a beam. He rubbed the spot. "How? And how do you know?"

"It appears I was unsuccessful in erasing Senia's memory," Mind said. "And when she was fighting Numen, she let her guard down. I caught a glimpse of Senia's vision in her thoughts. Elenyr wonders if we will stand by her."

"Blasted oracle vision," Fire muttered.

Mind rose and stepped to the door. "We need to focus on the Stormdial. Then we can deal with Elenyr."

"What does that mean?"

"I don't know," Mind said.

He pulled the door open and left. Alone, Fire remained in his seat, rocking with the rise and fall of the boat. At first he'd wondered why she would hope they would fight together, but the more he considered, the more he realized that Elenyr was giving them a choice.

Until now the fragments had stood with Elenyr out of need. Without her aid, they would have destroyed each other ages ago. Now they were demonstrating their ability to stand for themselves, to be on their own. When Elenyr said she hoped they would continue to fight together, she was admitting there was a chance they might not. She was acknowledging that they were no longer the young charges she'd agreed to train. But what would they be without Elenyr?

Chapter 32: The Devil's Maw

Water sat at the back of the boat, watching his companions. When the message had arrived from Fire, in the form of a tiger bounding into his bedroom, Water had gathered the others. He and Lira, along with Shadow and Light, had departed north. Jeric had joined them at the last moment, but his usual humor was subdued, and he kept to himself. Just as they were attempting to find a Talinorian vessel, two additional passengers had shown up with their own ship—Sentara and Rune.

"You sure you didn't invite them?" Water asked Light.

"Huh?" Light asked. He was watching the clouds.

"Never mind," Water said, and glanced to Shadow, who winked at him.

"We both know it was me," Shadow said.

"Why?" Water asked. "Why did you invite them?"

Shadow shrugged. "They had told me they wanted to see Elenyr the next time I would meet her. Sentara seemed rather angry with Elenyr."

"So you *brought* her?"

Shadow grinned. "I was curious."

"Your sense of mischief is going to cause conflict," Water said.

Shadow's smile widened. "I know."

Water's eyes settled on Sentara. The woman was just as much an enigma as Shadow had said, with Rune only a little easier to understand. The old woman insisted on managing the helm, while the young woman expertly worked the sails. Across from them, Shadow lounged on the railing, calling encouragement. Lira stood by Water, eyeing the strange group.

251

"Did we have to bring everyone?"

"Fire's message said it was urgent," Water said.

Light abruptly leapt into the sky, and soared in the sunlight, passing Jeric, who sat in the crow's nest, where he'd spent most of the voyage. Water disliked his behavior and wondered what had occurred between him and Elenyr.

Water frowned, his eyes again on Sentara, wondering if she could be a member of the Order. It was an unlikely gambit by the Order or Wylyn, but Serak had no qualms about using spies. Still, how much harm could she even do? There was no way she could best three fragments, an Eternal, and Jeric. Then he recalled something else Shadow had said, and stepped to his side.

"What did you mean when you said Sentara was formidable?"

Shadow was abruptly very interested in Light, his silence only heightening Water's concern—concern that increased when he recalled where they'd gotten the ship. Sentara had insisted they use her private vessel. Water had expected a fishing vessel, but it was a full Azure warship.

In the ensuing days he watched the new companions, still confused by their presence. Shadow had insisted his assassin friend knew Sentara and Rune, but Water didn't trust them, not yet. Sentara spoke little, and often to a pouch at her side.

They sailed north for several days, watching a great storm in the east. It had likely hit Terros hard, and Water hoped it had slowed the Order's effort to reach the Stormdial. He spent most of the voyage keeping Light from destroying their ship by accident, and the rest of the time he talked to Lira. The tension mounted the closer they came to the Azure islands, and Water wrestled with a sense of ending, as if the last few months were building to this, a final confrontation with Wylyn.

A week after leaving Herosian, their ship rose and fell, crashing through waves as it worked its way east. They'd passed a hundred islands of various sizes, but Sentara kept her distance from all of them. Then suddenly her sailing turned erratic.

252

She turned east, then north, then south, then east again. Shortly afterward she went north, and then back west. Unable to take it any longer, Water strode to the helm where Sentara stood, blissfully spinning the wheel.

"Where are we going?" he demanded.

"Where the waves fear to break."

"That's just a legend."

"Is it?" she asked.

"What's she talking about?" Lira asked, joining them.

Jeric, who was fishing over the rail, answered first. "It's an old Azure tale," he said. "The islanders speak of a place on the lake where waves never rise or fall, even in the greatest of storms."

"It's called the Devil's Maw," Rune said. She was sitting on a crossbeam of the mast, whittling a piece of wood.

"I've heard tales of such a place," Water said. "What does it have to with the Shard of Midnight?"

"The Devil's Maw is where the Shard of Midnight once stood."

All eyes turned to Jeric.

"And you know this *how?*" Water asked.

Jeric dodged the question. "I admit I never thought it would be found—or raised."

"So it *can* be raised?" Water asked.

"It can," Jeric said.

"Just how long have you known the location?" Shadow asked.

"Does it matter?"

"We spent weeks reading archives," Shadow said, and his tone turned disgusted. "I actually read a *book*."

"—part of one," Light interjected.

"I hoped Wylyn would be dealt with before it became an issue," Jeric said.

Before Water could demand more answers, Jeric strode away, his shoulders hunched. Water folded his arms in confusion, and then noticed Light mimicking his features and stance. His brother noticed his expression and flashed an apologetic look before moving to copy Shadow.

"But how do *you* know where to go?" Lira asked, turning to Sentara at the helm.

She regarded Jeric with a curious expression. "Jeric gave me a map."

Sentara withdrew a map and tossed it to Water. When he unrolled it, he saw it was a map of the Azure islands, only the map was different than maps Water had seen. The islands he knew were present, but so too where other islands, thousands of them.

"What is this?" he asked.

"Jeric said it was a map of the islands," Sentara said. "Those above . . . and those beneath."

Water bent to examine the old map, surprised by its clarity. Many of the islands he'd visited before, but the ones close to the center of the lake were sharp and tiny, almost resembling teeth, all pointing inward. Then Sentara banked again and Water stepped to the railing, looking into the depths. With his magic he saw what lay beneath the surface.

Rising from the deep, a great needle of stone extended, its peak scratching the surface. Then he spotted, another, and another, each capable of sinking their ship. Sentara was navigating the teeth of the Devil's Maw.

"The Azure fear the area in the center of their islands," Rune said. "And only a handful have mapped the extent of the teeth." Her gaze never left Jeric, suspicion in her eyes. "Fewer still have seen the center, the place where waves fear to break."

254

Water returned his attention to the map, examining the Devil's Maw in a new light. The needlelike islands pointed inward, to a circle of open water. The islands from the Devil's Maw seemed too exact to be natural, all placed as if by intent . . .

"It's a pattern," he breathed.

"The islands were not born of earth," Sentara said. "They were *created.*"

"How could we not know this?" Shadow asked, looking to Water. "And how does *he* know it?" he jerked a thumb at Jeric.

"Most of the islands of the Devil's Maw are beneath the surface," Rune said as they sailed past a needle of stone rising from the sea.

"Still," Water said. "We've lived for long enough that we should have known."

Sentara laughed, her tone filled with scorn. "Those as old as you always think they know all. For all you know, I could be older than you."

"Not likely," Shadow said.

Lira took the map from him. She examined it before turning it one way and then the other. "I do not see a Stormdial."

"Can someone please stop talking in riddles?" Shadow complained. "What *is* a Stormdial."

"Every krey world has a Stormdial," Lira said. "It's a massive tower that controls the precipitation."

"The *weather?*" Water asked. He couldn't imagine such power.

Lira nodded. "Water is life, and the Stormdial controls its flow. It's always built in a large lake, and because it draws so much water, it tends to create islands around its epicenter." She pointed to the larger islands, all curved around the Devil's Maw. "I've never seen one create islands like these, though."

"Our ancestors called it the Shard of Midnight," Water said.

Light grew bored of copying Shadow. "Why does any of this matter to us?"

Jeric leaned over the railing and pointed. "We're almost there."

Shadow joined him, offering the same languid pose. "I just hope there's someone to fight."

"There will be," Sentara said confidently.

"What are you even doing here?" Water asked.

"I must ensure Elenyr survives," Sentara said.

Lira, who'd kept her distance from the woman since their departure, frowned. "You keep more secrets than a thief."

"My secrets are mine, *Eternal*."

The sudden hatred in her voice was evident, and Lira looked to Water helplessly. Water turned to Sentara, intent on demanding the truth, but abruptly she spun the helm and pointed ahead, her eyes bright with excitement.

"We are here!"

The ship passed the last of the teeth and entered the center of the Devil's Maw. The wind continued to blow, but the sea abruptly went still, the waves dying until the water resembled smooth glass. Water leaned over the edge and watched their warship's reflection pass across the smooth surface, sending ripples that died close to the hull, the water returning to glass.

The circular Maw was gigantic. Waves from the dying storm lapped at the edges but nary a ripple breached the center. He peered into the depths and saw nothing in the depths. Apparently the teeth islands were only around the outside of the Maw.

The other fragments lined the rail, with Shadow flitting from one side to the other so he could watch the ripples caused by the rocking ship. Rune had fallen silent and gazed on the still water, her brown eyes filled with wonder. Water simply stared, the supreme tranquility affecting him deeply.

"I can *feel* the stillness," he said.

Water had never felt such peace. The water of lakes and streams was always in motion, always moving or changing form, and he'd grown used to feeling the constant ebb and flow. But here the water was still, brought to a halt by the teeth of the Dragon's Maw.

"We're slowing down," Sentara called. "There's not enough wind."

Water made his way to the rear of the ship and added a charm at the base of the hull, a touch of propulsion so their ship continued forward. Sentara turned the helm, angling them for the center of the Maw.

"This place is beautiful," Light said, watching his reflection.

"It's disturbing," Lira corrected. "Where's the tower?"

Water frowned and squinted, attempting to pierce the depths with his vision. He failed to see anything solid beneath the surface. It was as if the tower had been removed, leaving only the teeth pointed at its absence.

"Perhaps it was destroyed," Shadow said.

"How?" Water asked.

Shadow shrugged. "The Dawn of Magic saw a great war. Perhaps someone like us destroyed the tower."

"It would be very difficult to do," Lira said. "Stormdials are built to withstand the mightiest of weapons."

"But not magic," Sentara said.

"Perhaps," Lira's expression was doubtful.

Sentara ignored her and turned to Water. "It *could* have been destroyed by magic, but I suspect if the Order seeks its rise, then the Stormdial may yet live."

"But there's nothing there," Water said, pointing downward. "And if a tower hid beneath the surface, I would be able to see it."

"One with eyes does not always see," Jeric said cryptically.

257

Sentara then cocked her head to the side as if listening. Frowning, she reached into a pouch and withdrew a small orb. Staring at it, she began to nod as if she were listening to another speak. Abruptly a frown creased her features.

"You always think impulsively."

She fell into a heated argument, oblivious to the fragments and Jeric staring at her. Rune scowled. "Don't stare," she said. "It's not polite."

"Is she okay?" Light asked, his tone uncertain. Then he noticed a reflection in the still water and leapt over the railing with a laugh.

"She'll be fine," Rune said.

"How intriguing," Jeric said.

Rune's expression darkened. "We got you here. The question is, what do we do now?"

"I guess we wait," Water said. "If we're right, Wylyn will come."

"And if we're wrong?" Lira asked.

"Then we spend a few days with someone who's lost their mind," Shadow said, jerking a thumb at Sentara.

The older woman laughed, the peeling sound echoing over the still waters. "She likes you," she said to Shadow. "You don't mince words like everyone else."

Sentara glared at Lira, who raised her hands in defense. "What did I do?"

"What didn't you do?" Sentara said. Then she looked skyward. "The storm's picking up. We'll be safe here."

Abandoning the helm, she ordered Rune to fasten the sails and then disappeared below decks. Confused, Water looked to the sky and saw she was indeed correct, and the storm was gathering strength.

Lighting burst across the sky and the clouds turned a dark black. As the light of day gave way to the storm, Light yawned and retreated into the hold. Rune took a stand at the helm, but her caution proved unnecessary.

The rain mounted, the wind howled, but none of it pierced the Maw. A scattering of droplets fell, turning to a fine mist that floated across their ship, and the falling rain revealed what lay hidden.

Water's voice was filled with shock. "Is that . . ."

"I think it is," Lira said.

Above them, the rain and wind passed around a column of air. Even the lightning arced around it, as if the storm itself feared to enter. The barrier rose from the edges of the still water, rising so far into the sky it seemed to cut the clouds, the unmistakable shape drawing a gasp from Rune.

Water stared upward, unable to take his eyes from the sight of rain sluicing away from an invisible barrier. They'd passed through it, so Water knew there was nothing solid, and yet the rain and wind refused to pass. The Stormdial may have been absent, but a piece of its power remained, and the very storm avoided where the tower had once stood.

Chapter 33: Into the Storm

Fire hated the rain. The wet, the cold, the wind, he loathed it all. After the storm lessened Elenyr had taken the helm and guided them out of the inlet, and Fire was forced to help with the sails. He wanted to burn the entire ship, char it to ash, but that would just leave him underwater, the only thing he hated more than the rain.

"Watch the line!" Elenyr shouted.

With Mind still recovering below decks, it fell to Fire to catch the loose line and tie it back in place. Then he trudged through the water running off the deck to another line, holding it tight as he lashed it to the wood. He yanked on the rope as if doing so would dispel the chill that had seeped into his bones.

At least Water was not present. Whenever it rained, he danced about like a child, excited to feel the water on his cheeks and hands, relishing the surge of power. Such a child. But beneath the irritation came a burst of regret, and he realized he missed his little brother.

The ship dropped into a shallow trough and then rose again, the prow piercing a wave. The water splattered across him and he cursed, wiping his face with his sodden hand. Then he strode to Elenyr.

"How long do we have to be in this?"

"Until we reach the Devil's Maw." She had to raise her voice to be heard in the storm. She glanced his way and her expression turned apologetic. "I wish we could wait, but we need to reach the tower before Wylyn."

"What makes you think they aren't already there?"

She swept her hand at the tumultuous sea. "The storm will slow them down, and we left before they did."

"Is Serak really King Numen's master?" He rubbed his hands and breathed fire into his palms, relishing the fleeting heat. "Or is he loyal to Wylyn?"

"He had no reason to lie," Elenyr said. "So I suspect he obeys Serak. However, I believe he will remain with Wylyn until she either builds her Gate or is killed. He has not yet finished his task."

"Of killing you."

She did not answer and he disliked the darkness to her expression. Even in the most dire of conflicts, she'd never lost her faith in those she served. Yet now her eyes looked much like the storm.

"Why would a king serve Serak?" He finally asked the question that had haunted him since leaving Terros.

"He fears us," Elenyr said. "He fears our power."

"But why?"

"Because our power threatens his," Elenyr said. "You must understand that for the nobles and kings, sometimes power is not enough. They become frustrated with those that disagree with them. That frustration boils into arrogance and ambition, and then action. Usually they turn into tyrants."

Fire caught the railing as the storm lifted the ship again, wondering about the change in Elenyr. She spoke as if she'd already endured such betrayal, and it had left a scar. It was a reminder of the betrayal she'd suffered during the Age of Oracles.

The boat rose through another wave, the lift permitting a glimpse of the horizon, where distant sunlight marked the end of the storm. Fire's relief was palpable, but Elenyr remained stoic, her gaze fixed on the waters ahead.

"I wager most of the people do not understand this war with Serak," he said. "They still need us to protect them. Do not forget that the Order represents just a fraction of the people."

Elenyr was silent for long enough that Fire shifted his feet, wondering what to say. Then she hit the helm with a fist, the anger startling Fire, who'd never witnessed such an outburst from the former oracle.

"I should have seen it coming," she said, her voice hard.

"You're not an oracle anymore," he said.

"You don't understand," Elenyr said. "I was betrayed before—by those I called family. Since that day I've watched every kingdom, intent on bringing every corruption to light. Yet still the Order rose to power, converting the very people I thought I could trust. It makes me doubt everyone."

"Us?" Fire asked, stung.

"No," she said, her eyes softening as she glanced to him. "I would trust the fragments with my life."

"Even after Senia's vision?" he asked softly.

Her response was quick. "Even then."

He looked out to sea, unable to meet her gaze. It was the first time she'd confirmed her knowledge of Senia's vision, and Fire hated the feeling of shame. He hadn't even done anything, but he felt guilt that he could.

"Mind didn't want you to see that vision."

"It's better that I know," Elenyr said. "It means I can help."

"So you don't blame us."

Elenyr reached up and put her hand on Fire's cheek. "I will always have faith in my sons."

He shook his head. "But you saw what we could become."

"I saw what *Draeken* could become." she spun the helm, turning them into a wave.

"Am I not him?"

"Of course not," she said. "You are your own, and I'm proud of who you are becoming—vision or no vision."

"I almost destroyed the King's Library," he reminded her.

She laughed, the sound brighter than her previous despair. "True," she allowed. "But you also saved my life in the king's castle."

"I didn't like seeing you like that," Fire said.

He recalled seeing her helpless and anger touched his voice, sparking flames across his fingers. Seeing Elenyr trapped by lightning had been terrifying, all the more visceral after Serak's latest attempt on her life.

"Everyone can be harmed," she said. "And all magics have a weakness."

"He is still dangerous," Fire said. "Especially now that you know his identity. Wylyn will likely bring him to the Stormdial. He may be a king, but he is their best weapon against you."

"I will be more prepared the next time we fight," she said.

"As will I," he replied.

Fire tightened his jaw and imagined King Numen standing within reach. If Fire encountered him in battle, he wouldn't hesitate, and the king of lightning would see how dangerous the lord of fire could be.

Mind appeared in the doorway and worked his way across the moving deck. When he reached the helm he grasped the railing, wincing as it stretched the bandage on his shoulder. Elenyr noticed the expression and frowned.

"You should be below," she said.

"I've been down there for days," he said. "And I'm almost whole."

Fire held his hand up to touch the falling rain. "I hope you're thirsty."

Mind pointed northwest. "How close are we to the Devil's Maw?"

"We passed through the outer ring of islands earlier this morning," she said. "Are you up to guiding the ship?"

Mind nodded and she relinquished the helm to him. Then she advanced across the ship to the prow. The storm gradually lessened, the rain slackening off like a horse fatigued from a run. The wind still blew, but it lacked the punch of previous days.

"I'll watch out the port side," Elenyr said. "You keep on eye to starboard."

Fire grasped the railing at the head of the ship as Elenyr advanced to the prow and stood next to the railing. Standing at the end, she clung to the sail line and gazed into the water. Sailors across the lake avoided the teeth, with many claiming that to reach their center would cause their ship to be swallowed by the sea.

He'd heard the rumors about the Devil's Maw but had never seen it with his own eyes. He leaned against the rail and squinted, attempting to spot the teeth before they pierced their hull. Then the sea dropped into a trough, revealing a shard of stone pointed upward.

"Bank to starboard!" Elenyr shouted.

The boat groaned as the wood turned, narrowly missing the spike of stone as the sea lifted the ship upward. A moment later another appeared, and then another. The motion of the sea revealed more of the Maw's teeth, one so close the hull bounced off its surface before the sea carried them away. Abruptly he realized exactly why the sailors feared it. If the ocean dropped them on top of a tooth . . .

He imagined the stone piercing the ship like a blade, trapping them in the midst of the Devil's Maw until the ship broke apart, plunging him into the wretched water. Fire gripped the wood until small flames curled upward, and the wood darkened from the searing heat.

"Bank north!" he shouted.

The teeth grew denser the further they passed into the Devil's Maw, and it took all of their skill to avoid being shattered on a spike of stone. Teeth rose and fell, their black material reflecting the dim light, their points appearing and disappearing as the waves rose and fell.

"I wish Water was here," Fire called.

Elenyr didn't take her gaze from the water. "Me too!"

"Where do you think they are?"

"Shadow should have told them were we're going," she called back. "It won't be long—port side! Bank south!"

The waves had hidden the toothlike island, and as the ship dropped into a trough it sliced upward, cutting across the side of their hull. Fire clung to the railing as the ship bounced away. He grimaced when he saw cracks in the wood.

"We're taking water!" he shouted.

"We're nearly there!" Elenyr shouted back.

Then suddenly the ship passed an invisible line and the waves died, the rain falling away like a curtain. The seas turned to glass and Fire's eyes widened, shocked to see the power of the sea brought to heel.

"We're through!"

Fire wiped rainwater from his face and then burned heat through his clothes, causing steam to rise from his body. He breathed a sigh of relief when the moisture faded, leaving him relatively dry. Then he looked upward—and his jaw fell open.

The rain had not stopped. It had turned aside as an invisible force barred the rain entry. In smooth lines, the invisible barrier rose into a four-sided obelisk that pierced the clouds, seeming to rise forever.

"Where are we?" Mind asked, joining them as Elenyr dropped on the deck. "This thing must be a mile across."

"It must be where the Stormdial stood," Elenyr said.

Fire looked over the edge to watch his reflection in the remarkably still water, but the mirror prevented him from seeing beneath the surface. "Can Wylyn really raise the tower?"

"She thinks she can," Elenyr said.

Fire craned his neck to examine the break in the hull. "I doubt we can take much more damage."

"Then let us hope Water and the others arrive first," she said.

"Then we are in luck," Mind said, pointing west.

Fire spotted another vessel floating near the heart of the Devil's Maw. Several individuals were aboard, but Light's excitement was unmistakable. Fire grinned, and felt a profound sense of relief at seeing the other fragments.

A distant crash echoed from the south, drawing all eyes in that direction. Through the storm wall a ship appeared and careened into the Maw, listing to the side from a recent impact. Then another vessel appeared, and a third. Then others appeared.

Huge dakorians lined the rails, and robed Order members worked the sails. One of the ships was dwarven, indicating it had come from the west, while the other two were of Azure make, their markings revealing they'd been owned by Griffin. There was no mistaking the krey woman standing at the head.

"At least we arrived before they did," Mind said dryly.

"Our prey has come to the trap," Fire said, excited at the prospect of a fight. "Let's make it their grave."

Chapter 34: Friends and Foes

After two days of waiting, Water was about ready to strangle Shadow and Light, both of whom had grown bored within an hour in the Devil's Maw. Then a ship had come through the storm and Lira called a warning from the prow.

"Someone's here!"

"That looks like Elenyr," Light exclaimed, pointing to the new ship.

Sentara scowled and pointed south. "She's not alone."

Water turned and spotted Wylyn's fleet entering the Devil's Maw. The battle he'd wanted had come and he yearned to close the gap, to bring justice to Wylyn. At his side, Light bounced on his feet.

"Don't get too excited," Water said. "We're outnumbered."

"This is going to be *epic*," Light breathed.

Water smiled and called to Sentara at the helm, but the woman was banking the ship away from the new arrivals, aiming to connect with Elenyr. Water glanced to the woman, still uncertain of her source of hatred toward the Eternals. The old woman's gaze was fixed upon Elenyr, who stood on the prow of her own ship.

The two ships converged and Lira gauged the distance to Wylyn's forces. They would only have minutes before they were close enough to strike, and when that occurred the woman's tactic was obvious, overwhelm them by sheer force. Water guessed there to be several hundred Order members and all the remaining dakorians, including Wylyn and Tardoq. His eyes narrowed when he spotted the dark glint of anti-magic weaponry.

Sentara banked them to the side, gliding them close to Elenyr's vessel, and abruptly Sentara sprinted to the railing and leapt the gap.

Drawing her sword, she glided up the prow and put her weapon on Elenyr's throat, her words a snarl that no one else could hear. Water's eyes widened when he spotted the crackle of power on the blade. Lightning magic.

"Elenyr!" Water shouted and converged on her.

Lira cast a trio of air stones and darted across the gap, landing on the deck. By the time she reached the pair Elenyr had not moved, or even gone ethereal. Elenyr looked to Sentara with sadness in her eyes.

"I cannot promise I will succeed," she said. "But I promise I will try."

Sentara held her at the tip of her blade, her eyes boring into Elenyr's. Then abruptly she withdrew and sheathed her sword. Ignoring the fragments gathering power around her, she swept a hand to Elenyr.

"I will hold you to your oath," Sentara said.

"Why did you bring her?" Fire demanded.

Water pointed to Shadow, who grinned. "I told you this would be exciting."

"Whatever your conflict, it needs to be resolved. We don't have much time," Lira said, leaning over the railing to survey the approaching warships.

"I'd like to know who she is," Mind said, his expression dark as he pointed to Sentara.

Sentara glared at him. "I was the one Elenyr and the Eternals destroyed."

"This is an old friend," Elenyr said, causing her to bristle at the term. "She will be assisting us in the battle."

"Do you happen to have any dwarven fire ale?" Light asked, craning his head to look towards the galley. When everyone stared he shrugged. "Never mind. I'll go check for myself." He flitted below.

"She's not going to do much good," Fire murmured to Water. "She looks ancient."

"She's more formidable than she looks," Shadow said, hopping into the rigging and climbing upward.

Water frowned. Sentara clearly had a history with Elenyr, and he didn't care for the tension when battling Wylyn. Elenyr stepped into the center of the ship and swept her hand to the gathering.

"We have little time to waste, and it will require all of us if we are to be victorious . . ." She spotted Jeric and her voice faltered.

"You didn't think I'd miss this." Jeric hopped the railing to Elenyr's ship.

"Jeric," she said evenly. "I thought you'd stay in Herosian."

Water raised an eyebrow at her tone. Irritation and doubt were mixed into her voice, and the elf came to a halt. Elenyr regarded him for several moments and then her eyes flicked south, where the fleet had finished entering the Maw and begun to advance. Water looked between Jeric and Elenyr, wondering what had caused the gulf.

"Are we going to just let them hit us?" Rune called, her tone annoyed as she motioned to the approaching fleet.

"She's right," Lira said. "We need to act fast. We only have two ships and they have nine."

"We have three," Water corrected.

Lira raised an eyebrow but Elenyr was nodding. "Sentara, you and I will take the east and west. Since Water will have the strongest ship, he can handle the center."

"Strongest ship?" Lira asked, glancing to him.

Water smiled as he retreated to the railing. "You'll see soon enough."

Water stepped to the railing and leapt off. He landed in the sea and conjured his favorite ship, the water flowing up around him, hardening into sleek aquaglass. Lira leaned over the railing—her eyes widening.

Water's ship resembled a curved dagger, the hull hardening into a wicked ram, sharp enough to slice even the beams of a ship. The stern of the ship was equally as thin, with room for only a single passenger at the center. Two arms extended away from the narrow vessel, connecting to two more hulls. These resembled swords, their front pointed and pulsing with magic. Smiling in anticipation, he banked his Waverider and aimed for the nearest ship.

***

Fire smirked as he watched Water conjure his ship. Water wasn't usually one for destruction, preferring a clean victory, but his ship was one that Fire envied. He loved what it could do. He noticed Lira gazing in wonder and pointed to Water's ship.

"A ship is a ship." He joined her on the rail. "But his Waverider is a weapon."

The still water churned in the Waverider's wake as it sped toward the fleet. Then the sound of cracking glass echoed across the Devil's Maw, and the right blade detached from the Waverider. It accelerated forward, speeding so fast it seemed to fly, and struck the side of the lead vessel, the blade cutting into the hull like a knife into a roast turkey. Distant shouts rang out as the sailors rushed to stem the water seeping into the gash.

"Impressive," Lira said.

"Let's get moving," Elenyr said. "Lira, you're with us."

She called orders and the group parted. Sentara and Rune returned to the warship and the old woman caught the helm. Light and Shadow followed. Fire frowned when Elenyr ordered Jeric to return to Sentara's ship, and did not give a reason. Jeric accepted Elenyr's direction, but his features were tinged with regret. Light cast three ballistae on the deck of Sentara's warship, the trio of weapons aiming for Wylyn's armada.

Fire conjured his own weapon, a long tube that extended over the railing. The flames hardened and he cast a detonation charm in his hand, the sphere pulsing with power. With a smirk of anticipation, he socketed the ball into the end of the tube and caught the handles at the end of the tube. Then he eyed the distance and aimed for the nearest ship. When he fired, the entire ship rocked, and the detonation charm exploded from the tube. It leapt across the gap and struck the prow of an Order ship where it detonated in a burst of shattered wood and smoke. When it cleared, the entire upper prow was gone, like a nose absent from a face.

Fire noticed Lira and smiled. "The best part of being a fragment is the toys."

"Lira!" Elenyr called. "When we pass them, get onboard and do some damage! We'll pick you up on the opposite side!"

Lira nodded and drew her sword. Elenyr used the smoke to hide their approach and banked them alongside the vessel. The billowing smoke parted and the Order members noticed their proximity. They scrambled for weapons as Fire sent another detonating sphere into the mast.

The fireball exploded against the wood, shattering it and leaving a swath of scattered flames across the deck. With a groan, the mast teetered and then toppled toward the stern, causing men and women to shout and dive away, the great beam crushing the helm and cracking the deck, the sails and rigging becoming tangled in a mess of burning ropes.

Lira leapt the gap and alighted on the deck. She whirled through the burning rigging, sweeping her sword through the Order members still standing. They raised their weapons but Lira was too fast, and she streaked through their attacks, her blade plunging deep. Fire admired her skill. He'd always wondered what it would feel like to possess body magic.

Lira leapt the burning stump where the mast had once stood and alighted on the fallen beam, carving her way through the remainder of the Order soldiers, her blade flashing in the sunlight. She leapt to a rope and swung around a burning piece of sail before landing again on the fallen beam. The captain appeared and lunged, but Fire aimed and fired, the fireball striking the captain in the chest, blasting him into oblivion.

Lira sped by and raced up the fallen mast, reaching the end just as Elenyr finished coming around the Order ship.

Elenyr had kept their ship close, and it passed alongside the burning ship. Lira leapt from Order ship just as Elenyr spun the helm, bringing their ship under her. Lira alighted on the deck and rose to her feet.

"Well done," Fire said, nodding in approval.

"Get down!" Mind shouted.

Fire lunged, catching Lira about the waist and throwing her to the deck. She grunted from the impact—just as massive spinning blade passed above them. Emitting a shrieking whine, it ripped through ropes and railing, even carving a line through the deck before it passed beyond their ship.

Fire cursed and climbed to his feet, pulling his fireball launcher free of the railing. "Is that what I think it is?" He leapt to the opposite side and set it on the railing, scanning the armada for the war machine he hoped not to see.

"How did they get their hands on a Carver?" Mind called.

"I thought those were all destroyed," Elenyr said, spinning the helm to swing them closer to the fleet.

"What's a Carver?" Lira asked rising next to Fire.

"A dwarven weapon," Fire continued to scan the fleet. "They launch a spiked, circular blade that spins fast enough to slice through wood, stone, steel, pretty much anything."

Fire spotted a vessel with a strange contraption on the deck. It resembled Fire's own launcher, but it was all gears and levers. A blade was spinning inside, turning so fast it became a blur of metal. Then the dwarf behind the mechanism aimed and yanked a lever, sending the blade streaking for them, only this time it was aimed at the center of their ship. Fire bellowed a warning.

Elenyr yanked on the helm, the boat spinning to port and slamming Fire and Lira into the rail. The Carver missed the mast by inches but sliced through their ship, the blade spinning a line across the deck. The ship groaned as the wood began to part.

"We're not going to last long against a Carver," Fire growled, aiming at the weapon.

He fired, and the sphere leapt across the gap, but the dwarf stepped away from the contraption and pointed at the fireball. His own magic leapt from his palm, nudging the sphere upward, just enough to pass over him and splash into the sea, where it detonated across the still water.

"Get us closer," Lira called, flicking her sword.

"I'll try," Elenyr said.

She curved them toward the vessel as Order members loaded a new Carver blade. Barbs extended from a circle of steel, each tip like a wicked dagger. The operators pulled and the blade began to spin, emitting a dull whine as it became a blur.

The rest of the fleet was in shambles, with Light's ballistae raking the ships on the opposite side. In their midst, Water streaked around, too fast to hit, his own blades cutting deep into hulls. Several ships had already succumbed, their masts disappearing as they slipped into the still waters of the Devil's Maw.

"We're taking on too much water," Fire warned, rushing to load his own weapon.

Lira sprinted to the front of the deck and stood on the prow, Mind at her side. The Carver was aimed right at them, and when it fired, it would slice Elenyr's boat right down the center. Across the gap the dwarf smirked and reached for the lever that would end them.

"Lira!" Elenyr called. "Try to stop it in the air."

She banked to the side, but the dwarf tracked their movement. Lira charged the gap and jumped, casting air stones as she sprinted above the sea, skipping across stones she conjured beneath her feet.

The dwarf fired, the spinning blade emitting a shriek as it leapt from the launcher. Lira was just ten feet away and she clapped her hands together, casting a wall of air—but the weapon cut through the barrier like it was paper, knocking her into the ocean. She cried out as she fell, and the Carver hurtled straight at Mind. Fire dove to the deck, but Mind had not moved . . .

Chapter 35: Sunken

From his Waverider, Water watched the Carver blast through Lira's wall. It narrowly missed her legs and streaked for Mind. Water's gut clenched as the weapon meant to destroy armies flew toward his brother, the ten-foot blade more than a match for the guardian.

Elenyr screamed a warning and Fire dived free, but Mind remained in place and raised his hands—and abruptly the blade slowed, and came to a halt. In midair, it continued to whine, the blade whirling its deadly spin, just feet from Mind's outstretched fingers.

Water stared in shock, his Waverider drifting to a stop. Order members, fragments, and the dwarven engineer stared. Water's eyes flicked between the deadly Carver and Mind, who stood with purple light arcing across his arm, and then Water realized what he was doing. The fragment had sought to control gravity before, but it had always ended in disaster, yet here he was, wielding it against the Carver.

Mind's lips curled into a sneer and his eyes fell on the engineer that had fired the weapon. The dwarf cried out a warning and dived away, just as the Carver leapt forward, the spinning blade aimed at the ship that held the machine.

The captain spun the helm, desperately calling orders, but the Carver struck the ship broadside, slicing through the deck, cleaving the ship in two. With only the lower timbers holding it together, the ship groaned and parted like a loaf of bread cut by a cleaver. The dwarf bellowed his fury and ordered his assistants to load another Carver. But he was out of time, and Lira was already climbing aboard. Drenched from the sea, she scaled the hull and stood on the deck. Flicking her sword, she advanced on the dwarf.

Water watched in awe as she cut through the Order members. Dancing across the tilting surface of the sinking ship, she parried and cut, killing the Order soldiers that rushed her. Then she reached the dwarf. Instead of fleeing, the dwarf gathered fire in his palms and struck the deck, blasting the remaining ship in half.

"I'll take you down with me," the dwarf growled.

The dwarf picked up a nearby chain and used a burst of fire to send it wrapping around Lira's legs. She sought to leap free but a hole opened beneath the dwarf, and with a bellow he fell in, dragging Lira after.

She caught the edge of the cracked deck, her body hanging inside the sinking ship, the chain around her body. Water swung his Waverider toward the ship and accelerated. He dodged ships and arrows, his gaze fixed on Lira, his gut clenching as their eyes met.

"Water!" she shouted.

"I'm coming!"

The section of decking she held began to break—and snapped. Lira disappeared, dropped from sight in a crumble of broken decking and a burst of seawater. The crumbling ship continued to sink, and she did not reappear.

Water's heart thudded in his chest as he closed the gap. He fired both blades of his Waverider, sending the weapons into the sinking vessel. The water sliced through the hull on either side just as the Waverider blasted into the breach. At the last moment Water leapt off his watercraft, falling into the sea.

The Waverider shattered against the hull into sparks of magic and steam. Water summoned his magic and dove, propelling himself through the hole he'd created. Inside the belly of the underwater ship, Water spotted Lira tugging the chains around her legs, her hair waving in the current. Then the dwarf climbed the chain and reached for her throat.

As Water pushed through the debris, Lira turned on the dwarven engineer, breaking his hand. But the engineer lashed her ankle with chains and wrapped the chains around a hook in the hull. A burst of his magic melted the hook and chains together, the water bubbling as it boiled. Lira drove her sword into the engineer, and the dwarf died with a triumphant smile on his lips.

Water found a gap in the debris and surged through two beams, but another section of hull sank in front of him, forcing him up and over. Lira pulled on the chain but even her strength could not break it. Lira fought harder as the ship dragged her down, further from the light on the surface. He caught a glimpse of the fear on her face. Then he spun through the debris from the galley and reached her side.

He grasped the chain and pulled, but the hook was deep in the decking, and it would not budge. Their eyes met and he saw the strain on her face, the effort not to breathe. She shoved him away and pointed upward, a signal to leave her behind. He jerked his head and wrapped his arms around her, pulling her into a kiss.

Lira stiffened in surprise, but Water used the contact to cast a breathing charm, allowing air to flow through a barrier in her lips. She clung to him as he completed the charm, the barrier permitting air to flow directly from the water into her throat, the air forming a bubble around her lips. Then he released her and leaned away, but she did not let him.

Inside the underwater ship, with her legs chained to the base of the hull and debris all around, she kissed him back, the contact quickly growing ardent. His heart hammered, his mind buzzed. Then she parted and gazed into his eyes, her hair swaying in the water.

"I'm not used to being saved," she said, her words muffled through the charm.

"Neither am I," he said.

"Think you can help with . . ." she motioned to the chain.

"Right," he said hastily.

He forced himself to look away from her captivating eyes and cast a blade of water, using it to saw against the chain. The water pressure gradually built as they were dragged into the depths, until he'd finally cut enough that she used her strength to bend a link and release herself.

Then he propelled them to the enormous gash in the hull, taking them into open water.

She shuddered as she watched the hull sink beyond them. "I would have drowned without you."

"I'm a guardian of water," he reminded her. "I would never let that happen."

"And the kiss?" she asked, looking back to him. "Was that necessary to cast the charm?"

"It was the fastest way," he said, squirming.

"I like the fast way." She coiled her arms around his neck and kissed him again, a fleeting contact, a tease of more.

When they parted a shadow passed over them and he looked up. The conflict had spread across the Devil's Maw, with ships burning and broken. Wreckage floated and debris sank. Elenyr's ship was damaged and listing to the side while Sentara's warship burned. But the shadow had come from a smaller ship. Unnoticed, it had passed beyond the battle and reached the center of the still waters. Although the distance was far, Wylyn's features appeared over the railing as she reached out and dropped a small object into the water.

"We're too late," Lira breathed.

Water caught her and they surged towards the object, but the distance was great. Water followed it down, and saw the object pulsing with power. It sank faster than normal, as if it was being pulled from below.

"What is it?"

"A power crystal," she exclaimed. "And I think we're about to see the rise of the Stormdial."

The power crystal dropped into the depths, only the blinking of its power still visible. For several seconds they rushed deeper, until abruptly the light winked out, and a dull rumble echoed beneath the sea.

The result was instantaneous. A chilling *boom* followed, so loud it made Water and Lira wince. The next moment a force was sent out from the Devil's Maw, creating a wave so large it rocked the boats of friend and foe. Water expected it to die when it reached the needles of stone, but instead it continued, spreading outward into the dying storm . . .

And the teeth began to move.

Water's eyes widened as the great stone pillars groaned, the thousands of tiny pillars grinding forward as they answered the summoning. They moved inward, the still waters shrinking as they pressed against its exterior.

"What's happening?" Water asked.

"The teeth aren't pieces of the Stormdial," Lira said, her voice tinged with shock and fear.

"What do you mean?" he asked.

Then he saw it and his eyes widened. Under the water the islands were coming together, the stone closing against each other, water gushing away, the islands merging and joining, the direction uniform, as if they all belonged to a single entity.

"They're part of the tower," she said. "They're coming together."

Even as she spoke, the islands began to rise, the shards coming together, merging and climbing, building and converging on the center. The sharp points rose through a sea in turmoil, the still waters continuing to shrink. Water turned a slow circle, shocked to disbelief by the truth. The Devil's Maw didn't hide the Stormdial.

It *was* the Stormdial.

The pieces collided and machinery clanked, locking the shards together. Other sections were lifted up, revealing jet black material, the water cascading off the surface as it lifted higher and higher. Still the pieces moved closer, the great sections of the tower looming in the underwater view.

"If we don't move we're going to be crushed," he said.

279

He caught her about the waist and wrapped them in a thread of magic, propelling them through the water. It was evident the islands were merging into four giant segments, all moving in perfect synchronized motion. The four segments were already colossal, the needles climbing and converging, becoming mountains that would come together into a single, giant obelisk. Water raced them towards the surface, scanning the approaching pieces for a point of escape.

"Can we make it to the surface?" Lira asked, pointing upward.

He spared a look at the ships far above, but they had sunk deep into the sea. "We won't make it to the surface, not in time."

One tooth rose beneath an Order ship, the stone piercing the ship and lifting it into the sky. Men and women leapt free as the section of Stormdial merged with another, the machinery chewing the ship to kindling. Any caught were crushed.

Elenyr's ship was bounced off a needle rising at its side, and the occupants leapt to Sentara's warship before it too was lifted and crushed. Three other vessels remained, and for the moment the battle was forgotten. All rushed to reach the shrinking spot of safety at the center of the Maw.

"Look!" Lira cried.

Another pillar had appeared, rising from the deep. Its summit was flat except for several curving arches that resembled four claws of a hand. The Stormdial climbed towards the surface, approaching Wylyn's ship. Caught in the current, Water and Lira were cast aside as the pillar breached the surface and lifted Wylyn's small vessel skyward. The remaining ships converged on the sides of the central pillar.

With nowhere else to go, Water pulled Lira toward the pillar, the outer shards uncomfortably close and getting closer. Now just a few hundred feet away, the water was pushed upward, lifting the boats above driving them inward. When the two sides came together, Water and Lira would be crushed.

"Look out!" Lira cried.

Water flinched as a large protrusion pushed out from the center tower, swinging open like a door, only this door was the size of a castle's keep. It leaned outward, a matching recess appearing in the approaching tower section. It breached the surface and picked up a dakorian vessel, lifting it skyward, whereupon the passengers fled the ship and raced into the opening, disappearing into the tower.

"That's our only shot," Water said, pointing to the tower. "We need to catch one of those ledges."

"We'd better hurry," she said, eyeing the narrowing gap.

Sentara's ship caught another protrusion but it was an awkward position, and it teetered on the side. Elenyr and the others dived for the safety of the ledge as the ship tipped and fell into the roiling sea. With just a hundred feet left between the center tower and the outer sections, Water sped toward the tower, searching for a ledge. There were several of the giant openings, but all were too far to reach, and the outer sections of the tower were closing fast. The water compressed in the gap, rising upward to drain through gaps in the outer supports, the current chaotic, pulling them in every direction.

"There!" Lira cried.

He spotted a section opening beneath them and dived, propelling them deeper and deeper, the light going dim as outer sections continued to approach. Fifty feet became thirty, and then twenty, and then ten.

With all light extinguished Water shifted Lira to his side and forced them faster, shooting the gap as the great sections of the ancient structure came together. Lira cried out as the two sides closed within two feet, the walls so tight Water could feel the pressure.

They reached the protrusion and shot into the opening, and Water sped into the doorway at the back as the machinery closed with a titanic *boom*. Seawater sprayed all the way into the clouds as the last of the pieces locked into place, the Stormdial whole for the first time since the Dawn of Magic. A mile high, it stretched to the heavens, its shockingly steep walls glistening with water. The machinery finally went still, the last great gears locking into place. From deep within the risen tower, a great power awakened, ready to serve its master's bidding . . .

Chapter 36: The Cleansing

Rynda strained against the loose bar, willing the stone to break. Muscles and sinews tightened, until the rock gave way. Rynda yearned to wrench the bar free but the sound might draw the guards, or wake the other monarchs. The bar scrapped across the stone and she bared a savage smile. Sweat poured off her forehead, dripping onto the dirt, seeping into the cracks by the bar. After weeks of effort, the bar finally pulled free.

She held the bar as she trembled in victory, but she gave no voice to her triumph. Instead she placed the bar against the center of the next bar, using it to pry. This time she shoved, using the bars as leverage to force the bar to bend.

The iron bar gave a squeak of protest as it bent at the center, pulling inward, the end pulling up from the floor, cracking the already weakened stone. The bar pulled inward, bending, opening wider and wider.

Careful to not drop the bar in her haste to escape, Rynda withdrew the bar and stepped to the other side of the gap. Threading it through, she placed the bar on the right side of her escape route, and pulled her leverage bar, forcing the bar to bend outward. Inch by inch, the bar bent, opening wider and wider. Her leverage bar bent as well, but not before the opening was wide enough for her large frame.

She withdrew the bar and examined the breach. The bar on the right was bent outward while the bar on the left was bent inward. With the missing bar in the center, there was just enough space for her to slip through.

Casting a glance toward the empty common room of the prison, she noticed Queen Erisay's door, which remained shut. Since her duel with Tardoq, she'd spoken with the dark elf on several occasions, but Rynda disliked the growing attachment. Her best chance to escape would be alone, and let the other monarchs fend for themselves. Still, she hesitated.

Growling, she turned away from the prison and reached through the gap. With great care, she worked her head and shoulders through, bending at the waist in order to pass her upper body. She had to suck in her breath, and contort her shoulder and arm to gain the necessary space. Her armor caught, and her back scrapped across the bent bar, but she came free. Catching one of the other bars, she pulled her waist after, and then her legs. Her boots passed through and she straightened, free for the first time in weeks.

"You'll need a weapon."

She whirled, and found the dark elf queen with the bar in her hand. She extended it through the gap and Rynda took the makeshift weapon, annoyed that she felt shame. She clenched her hand on the bar and reminded herself that the other monarchs were not her responsibility. But the shame proved sharper than her will.

"I'll stand a better chance on my own," Rynda said.

"I know."

"And you can use the breach after I'm gone."

"I know."

Rynda growled and stabbed a finger to her. "We are not the same race, elf. Why do you expect me to lead these fools?"

"Because you are a general," Erisay said simply. "And a general cares for those under her command."

"They are not in my army," she hissed.

"A king protects all life," Erisay replied. "It is your responsibility and mine. We protect more than just our race and culture. We protect the people—of every race. When we fall to our baser instincts, our world suffers, our people suffer."

Stung, Rynda swept a hand at the elf. "I care nothing for your kind."

"Well I care about you," Erisay said with sudden heat. "We may not be the same race, but we are sisters in every other respect. If you were injured or hurt, I would care for you. If your son or father came to me, I would house them and feed them."

"Why?" Rynda demanded.

"Because what else is there?" Erisay asked, her voice challenging. "Trade agreements? War? Shipping manifests and inventory? You are a queen, Rynda, and your duty is to serve the people—all people."

"Your words mean nothing to me." Rynda struggled to keep her voice quiet. "I am a rock troll, trained for life, to fight to the death. I am the very flesh of war, and will claim the vengeance that is my due."

Queen Erisay regarded her with pity in her eyes. "Then you are no better than Bartoth."

Rynda wanted to reach through the bars and strike the elf, to silence her words, because they pierced her deeper than any blade. Bartoth was a cruel king, exiled by the shedding of blood, and now he'd joined with Serak and Wylyn, gathering goblins and giants to his banner so he could seek vengeance.

But there was truth to Erisay's words, and Rynda realized she'd been selfish. She wanted revenge on Bartoth and Serak, even Tardoq. But was that all she was? A warrior? A killer? Is that all she would ever be?

Seized with a different sort of anger, she released a barked order. "As you will. Wake them up."

Erisay smiled knowingly and whistled. The sound was not loud, but it seemed to reverberate in the cells of the prison, eliciting several muffled curses. A clatter came from the rooms, and the other monarchs stumbled out. Dothlore appeared first, cinching his belt as he looked about. He caught sight of Rynda standing on the other side of the bars. As the other kings piled from their rooms, he darted to the opening, a smile appearing beneath his beard.

"I thought you'd go alone."

"I would have," she said. "But someone talked me out of it."

"We should thank that person," Queen Erisay said, slipping through the gap with ease.

"We should," Dothlore agreed, working his way through the gap.

King Porlin was next, and he looked up to Rynda with hope in his gaunt eyes. "You have my gratitude, good queen."

"Don't make me regret this, human."

"I won't." He paused on the threshold. "What about Numen?"

"We haven't seen him in weeks," Justin said, pushing him through. "He's probably dead."

Then he looked up to Rynda and thanked her with a nod. Rynda returned the gesture, a mark of respect between monarchs. For all their faults, they were men and women that aspired to honor. Then the two goblins passed, and one scowled as he came through the breach. The second bore a matching expression.

"We still hate you."

Rynda chuckled in amusement. Perhaps not all of them had honor. But at least she would not have to endure the regret if she'd left them behind. As King Justin stepped through the opening, he nodded.

"Where do we go now?"

"We climb," she said.

"You want us to climb *that?*" King Porlin asked.

He pointed to the outside of the suspended fortress. Rough and lined with cracks, the surface angled up and out, leading to another ledge thirty feet above. Under normal circumstances it would be a relatively easy ascent, but climbing while hanging above a live volcano made the attempt dangerous.

Crowded on the small ledge, the other kings eyed the exterior. Across from them, the inside wall of the volcano was pitted with crags and glowed red with heat, the surface raw and broken by past eruptions. The air reeked of sulfur, and magma glowed below, uncomfortably close.

"You're free to return to your prison," Rynda said. "But I'm not staying."

She reached for a crack and leaned out over the drop, her gut clenching in fear. Ignoring it, she reached for another crack and swung her feet upward, finding a knob. Then she began to climb. Comfortable with underground terrain, Erisay came next, followed by Dothlore. After a hissed conversation, the other humans followed. King Justin taking the lead. King Porlin wiped the sweat from his brow, glanced backward, and then began to climb. The goblins snapped at each other and then joined them, while the orc king took up the rear.

"What's on the level above?" Dothlore called, his voice subdued.

Rynda recalled her flight through the fortress. "Living quarters," she said. "But the fortress is only partially occupied. We are likely to find it empty."

"And if it's not?" Erisay asked.

"Then I handle the threat," Rynda said. "And you silence the struggle."

Rynda reached for another crack—but froze when a barked order came from above. The other monarchs reacted in kind, the line of escaping prisoners coming to an abrupt halt. Rynda listened, waiting for other orders, mapping the last few holds to the top. If she could get her feet on the floor, she would stand a chance.

"The order was not for us," Erisay whispered.

"What did they say?" Rynda murmured

"Place the barrels at the ledge?"

Her tone made her confusion evident, and a moment later the same order was echoed across the fortress, repeated over and over again, muffled by the sound of thousands of barrels being set on the floor.

"Whatever is going on," Rynda reached for a hold and hurried upward, "we need to move quickly."

She climbed from hold to hold and didn't stop when a pair of barrels appeared on the ledge above. Other barrels were pushed into other openings, dotting every balcony on the exterior of the suspended fortress.

"What are they doing?" Dothlore hissed.

Just feet from the ledge, Rynda didn't care. She scaled to the top and then used the barrels to hide her ascent. Inside, four soldiers stood with two golems, all working over a quartet of barrels, removing the lids and pushing them close to the drop. All looked up when Rynda's large frame rose into view.

"The prisoners have—"

The leader shout was extinguished, and his mouth moved in vain. Rynda recognized the muffling charm and leapt over a barrel, catching a man by his throat. She raised him, using the man's body as a shield against the other guards, who drew their weapons and swung, striking their comrade. Rynda darted to the side and hurled the man's body, knocking all but one sprawling. Then she whirled and caught the golem reaching for her back. She grabbed his wrist and placed a boot on his chest, ripping the arm from the body.

Wielding the arm like a club, she bashed the golem in the head, and then struck the second golem, knocking them both towards the opening. Erisay rose and slipped to the side as the two golems tumbled out the window. They fell into the volcano.

286

Rynda leapt to the downed guards, using the golem's arm to finish the fight. The final guard stood at the door, his expression one of horror as he fought to pull it open. Just as the door handle turned, Erisay whistled.

Harsh and grating, the sound caused Rynda to wince. Dothlore was just pulling himself over the ledge and he too cringed. But the guard at the door released a silent shriek, his eyes going wide in pain. He reached for his ears but the whistle pierced his hands and assaulted his skull. With a final, soundless shudder, he slumped to the floor.

Dothlore stared at the body and then looked to Erisay, who shrugged and turned to King Justin, just stepping over the edge. The human reached back for King Porlin, helping him over the ledge.

"We need to move," Erisay said. "Quickly. Whatever they are doing will provide a distraction for our escape."

"What's in the barrels?" Justin asked.

"Looks like stonesap," Porlin said, gasping from the climb. Rynda elevated her opinion of the man. She'd been certain he would fall.

"Stonesap?" Dothlore touched the liquid in surprise. "What is Serak doing with stonesap?"

"He has a lot," King Justin said.

He stood at the window, peering upward. Rynda joined him, and eyed the nearest balconies, all of which contained more barrels, all being pushed to the edge, the tops being opened.

"It's been tainted somehow," Dothlore said, examining the barrel. "But it looks like he's going to pour it into the volcano."

"Why would anyone do that?" King Porlin asked.

"We're about to find out," Rynda said.

She watched as the barrels tipped, pouring over the edge in a cascade of dark liquid. More and more, and still more. Tens of thousands of barrels were poured into the mouth of the volcano, the stream splashing off the stone and pouring towards the magma.

287

"Hurry!" King Justin hissed to the two goblins and the orc.

All three scrambled upward as the liquid approached the magma, and the orc gave up. Turning, he fled downward, attempting to reach the cells before the stonesap ignited the volcano. The other two goblins raced up the slope, the first reaching the balcony as the stonesap touched the magma . . .

Chapter 37: Serak's War

The explosion rocked the fortress, the fire devouring the stonesap in a streak of crimson flames, filling the interior of the volcano. The tidal wave of liquid fire burst upward, swallowing the hanging citadel.

Porlin and Justin yanked one goblin chief over the edge, but the second was not so fortunate, the flames catching him, his shout barely audible in the roar of the stonesap-fueled flames. The monarchs dived away from the blast of heat but Rynda stood her ground, watching the protective charms of the dwarven fortress funnel the heat up and out. Building a fortress inside a volcano carried inherent risks, and the dwarves had obviously prepared for an eruption. But this eruption was created by the hand of Serak, and the fire continued to blast upward, reaching the top of the fortress and exploding into the sky. Rynda went to the door and shoved the guard's body aside so she could ease the door open. The interior space was unoccupied, with hundreds of forges surrounding the empty shaft. It too was filled with fire, the red glowing against the walls, filling the pipes to the forges, igniting each in a burst of fire.

"He's reigniting the volcano and the forges," Dothlore said from beside Rynda. "But why alter the stonesap?"

"Doesn't matter," Porlin said. "We can escape now while the guards are at the balconies."

"He's right," Justin said, crowding the door. "We should make a run for it."

Rynda nodded her agreement. "Stay with me. Don't fall behind."

She stepped into the corridor and raced for the stairs leading upward. Cheers were heard from the rooms they passed, guards and servants to Serak exulting in their accomplishment. Whatever they'd done.

She scowled, disliking her lack of understanding. The more she learned about Serak, the less she understood. Why ignite a volcano? Why kidnap the kings? Why let Wylyn take the Order of Ancients? The questions only had two possible answers. Either the man had gone mad. Or he was fighting on a battlefield she didn't understand. And he didn't strike her as one who'd gone mad.

They rushed up the empty stairs, following the same route she'd used during her duel with Tardoq. One level led to the next set of stairs, the staircase a giant spiral that circled the fortress. The fire continued to rise outside the fortress, a great roar of fire and sound. Except this wave was being fed, and more stonesap continued to pour, the liquid cascading through the enchantments and fueling the eruption.

Rynda slowed as she reached the topmost level, ascending the final steps on soft toes. She came to a halt and scanned the top courtyard, her gaze drawn to the walls of fire that reached into the sky. At the center of the fortress a column of empty space extended straight down, and fire filled it as well, a geyser of superheated fire that reached the clouds.

"By the gods," King Justin breathed, his hair whipping about his head. "It's practically burning the heavens."

The flames filled the clouds, the sky itself seeming to burn. But such fire could only be fed for so long, and it had begun to fall. In moments the distraction would be over, and they would be trapped.

Rynda eyed the bridge that connected to the outer wall, the sole point of access that barred the wall of fire. Only a few guards were present, all climbing to the outer and inner walls to view the awesome spectacle. Rynda scanned the surface of the fortress one last time, and this time spotted another object.

The large oval rested on a pedestal, the outer material dark, seeming to absorb the light from the fire. A solitary figure stood before the strange object, and when he turned, she recognized him.

"It's Serak," Justin hissed. "He's here."

"Of course he is," Rynda said, her metal hand clenching into a fist. "Erisay, you're on your own. I have a debt to repay."

"Don't be foolish," Dothlore said. "You can't kill him alone."

"Watch me," she snarled. "And don't call me a fool."

She rose and began to walk towards Serak. Porlin hissed at her back. "But you don't have a weapon."

She cast a look back. "I *am* the weapon."

She kept her gait slow, purposeful. Men could sense hurried motion. Thirty paces became twenty, and then ten. As she stalked her prey, she unclenched her metal hand, imagining what Serak would do when her hand closed about his neck, burning his flesh until—

"You surprise me, Queen Rynda."

Discarding her surprise, she leapt forward, closing the gap in three quick steps. But a hand of stone rose between them, holding a large, glittering sword. Her soulblade. She came to a halt upon seeing her weapon.

"Serak," she said evenly. "You have my gratitude for bringing me my sword."

"I did not expect you to escape for another fortnight," Serak said. "And using the cleansing as a distraction? Brilliant."

"Cleansing?"

Rynda spared a glance to the side, and found Dothlore standing on Serak's flank. He held a weapon he'd picked up from one of the guards below. King Porlin joined them, as did the other monarchs. Serak chuckled as they surrounded him.

"And you all followed the rock troll."

"We are allied against *you*." King Justin spit on the stone.

"I don't need help to kill him," Rynda growled.

"Once you start a war, you do not get to choose your allies," Queen Erisay said, taking position between Rynda and Dothlore. Rynda noticed a slim, orange dagger in her hand. An echo blade. Rynda raised an eyebrow to the queen, and she shrugged. Such a weapon required

291

great skill to cast because it followed sound to its target. Rynda had once seen such a dagger through the mouth of an orc. The blade had pierced to the back of the skull. The weapon had been thrown from half a mile away, and tracked the orc's voice across hills and through a forest.

Serak noticed the weapon and chuckled. "Queen Erisay, a sound mage? You are far more clever than I anticipated to keep such a secret."

"Some weapons are held in reserve for the right battle."

"Even your own daughter didn't know," Serak said.

"Melora was not one to trust," Erisay's voice hardened.

"Indeed," Serak said.

He motioned to the stone at their feet and golems rose from the stone, shaping into living weapons. Each stepped free and faced the various monarchs while one rose and claimed Rynda's sword. She gauged the distance, eyeing the weapon. If she could get her hands on her soulblade . . .

The golem flipped the giant sword in its hands and offered the hilt to Rynda.

Dothlore growled. "Why would you—"

Rynda snatched the blade and struck, slicing the golem in two. Then she leapt for Serak. The speed of her attack shocked everyone, and her greatsword cut through his neck. Instead of blood, water spilled to the stone. Confused, Rynda watched as Serak reached up to the wound, an annoyed expression on his face. His body turned translucent, like clear water on a still beach, and then reformed into flesh.

"Rock trolls," he said. "Always so quick to swing a sword. Have you forgotten that I am a guardian? My body is *made* of water and earth. Your blade may hurt, but it will not kill me."

"I'll put that to the test," she said evenly, retreating several steps.

"I'm sure you would," Serak said. "But it's time you understood why you're here."

"I don't care," Rynda snarled.

"Come now," Serak said, "You're smart enough to understand the truth, and I suspect you wonder what battle I'm preparing for."

She shifted her feet, unable to deny it. He smiled and swept a hand to the wall of fire, which was falling, its fuel spent. The fires fell below the edge of the fortress, leaving waves of heat and smoke billowing across the top of the fortress. Soldiers appeared in the haze, returning from pouring the stonesap. They caught sight of the standoff and rushed to arms, but Serak waved in dismissal.

"You are not needed."

Zenif appeared and sprinted forward, but again Serak motioned in dismissal. "Go below, Zenif."

"But it's Queen Rynda—"

Serak cut the captain off. "Open the gates and allow the monarchs to take whatever they need from the stables."

"But Master Serak . . ."

His eyes flicked to Zenif, who glared at Rynda, his eyes filled with hatred. Barking orders, he withdrew, taking his men with him. Rynda had the satisfaction of seeing him limp, obviously still sore from when she'd broken his ankle. In seconds, the entire courtyard had emptied, and the gates opened in both the inner and outer walls. Through the smoke and cinders, the evening sky was visible, a clear moon falling on a wide valley.

"It's a trick," the goblin hissed.

"No trick," Serak said, gesturing to the gate. "You may go at any time."

"So why take us in the first place?" Justin demanded.

"You are kings and queens, rulers over many peoples," Serak said. "But that land you call your own is claimed by the Krey Empire. One day they will come here, and when they do, your kingdoms will be torn down as easily as a rock troll kills a man."

"*You* are the threat," Dothlore growled.

"Am I?" Serak asked. "Behind me is the Dark Gate, a portal I have spent lifetimes preparing. When it is opened, we will have access to a nearly infinite army, one capable of standing against the krey."

"Ero will protect us," Porlin said.

Serak burst into a mocking laugh, causing King Porlin to flush. "You think of Ero as a god, but he is just a member of the ancient race—one with a gift for deception."

"Why the stonesap?" Dothlore asked. "Why ignite the volcano?"

"The fiend army is not the only thing behind the Dark Gate," Serak said. "The entity that created the fiends would be lethal to our world. The cleansing has prevented it from passing through the portal."

"That's why you altered the stonesap," Dothlore guessed.

Serak swept his hand to the haze across the summit of Xshaltheria. "Do you smell the bitter wind? The vestiges of the stonesap have stained the very air, and not even the Dark will be able to enter. Its army is now ripe for the taking—for one with enough might."

"You speak nonsense," King Porlin spat. "You have gone mad."

Serak regarded him with thinly veiled disgust. "Go, prepare your armies and return if you wish. You can bear witness to my new army, and kneel before your master."

"I do not kneel," Rynda said.

"All kneel to a superior power," Serak said.

The kings exchanged looks before Porlin abruptly turned and fled. The others were quick to follow, leaving only Dothlore, Erisay, and Rynda. Rynda held her blade, gauging the distance, wondering how to kill the guardian.

"When I return, you will not survive," Rynda warned.

"When you return, you will kneel."

"We should depart," Erisay said. "Let us be wise."

Rynda understood her intent. Whatever Serak's purpose in releasing them, they could do more damage outside of captivity. Erisay and Dothlore turned and followed the other kings, but Rynda paused, her sword pointed at Serak.

"You are a fool to think I will trust you."

"I do not need your trust," Serak said. "I need your army, and your leadership."

"They are mine," Rynda said.

He reached into a fold of his cloak and removed a small mirror. He tossed it aside and the glass shattered. Rising from the shards, light bent and shaped, rising to reveal a view of a sunlit boat. The viewpoint turned, as if they were looking through the eyes of another.

The viewer was on a boat, one rocking with large waves. But there was no storm, and the sun shone upon the sea. Beyond the waves a massive tower rose from the sea, its converging pieces coming together, growing higher and higher, all the way to the clouds. Its sheer size defied belief, a mountain, built by hand rather than nature.

"What is this?" Rynda asked.

"Wylyn has raised the Shard of Midnight," Serak said. "If the fragments of Draeken do not stop her, she will open her own Gate, and her house army will cascade across these lands, enslaving all, and butchering those who fight."

"Is this a memory?"

"What you witness occurs now." Serak pointed east. "The tower has been raised in the heart of Blue Lake. By the time you reach Griffin cities, you will hear the rumors of its rising."

"Why show me this?" Rynda asked.

"So you can accept the true threat," Serak said. "The krey are the enemy, and in time you will see that I am your ally."

"Never."

Serak smiled and his body turned to water. His limbs and legs pooled into liquid and he dropped to the floor like rain. Alone, Rynda cast the giant tower a last look and then joined the others. They had gathered a wagon and supplies, and were hastily mounting horses. Rynda stopped at the last gate and looked back, hating what she'd heard in Serak's words.

Truth.

Chapter 38: The Stormdial

"Jump!" Elenyr called.

She caught Mind's tunic and shoved him across the gap to Sentara's warship. Fire followed, and she leapt after, landing as the vessel they'd purchased ripped in half like a paper toy, caught between two sections of the tower.

"Did you have to shove me?" Mind asked, dusting himself off.

Elenyr's eyes swept the deck. "Where is Water?"

Light was leaning over the rail, a beam of light reaching from his eyes into the roiling sea. "He's down there with Lira." His voice was anxious, worried. "I'll go after him."

Light stepped on the rail but Elenyr grabbed his arm. "He will be fine," she said, both stumbling as their ship heaved. She caught a rope and called to Sentara, "Can you get us out?"

"We cannot escape," she exclaimed. "Not through that."

Sentara pointed to the rising teeth, each a sliver of the tower. The sea was in turmoil, the waves crashing against the towers and being pushed out of gaps, a lethal maze of rising and falling tides.

"We must reach the center," Mind called.

Sentara spun the helm away from the closing jaws of the Devil's Maw and sailed toward the tiny boat at the center of the stillness. Elenyr cast Mind a glance, mentally asking the question, *How did you stop the Carver?* But the fragment merely shrugged, a faint smile appearing on his features.

She'd never seen him control the magic of gravity, yet he'd wielded it to devastating effect against the Carver. When had he solved his previous doubt? When had he begun to master the magic? She wanted to ask more but they were trapped in the Maw, and there was no time to waste.

All the fragments on the ship lined the rails with Jeric and Rune. Light and Shadow both seemed excited. Light caught Elenyr watching and rushed to her side, motioning to the closing jaws of the Maw.

"Isn't this exciting!" he cried.

"It's about to crush us," Elenyr said.

"It will if we don't get out of the way!" Jeric called.

Elenyr spared him a look, wondering again why he was here, and what his real identity was. "Get to the prow and tell me what you see." She called to Light.

"Wylyn is waiting for—"

The tower burst from the still water, rising so fast that Wylyn's ship settled on the relatively flat surface. Elenyr caught a glimpse of the krey woman before the tower carried her skyward. Water cascaded off the flat exterior as the tower rose from the sea. In minutes the outer sections would join to create a great obelisk. When the sides and center came together, the machinery would crush anything caught between them.

"The ledge!" Mind shouted. "It's our way in." He pointed to a ledge extending from the center tower, rising towards them from beneath the surface of the sea.

Sentara banked her way towards it. "High oracle," she said. "If I get killed, she's going to come for you."

"I know," Elenyr said. "So we'd better survive so I can figure out a way to heal you."

The old woman followed Light's direction to the central tower. It continued to rise, the smooth, black stone spilling water as it extended into the sky. Whatever enchantments had been placed on the water had broken, and the surface roiled in fury, lifting and tossing them about.

298

Elenyr spotted the last two Order ships coming to a stop against the main tower, and a moment later a giant ledge burst from the water, lifting the dakorian ship into the sky. They disembarked and entered the tower while the second also caught a lift. Sentara barked an order to Rune and the girl leapt to secure the sail, her eyes bright with fear and shock.

"Water and Lira haven't come up," Mind exclaimed. "He says he's going deeper to find a way into the tower."

Elenyr grimaced. "They will have to fend for themselves."

Rune called out a warning from the prow and Sentara swung their ship against the center pillar. The ledge Mind had spotted appeared beneath them. Elenyr was knocked to the deck when the ledge slammed into the hull and lifted them upward. Dazed, she stumbled to her feet.

But the ship began to teeter.

The prow had not made it onto the buttress and it was tipping down, the hull beginning to slide off the edge. In seconds it would balance too far and the entire ship would tumble hundreds of feet to the sea.

"OFF!" she bellowed, and then phased to ethereal. Dropping through the hull, she reached the smooth black stone and sank her ankles into the ledge. Gritting her teeth, she reached up and let her ethereal hands sink into the wood before turning them partially solid, using her body as an anchor.

She gritted her teeth against the strain, and grimly held the ship from falling. With her holding the stern of the ship, the keel tipped over the edge. The others scrambled off the hull and dived onto the ledge. The sheer weight of the ship threatened to pull Elenyr in half.

Rune sprinted up the angled surface, leaping for the railing and then jumping. The wood of the hull groaned, and began to come apart. Elenyr released the ship and it tipped over the edge, falling into a tumble. She darted to the edge and watched the ship fall three hundred feet. The ship splashed into the sea, flattening the hull and sending debris in all directions.

"Blast," Sentara muttered. "I really liked that ship."

Jeric motioned to the doorway further inside. "Perhaps we should retreat? I'd rather not experience what's it's like to be crushed between sections of a krey citadel."

The group ran for the central tower. The locking mechanism was shockingly huge, easily as large as the entire castle at Terros, and entirely smooth. The surface slick with water and grime, they all skidded as they hurried into the giant tower.

A shadow engulfed them as they raced inside the enormous opening, a matching ledge on the opposite side gliding into the cavity, only the position was inverted. Clearly intended to interlock, the two would join and seal, binding the center tower to the outer support. The group raced inside as the view darkened, the outer buttress closing the gap. They were still rising, both towers moving in perfect synchronization as they came together.

"There!" Fire pointed toward an opening at the very end.

Light cast a wolfsteed that illuminated the way, the beast dancing ahead to show their destination. With the increased darkness, Shadow sent a thread of shadow into the air. When it fastened to the ceiling, he yanked and soared over all of them to reach the door first.

"Why are we running?" he asked as he sailed by.

"Is he laughing?" Rune growled. "This is no time for amusement."

"It's always time for amusement," Light said, mounting his wolfsteed. "Isn't that what Jeric always said?"

"Not this time," Jeric said.

Jeric dove through the doorway. Fire and Mind followed, and Rune next. Elenyr spotted Light lagging behind and stopped on the threshold. His horse growing fatigued in the darkness, the fragment sprinted the remaining distance as the outer section of the tower loomed behind him.

"Hurry!" Elenyr shouted.

He glanced back once and then accelerated, reaching the doorway just as the outer section filled it, the two enormous pieces coming together in a *boom* that rattled Elenyr's teeth. The distant thumping of machinery echoed as the two locked together, and then suddenly the floor thrummed with power.

Lights appeared in the ceiling and walls, the whitish glow coming to life to show a hallway extending away, seeming to go forever. Over a hundred feet in height, the corridor was massive, with several other corridors branching off. Although the outside of the Stormdial was pure black, the interior walls were blue accented with white. Dark purple lines pulsed in the wall like veins in a body, making the tower feel alive.

Elenyr hurried down the hall. "We must reach the summit before Wylyn assembles the Gate."

"I'm tired of running."

Light drew from the illumination and a wagon took shape, lifting the entire group off the floor. Fire jumped to the back and added his own magic, making it leap forward, accelerating down the hall.

"Find Water and meet me at the summit," Elenyr said.

"What do you intend to do?" Mind asked.

"We can't go in blind," Elenyr said. "Gather the others and find a way up the tower. I'll take a look."

"Maybe you should wait," Jeric said.

"I don't listen to those I don't trust," she said.

She crouched and leapt, phasing to ethereal as she passed into the ceiling. Moving through the inner workings of the tower, she went straight up, bursting through another corridor filled with Order members and dakorians before passing beyond, their shouts of dismay going unheeded.

She regretted what she'd said to Jeric. It may have been true, but she could have found a kinder way to say it. She scowled as she passed through a beam of white material, and shook the regret free. Jeric was the one who had lied.

Energy pulsed in conduits of power, forcing her to avoid the magic. As she flew through the Shard of Midnight she gradually understood its

301

shape, and realized just how much power was being funneled toward the summit.

The bulk of the tower was all machinery, power and gears and locking arms allowing the Stormdial to reassemble. Strange machinery dominated each level, the workings complex and foreign.

Several levels allowed passage from the exterior to the interior, which would permit workers to make repairs on the massive edifice. At a mile in height, its sheer size defied belief, while the interior was no less breathtaking.

Thousands of chambers were placed on perfectly ordered levels, each built to serve the needs of laborers. The living chambers were spaced apart and segmented, with no obvious method to descend or ascend. Then Elenyr passed through a room and spotted a mirror. She frowned and alighted on the chamber floor, striding to the mirror. It was large enough for a dakorian and contained symbols on the sides. She recognized a handful of the symbols from the krey language and pressed the one with the highest number.

The mirror rippled and went still, and she stepped through the glass. Passing through the barrier, she entered the summit of the Stormdial. She gasped for breath and looked upward, spotting four great arcs rising to a single point in the sky. The Gate she'd used was placed at the base of one of the arcs.

They were above the vestiges of the storm, the gaps in the clouds allowing her to see the blue water far below. Islands were visible in the distance, and the Azure people were probably panicking at the sudden appearance of the fabled tower.

She heard a barked order and turned. A dozen dakorians and a handful of Order rushed to assemble the Gate while Wylyn looked on, her features bearing a smile of triumph. Elenyr scanned the group. She thought she'd spotted King Numen on one of the ships, and if he was present, he would be the most dangerous . . .

She heard a scuff behind and whirled—as the lightning net fell upon her. The energy crackled into her bones, and she cried out, more in anger than in pain. She realized that by taking the tower's Gate instead of the slower route, she'd stepped right into the trap.

King Numen caught the end of the net and dragged her toward Wylyn. "I told you I'd kill you," he growled.

His face was scarred, a legacy of the burns Fire had inflicted. The scars gave him a dangerous and manic look, his smile twisted, filled with rage and pain. She would have felt guilt if he hadn't scarred her in turn.

"You are too late," Elenyr shot back. "The fragments are nearly here."

"Then I will have to kill you quickly," he said.

"No," Wylyn said, turning. "I'd like her to witness her failure." The krey woman looked down on Elenyr with triumph in her eyes. "The human thought you would seek to scout ahead. I must say his study of you is proving to be an advantage."

"Did you know Numen is here on Serak's order?" she asked, wondering when she had grown so easy to capture. "He will betray you."

"She lies," Numen growled.

"Doesn't matter," Wylyn said with a haughty laugh. "In moments I will return to my house, and my entire fleet will embark from Drendelin and set course for Lumineia."

Elenyr strained against the bindings but Numen dragged her to the base of one of the four great arcs. The net reformed, wrapping around her waist, legs, wrists, and throat, holding her fast.

"You have no idea of the power of my fragments," Elenyr growled.

"Actually I do," Wylyn said. "Which is why I chose the Stormdial as the place to build the Gate. You see, not only does it contain an enormous gravity sphere, it also has a special soldier to guard the tower." She smiled. "I'm sure you've heard of a construct . . ."

Chapter 39: The Mastery of Mind

"Elenyr should have been back by now," Mind said.

"You think she got caught?" Light asked, his expression fearful.

Annoyed by their doubt, Fire jerked his head. "It's Elenyr. She'll be fine."

Their wagon reached the center of the tower to find it was hollow. Fire jumped off Light's wagon and approached the shaft, peering upward. Air blew down the empty shaft, and far above he spotted light coming from the summit. They'd explored down several of the other great tunnels, but they only led to empty living quarters and what resembled meal halls.

The entire tower was empty yet pristine, its sheer size and enormous corridors making it haunting. Fire leaned over the rail and peered into the depths of the tower, but it seemed to go on forever. Then he spotted movement and squinted.

"Looks like Water made it inside," he said.

Water rose into view. The fragment had cast an ascender that clung to the side of the shaft, and rose with Lira on his side. The other fragments gathered on the railing and Light actually shouted in excitement.

"We weren't sure you made it!" he cried.

Water waved downward. "It was close. Glad to see you all here." Then he frowned. "Where's Elenyr?"

"She scouted upward," Jeric said, his tone worried. "She has not returned."

Fire frowned and glanced his way, attempting to gauge the elf's demeanor. He'd never liked the elf, mostly because he represented an unpredictable element. At any moment he could side with the enemy simply because he found it amusing, and such whimsy could not be trusted. But over the last few weeks he'd been different, ever since Elenyr had been hurt. It was almost as if he was a different person entirely. Did he care for Elenyr that much? Or was it something else?

It's something else, Mind thought to him.

What do you mean? Fire didn't like talking through thoughts, but in this case it seemed prudent.

If I knew I would tell you.

Fire heard the honesty in his thoughts. Mind truly didn't know, likely because both Elenyr and Jeric possessed significant mental shields. But Mind was suspicious of Jeric, that much was evident.

Water's ascender, which resembled a spider, reached their level and clambered over, allowing Water and Lira to dismount. Water reached up to help Lira down, his expression revealing a fleeting tenderness. Fire grinned. Perhaps he was not the only fragment of passion.

"We must hasten to the summit," Lira exclaimed. "The tower possesses a large gravity sphere, one with the capacity to power the Dark Gate."

"Gravity sphere?" Rune asked.

Fire glanced her way. He'd almost forgotten the girl was present. She stood with her arms folded, her features hard, as if she was trying not to show her discomfort. Sentara stood at her side, and again Fire wondered as to her identity. It rankled to have so many strangers in their midst.

"Gravity binds our feet to the ground," Lira said, "and its power can be tremendous. I didn't realize Mind had such magic."

"Him?" Fire asked.

"When he stopped the Carver," she said with a nod. "It's the same power used throughout the Krey Empire to feed their machines."

Did you know? Fire mentally asked.

I felt it, he said.

And you controlled it. How?

Mind shook his head, a tiny motion, as if he didn't want to answer. Then abruptly he sent, *I think it comes from Draeken.*

Fire scowled. All the recent events had changed the dynamic between the fragments, and Fire also felt the stirrings of Draeken. He *wanted* to come forth, to stand in power, to be in control.

"The krey have beautiful architecture," Shadow exclaimed. "But it's too bright for my tastes."

His words broke the spell and Fire noticed he and Mind had fallen behind. He sent a thought to Mind that they would discuss it later and he agreed. Searching for a way upward, the group followed Lira down another corridor to an intersection.

"I hate this place," Rune muttered. "How can we know where we're going?"

"You're in luck," Light said brightly, and pointed down the hall. "Maybe they can give us directions."

The group whirled as dozens of dakorians and Order members appeared from a nearby corridor. Aradig smirked at them and drew his sentient bow, but it was the other person that drew Fire's gaze.

Tardoq.

"Kill them," Aradig said.

With a shout, the group charged, and Mind barked orders. "Fire and Light, you have the flanks. Jeric and Sentara, you're with Light. Water and Rune, you're with Fire. Lira, you're with me. Shadow, have some fun."

The smaller fragment smirked. "How I love to hear those words."

Water raised an eyebrow at the unusual arrangement. In such a setting, Fire, the strongest of the group, generally anchored the line at

306

the center, yet Mind was taking that position. Mind ignored the questioning looks and started forward, purple light swirling across his arms.

The two sides closed in a rush. Fire conjured a full chariot of flames, the horses breathing fire. Water and Rune leapt aboard and Fire whipped the reins, charging right through the line of Order members, setting them ablaze.

On the opposite side, Light came to a halt and cast a giant ballista, but instead of the standard bolt in a single groove, it contained a dozen bolts. His eyes gleamed as he took aim at a knot of dakorians and opened fire, sending shafts of light into their flanks. Others charged, seeking to reach the weapon, but Jeric and Sentara took up position on either side of the war machine, their blades working in tandem to keep the Order from reaching the ballista.

The corridor dissolved into chaos, magic and swords clashing as men and women cried out in pain and rage. All the while, Mind advanced into the center of the battle. Lira at his side, cast him uncertain looks. Fire too watched Mind, eyeing his brother.

Aradig launched his sentient bow into the air and it fired a bolt at Mind, but Mind reached upward, warping the gravity that held it and yanking it to the ground. It exploded, blasting a pair of dakorians reaching for Fire's chariot, which he'd swung back for another pass. Aradig's eyes widened and he shouted orders, sending dozens to Mind.

Lira scowled. "I hope you have a plan."

"I do," Mind said. "Kill them all."

He surged into a sprint and pointed to the nearest Order member. From twenty feet away he caught the man's throat and lifted him off the ground, using his body to catch the next arrow from Aradig's bow. The detonation filled the air with smoke and the body tumbled into his companions, lifeless.

The man's discarded sword lifted into the air, and another man rose as well. He shrieked and sought to dislodge himself from the invisible grip, but the blade and the body came together, and then were tossed him away like trash.

307

A dakorian charged and raised his hammer, and Mind reached out with both hands. The dakorian growled as his feet came off the floor. He bellowed as he was thrown into a bolt from Light's ballistae. The dakorian cried out as it pierced his body.

Fire watched it all, exulting in his brother's newfound power. Then his saw his eyes, the purple tinge to the irises, the cruel twist to his mouth. Mind didn't enjoy a battle, not like Fire, but this time he did, and Fire found the view disturbing. Fire had only seen that expression in the mirror. When they were Draeken.

Fire pulled the reins on his chariot, aiming for Mind. But his attention was drawn to the conflict, and he was forced to focus on closer threats. A dakorian cut Light across the shoulder, another stabbing Shadow in the hand. The injuries would have been minor, but the anti-magic blades dug deep, and Light lashed out, quickly losing control.

Fire pulled on the reins to go help. A dwarf got to him first, shoving an axe through the wheel of his chariot, making it flip. He caught a glimpse of Sentara flipping in midair and landing with ease, Rune tumbling at her side. Then his face struck the floor and his vision flickered. Fire dribbled down his cheek and he rose to his feet, spitting sparks. The dwarf came at him, and Sentara stepped in his path, deflecting his second axe and driving him away.

"I could have taken care of him," Fire said.

"I doubt it," Sentara sniffed in disapproval.

Fire rose to his feet and conjured his sword of fire. Just as he faced another dakorian, he spotted Mind. The fragment lifted a fallen dakorian hammer and sent it slamming into a trio of order members, crushing one against the wall and sending the others flying.

Fire deflected the dakorian's sword and retreated, but another lunged at Fire, his hammer grazing his arm. Fire growled and darted close, striking the dakorian a scorching line down his chest. The dakorian retreated, and Tardoq took his place, striking Fire in the chest with his full might.

Fire tumbled down the corridor and hit the wall, gasping for breath. Tardoq stalked forward. Mind jumped between them, and threads of purple bonding him to Tardoq. He jumped, and then fell sideways, slamming into Tardoq's back.

The dakorian rose and spun, his features contorted in anger. He bellowed an order, gathering the remaining dakorians in the hall. Mind expected them to charge but instead they retreated, sprinting back to the chamber from which they had appeared. The Order members followed suit, leaving their dead as they retreated.

Fire coughed and reached for Mind, who helped him to his feet. *You still with me?* Fire asked.

I'm still me, Mind replied, the tone of his thoughts annoyed. *I just wanted them to think I was losing control.*

Not entirely convinced, Fire limped toward the others. Most were wounded. Light's shoulder was injured, and Shadow bandaged his hand. He smiled as he put what looked like a dakorian's horn into his pouch.

"When did you learn how to do that?" Water asked Mind, motioning to a man bound on the ceiling.

Shadow grinned. "That was me." He snapped his fingers and the man fell, grunting when he hit the ground.

Mind pointed to the room their foes had entered. "They had the advantage and should have pressed it. I suspect they are leading us into a trap."

"Let's not disappoint," Fire said, curling flames in his palm.

"You *want* to walk into a trap?" Rune demanded.

Shadow leaned over, his eyes gleaming. "They may have set a trap, but they do not know what *we* can do."

Water nodded. "Exactly. Light?"

"They hurt me," he said, rubbing his shoulder. "I'd like to hurt them back."

Fire shot Mind a look. *Are you certain it's wise to become Draeken? After what we saw in Senia's vision?*

He didn't say that he was worried about Mind. The way he'd acted during the fight, his recent control over gravity magic, both spoke to an increase in Draeken's power, and Fire didn't want to think of becoming a dark Draeken.

I can hear your thoughts, Mind sent, annoyed. *Stop worrying about me. The timing of the vision is off. We should be safe.*

I don't like it, Fire said.

Would you rather let Wylyn open her Gate? Mind demanded, and then aloud. "I think you're right. Fire?"

Jeric glanced between them. "Are you certain you can hold Draeken together?"

"More than ever." Mind didn't take his eyes from Fire, who now regretted his inability to close his thoughts.

"Let's just make sure Wylyn is dead this time," Fire said.

"And our friends?" Water asked.

"I'm not your friend," Sentara retorted.

Mind looked to Jeric. "You, Sentara, and Rune should locate an exit."

"There are probably krey vessels at the base of the structure," Lira said. "Find one and get outside the tower."

"We're not leaving," Rune said, folding her arms.

"Yes we are," Sentara replied.

Rune rounded on her. "You wanted to make sure Elenyr survives, and now you're just going to leave?"

"She can't fix what she did if I'm dead," Sentara said.

Rune stared at her and then released an annoyed breath, and nodded. Sentara cast them a look and then departed with Rune, but Jeric merely folded his arms.

"I'm not leaving." His tone did not allow for argument, and Fire noticed a steel in his eyes he'd never seen before.

"What's your plan?" Water asked Mind.

Mind pointed downward. "I can feel the gravity sphere at the base of the tower. It hasn't been used for ages, and there's a touch of decay, an instability that could be exploited. If we could damage the sphere, the entire tower would come down, this time for good."

"Let's get this done," Fire said, for once unhappy about the coming battle.

Mind looked to the others and they phased to their elemental state, the fragments reaching for Mind's arms. Light disappeared first, and Mind smiled when the golden light seeped into his flesh, his features altering slightly to become Draeken. Shadow came next, causing his smile to turn mischievous. Fire merged, and his consciousness blended with the others, the fire burning with the fragments he called brothers. Last to join, Water's magic swirled up his arms and sank into his flesh. Fire felt a touch of honor and worry before his thoughts abandoned him, and another mind claimed them all . . .

Whole for the first time in ages, Draeken flexed his fingers, feeling the rush of power, the supreme might at his command. He could feel the fragment's memories, their magic, their doubts and concerns. But they were not present. There was only Draeken. Jeric and Lira stood across from him, Jeric's expression one of doubt, while Lira looked worried.

Draeken motioned toward the doorway leading to the chamber. "Are we ready?"

"Are you?" Lira asked.

"They expect five guardians," Draeken said. "They cannot be ready for me."

"How long can you last together?" Jeric asked.

It had been centuries since they'd all merged together, and they'd crumbled in minutes—but this time Draeken did not sense the same instability. He felt complete. It seemed the magics were in tune for the

311

first time in his life, and he wondered if it was due to Mind's acceptance of self. He felt powerful. He felt hungry.

"Long enough," he replied.

Chapter 40: Draeken

Draeken stepped through the Gate onto the summit of the Stormdial, his gaze immediately drawn to the four great arcs ascending to a pinnacle high above. The top of the Stormdial seemed to rest on top of the world, with clouds below and beyond, stretching to the horizon.

The summit was devoid of railing or barrier while the surface contained an assortment of debris. Wylyn's ship, as well as pieces of wreckage from the battle, lay strewn about the smooth material. At the center, the handful of surviving dakorians rushed to complete the Gate, the large arch of black stone nearly finished. Pulsing purple lines fed the material.

King Numen stood with Tardoq. The pair flanked a bound Elenyr, her bonds sparking like living lightning, holding her fastened to the base of one of the other arcs. Aradig too, was present, although he'd endured a wound from Shadow in the tunnel below. All eyes turned to Draeken's entrance. He smirked at their attention and turned his gaze to the final member of the group arrayed against him.

Wylyn, wife to Skorn, leader of the invasion, stood next to a strange statue. The statue was not large but it exuded power, the muscular arms and armored body so vivid it seemed ready to leap from the stone which held it bound.

Lira came to a halt at Draeken's side and muttered a curse. "It's a construct," she growled.

"A what?" Draeken asked.

"A weapon of pure power," Jeric said.

Lira spared him a confused look. "A construct is much like you and Serak are guardians, except more stable. They can be unbound, or bound to a mind, allowing a wielder to become the construct. Very rare, very lethal."

313

"So am I," Draeken said.

"You don't understand," Lira said. "Constructs are fashioned from a particular type of energy, fire, light, even water."

All watched Draeken and his companions except the dakorians completing the Gate. Tardoq and the handful of surviving Order members stood with them, making no move to advance. Wylyn examined Draeken with a haughty expression before motioning to the bound Elenyr.

"Your magic is impressive," she said. "But you are no match for the might of the Empire."

"Says the woman about to die," Draeken said.

Wylyn laughed and motioned to the construct. "You may have had a chance against flesh, but this weapon cannot be destroyed. It draws its power from the well within this very edifice, and its power is beyond your comprehension. Normally a dakorian would wield such a force, but this time, I'm inclined to kill you myself."

Tardoq scowled at Wylyn's words, and Draeken smiled, pleased at the woman's pride. A dakorian would know how to use it, but Wylyn was too arrogant to make the smart choice. She was just like her son, Relgor, and one of Draeken's fragments had taken care of him.

Wylyn reached to the back of the construct and turned a key, and her body went limp, falling to the summit of the Stormdial like her life had been extinguished. The next moment the eyes of the construct snapped open, bright purple and rigid. The statue stepped free of its base and strode forward, the features remolding to those of Wylyn, the stone exterior falling away to reveal a body of purple light.

"A construct of gravity," Lira said, her tone filled with dread.

Draeken reached to Wylyn and sought to manipulate the gravity contained within her body, but the construct's flesh did not yield to Draeken's power. But it was still made of flesh, and that meant it could be broken.

"Get Elenyr and stop the Gate," he said to Jeric and Lira. "I'll handle the construct."

314

"And if you die?" Jeric asked.

"I won't."

Wylyn stepped into the air and soared upward, climbing into the sky as purple light sparked on her arms. Draeken gathered his magic around himself and did the same, warping the gravity in order to lift himself skyward, his boots coming free of the Stormdial.

Excitement burned in his veins as he rose from the summit, the might of the earth obeying his will. Even the dakorians stared in shock while Numen's eyes nearly burst from his skull. Tardoq merely scowled.

"Your magic cannot defeat a construct," Wylyn called, her voice warped by the power in her body.

"Come and find out," Draeken exclaimed.

The construct reached to him and Draeken felt his body yanked downward. He fought the pull but it was far superior, and he cast a wall of fire to cushion the impact. Sparks and cinders scattered as the flames softened his landing, but the blow left Draeken dazed. He felt another tug and his body was launched into the neighboring arc, slamming him brutally on the surface before he went tumbling over the edge.

Panic engulfed him, and he caught a glimpse of Jeric fighting to reach the Gate while Lira battled the dakorians. Then Draeken lost sight of them as he plummeted down the side of the tower. Wylyn aimed downward and came after, purple light pulsing in her hand.

***

Elenyr screamed as Draeken fell, her heart constricting in her chest. King Numen actually laughed. The rage within Elenyr mounted and she fought against the bonds, sending lightning arcing into her flesh. King Numen leaned in, half his face scarred from their last battle.

"How does it feel to watch them suffer?"

"I thought your master wanted Draeken alive."

"He does," Numen said. "But he won't mind if Draeken comes a little broken."

His sneering comment elicited a memory of another cage, one that had trapped Elenyr's daughter. In the end she'd shattered her prison and escaped, wreaking havoc on her captors until they fled in terror. She'd escaped because she had the will to fight, and Elenyr drew courage from her daughter's memory.

Elenyr phased to ethereal and pushed her arm against the bindings holding her wrist. She screamed again as the lightning pushed through her flesh, but this time she did not retreat. Gritting her teeth, she inched her arm forward, the lightning burning her wrist and arm, leaving them blackened, but the bond passed through her skin and bones, sliding out the opposite side.

Her hand pulled free. The man's eyes widened. He cried out and reached to the sky for lightning, but Elenyr already had her hand around his throat. He fumbled for a dagger but she yanked him close and growled into his ear.

"Never cage what you should kill."

He fought in her grip but Elenyr pulled King Numen into the lightning bonds, pressing him against the powerful ropes. He shrieked as his own power rippled through his body. Although he fought to control it, the man's fear robbed him of his magic and the lightning scorched him to the heart. By the time he wrestled himself free, the lightning had burned his skin from cheek to waist.

His clothes steaming, he fell onto his back. He dragged himself away while Elenyr pushed her other hand against the bonds. Half of her bindings had been damaged from the contact with Numen, and she pushed her way through, driving her body through the ropes of lightning until she stood free.

Pain lanced through her but she turned solid and stalked forward. Elenyr came to a halt at King Numen's feet. Remarkably he was still alive, and Elenyr knelt at his side, drawing the sword from the king's sheath.

"You picked the wrong side, your highness, and I warned you what would happen the next time we met."

He raised a hand, his features contorted with desperation as he sought to harness a lightning bolt. Elenyr leaned down and plunged the sword into his body, and then dived away as the expected lightning bolt landed. It struck the hilt of the sword and coursed into his body. He shrieked in agony, all but disappearing before the lightning faded.

He lay with his eyes closed, his body still shaking, and Elenyr turned away in disgust. Then she turned and sprinted toward where she'd last seen Draeken—but he burst into view, soaring upward with the construct in pursuit. Relief flooded her veins and she slowed—and then spotted Jeric.

Jeric fought for his life. With his aquaglass swords, he battled nearly a dozen Order members while dodging arrows from Aradig's sentient bow. Elenyr grunted in irritation, annoyed at the twinge of loyalty that stirred in her heart.

She swept into the battle with all the fury of a vengeful wraith, her blade slicing deep as she twirled and spun, the sheer speed of her assault slaying three before the others could react. She slid to a halt next to Jeric and the elf nodded his gratitude.

"I wasn't sure you'd fight with me."

"You're still an ally," she said. "Even if I don't know your identity."

"You will," he promised.

"Why did you come back?" she demanded.

"Sometimes one is compelled to fix what one has broken," he said.

She phased to ethereal as a battle axe from a dwarf passed through her body, and then drove her sword into his chest. Flipping over his body, she brought her sword down into the woman beyond.

Jeric morphed his shield into a spear and used it to strike a man that sought to keep his distance. Then he recast the shield and deflected an

317

arrow from Aradig's bow. He winced when a woman darted in and sliced his waist. She danced out of reach before Jeric could retaliate.

"I'm uncertain it can be fixed," Elenyr said.

His smile fell and the distraction cost him as a detonating arrow landed nearby, knocking him flying. Elenyr spun and saw Aradig smirk, so she turned ethereal and dropped into the tower. Accelerating through the summit, she gathered herself and leapt.

Elenyr burst from the roof next to Aradig. She turned solid and smashed her knee into his chin. The surprised troll fell on his back, and she landed on his chest. The troll managed to roll, avoiding an expected strike, but she was not aiming for him. Rebounding off his body, she leapt upward.

And caught the sentient bow.

Landing hard, she turned to face Aradig and placed her sword against the bow, an unspoken threat.

He pointed his sword at her. "Release it, or I'll kill you."

"You chose the wrong side, Aradig," she said.

His next threat died on his lips as she sliced deep into the curve of the bow. The taut string yanked the weapon together, snapping it in half. Aradig roared his fury and lunged, but she tossed the fragments into his face and dropped into the roof of the tower. Then she rose behind him, her blade slicing from foot to neck. Aradig went down with a mortal cry, never to rise again. The sight of his fall caused the other Order members to retreat in fear, and Elenyr strode to Jeric.

"No more games," she said. "Tell me the truth."

They were both knocked to the side as the construct plunged through the roof nearby. Wylyn tore through the structure and fell into the hollow shaft of the Stormdial. Draeken dropped after her, smoke rising from both forms.

"I could use some help!" Lira shouted.

Lira sprinted up and around them, air stones appearing to support her. Elenyr realized Lira had kept the dakorians occupied, but they were driving her back, and the Gate was nearly finished.

"Later," she said to Jeric. "If we survive."

Suddenly a thrum went through the summit, drawing all eyes to the Gate. Purple light flowed through a small triangle hovering a short distance from the Gate, the threads of power streaking into the dark material. A silvery surface shimmered under the Gate.

The Gate was activating.

Chapter 41: Construct

Draeken fell down the outside of the tower, air battering his frame. His body spun, the clouds and the black tower hurtling through his vision. Panic engulfed him but anger surged, and he clenched his fist, summoning the gravity by sheer will. He slowed and came to a halt, and he looked up to see Wylyn streaking toward him. She extended a hand and the lines of gravity warped around him, but this time he was prepared, and he slipped out of the trap. Then he aimed upward and sent a burst of fire, the flames forming a fist that struck Wylyn into the tower.

The construct disappeared behind the flames and slammed into the wall. Draeken used the moment to rise beyond her and watch Wylyn emerge from the smoke. It looked nearly unscathed, but Draeken noticed a spot on her side that looked dimmer than the rest. Whatever made up the construct's body, it could still take damage. The question was, how much?

"You think to harm me with fire?" Wylyn shouted. "A construct is built to destroy *armies*. And you are just an insect."

Wylyn reached to him and Draeken's arms snapped outward, the gravity pulling his fingers to the extreme. Ligaments and tendons popped and Draeken shouted as the construct sought to rip him in half.

He managed to conjure a bird of light and add a detonation charm, the small creature flitting to Wylyn, exploding on impact. The hold lessened and Draeken sucked in a grateful breath, and then cast a horde of birds, each carrying an explosive detonation charm. They pummeled Wylyn, driving her back against the wall, forcing her to relinquish her hold on Draeken. She crossed her arms and screamed before ripping the remaining birds in half, filling the sky with fire and smoke. When it cleared Draeken was flying upward, toward the arcs.

Draeken caught a glimpse of his friends fighting, of Elenyr free, and Lira battling three dakorians. He slowed, struck by the lethal beauty of her movements, of her grace and skill, and a surge of attraction pooled in his gut. It didn't come from him, rather it came from a part of him, and for an instant his soul began to fragment. He gritted his teeth and dropped in the air until he managed to hold them together. By then the construct had caught up and Draeken turned.

The construct reached for him but Draeken darted aside, flipping around an arc and streaking for the construct. Blasts of light and gravity echoed like thunder, reverberating off the arc as they dueled.

Out of the corner of his eye he spotted the Gate coming to life and knew he was out of time. He ducked a blow and dove straight down, but the construct pursued and caught his shoulder. A blade of pure gravity appeared in her hand. Draeken rolled to avoid the weapon, and used the momentum to send Wylyn plummeting into the roof of the tower.

He cast a spear of gravity and launched it at the woman. It dug into her belly and then accelerated, driving her into the roof, blasting through to the air shaft below. Draeken turned toward the Gate but a thread of gravity reached out and looped around his ankle, yanking him down after her.

He bounced off the edge of the hole and dropped into the tower, falling above Wylyn. Using the rope attached to his ankle, he sucked the moisture from the air and funneled it around the rope, sending it crashing into her, wrapping around Wylyn's body and arms, the liquid ascending to cover her mouth and eyes. Still falling, she gathered herself and spread her arms wide, shattering the water in all directions.

She slowed to a halt and looked up at Draeken, her purple eyes gleaming. "I don't need air," she said, her tone mocking. "And your little magics cannot harm me."

"Perhaps," he said, and then flashed a very Shadowlike smirk. "But let's see what else I can damage . . ."

Draeken released his magic and dropped. Air buffeted him and he angled his body downward, falling down the giant air shaft. The construct turned and followed but Draeken lashed the gravity to himself, propelling himself even faster. The wind battered his face as he plummeted down the central shaft of the Stormdial.

Wylyn tried to catch him, to slow him, the threads of gravity reaching, but none managed to take hold, Draeken's sheer speed preventing any attack. Despite the conflict and fate if he failed, Draeken found a smile on his face, and blood thundered in his veins.

The levels of the tower blurred by as he fell, the great height of the tower passing in a blur. He passed below where he thought the surface of the lake would be and still he fell. The air gained a dull whine as he continued to propel himself faster, diving in the depths of the tower and the sea.

He spotted a purple glow and released his magic, and then gathered himself to slow his descent. The base of the tower approached with shocking speed and he fought to bring his body to a stop, the sheer effort causing his joints to pop. Then he passed through the base of the tower and entered a massive chamber.

The space was as large as the entire underground city of the dwarves, but flat on the bottom and rounded across the top, resembling an upside down bowl resting on the floor of the seabed. The walls were vaguely translucent, the depths of the sea visible on the opposite side. At the center of the chamber, a giant sphere floated off the ground, purple light seeping through the dark surface. A trio of pillars extended from the sphere to the tower, the conduits of power rising into the Stormdial.

The chamber was pristine except for the wreckage of a handful of ships. Draeken recognized the hull from one of the dakorian vessels while a nearby keel lay in a corner. Other pieces of wood and broken sails were scattered about, picked up when the tower had risen.

Draeken reached for the power of the sphere but flinched in shock. Just brushing its power was like dipping a finger into a bonfire the size of a house, and he retreated. Then Wylyn came to a halt beside him and Draeken turned.

"You think you can damage the tower?" She gestured to the enormous edifice. "Your pitiful race are like rodents compared to our might."

"Have you seen what a rat can do?" Draeken scoffed.

She scowled and flew at him. He tried to dodge but she'd cast a net of gravity that snared him and sent him falling to the base of the chamber. He managed to cushion the blow and cast a spear of light, using it to shred the bindings. Then he turned and hurled it at Wylyn.

She laughed and dodged the spear. "You are such a fool—"

The spear reached the end of the gravity thread and reversed direction, plunging into Wylyn's back. She screamed, her expression shocked as she fell to the floor. Wylyn rose to her feet and reached to her back, yanking the weapon from her body with another scream. The wound healed, but the injury remained dark, like flesh gone dead. She lifted her eyes and glared at him, but Draeken merely smiled.

"What happens if I kill the construct?" he wondered aloud.

Her features hardened, revealing the truth. It would kill her. Draeken smiled and he started forward, gathering the water into a wall to obscure his path. Then he wrapped himself in shadows and dived behind a ship's keel. The construct burst through the water, stepping into a quartet of spears hovering above her head. They fell upon her, forcing her to evade, driving her towards the gravity sphere.

The woman was stronger than he, that much Draeken knew. Although her raw power exceeded his own, she did not have what he possessed. Draeken knelt behind the keel and released the fragments. He grimaced as the power left his flesh and they fragments took shape.

"You saw what I saw," Mind said.

Water nodded. "We know what to do."

"Does anyone have any cheese?" Light asked.

Fire gathered magic in his hands. "Stay focused, Light."

"Let's hunt some krey," Shadow said with a smirk.

Chapter 42: The Fragments of Draeken

"Don't get arrogant," Fire said to Shadow, eying Wylyn, who'd retreated beneath the sphere.

"Coming from Fire?" Water asked.

"It's too dark in here," Light said, annoyed.

Mind gazed on the fragments, his brothers, and was suddenly overwhelmed with a surge of pride. The bond between them went beyond friendship, beyond family, and moisture welled in his eyes as he thought of how much they meant to him.

Water noticed his expression and nodded, offering a faint smile. "You ready?"

"Ready," Mind said. "You know what to do."

Already knowing his intention, they darted away, and Mind leapt from behind the keel just as the construct pointed to the ship. The wood snapped as it was struck by an unseen force, sending the ship tumbling away. Mind reached for her with threads of gravity but she slapped them high and retaliated, binding him to the ground. He dropped to his knees, his arms spread apart. He cried out as the gravity chains thickened.

"Your magic is no match for my might," Wylyn growled, striding forward.

Mind managed a laugh. "Power is blind," he said. "Lucky for me, I have more than two pairs of eyes."

Wylyn's eyes widened—just as Shadow burst from behind Mind. His features contorted into a terrifying mask, he streaked at her with a haunting shriek. She flinched, the sudden shock causing fear. Her fear morphed to anger when Shadow began to laugh.

"You frighten so easily," Shadow taunted.

Wylyn screamed and flung her arms up, sending threads of gravity reaching for Shadow—and passing through his body. His body like smoke, Shadow raised a hand through the purple thread attempting to tie him down.

"Hm," Shadow grunted in amusement. "Looks like your magic doesn't work on shadows."

Wylyn stared at him in shock, and didn't see Fire slip behind her back and conjure a weapon. The flaming maul smashed her to the floor, and then a spear of light plunged through her body, binding her to the ground. Water gathered the liquid on the floor and wrapped it around the trapped woman.

"ENOUGH!"

Wylyn's scream reverberated throughout the chamber. She flung her hands out and ripped her body from the bindings. Water, Light, and Fire were launched backward, their magic shattering. With sparks spilling from the spear in her body and half her face dim, the construct looked truly frightening.

"It's time you learned to be a slave!"

Her power had faltered during the assault and Mind had managed to free himself, but Wylyn leapt into the air and aimed her power at him. He cast his own magic, much weaker without the other fragments, and darted into the darkness, running from her barrage of attacks . . .

***

Light sucked the light from the room and cast a large ballistae, which he rolled under the gravity sphere and out of sight. Then he turned and sent the remaining light at Wylyn's back. Her strikes narrowly missed Mind, her aim off due to the shadows cast by Shadow.

Wylyn screamed again, her fury causing Shadow to laugh in delight. Light jumped into the air and cast wings. Wylyn whirled and sent threads of gravity at him. Light spun, evading the threads before tossing a spear upward, where Mind caught it with his own magic and sent it into the woman's body.

325

The construct's torso was a patchwork of cracks and dark lines. Like a disease, the damage covered her arms and legs, and even into her face. Sparks spit from the wounds recently healed. She dropped to the ground and struck the floor. Light cried out as the gravity mounted, yanking him downward. He landed on a wing, the magic crumbling from the impact and leaving him dazed. As Wylyn stalked towards him he managed to lift his head and see Fire . . .

***

Fire caught the ballistae Light had conjured and reached to the shaft of light. Gathering heat from the room, he added detonation charms along the spear, the flames turning white with heat, and then the supreme blue. The air gained a chill as the heat was siphoned into the spear, and ice formed on the ground beneath the ballistae.

"Water!" he shouted.

He kicked the ballistae to him and then charged under the sphere. He jumped and flipped, landing on the gravity sphere. Running upside down, he approached Wylyn as she reached Light. Gathering fire into his fists, he brought them down on Wylyn—but the woman turned.

Fire caught a glimpse of her haunting features before she caught his throat and slammed him into the ground. Fire's vision clouded, and when it cleared he saw Wylyn with a shimmering purple sword in her hands.

"Die apart or die alone," she said. "It doesn't matter to me."

"At least I won't have to see your face."

Fire squirmed against the invisible bindings but they might as well have been made of dwarven mithral. The weapon dropped towards his chest—and then slowed to a halt. Out of the corner of Fire's eyes he spotted Mind. He was on his knees, his arm reaching for Wylyn. Sweat beaded his forehead and he grimaced, fighting her power—but the blade continued to descend until it touched his chest, and began to enter . . .

***

Water caught the ballistae and rotated the weapon, cringing from the proximity to such heat. He'd already cast a ball of water underneath

326

the gravity sphere, the ball of liquid deforming and expanding onto the smooth surface.

Water took aim towards the ball of water and fired the ballistae. The tremendous heat of Fire's spear pierced the water, turning the entire mass into steam. Spear and target exploded with such force that Water was sent tumbling backward, his body sliding twenty feet before he came to a halt. Out of the corner of his eyes he spotted Wylyn looking up, her expression one of horror.

"It's not possible," she breathed.

When the smoke and steam cleared the shell of the sphere contained a crack, and purple light spilled from the interior. Wylyn abandoned Fire and leapt to the opening, flipping upside down to land next to the crack. Her body contorted with the effort, she grasped the two sides of the crack and pushed them together. But a burst of delighted laughter caused her to look up—and her eyes widened when she spotted Shadow.

***

Shadow sprinted away from Wylyn, pleased that the gravity magic did not affect him—at least when he was in ethereal form. He reached the broken ship and slipped into the darkness inside. He came to a halt and smiled when he found what Draeken had spotted upon entering the chamber.

The Carver.

"Hello beautiful," he crooned.

Grasping the handles, he worked to dislodge it from its moorings. The machine had miraculously survived the destruction of its ship, and Shadow sought to free it from the beams and wreckage holding it pinned. He grunted as he lifted it free and tried not to listen to the sounds of pain from the other fragments.

The entire machine slid into the open and he dragged it out of the ship. Then he checked the weapon for damage and recalled watching the dwarf work the controls. He reached for the lever and pulled.

And the Carver began to spin.

Shadow cackled in glee as the spinning blade became a blur, the barbs all but disappearing, the weapon whining as if eager to be sent forth. Shadow flinched when Water sent the spear into the gravity sphere and looked up at the blast. When the crack was revealed he smiled and patted the machine.

"Your target is ready," he said. "It's time to see what you can do."

Turning the weapon, he took careful aim, his anticipation building. Fire, still bound on the floor, glared at him, while Light's features lit up with excitement. From nearby, Mind bellowed an order.

"Just shoot the blasted thing!"

Across the gap Shadow met Wylyn's gaze, and it was the first time he saw fear in her eyes. Offering a mock salute, he pulled the lever, and the Carver leapt away. It passed over Mind and blasted towards Wylyn.

The woman was forced to leap aside as the weapon hurtled towards her body. Her scream was filled with rage and disbelief as the Carver struck the crack on the gravity sphere, and plunged inside.

Chapter 43: Deep Wounds

The Carver pierced the sphere, disappearing for an instant before bursting from the opposite side. It soared away and then slowed, the power of the sphere bringing it to a stop, and then pulling it back in. The shrieking weapon carved a new hole on the top of the sphere, again disappearing, and again bursting forth. Wylyn's cry of dismay was lost in the *crack* of the gravity's casing, each new hole spilling forth more power.

"Do you have any idea what you've done!" she screamed.

"Behold the power of a rat!" Shadow shouted.

Mind stared in shock at the broken gravity sphere, watched as the threads of gravity seeped out of the rents and fastened to a section of the floor, ripping a great chunk upward. It crashed into the underside of the sphere. A moment later the ballistae Light had crafted did the same, shattering into sparks of light and magic.

The keel of the boat slid toward the sphere and then lifted off the ground, and Mind retreated when they reached for him. Then a section of roof came free, ripping apart as it collapsed toward the damaged sphere. And still the Carver burst into sight, slowed, and then plunged back inside, spinning so fast the edge had turned red with heat.

"We must go!" Mind shouted.

He tried to step into the air but merely floated off the ground before returning to it. As Draeken he had the power of flight, while Mind lacked such ability. Shadow was already ascending his way out of the tower, climbing the walls on the back of a reaver entity, the beast's claws finding purchase in the darkness. Light too, was leaping into the air, repairing his damaged wing enough to soar around Wylyn, who stared at the damaged sphere in disbelief.

Water cast a thread of moisture on the ceiling and it carried him into the air shaft and out of sight, leaving only Mind and Fire. Still partially trapped, Fire worked to set himself free, struggling to break the bonds of gravity that held him bound. Situated the closest to the sphere, he was in the most danger, with a section of floor tearing nearby. Mind spotted the other fragments clinging to the wall of the shaft.

"Go!" Mind shouted to his brothers, and sprinted to Fire.

"No."

Wylyn's voice was quiet, but it carried lethal intent. She turned to Mind with rage spilling from her gaze, and then reached a hand outward, the palm upward. Mind dodged, but the attack was not for him.

"You think yourself powerful?"

She brought her fingers inward, and the stone beneath Fire turned into a hand, the fingers rising around him. He struggled all the harder, getting an arm free before the fingers closed about his body.

"You think this victory?"

Slowly, she closed her fingers, and Fire roared as the hand began to squeeze, compressing his flesh. He turned to pure flame, and sparks sputtered from the gaps in the fingers. Mind slid to a halt and caught Fire's extended arm.

Anger and fear lanced into Mind's gut and as he sought to merge Fire to him, but the fingers closed tighter, pulling Fire's arm from his grip. With all his might Mind caught the stone hand and pulled, exerting every ounce of magic he possessed, but still it tightened.

"I'll kill you," Mind snarled, the sound drowned out by Fire's bellow.

"You will never win," Wylyn said. "The Empire is greater than you can imagine, and all your magic will be like cinders in a storm. *My* storm."

She descended and crafted a spear of gravity, placing the tip in a gap between the fingers, putting it on Fire's heaving chest. Mind lunged for her but she slapped him away, and he tumbled to a stop. When he rose their eyes met, and the woman drove the spear through the fingers and into the fragment of Fire.

"A slave with power is still a slave," she spat.

Water slammed into her back, carrying her to the floor, where she splashed in a puddle. A section of the outer wall had been pulled in and water streamed through cracks in the earth, the pressure of the sea forcing it into the chamber. The liquid poured in through the outer cracks, quickly flooding the floor.

With so much water at his command, Water brought his hands together into a tremendous clap, the water responding to his summons, crashing into Wylyn and sending her across the chamber. Mind leapt to Fire, and with Water's aid they managed to pull the stone fingers apart. Inside, Fire lay broken, his body like a dying ember.

"Fire!" Water shouted, his voice tight with anguish.

Fear and anguish rippled through Mind and he reached out to his brother, but his body was cold and getting colder. Mind then reached to his hand and squeezed it, willing him to awaken. Fire's eyes fluttered open.

"Fire!" Mind shouted, his stomach lurching with relief. Was he crying? But his hope was in vain as he saw Fire's eyes going dim. The fragment smiled, the expression one of grim satisfaction.

"Join with me," Mind urged. "Quickly."

"We called ourselves fragments," he murmured, his voice hauntingly quiet. "But I liked being brothers."

"Fire," Water plead. "You're the strongest of us."

Fire coughed and grimaced. "It's time for you to be the strong one."

Water looked to Mind, his expression desperate. "Can't you force him to join?"

"I'll try," Mind said.

Mind clenched his hand and reached for Fire's mind, but the memories were weak and fading. He tightened his grip, oblivious to the floor ripping apart, and willed Fire to merge, to become Draeken. Fire's eyes fluttered shut for the final time, and his memories faltered.

The flames poured around Mind's arm, seeping upward like a dying fire clinging to life. Mind felt Fire's strength merged with his own, felt the familiar surge of power . . . and the host of injuries.

Water looked to him with a desperate hope. "Is he alive?"

Mind shook his head.

Mind could feel Fire's magic, but not his thoughts, not his anger, not his defiance. Mind rose from the scorched ground and turned to Wylyn, who'd finally managed to free herself from the water. Her expression of satisfaction sent Mind's fear into rage, and he raised his hand toward her.

"You cannot harm me," she said, striding forward even as the ground ripped apart, and pieces of wall crashed inward, the great chunks colliding into the sphere.

Mind snarled the words, "But I know what can."

He caught a thread of gravity from the gravity sphere and lashed it to Wylyn's body. Then he tossed the other end of the gravity rope upward—right as the Carver cut a new hole in the sphere. It soared outward and slowed, the gravity already pulling it back in. The thread of magic attached to Wylyn caught around the Carver. The cord went taught and the shrieking blade was drawn to Wylyn.

She raised her hands but not fast enough, and the Carver hurtled into her, the blade spinning into her body. Purple sparks burst from her torso as it tore into the construct, and Wylyn's scream reverberated throughout the chamber.

"That's not going to kill her," Water said.

"It doesn't matter," Draeken said. "The sphere will finish the job."

"Then we need to leave."

332

Without a word, Water stepped to him and merged, his body fading up Draeken's arm to blend with him. Draeken felt Water's piercing sorrow merge with his own, the sense of grief so vivid it brought tears to his eyes. With the power of Fire and Water, he stepped into the air and flew upward, rising toward the air shaft. The pull from the sphere was tremendous, and it took all his strength to break free. When he did, he looked down, and watched as chunks of the building began to rip apart and tumble into the abyss.

He caught a glimpse of Wylyn, her body a patchwork of cracks, sparks cascading off her form. She fought to fly free of the gravity well but it had become too strong, and she dropped onto its surface. Her final scream echoed up the air shaft before an enormous piece of tower slammed into her and all was silent. Alone, Draeken turned and flew upward as the tower ripped itself apart.

***

Elenyr, Jeric, and Lira fought to reach the Gate but the four surviving dakorians refused to break the line. Many glanced to Wylyn's body, which had been placed on the threshold. Even Tardoq didn't attempt to flee.

Then the tower shuddered.

Elenyr felt the tremble through her boots and glanced downward. The next shake knocked her to her knees. When she looked up, the surviving dakorians stared at the roof of the Stormdial in horror, and the entire battle came to an abrupt halt.

Elenyr, Jeric, and Lira all sported numerous wounds, with Jeric suffering the worst of it. Blood dripped down his cheek and he leaned against one of the spires, his face white. Elenyr stared downward, her expression tight with worry.

"The gravity sphere has been damaged!" one of the dakorians cried.

Another motioned to the Gate, the light of which had stopped growing. "The Gate lacks the power to escape this world!"

The dakorians shifted their feet uncertainly, all looking to Tardoq. Lira exchanged a look with Elenyr and guessed Elenyr was thinking the same thing. If the sphere had been damaged, had Draeken triumphed over Wylyn?

"Connect to Wylyn," Tardoq growled.

"The communicators are all destroyed," came the response.

Tardoq glared at Elenyr, who raised her bloodied sword. "How long before the tower is destroyed?" she asked. "Will you fall with the tower?"

As if in response to her question, the tower trembled again, more violent than before. A crack appeared in one of the arcs, stretching for several feet. Elenyr suppressed the spark of fear. The gravity sphere for the Stormdial would be enormous, and if it detonated, several miles in every direction would be destroyed in seconds.

Tardoq must have realized the same thing, because he pointed to the Gate. "Retreat."

"But captain," another protested. "Wylyn could still be alive."

"If she is, she has the Construct," he said. "And she knows to flee."

The soldier nodded and the line began to retreat across the surface of the tower. Lira glanced at the edge of roof just ten feet behind her. Prior to the trembling, the dakorians had been intent on forcing them over the edge, and only Elenyr's ability to rise in their midst had kept them from completing their design. But if they stayed and fought, they risked the Gate losing power and leaving them stranded.

"Do you have no loyalty?" Elenyr asked, gliding forward. "You flee your master at the first sign of loss?" It was an attempt to goad Tardoq into staying, but he did not take the bait, and the tower shook anew, more cracks appearing.

Tardoq met Elenyr's gaze and wiped the blood off his lip. "We would stay and fight, but I think we'll let the tower end your lives."

A section of the roof crumpled, taking two dakorians with it. They bellowed in surprise before they plummeted from sight. Another hole appeared, and then another. The last nearly claimed Lira, but her enhanced agility allowed her to jump free. Tardoq and his last dakorian companion sprinted for the Gate, but another figure reached it first.

Numen.

The king stumbled into the Gate, casting Elenyr a baleful glare as he disappeared. The tower trembled again, this time with a touch of violence. With no other option, Tardoq sprinted for the Gate. His final companion did not make it, and a hole opened to swallow him. Alone, Tardoq disappeared through the Gate.

"Did Tardoq leave Lumineia?" Elenyr asked Lira, using her chin to point to the Gate.

Lira eyed the flickering power on the Gate and shook her head. "As they said, it didn't get enough power to reach the Empire."

"That means they're still on Lumineia," Elenyr said.

Elenyr slumped to her knees, the relief piercing. If they had reached the Empire, all would have been lost. Lira was at her side, but she shook her head and pointed to Jeric. The elf's features were weak but his smile was bright. Lira stepped to his side and used a strip of cloth to tie a bandage around his leg.

"You always have a way of finding victory," he murmured.

Elenyr shushed him and tightened a bandage on his arm, but the blood-soaked clothing did little but make him wince. He reached up and touched her cheek, a smile on his face. Elenyr's gut tightened and she shook her head.

"You'll be fine," Elenyr said.

"I need to tell you the truth," he whispered.

"Not here," she said. "You can tell me when we're off the tower."

The conversation hid her fear as she watched the life drain out of Jeric. He smiled as if he understood her ruse, but the expression only heightened her fear. She tore a strip of cloth from her tunic and tied it around another wound.

335

"Elenyr," he said.

"You're not going to die," she said, ashamed that tears were in her eyes.

"I need you to understand my regret."

The trembling of the tower was nearly constant now and cracks marred the roof. A mile in the sky there was no way they could escape the tower before it collapsed, and so she leaned in and embraced him, the contact blossoming regret in her stomach.

"I'm sorry," she murmured when they parted.

"It is I that must beg for mercy," he said.

A groan came from behind and Elenyr spun to find Shadow climbing through a hole in the roof. Relief flooded her frame when Light climbed through the hole, obviously injured, but alive. Then Draeken appeared, his body and face weary, his features broken. She recognized the touch of heat to his frame, and the carriage that indicated Water, so why the despair?

"Where is Fire?" she demanded.

"I have his magic," Draeken said, his voice hollow as he limped forward. Their eyes met and the agony in his eyes revealed the truth.

"No," Elenyr breathed, shrinking from Draeken's words. "It's not possible."

"He did not survive," Draeken said.

Elenyr passed a hand over her face, the grief so sharp she could taste it. Draeken's tone was tight, filled with anger, grief, and regret. Then the tower began to shake without stopping, the trembling rising as the tower gained a dying keen . . .

Chapter 44: The Fallen Shard

"We must depart," Draeken said.

He held his side, where Fire's wounds were now his own. The searing pain leeched through his body, feeling like every bone was cracked, yet it still did not compare with the agony he felt at Fire's loss.

"Can you fly us out of here?" Elenyr asked.

"I don't think so," Draeken said. "Not like this."

"Then we go down the side of the tower," Elenyr said, and looked to Lira. "You craft the vessel. Water can help us when we reach the sea." Her tone was distant and wooden.

Draeken nodded and groaned as Water pulled away and fell to his knees. Then he merged with Shadow and Light, grateful for the rush of power they provided. Light was hurt but Shadow was relatively unscathed from the battle, and he helped to numb the pain. As they did, Lira used her magic to shape a thin ship out of air, the wind tightening together into a long hull and a flat keel. Together, the five of them pushed it to the edge and Water climbed into the front. Lira took her place behind, while Elenyr and Jeric stood in the center. Draeken grimaced as he eased himself into the back of the ship.

His gaze swept the summit, where dozens of Order soldiers and dakorians lay dead. He wanted to take solace in the victory, but the pit in his chest did not leave. Fire was dead, and Draeken was broken.

"We have been victorious," Elenyr said, her voice empty.

Draeken's hand clenched into a fist and he shook his head, the shaking of the tower thudding in his body. He reached out to the gravity and lashed it to the vessel, pulling them to the edge until the keel of the air boat teetered down the steep slope.

"You sure about this?" Water called back.

Elenyr stabbed a finger toward the edge. "We either take our chances or go down with the tower."

Water looked back to Draeken and their eyes met, an unspoken accord passing between them. The tiny ship contained everything they cared about, and they weren't going to let it shatter. Then Draeken gave a final shove and they slipped free.

The vessel tipped down the slope, the air slamming into them as they fell. Faster and faster they plummeted until the flat-bottomed boat struck the smooth side of the Stormdial. They bounced and started to spin. Lira used a gust of wind to keep them straight, but the air buffeted them as they plummeted down the tower's side. Draeken bent the gravity, wrestling the magic to keep them headed straight down.

Cracks in the tower burst into view on all sides, and abruptly the outer wall exploded ahead, venting into a cloud, turning it crimson. Flames and purple light spilled forth. Another geyser erupted, sending more debris into the clouds.

The air on the bottom of the boat glided down the tower's exterior, dampening the violent shaking from the tower. Draeken winced when another hole exploded to their right, gushing debris and stone in the burst of fire.

"We need to go faster!" Lira shouted.

Draeken lashed threads of gravity to their vessel and to the tower. The ship accelerated, flying down the slope with such speed the wind bashed their hull. Only Lira kept them upright. They reached the clouds and passed into them, the air darkening and gaining a chill, moisture gathering on their faces. Draeken wiped the water away as a shadow passed overhead. He spun to look, and his eyes widened.

The tower was leaning.

Tipping toward them with a groan, the entire Stormdial had begun to fall. Draeken lashed more threads to the already unstable boat and Lira added a burst of wind, driving them straight down the slope.

338

Draeken's heart lifted in his chest as their boat began to tip further downward, and he gripped the sides of the hull, his fingers so tight the magic cracked. The stern of their ship tipped further than the prow . . . and they slipped free of the side of the tower.

The ship fell freely. Explosions ripped the tower apart, blasts of power rending the great tower into chunks of stone. One explosion was close, sending sizzling shards into their boat and knocking it askew.

"Hang on!" Lira cried.

"I already am!" Draeken shouted.

Their ship spun, flipping end over end, and Draeken's stomach sought to leap for safety. The spinning gradually slowed and Lira righted them, but cracks littered the ship on the side of the impact, and Draeken knew they could not take another hit.

A geyser of fire erupted ahead of them and Draeken pointed to it, splitting the flames to form a narrow path. Their ship burst through the smoke and fire and continued to fall, just as the roiling sea came into view.

Rising in huge swells, the sea felt the turmoil in the looming tower. Water reached to the sea and it rose at his summons, climbing the side of the tower. Higher and higher it rose, becoming a long ramp leading to safety.

The tower groaned anew and a massive explosion ripped apart the corner, an entire section disappearing in purple fire. Draeken shielded his gaze, his heart hammering his ribs as he imagined what would happen to their ship if such an explosion caught them . . .

The vessel reached the end of the water ramp and struck hard. The ship careened down the ramp toward the sea, speeding so fast that Draeken was pressed into the base of the boat. He heard a crack and looked back, and watched the wall split next to the ramp.

"Go!" he roared, and drove his magic into the stern, propelling them even faster.

They reached the end of the ramp and dropped into a trough of the sea—as the lower tower detonated. Purple flames shattered the ramp and reached for them, the debris battering the ocean and the wall Draeken had raised.

"We need to get as far away as possible!" Lira shouted. "It's going to incinerate everything within a few miles of—"

BOOM

An eruption shook the very earth, and the entire tower seemed to lift. Then it dropped into the cavity that had appeared beneath the tower. Draeken banked their ship to the side as the shadow of the falling tower enveloped them, and the tower plummeted to the sea. Another explosion ripped the center of the tower apart, sending the top half spinning away.

The massive section of tower struck the water just a few hundred feet from their ship, landing in a tremendous splash. Waves rose and fell, buffeting their ship as they fought to get away from the tower.

Draeken looked to the base of the devastated structure. The gravity sphere glowed with power beneath the sea, the walls gone, the base of the tower ripped apart. Like a sun beneath the waves, it brightened until he had to shield his eyes. And then it detonated.

Instantly the sea rose upward, rising into a tidal wave. The sea rose up like it sought to devour them whole, a roaring monster of wind and water. Draeken managed to cry out a warning, and all within the boat gripped the hull. The wave picked them up, lifting them up and tipping them forward, until abruptly the wave slowed, and the ship bounced down the lower part of the gigantic wave. Impossibly, the entire wall of water came to a halt—and then began to retreat.

Waves, bits of stone, sections of tower, all of it, was drawn inward, the gravity sphere reaching out and sucking it all in. Threads of purple light the size of tree trunks latched onto their ship and brought them to a bruising halt, and then yanked them under the surface. Water managed to cast a bubble overhead to keep them from drowning but the enormous threads swept them backward.

Draeken reached to the giant thread of power and cast a gravity blade, hacking at what dragged them under, his own magic cutting deep. Abruptly it snapped and they popped to the surface like a cork. But the water was still going backward, spinning into a giant vortex.

340

"I can't push anymore!" Lira cried, her voice strained.

"Neither can I!" Draeken shouted.

"Need a hand?"

All five whirled to find Sentara and Rune aboard a sleek, white vessel. Sentara stood at the odd helm, her smile smug as she floated, not on the water, but above it. Jeric climbed aboard, and the others scrambled to follow. Their crumbling air ship was instantly pulled into the whirlpool. Sentara pressed a rune on a pedestal and the ship leapt away.

Draeken cursed as he fell to the deck, the acceleration so swift he almost tumbled out the stern. Elenyr alone managed to keep her feet as the wind whipped her face, her features frozen with suppressed emotion. Sentara shrugged apologetically.

"Sorry."

"It doesn't matter," Elenyr said.

The krey ship streaked away from the vortex, bursting from the lip and speeding away. As it did, the sinking length of tower crumpled, and a blast of power cascaded away, rising into the clouds and across the sea.

Everywhere it touched, the storm evaporated, the waves stilled, and the rain ceased to fall. Then the Stormdial sank beneath the surface, the pieces folding in on itself, the walls flattening and compressing. The swirling vortex finally began to quiet, a plume of water rushing to fill the void.

Draeken gazed on the sea that washed away the final vestiges of the ancient structure. A fine mist sprinkled across them, the remains of the storm that had existed just moments ago, the absence allowing a stunning view of the sunset.

"It's over," Jeric breathed.

Elenyr crumpled to the deck. Emotion clogged Draeken's throat and the fragments parted, each stumbling in the boat. Mind remained

341

standing, unable to move, to think, to understand. Wylyn was gone, but the cost was more than he could bear.

He'd sworn an oath, that he would guard the fragments with his life. He'd failed. He caught Elenyr's gaze and the woman seemed to stare through him, to see the emptiness he felt. She did not speak, and he wished it was him the Stormdial had crushed.

Chapter 45: Jeric's Truth

Elenyr stood on the balcony of the abandoned inn. The location had once been a thriving collection of homes, with two inns, a tavern, and a blacksmith. Then a flood had washed away three of the buildings, leaving the lone structure still standing. Fearful that the inn would be swept away in the next flood, the settlement had been abandoned, leaving a graceful structure empty.

Built adjacent to the mouth of a river, the inn lacked furnishings, and anything of value had been stripped. What remained were bare walls, cold hearths, and creaking stairs. Forgotten by anyone except a handful of locals, the location served as a place of respite for travelers who knew how to reach the hidden structure.

The krey vessel bobbed on the sea, the moonlight casting it in silvery light. A recent storm had dusted the ground and roof in snow, and the air carried a chill. Two of the fragments worked to light fires in the hearths, the action sober, as Fire would have done it in seconds. His absence left them all silent.

"May I come in?"

Elenyr turned to find Jeric standing in the doorway. She shrugged and turned back to the view, staring into the distance where the Stormdial had once stood. Its destruction and Wylyn's death were victories, but she'd never felt so defeated.

"I'm sorry about Fire." Jeric took a spot at her side.

"I always feared one of them might be killed," she said distantly, "but I don't think I ever thought they would fall."

"The other fragments are arguing with Sentara and Rune," Jeric said. "They need to know what to do now."

"Serak remains alive," Elenyr muttered. "We will have to go after him, before he reclaims the Order of Ancients." The answer was automatic, but she didn't care. Nothing mattered except the ache in her chest.

"Elenyr," he groaned. "You need to talk about what happened."

"To whom?" Elenyr asked, her voice turning hard. "To you? I don't even know who you are. I've just lost my son and . . ."

Her fleeting anger evaporated and tears leaked from her eyes. She wiped at them furiously, struggling to contain the wave of grief. Her son had perished, and she had not been there to protect him.

"I'm sorry I have not been truthful," Jeric murmured.

"Have you always lied to me?" she asked, ashamed that her anger shifted to him.

"I have," he replied.

"*Why?*" she ground the word out.

She spared him a glance and his expression was somber, even pained. She wanted to lash out, to scream and shout, to hurl obscenities at Jeric. Instead she stood silent, glaring at the one she'd once loved. Or thought she'd loved.

"Because I never thought I would meet you," he said softly. "And I never imagined I would fall for you."

She folded her arms, as much to display her doubt as to hold her emotions from spilling out of her mouth. "If you would ever speak the truth, do so now. Or be gone from this place and never return."

He regarded her with heavy eyes. Then he inclined his head and looked out to sea, leaning against the railing. For a long moment all was still except for the lapping of the water on the rocky shore below.

"I have worn many personas here," he said. "All were fleeting, meant to be discarded when they had served their purpose."

"And what was that purpose?"

344

He raised an eyebrow at the acid in her voice. Annoyed, she raised her hands as if to say she would wait for him to speak. Despite her anger, a touch of curiosity appeared in her mind. Was he really going to speak the truth?

"I wanted to learn," he said. "To learn of the people here, the races and their customs. It was something I was unfamiliar with, and craved to understand. Then I created Jeric, and relished the freedom such a persona provided. I quickly gained a reputation as one with knowledge and a sense of adventure, both of which appealed to me. I knew it was dangerous to continue and prepared to discard Jeric as I had before. Then I met you."

He turned and held Elenyr's gaze. Struck by his words, she remained silent, her grief and anger momentarily distant. Not forgotten. Never forgotten. He spoke freely, more openly than ever, and her curiosity continued to rise.

"You knew me as Jeric, and I was surprised by my attraction to you." His lips twitched in a faint smile. "You were and are captivating, and by the time I realized what I felt, it was too late to change personas to another. I kept Jeric because of you, because I wanted to be with you."

"Then who are you?" she asked, a touch of foreboding creeping into her heart.

"You must understand," he said, grimacing. "This truth is one long kept, and to share it will put you in danger."

"I don't care." Her anger was back. "You owe me an answer."

He inclined his head and then murmured. "Please do not be angry."

"Why would I be angry?" she scoffed.

"Because I am not an elf," he said.

"A human?" she asked, confused by the omission.

He shook his head, and then slowly reached up to his tunic. Withdrawing a small, glittering pendent, he pressed the embedded rune, and then closed his eyes as if in pain. Just as Elenyr was about to ask the purpose of the pendent, his skin shimmered, and began to change.

From light elven skin, his flesh began to darken, turning grey. His arms thinned and his chest shrank. His body grew shorter, and she heard a faint grinding of bones. Her jaw fell open as she realized it was not an illusion. His physical body was changing.

Distantly she recognized that Light would have recognized an illusion in an instant. She also knew of no magic capable of altering the physical makeup of a body. Not even the Verinai had obtained such magic, even though they had tried. Yet here Jeric was, his body shrinking to her height, his blonde hair growing white and hanging about his head.

She gasped and retreated a step when she recognized his new form. It was not elf or human, dwarf or orc. It was not even a race of Lumineia, and his body resembled the woman they had just killed on the Shard of Midnight.

He was krey.

The transformation complete, he sighed and opened his eyes, the light blue of elven gone, to be replaced by a deep blue, a startling color that seemed to pierce her to her soul. She stared in shock, bewildered and stunned. Then she recognized him.

"It cannot be," she breathed.

"Please do not be angry with me," he said in a voice that belied his ancient identity.

She continued to stare, bound by disbelief. The krey standing before her was not just any member of the ancient race, but the principle protector of Lumineia, the architect of the different races, and the very father of magic.

Ero.

Epilogue: The Master

King Numen awoke screaming, the pain arcing through his body, his numerous wounds demanding to be heard. He felt a healer's touch and grimaced, before a welcome numbness spread across his flesh, allowing him to sit up.

The small room contained only a bed, the brown stone uncomfortably warm. A window set in the opening looked into a haze of heat, a distant wall of rough rock just visible. He was back in Xshaltheria. The healer stood and departed, revealing another visitor.

"You've been asleep for days," Serak said.

Numen spotted a mirror nearby and snatched it up, raising it to see his reflection. Ugly scars covered half his face, extending to his shoulder and arm. The purple and mottled skin was hideous to behold, and his stomach heaved.

"Elenyr did this to me," Numen growled, his voice raspy.

"She left you for dead," Serak said.

Numen's eyes hardened. "I will rip her to shreds."

"You've tried three times and failed," Serak said. "And I'm tired of being disappointed."

He heard the threat in his voice. "Tardoq—"

"Has taken your place," Serak said.

"You would replace me with an outlander?"

"I would replace you with *anyone* who could kill the Hauntress," Serak said.

Numen ignored the dangerous glint in his eyes. "I will kill the Hauntress *and* Draeken's fragments for what they've done to me."

"I am the Father of Guardians," Serak snarled, causing Numen to recoil. "And my plan is nearly complete. I will not let your failures destroy what I have built." He reached outward, and a length of water grew from his hand, hardening into a blade.

Numen's eyes widened. "You would help me live, just to kill me?"

"I cannot permit failure," Serak said. "And after all you have done, I wanted to kill you myself."

"But Elenyr lives," Numen cried, retreated against the wall.

"And I have the weapons to destroy her," Serak said, gliding forward.

Numen tried to stand. The pain from his wounds lanced across his limbs and he groaned, falling back onto the bed. Breathing hard, he called out to Serak, and raised a hand to placate the man he'd called master.

"I saw Draeken fight Wylyn," he said. "I am uncertain he will join you."

Serak paused and looked back, his smile sending a chill into Numen's gut. "You may be a king, but he is a lord, and in time he will accept his rightful place."

"As your servant?" Numen managed to keep his voice. "He will never follow you."

Serak regarded him with cold eyes. "After everything you have witnessed with the krey and the dakorians, all their superior technology, you still do not understand. The threat we face is greater than even I can defeat."

"So why Draeken?"

Numen hoped to keep Serak talking, and desperately sought to reach for his magic. But they were deep in Xshaltheria, and no power was close enough to wield. Then Serak smiled, his expression so dark it made Numen shudder.

"You think I wish Draeken to be a weapon?"

Numen nodded vigorously. "What else could you need him for?"

"I do not seek a *servant*." Serak advanced and placed his sword on Numen's chest, his eyes lit with fervor. Then he struck a lethal blow. As Numen died, Serak's eyes glimmered with dark anticipation. "I seek a *master* . . ."

The Chronicles of Lumineia

By Ben Hale

—The Shattered Soul—

The Fragment of Water
The Fragment of Shadow
The Fragment of Light
The Fragment of Fire
The Fragment of Mind
The Fragment of Power

—The Master Thief—

Jack of Thieves
Thief in the Myst
The God Thief

—The Second Draeken War—

Elseerian
The Gathering
Seven Days
The List Unseen

—The Warsworn—

The Flesh of War
The Age of War
The Heart of War

—The Age of Oracles—

The Rogue Mage
The Lost Mage
The Battle Mage

—The White Mage Saga—

Assassin's Blade (Short story prequel)
The Last Oracle
The Sword of Elseerian
Descent Unto Dark
Impact of the Fallen
The Forge of Light

Author Bio

Originally from Utah, Ben has grown up with a passion for learning. Driven particularly to reading caused him to be caught reading by flashlight under the covers at an early age. While still young, he practiced various sports, became an Eagle Scout, and taught himself to play the piano. This thirst for knowledge gained him excellent grades and helped him graduate college with honors, as well as become fluent in three languages after doing volunteer work in Brazil. After school, he started and ran several successful businesses that gave him time to work on his numerous writing projects. His greatest support and inspiration comes from his wonderful wife and six beautiful children. Currently he resides in Missouri while working on his Masters in Professional Writing.

To contact the author, discover more about Lumineia, or find out about the upcoming sequels, check out his website at Lumineia.com. You can also follow the author on twitter @ BenHale8 or Facebook.

www.ingramcontent.com/pod-product-compliance
Lightning Source LLC
Chambersburg PA
CBHW020826180626
46814CB00001B/119